A King's
Commander

THE ALAN LEWRIE NAVAL ADVENTURE SERIES
BY DEWEY LAMBDIN

The King's Coat
The French Admiral
The King's Commission
The King's Privateer
The Gun Ketch
HMS Cockerel

A PRIMUS OMNIBUS EDITION

For King and Country

A KING'S COMMANDER

AN ALAN LEWRIE NAVAL ADVENTURE

DEWEY LAMBDIN

DONALD I. FINE BOOKS
New York

DONALD I. FINE BOOKS
Published by the Penguin Group
Penguin Books USA Inc., 375 Hudson Street,
New York, New York, 10014, U.S.A.
Penguin Books Ltd, 27 Wrights Lane,
London W8 5TZ, England
Penguin Books Australia Ltd, Ringwood,
Victoria, Australia
Penguin Books Canada Ltd, 10 Alcorn Avenue,
Toronto, Ontario, Canada M4V 3B2
Penguin Books (N.Z.) Ltd, 182-190 Wairau Road,
Auckland 10, New Zealand

Penguin Books Ltd, Registered Offices:
Harmondsworth, Middlesex, England

First published by Donald I. Fine Books, an imprint of
Penguin Books USA Inc.

First Printing, February, 1997
10　9　8　7　6　5　4　3　2　1

Copyright © Dewey Lambdin, 1997
All rights reserved

Library of Congress Cataloging-in-Publication Data
Lambdin, Dewey.
A king's commander : an Alan Lewrie Naval adventure / Dewey Lambdin.
p.　cm.
ISBN 1-55611-504-0
1. Great Britain—History, Naval—18th century—Fiction. I. Title.
PS3562.A435K53　1997
813'.54—dc20　　　　　96–31029
CIP

Printed in the United States of America
Set in 11/13 New Caledonia
Designed by Irving Perkins Associates

For Bill Wiles, Rick Newlon, Terry Fox, Tom Skalsky, and Jon Drake, my old pack of college runnin' buddies back when we were learning how to become a Nelsonian "Band of Brothers."

And, for Bob Enrione at CBS, who gives the best "loan" of obscure research books, and supplies the finest period details for the ambience, ever I did see.

Full-Rigged Ship: Starboard (right) side view

1. Mizzen Topgallant
2. Mizzen Topsail
3. Spanker
4. Main Royal
5. Main Topgallant
6. Mizzen T'gallant Staysail
7. Main Topsail
8. Main Course
9. Main T'gallant Staysail
10. Middle Staysail

11. Main Topmast Staysail
12. Fore Royal
13. Fore Topgallant
14. Fore Topsail
15. Fore Course
16. Fore Topmast Staysail
17. Inner Jib
18. Outer Flying Jib
19. Spritsail

A. Taffrail & Lanterns
B. Stern & Quarter-galleries
C. Poop Deck/Great Cabins Under
D. Rudder & Transom Post
E. Quarterdeck
F. Mizzen Chains & Stays
G. Main Chains & Stays
H. Boarding Battens/Entry Port
I. Cargo Loading Skids
J. Shrouds & Ratlines
K. Fore Chains & Stays

L. Waist
M. Gripe & Cutwater
N. Figurehead & Beakhead Rails
O. Jib Boom
P. Bow Sprit
Q. Foc's'le & Anchor Cat-heads
R. Cro'jack Yard (no sail fitted)
S. Top Platforms
T. Cross-Trees
U. Spanker Gaff

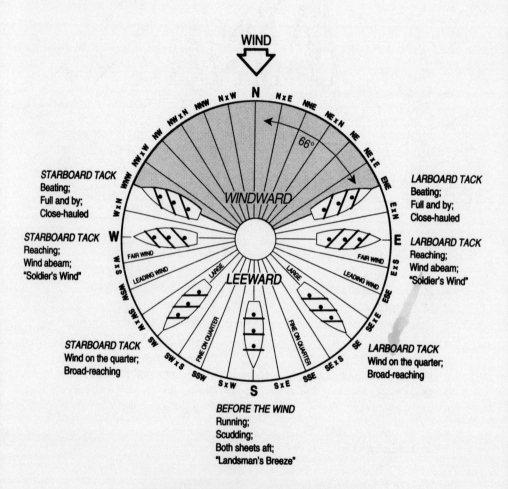

POINTS OF SAIL AND 32-POINT WIND-ROSE

A King's
Commander

BOOK I

An socia Iuone et Pallade fretus
armisona speret magis et freta iussa capessat,
siqua operis tanti domito consurgere ponto
fama queat?

Or shall he trust rather to the aid of Juno and Pallas
of the ringing armor, and launch forth at the king's
command, if haply, the sea subdued, some renown
could arise from so great a task?

—*Argonautica*
Book I, 73–76
Valerius Flaccus

CHAPTER

1

"DEAREST!" LEWRIE WHISPERED into her sweet-smelling hair.

"Oh, dearest God, Alan . . . !" Caroline responded in a like whisper. Though they could have shouted, for all the clamor of a sloop of war readying to set sail. "My only love."

A few more minutes, Lewrie squirmed in rising impatience; just a few minutes more, and I'm safe—I think. Mostly, anyway!

There were limits on how even the fondest captain and his wife could behave in public; quite unlike the open bawling of "wives"—the real helpmates, or the feigned for profit—had made when HMS *Jester* had at last lowered the "easy" pendant and put herself back into Discipline, and the men of the lower deck had bade farewell to their loved ones, perhaps forever. Squealing, mewling brats, snuffly seamen, and howling harridans, appearing far older and weathered than their years, cursed by Fate they'd wed with sailors. Saying their own good-byes—also perhaps forever; left with a new babe-to-be, a dubious pay certificate that would go for a quarter of its value with some agate-eyed jobber, a portion of their man's pay signed over with the Councillor of the Cheque, and always, and purposely, six months in arrears. A handful of solid coin, perhaps, since *Jester* had been formally commissioned in a home port. Paid just before sailing, so they'd not desert.

And, of course, the drunken shrieks of those harpies who'd come aboard as "wives," as they would every vessel Out of Discipline that they could reach, too drunk to know their tour of duty was over, and shoveled back into the bumboats, complaining loudly that they'd been shorted their due fee from their temporary "husbands."

Yesterday had been the hands' turn for partings; today it was the gunroom's. Unseemly weepings, wailings, and gnashing of teeth was not their way, not in public, at least.

" 'Tis been so *good* to have you home, even for a few scant . . ." Caroline shuddered. "I thought 'twould have been longer. I wished!"

"I know, dearest!" Alan sighed, shuddering himself as he used the wide brims of her stylish bonnet to screen them from the men in the waist—to kiss her soft, sweet lips just one more time, though they'd sworn to settle for last-minute affection in his great-cabins. "But things went so hellish good, so quickly, I . . ."

From the corner of his eye, Lewrie espied their new charge, young Sophie, Vicomtesse de Maubeuge, that unfortunate frail orphan of the Terror, and the evacuation of Toulon. Wan, pale . . . well not *that* wan any longer. In fact, she was eyeing him with a suspicious—yet sad—well, call it a leer, damme if he couldn't!

He gulped down his terror of her. Should she ever reveal to Caroline his carousing in the Mediterranean with Phoebe . . . ! Quick turn, hugging Caroline harder, turning her so her back was to Sophie and her almost-mocking brow. And to escape that lifted brow as well!

A few more minutes, pray God! he thought fervently. Off and away, then! And if it comes out, I'm a thousand miles alee!

"I'd hoped to be in port longer, as well, love. Get back to Anglesgreen. Let you show me off, hmm?" Lewrie said, essaying his most fetching grin; to tease and dandle his way free. And leave his lovely wife laughing. "Get everything settled before . . . *Damme*, sir! Down! Get down, this instant! What the bloody *hell* you think you're playing at, young sir?"

"*Mon Dieu, merde alors!*" Sophie gasped.

"Hugh!" Caroline shrieked. "Baby, don't *move*!"

Lewrie's youngest son had gotten away from his watchers once more, and had scaled the starboard mizzenmast ratlines. Again! This time, he was halfway to the fighting top!

Alan sprang to the bulwarks, getting a foot up on a carronade slide-carriage, then the blunt iron barrel, to swing into the shrouds and go aloft. "Hang on, lad. Don't go an inch higher, hear me?"

Taut as the mizzen stays were set up, as tensioned as they were through the deadeye blocks, the shrouds thrummed and juddered as Alan fearfully climbed, ratlines quivering with each rushed step.

"But, *Daddy* . . . !" Hugh protested. Aye, he *did* have a good grip on stays and ratlines, leaning into them; his pudgy little fists were a pink pair of vises on the tarred ropes, yet . . . !

Lewrie reached him, came eye level with his son.

"I *told* you," he panted, fuming. "I *told* you, you will *never* do this. It's for seamen, *grown* men . . ."

"But, Daddy, t'other boys . . . !" Hugh whined, gesturing briefly to the clutch of snot-nosed ship's boys, the usual mob of Beau-Nasties carried on ship's books as servants; some of whom were only double the total of Hugh Lewrie's precocious, and terrifying, four years.

"Down, I say!" Lewrie barked. "Now! And, carefully!"

"Aww . . ." Hugh grumbled, casting one more wistful glance aloft to the topmast truck, which had been his intent. Well, at least the cross-trees, if truth be told.

On deck at last, smudged with tar and slushes, Caroline knelt at his side in a twinkling, to coo and fret, wondering whether Hugh needed cosseting, or another sound thrashing. For foolishness; and for smutting his best suit of clothing, if nothing else.

"M'sieur, pardon!" Sophie reddened. "Ah tak' ma eye off 'eem jus' *une moment*, et . . . forgeev, *plais*."

Hmm, I could *use* this, Lewrie thought, though wishing to tear a strip off her hide, as he would the merest menial. No, he decided; jape his way out. Tug at her heartstrings. And her remorse.

"A thousand pardons, Captain," Lt. Ralph Knolles said, doffing his hat in concern that he might be found remiss. "I should have assigned a hand to shepherd the lads. A topman, it appears."

"A topman, indeed, Mister Knolles." Lewrie grinned. "Damme . . . he's a little terror, isn't he? Now we know where the next sailor in the family's to come from, hey?"

"*Indeed*, sir." Knolles smiled in return, with infinite relief.

"Mademoiselle Sophie," Lewrie said, turning to the girl. "Of course, you're forgiven. Nothing *to* forgive, really. As you become more familiar with us, you'll learn that Hugh will ever be our mischievous little imp. And a prankster. You must watch out for that, so he doesn't use you ill, as boys are wont to do—with sisters. From Sewallis, well . . . he's the quiet sort. I'm hoping you'll be a civilizing influence upon Hugh. And an edifying one 'pon Sewallis. As one more beloved member of our house. *Dear* as an elder sister."

"*Merci, m'sieur*," Sophie replied meekly, all but chewing her lip in contriteness.

"Well, then . . ." Lewrie concluded heartily. "My dear, perhaps we should bundle everyone into the buoy-tender before Hugh discovers the powder room, and erects a sand castle out of cartridges."

It was the perfect note to strike, Lewrie thought; if he did say so himself. Dear as he loved his wife and children—and he did in spite of his dalliances—sweet as it had been to have them down from the country to Portsmouth while *Jester* had recruited and manned, and as tender and passionate as Alan and Caroline's reunion had been—well, damme if I'm not glad to see the back of 'em, he thought, a touch rueful.

"Hugh!" he called, picking up the lad to bring him eye level again. "You be as good a boy as you can be . . . consid'rin'. And, I promise you, when you're older . . . next time I'm home, hey? There'll be all the climbing aloft you want. But not before I say, hear me?"

"I promise, Daddy," Hugh replied. And thank God he'd finally learned how to pronounce his R's. "An' then *I'll* be a sea officer, just like *you!*" the boy cried, wriggling with delight.

"That you will," he agreed, setting him down. God's teeth, what'd the boy expect, anyway? Second son, and all? It was naval or military service for him. "And Sewallis?"

"Yes, Father?" his eldest replied, ignored in all the confusion, and almost shrugging into himself as the hands of the after-guard trudged by to stations, as sailors and marines prepared to breast to the capstan bars to hoist anchor. Eyes darting constantly, not out of boyish curiosity, Lewrie was certain, but to see if he would be in the way! There'd been moments of folderol, of high cockalorum between them—but only a few—since he'd been "breeched."

Such a *grave* li'l man, Lewrie thought, with a trace of sadness, as he knelt by his side. "You make us proud at your school, now, hear me? Mind your mother . . ."

"I will, sir." Sewallis gulped, tearing up.

"Help make Sophie feel welcome and one of us."

"I will, sir."

"And keep an eye on Hugh. God knows, it takes more than one pair, now, don't it," Alan joshed.

"Good-bye, Father!" Sewallis suddenly wailed, tears flowing for real, and his solemn little face screwed up in pain. He flung himself at Lewrie, who hugged him close. "Wish you didn't have to go!"

"Growl you may, but go ye must, Sewallis," Lewrie told him as he patted his back. "Hush, now. Young gentlemen don't *cry*! Not in public, at any rate. Talk to your puppies, mayhap, when things are dreadful. They'll always cock an ear to you. That's why I have that damned Toulon. He's a good listener, in the main."

Sewallis, perhaps with good reason, had an abiding fear of cats. Old

William Pitt, sensing his shy nature, had taken a perverse delight in tormenting him before he'd passed over. Sewallis's happiest words, all during Lewrie's too-short spell in harbor, had been about dogs; specifically the litter of setter pups a stray bitch had whelped in their barn. Toulon, not to be outdone by his noble predecessor aft in the great-cabins, had spent half of Sewallis's times aboard playing panther-about-to-pounce from any convenient high place, or edging in close to *stare* at him when the family had dined aboard.

"Daddy . . . !" Sewallis shivered, trying to form a thought that simmered in his little head, some last meaningful declaration.

"There, there, little lad," Alan said without listening as he let him go and stood up. "Mind your way down the battens, into the tender. You're big enough, now, not to need a bosun's sling."

"I'll see to 'em, sir," Maggie Cony suggested, with a knowing wink. "Will an' me c'n cosset 'em inta th' boat."

"Aye, thankee kindly, Ma . . . Mistress Cony," Lewrie amended.

Her and Cony's own git birthed, and back on her pins nigh on a year, she was a handsome young wench; thatchy-haired like her new husband, blue-eyed, with a face never meant for true beauty, but a strong, open and honest, and pretty, face after all.

"And I'll keep a weather-eye on 'em, sir," Maggie promised. "As Will is wont t'say."

"And I on your man, mistress," Lewrie promised in turn. "Get him back to you, a warranted bosun someday, safe and sound."

That had been a proud and happy moment, to stand up for Cony in a dockside chapel as he took his bride, at last, four-square in his best rig as boatswain's mate, a petty officer, now. Though his swaddled son, born during their last cruise aboard *Cockerel*, had not taken well to the festivities, and had wailed through half of it.

"*Adieu, m'sieur,*" Sophie said, wan and weepy once again, her green eyes brimming. "*Bonne chance.*"

"Adieu, mademoiselle . . . adieu, Sophie," Alan replied, giving her a hug, too. "I trust you'll fall in love with little Anglesgreen. And find peace and contentment there. Fall in love with our family, too. As they already have with you," he stressed, hoping to get one last hint driven home.

"*Bonne chance,*" she said again, stepping back and dropping him an aristocratic curtsy in *congé*. "An', *merci beaucoup* for aw' you do *pour moi, m'sieur.*"

She rose, and fixed him with a curious, hard stare for a trice, her fine reddish-auburn hair flickering about her face and the shroud of her traveling cloak's hood, her green eyes intent in her slim and gamin face. "Poonish ze Republicains zat tuer . . . zat keel ma Charles, *m'sieur* Lewrie. Ah pray fo' you' success."

"*Merci.*" He nodded. "*Merci, beaucoup.* Caroline . . . ?"

He gave her his arm to walk her to the starboard entry port, and a waiting bosun's chair slung from aloft on the main-course yard.

"Alan, should the wind not serve . . ." she hinted desperately.

"Beat down to Saint Helen's Road, my dear, a few miles, and lay-to, till one comes fair," he said, a touch of severity in his voice. "Admiral Howe was lucky he had a favorable slant, t'other day. And then, off for Gibraltar, quick as dammit."

Out of long habit, he cast his eyes aloft to the impossibly long and curling coach whip of a commissioning pendant atop the mainmast truck. Then aft, to the Red Ensign that flew over the taffrail on the flagstaff. Red, for an independent ship, one sailing free of fleet or squadron, under Admiralty Orders. A few days before, Portsmouth Harbor had teemed with warships; stately 1st-Rate 100-gunners, 2nd Rates, 3rd-Rate 74's, and frigates, from the mouth of Southampton Water down into Spithead, west into the Solent as far as Buckler's Hard. Now, it yawned vast and empty. The French were out. And so was the Channel Fleet, under elderly Admiral Howe.

"But, if . . ."

"Admiralty Orders, dearest." He sighed. "With dispatches aboard. 'Make the best of my way, with all dispatch' . . . Should the wind come useful, we'd cut cables, instanter, and scud out under jibs and spanker, and no one'd mind us losing our anchors, 'long as the dispatches were on their way. I'm sorry. I truly am."

Didn't mean t'sound harsh, he told himself; mean ev'ry word of it, swear I do. But, there it is.

"I'm sorry, Alan," Caroline replied weakly, her lips atremble. " 'Tis just that I'm selfish for one more hour, half a day . . ."

" 'Tis just as hard for me, Caroline," he said with some heat. Meaning that, too. "God help women who marry sailors. Even in time o' peace, we're an undependable lot."

God help sailors six months from home, too, Lewrie told himself ruefully; them that can't keep their breeches' flap buttoned! Or their hearts content with what waits for 'em at home.

He'd played up bluff, hearty and cheerful, from his first sight of her, praying he wouldn't give the game away some night in his sleep. By muttering the wrong name in a moment of ecstasy, or those first few muzzy moments 'pon waking. Why, a man'd be a *fool*, who . . . !

Right, then, I'm a fool, he thought; always have been, probably always will be! A proper wife, the mother of three fine children (and thank God for small mercies that little Charlotte was left ashore today at their lodgings—the squally, squawly chub!).

He took Caroline's hands in his, looked deep into her beautiful hazel eyes; those merry loving eyes with the riant laugh-folds beneath which reflected her warmth, her caring, giving cheerfulness. In a face as slim and patrician as anyone at Court. For a year over the dreaded thirty, Caroline was as graceful, as lithe and lovely as a swan, sweet as swansdown to touch. No, this was no frumpy matron he'd married; not one to surrender easily to hearty country cooking and stoutness.

Caroline ran the farm better than most men, presented him with a clean, orderly, well-run household as gracious, as stylish, as any greathouse in England. Though there had not been time to see it, she swore that the gardens, the new furnishings, the finally finished salon and bedchambers for guests, were marvels. Everything Caroline turned her hand to was marvelous; *everyone* said so! Since their first tumbledown gatehouse home on New Providence, she'd been a wonder when it came to housewifery, at hosting—a spectacular blend of practical frugality when called for, a commonsensical North Carolina plantation domesticity, allied with a rich planter's, a rich squire's, easy and noble airs.

A sensible woman, well-read and so easy to talk to, about silly things, about matters of import beyond the stillroom, nursery, and bloody fashion! Tongue-in-cheek waggish, she could be, too; a grown woman's wry and witty waggishness, not the prattlings of some girlish chit fresh in her first Season in Society, still redolent of milk-pap and primer-level humor.

Light brown, sandy-blond hair, still distressed into stylish witches' ringlets, for "*à la victime*" was still all the "go"; a style that bared a graceful but strong neck and shoulders.

And I've cheated on *her*? he wondered; to himself, of course! Why, a man'd be a *total* . . . !

"It's time, I fear, beloved." He sighed heavily. "Else we'd never, and . . ."

"I know," Caroline whispered, patting the broad dark blue lapels of his new uniform coat. One last stroke of her gloved hand on his cheek. One last proper, public, buss . . . soft and fleeting on the lips, at a proper distance at the entry-port gate. An incline of her head for a departing bow. A doff of his new gold-laced hat with the wide gold tape about the brim so new it hadn't gone verdigris in salt air yet.

She accepted his help into the bosun's chair. One last squeeze of adoring fingers, as they had together once before, so long ago, at Charleston, after he'd evacuated her family from the impending Rebel takeover of Wilmington . . . twelve bloody years ago, and a bit, Alan marveled in reverie! Winter o' '81, and Fated t'be husband an' wife e'en then? Damned if we didn't both *know* it, too! Straightaway!

Then, up and away, to a falsetto squeal of the stay-tackle's blocks, the creak of the main-course yard as it swung her outboard of *Jester*'s hull to dangle over the buoy-tender that was below the mainmast chain platform.

Down there, Hugh was squirming against Mrs. Cony to crane and see everything about a ship getting underway. Sewallis . . .

Poor, *sad* Sewallis, Lewrie thought, still doffing his hat to them all, finding something new to be rueful about as he attempted to recall how much attention he'd really given the lad.

Prim as a parson, face reddened by wind and emotion, and about as screwed up as a hanged spaniel's—looking just about that happy, too! Slim little scholar's hands clasped tight below his waistcoat as if in supplication.

Sophie de Maubeuge, dabbing at her eyes with a handkerchief, too tearful (thank bloody Christ!) to recall her earthly savior's—ahem—Fall from Grace! And pray God it don't suddenly come to her, either, Lewrie asked his Maker most earnestly! Poor chit; not a relative left alive, either guillotined—or killed in that last sea battle that got me this ship as prize. Fate's been slamming her doors on Sophie's fingers everywhere she turns. Titled aristocrat—*slam*. Marryin' Charles de Crillart? Slam, he was killed when we took *Jester*. Now she's off the ship for a strange house in a strange new country. Catholic convent girl. Slam, slam, slam. Have to pretend to be—or *learn* to pretend to be—the same as any country-raised English girl. Go for Church of England in a year'r two . . . if she has *any* sense at all.

God save her; in my house? Part o' my family? He shuddered suddenly. Poor little mort! Nigh a daughter, to the likes o' *me*?

"Good-bye!" he called down, once Caroline was safely settled on a thwart amidships of the sturdy buoy-tender. "Write often, as will I! All of you! You mind what I say, Sewallis?" he cried, meaning to offer the lad a crumb at the last, to atone. "I wish to hear all about your progress. *And* your puppies! They should be good hunters, by the time I'm back, hey?"

"Uhm, excuse me, sir, but . . ." Lieutenant Knolles interrupted with a sorrowful cough into his fist. "There's a veer to the wind, and . . ."

"I saw, Mister Knolles," Lewrie replied from the corner of his mouth, still posed at the bulwarks with a gay grin plastered on his "phyz" for his family. "Hands to stations, then. Heave us in to short stays."

A Marine drummer began a roll. A fiddle screeched as one of the idlers tried his tuning and sought the proper key. Spithead nightingales began to peep, as newly warranted Boatswain Porter and his Bosun's Mate Will Cony, both off that ill-starred *Cockerel* frigate, piped the commands for stations for leaving harbor, and up-anchor.

A precious, breathless moment more, as the buoy-tender's oarsmen stroked the boat away, clear of *Jester*'s side. "Give way, together!" her midshipman called from the stern sheets and tiller-bar. One moment more to lift his cocked hat in salute to kith and kin, then put it firmly back upon his head and turn, dismissing them, as he *must*, and stride purposefully to the center of the quarterdeck.

His quarterdeck!

He let out a heavy, lip-puffing sigh that bespoke both his impatience, and his relief. Swung his arms and clapped his hands before him unconsciously, to release a scintilla of how tautly he'd forced himself to pose, this last day in harbor.

Relief, that he'd not blown the gaff. Relief, that, no matter how dear he cherished them all, he was off to sea, and they were no longer the center of his universe. Not when a greater, wider world awaited.

Impatience, of a certainty, to be off and doing in that greater world, which was now filled with strife and the stink of gunpowder; in a proper ship, well-armed and able. A ship he'd already proved on the passage home, which could take the worst of the Bay of Biscay gales and swim as proud as any 5th-Rate frigate. Fast, sleek, with a clean entry and forefoot; not so fine as to bury under opposing waves, but cleave them and ride up and over. Deep enough in draught to grip the seas, resist slippage to leeward; long enough on her waterline to tear across the seas like a racehorse. Wide enough in beam to carry her artillery and stores safely, to be sea-kindly as well as fast . . .

And for himself—for the first time in his career, he would command a real warship, not a gun ketch converted from a bomb vessel, nor a hostilities-only, hired armed brig or dispatch schooner. This marvelous Sloop of War was 380 tons, eighteen-gunned, a French corvette—a swanlike and lovely three-masted miniature frigate!

And, he was a step closer to post-captain's rank, when he could be eligible for command of a true frigate, a rated ship. Crews called the commander appointed over them in any warship their captain. Now, as an Admiralty-confirmed commander, he was uniformed almost like a true post-captain, and *was* a post-captain in all but name.

White breeches and hose, white waistcoat and shirt, legs now encased from the knees down in a spanking-new pair of Hessian boots. He could not resist the temptation of having the London shop sew on tiny gold-fringed tassels. A dark blue coat, with a dark-blue stand-up collar and broad blue lapels, instead of a lieutenant's white ones. There were two bands of gold lace encircling his cuffs, set with three gilt fouled-anchor buttons. The collar, front, top, and bottom, bore a wide band of gold lace; as did the two outside pocket flaps, along with even more set-in-three gilt buttons. The lapels' outer edges, and tops and bottom seams, were gold-laced, and nine gilt buttons to either lapel allowed it to be worn open, or closed in foul weather.

Another thing to rue, he thought suddenly. Going to London to assure his confirmation, and smarm his way through the junior clerks below-stairs, the basement moles who had pored over all his records of service, "tsk-tsk-ing" over every undotted I or slovenly crossed T.

Then off to Coutts's Bank with prize-money certificates, off to see his solicitor, Matthew Mountjoy, who handled his affairs ashore; both the farm and his dealings with the financial side of the Admiralty—and his creditors. Feeling relief, and guilt, that he was called by duty from the bosom of his family after only one night with them in hired lodgings in Portsmouth. And before any trace of his affair with Phoebe showed on his face!

The pleasures of shopping, like a wealthy gentleman, free of a demand upon his time. Of *course*, he needed new hats from Lock's, new full-dress and undress coats, pristine white breeches and waistcoats, shoes and boots—that was required! Pistols, too, from Manton; his had gone down with *Zélé*. A new sea chest in which to store all his new finery . . . and a new sword.

He'd have a Gill's, no other. Wilkinson was all right, he thought, but a Gill's he'd had before, and it had never failed him. Until he'd been forced to surrender it to that puffed up, piss-proud young Frog, Col. Napoleone Bonaparte. Oh, there was the slim, straight rapierlike smallsword he'd taken from the French captain, when he'd taken *Jester*—back when she was named *Sans Culottes*. But it was much too ornate, a bit *too* slim and elegant a blade, fit for full-dress occasions, not a real bare-knuckle brawl. He wanted a fighting sword, and that was what he'd found.

It *was* a Gill's—at thirty-one, he sensed he had already developed a conservative streak, and some positively rigid prejudices—less elegant than his lost one, but more fit for the melee. His old hanger had been slimmer, a true gentleman's "hunting sword," slightly curved. His new blade, the cutler had told him, was patterned upon a French grenadier's hanger. The blade was wider along its entire length, a tad thicker in cross-section, and only slightly curved; much less like a Light Cavalry saber than most, with all but the first two inches before the guard honed razor-sharp, and the first eight inches of the top behind the wicked point as well. It fit his hand, felt solid and durable, yet nowhere near as heavy as a humbler cutlass. Like all hunting swords or hangers, it was shorter than a smallsword—only twenty-six inches of blade—but he preferred that in the confusion of a shoulder-to-shoulder, nose-to-nose melee. And it was reassuringly heavy close to the guard, but wickedly light and quick as it tapered to the point.

Black leather grip wrapped in gilt wire, a slim, gilt-steel swept hilt with a large oval guard to protect his fingers. There were no seashells this time, but a fairly plain pattern of stylized oak leaves. The scabbard was black leather, with gilt furnishings. They had soldered a coin-silver plaque to the outer face of the upper furnishing, with a pair of crossed cannon over a fouled anchor engraved, wreathed in oak leaf. Almost like the design of his old watch fob . . . which was now the prize of some garlic-breathed French sergeant of Lancers, too, unfortunately!

New watch and fob, new grogram boat cloak, shaggy watch coat, dressing robes for warm or cold weather . . . it had turned into *such* an orgy of Spending and Getting! And guilt over his pleasures had driven him to purchase even more, for Caroline, the children, Sophie . . . even a pair of bosun's pipes for Porter and Cony, to mark the warrants he'd gotten Porter and Bittfield, and the Admiralty's recognition of his own prerogative to promote Will Cony to bosun's mate.

Then, recruiting drove him from their arms, setting up his own rendezvous, printing fliers to summon calf-headed cullys who wished to go to sea, dealing with the local regulating captain of the Impress Service. The dockyard officials, the port admiral . . . to find the rope and timber to restock *Jester* with spare topmasts and yards, stuns'l booms, miles of cable and rope, fresh paint, gunner's tools . . . and the reams of correspondence necessary to beg for permission, to justify any slight alteration that might cost the Crown tuppence! Why, it was so odious, so all-encompassing an endeavor, that he'd been lucky to get a *meal* ashore with Caroline and . . . !

"Anchor's hove short, sir. Up and down!" Knolles called Lewrie from his reverie.

"Very well, Mister Knolles. Brace for the heavy heave. Topmen aloft. Free tops'ls only. Spanker, jibs and tops'ls. Inner, outer flying, and fore topmast stays'l from the foc's'le . . . main topmast stays'l and mizzen t'gallant stays'l. Should this perverse wind head us, I don't wish us fighting the square-s'ls all the way aground, on the Isle of Wight. Rough on the quick-work. *And* the career, hmm?"

"Aye, sir!" Knolles grinned in agreement.

"Wait to ring up or fish the anchors to the catheads, Mister Knolles. *Should* we get headed, we may have to anchor again, quickly. At the southern end of Saint Helen's Road, for certain, if a clear wind can't be found in the Channel."

"Aye aye, sir. Mister Porter, Mister Cony!"

"Won't be elegant, but . . ." Lewrie shrugged to his sailing master, Mister Edward Buchanon, a swart and laconic-looking soul come down from the Medway to be appointed into *Jester*, fresh from years aboard other ships as a master's mate, and fresh from his Trinity House examination at Tower Hill. So far, Lewrie had found him slow in speech, dull as dishwater in conversation. But that, he suspected, was the man's innate caution, as an experienced seaman first, and as a "newly" with his first senior warrant, in a strange ship, second.

"Aye, Cap'um." Buchanon nodded solemnly, with only a glint of delight in his eyes to betray him. " 'Tis better t'be safe'n sorry, I says. Sloop o' war's *meant* t' dash, now an' agin. But, 'tis many a *dashin'* cap'um laid himself all-aback b'cause o' it. You'll be tackin', soon's we have steerageway, I suggest? Larboard tack'll take us too far t'loo'rd, toward the island."

"I most certainly will, Mister Buchanon, and thankee kindly for your wise suggestion," Lewrie happily agreed.

"Heave, and in sight!" The call came from the forecastle, as the best bower arose from the depths, trailing a storm cloud of mud and sand, and the stench of weed. Pawls clacked in the capstans, now rumbling as the hands trotted around them, bare feet drumming. Sails rustled and blocks cried as canvas sprouted on standing stays and on the tops'l yards high aloft. *Jester* heeled slightly to the pressure, stirring and shuffling sidewise, crabbing to the wind, with her tall rudder hard-over to windward, two quartermasters, Spenser and Brauer, maintaining their full weight on the double wheel. A gust, and she heeled a bit more, but a gust that backed more abeam this time, and Lewrie saw the quartermasters ease the helm a spoke or two, smiling.

"Der rutter, ve haff, Kapitan," Brauer, the pale-blond Hamburg German informed him. "*Genug, aber* . . . she bites, zir."

"Lay her full-and-by, close to the wind as she'll bear, till we have a goodly speed, then," Lewrie told him, with relief in his voice. They *weren't* going to be blown sidewise onto the shore to their lee! "Ready to come about to the starboard tack."

"Well, the lee tops'l braces, and belay!" Lewrie could hear Cony shouting from the waist to the gangway brace-tenders. *Jester* did not rate a yeoman of the sheets in her muster book, so a bosun's mate was called upon to supervise several chores beyond the duties of one aboard a larger ship.

Lookin' fine, Will Cony, Alan told himself proudly; lookin' fine.

Cony had filled out a bit from the stripling volunteer he'd met aboard the *Desperate* frigate during the Revolution. Dressed now in a little style, with a white-taped short seaman's coat with gilt buttons, a dark blue waistcoat, and tailored slop trousers; good sturdy shoes on his feet, well-blacked, with silver buckles—solid silver, not coated "pinch-beck." A petty officer's plain cocked hat instead of a round hat with low crown and flat, tarred brims. The former poacher lad from Gloucestershire had risen in the world. And would rise even further, if Lewrie could do anything about it. The fleet needed men like Will Cony.

"Three knots, sir!" Mister Midshipman Spendlove shouted from the taffrails, where he and his new mate, Midshipman Hyde, had just taken a cast of the log.

"*Verdamt!*" Brauer groaned, and the sails aloft rustled, losing their luff, as the commissioning pendant streamed farther aft, to the starboard quarter.

"Headed, by God. Mister Knolles, ready about?" Lewrie called.

"Ready, sir."

"Helm alee! Tack her, Mister Knolles. New course, due east."

And *Jester* came about. Logy at slow speed, but her bows came around sweetly, the harbor sweeping by in an effortless pirouette. Seawater began to chuckle and gurgle under her forefoot, to murmur down her sides. From aft, there was a burbling, high-throated sound of chuckling from around her rudder as she settled on her new course and found new strength in a wind now come more from the south. From France, where she'd been born.

Across the harbor she trundled under reduced sail, Ride Sand and No-Man's-Land astern, and Horse Sand, and the Horse Tail, off her bows, in the narrows.

Directly the wind backed more from the east, she fell off and tacked again to larboard tack, with the wind striking her left side, with Warner

Sand and St. Helen's Patch well to their lee. Monkton Fort was the stern range-mark, up to the nor'west.

Damme, can we do it in one long board? Lewrie exulted within. It would be a hellish comedown to chortle too soon, if he all but promised an easy departure, then was forced to come to anchor, after all. Best keep silent, for the nonce. And fret, while appearing a paragon of equanimity.

No, they were headed again as the fickle breeze swung back to the South. Larboard tack would force them down below St. Helen's Patch and toward Denbridge Point, into the cul-de-sac of Nab Rock, the New Grounds, and Long Rock.

"Ready about, Mister Knolles! Quartermasters, new course east-sou'east. Mister Buchanon, I propose to go east-about the New Grounds, and stand out into the Channel to make our offing, before we come about to west, in deep water."

"Aye, sir, that'd be best, I think." Buchanon nodded, after he'd pored over the chart pinned to the traverse board on the binnacle cabinet. He looked relieved, that his expertise would not be tested in those narrow channels, for below Denbridge Point there were also the risks of Betty's Ledge, the Denbridge Ledge close inshore, and North Offing, or Princessa Rock. They were day-marked, supposedly lit at night, but it was still a chancy business.

Around *Jester* came to the starboard tack, shallow Langstone Harbor and Cumberland Fort abeam to larboard. Chuckling again, as she passed four knots. There was a bit more chop now, the promise of the Channel's lumps to come. Current flowing one way, tide race opposed to it, and a southerly wind cross-patched atop it all, they would be careening and bounding like a coach on a winter-rutted road soon enough. *If* the wind stayed from the south, and they remained at ESE, close-hauled as dammit, right up against it.

Finally, St. Helen's town, and its creek on their starboard quarter! The last spit of New Grounds abeam!

"Ring up anchors, Mister Knolles, we've no more need of 'em. Ring up and fish, then buckle the hawseholes. Idlers! A tune, there!" Commander Lewrie demanded, utterly relieved, now that he and his fine little ship were safely on their way to making their offing.

The fiddle screeched again, in harmony with a tuning box and a fife. *"Heart of Oak,"* they began, and everyone knew it by heart—the former *Cockerel's*, the fresh-caught merchant seamen from the press, the hands turned over from the guard ships, those that Howe hadn't put to sea aboard his line-of-battle ships; the ships' boys second class down from

London and Mister Powlett's Marine Society, the Marines, and the sailors lent to him off Nelson's *Agamemnon*, off *Victory* and *Windsor Castle* to work her passage home; the midshipmen, of a certainty, and the brace of nine-year-old boys first class gentlemen volunteers who'd signed aboard as cabin servants to learn enough of the sea so they could become midshipmen someday themselves.

And the landsmen from the hulks and debtor's prisons, the volunteers from some rendezvous tavern inland, the sprinkling of Maltese seamen hired out by the Grand Masters he'd ended up with—soon they all would learn it, and know it by heart.

> *Come cheer up, my lads, 'tis to glory we steer,*
> *to add something more to this wonderful year;*

Add *something*, Alan vowed to himself. Something writ large. I've never known a peaceful commission, a voyage that was "all claret and cruising." Trouble . . . well, damme, trouble has a way of findin' me. This time, though . . . this time I'm all *but* a captain, on me own bottom with a ship and crew seasoned just enough for starters. And I'll make 'em even better. God save me, but I *love* this ship! What she's capable of, given half a chance. What I think this ship, and I, together, can accomplish. Father, Fate . . . the Navy, *beat* me into a sailor. Well then, so be it. A damn' good'un, too, I believe, at last. And who'd have ever thought it!

> *To honor we call you, not press you like slaves,*

Oh, yes, we do press! Pressed *me*, in my own way, he laughed.

> *For who are so free as the sons of the waves?*

Free? he scoffed. Mostly, yes, I am. At last! To run a ship my *own* way. Take her in that Rebel John Paul Jones's "harm's way." And win! Damme, that's been my main fret—that I wanted *this* just as much as family . . . maybe more.

> *Heart of oak are our ships,*
> *heart of oak are our men,*
> *we always are ready;*
> *steady, boys, steady . . .*

Alan Lewrie had never been known as much of a singer, but this time he lolloped out the chorus in a bellow, along with the hands of the after-guard and the quarterdeck people.

We'll fight and we'll conquer, again and again!

A first lift of the bows to the Channel chops, a sluice of sea breaking over her forecastle. The rush of water creaming alongside of her impatient flanks. A sibilant, silken respiring, it was, of a live being made of oak and iron. Wind coming stronger aloft, keening among a maze of sheets, braces, jears, lifts and halliards, an Irish banshee's crooning moan among the stays and shrouds, with frolicsome flutterings, as luffs and ratlines danced.

HMS *Jester*, eighteen-gunned Sloop of War had been reborn; and reborn English. And around her beak-head rails, and new figurehead of a gilt-crowned fool, an English Channel now christened her with salt.

"OFFING ENOUGH, MISTER Buchanon," Lewrie decided, one hour later. "Mister Knolles, come about to larboard tack, then make sail. Fore and main courses to the first reefs. Take in the main topmast, and the mizzen t'gallant, stays'ls."

"Aye, sir . . . all plain sail. Bosun Porter? Ready about!"

More canvas—more speed; white-hued virginal canvas never exposed to weather except at sail drill during their working-up period of River Discipline. Course-sail brails undone, drawn down by their clews to sheet them home, with a wary portion gathered in reserve about the yards to the first line of reef points. Long yards creaking around to the best angle for a beam wind—a "soldier's wind"—powerfully long English yards, and wider, fuller-cut sails than the more-timid French practice.

More flutings and keenings aloft, more moans and whisperings. *Jester* began to bound over the sea, her wake-breath sonorous yet insistent. As Commander Lewrie left his quarterdeck, at last satisfied, to go below, he could almost believe he could hear her singing to herself—a chorale of freedom and power.

While around her forefoot and cutwater, around her transom post, that chuckling, gurgling rush . . .

HMS *Jester*, he could almost conjure, was laughing softly with delight, as she stood out to sea. Stood out to find the war.

CHAPTER
2

JESTER'S FIRST SUNSET spent upon the sea, a rare and rosy-hued wonder to the west, the end of a pleasant and bracing late May day of sailing. Lewrie had no time to go on deck to appreciate it, however; he was concluding the last of his voluminous paperwork with his clerk and the purser.

"I think that should be all for today, at least, Mister Mountjoy." He sighed, after looking over the last revisions to what was now the *thrice*-amended watch-and-quarter bills, and the sheaf of instructions to guide quarterdeck watch-standers as to his personal idiosyncrasies, his Order Book. "A fair copy of watch-and-quarter bills for Knolles, Mister Buchanon, Bosun Porter and Cony, and the purser here, by, oh . . . say, four bells of the forenoon. Order Book by the beginning of the First Dog Watch, tomorrow."

"So sorry, sir, but that would be . . . ?" Thomas Mountjoy asked, a quizzically amused, and sheepish, grin on his face (which seemed so far his only expression) becoming even more pronounced.

"Umphh," commented Mister Giles, the purser, from the offhand side of the well-polished cherry-wood desk at which they sat in Lewrie's day-cabin. But Giles was, even for one as young as his hapless captain's clerk, a "scaly fish," with years at sea, to Mountjoy's "new-come."

"Ten in the morning for the watch-bills, Mister Mountjoy," Lewrie explained patiently. "And four p.m. for the Order Books."

"Ah! Comes the dawn, so to speak, sir!" Mountjoy japed, with a theatrical overplay of voice and "phyz." "So much to take in, d'ye see. I should have thought, though . . . once away from all those pettifogging shore officials, there'd bit a bit less, uhm . . . correspondence."

Alan hoped he wouldn't be sorry that he'd done his solicitor a favor, in taking his ne'er-do-well younger brother aboard. He needed a clerk, and when offered . . . Perhaps he'd agreed too readily!

But, he'd been fit and full of cream at the moment; and full of himself with being confirmed, fresh from Coutts's and the deposit of his officially honored prize-money certificates, smug with his acclaim in the London *Gazette* that had made much ado over his most recent action in the Mediterranean, which had won him *Jester*, and having saved those Royalist French *émigrés*—men, women, and children doomed to slaughter on the spot, or beneath the guillotine, had he not been victorious.

And, full of a rather good claret, he recalled, at Matthew Mountjoy's office. This younger Thomas, though, was a hopeless legal student, a "Will He—Nill He" sort only *playing* at reading law around Lincoln's Inn Fields, and so *easily* drawn from his studies! Might a gallant captain—to wit, Lewrie!—prevail upon the Admiralty, and obtain Thomas an appointment? Take him to sea, away from venal amusements . . . why, he could clerk, continue to read his law, profit financially, and return a man, with more self-discipline, hmm?

Daft, Alan thought, studying Mountjoy. He's the forehead of an *addled* hen, and that, in the clouds! Writes a fair hand, though . . . He puffs and pants his way through, but gets there, in the end. Mountjoy had at least appareled himself for sea (with some delight). He wore a dark blue plain undress coat, waistcoat, and breeches; though he clung to land in his choice of hats—a tall, tapering, narrow-brimmed high-crowned civilian style. He'd made sartorial concessions to the fleet, while, it seemed, not one whit of effort to accommodate himself to its lore and lingo.

"Should've thought, 'fore *joining*, sir," Giles snickered, removing his square-lensed brass spectacles to polish on his handkerchief. " 'Cause once back in the pettifoggers' reach, a man'd think the Papist Inquisition's got him, if his accounts and books don't make sense. Oh, whoa-up, there, young sir. *That* book'd be one o' mine. The green'un, there, I believe?"

"Oh, so sorry, Mister Giles." Mountjoy gaped, looking sheepish and hopelessly muddled anew, as he gathered up all his untidy piles of rough drafts, books, and forms. "But they do appear all of a hellish *piece*, so far, sir."

Alan suspected that Thomas Mountjoy was too hen-headed to come in from out of a driving rain, a harmless but will-less mote who would waft through Life on the first wind that found him.

Giles, though . . . Same age, same build, same ink-stained stricture to his career; but there, all semblance ended. Giles had come up from the orlop, first jack-in-the-bread-room, then assistant and clerk to some purser, apprenticed since his early teens to a dour, penny-pinching trade far longer than Mountjoy, all ledgers and finger cramp; fretting over ha'pence per gallon and stone, Lewrie shouldn't wonder, since his voice broke.

He played the cynical, "wise beyond his years" wizard with his records and sums, an able and efficient administrator down from the Victualing Board at Somerset House, though he sang his "old tarpaulin man" song a bit too often for Lewrie's taste. Confident in his first warrant on his own, wry and acting just a touch "fly," as if it were all a nudging, wink-tipping, cheese-paring game; he reminded his captain of an East End confidence man, with his three walnut shells, and a single pea on a blanket, and suspected Giles had had mentors who'd been *real* "Captain Sharps," archetypical "Nip-Cheeses"—*and* quite possibly crooks!—as his teachers.

Sadly, Lewrie could dismiss Mountjoy should he not work out, but he was stuck with Giles. Mountjoy served at the captain's pleasure, paid the same as a midshipman (which wasn't much worth bragging about!) and had no protected status. Giles, though, had an Admiralty Warrant, after performing Mountjoy's job for at least a year aboard another ship, in addition to his long period of training in dispensing food, drink, clothing, and sundries. Should *Jester* pay off after a three-year commission, officers and crew would depart, while the purser, gunner, boatswain, cook, and a few others with senior warrant would remain aboard to await a new captain and crew. Or should she be laid up in-ordinary, Giles would live aboard, at full pay. Like the Church, it was a lifetime living.

A good purser went far toward developing a reasonably happy ship; a dishonest one could ruin even the best. Giles could be the sort who could, with dexterous and creative ledgering, "make dead men chew tobacco," and continue to purchase china mugs, plates, slop clothing, hats, shoes, and . . . and, well—plug or twist tobacco, long after they'd been discharged-dead, discharged, or run!

So far, Alan had kept a wary eye on Giles and his ledgers, and could find nothing out of the ordinary, insisting to see, and help account for, the quality and quantity of everything that had come aboard, which Giles would issue in future.

Giles had become even more "salty," more affably wise. But also more amenable and agreeable, as if he'd taken Alan's warning to heart, and realized that he'd met his equal. And would settle for legitimate profits. God knew, that was enough for most pursers, when the Admiralty paid for sixteen ounces, and let him issue at twelve to the pound; and that at twenty-eight days the lunar month, not thirty or thirty-one to the calendar month. Giles should have quite *enough* profit, thankee!

"Right, then . . ." Lewrie said, by way of dismissal.

Giles, more used to a captain's ways, rose at once. Mountjoy, however, cast a disappointed (and hopeful-but-sheepish, it went without saying) glance over Lewrie's shoulder to the wine cabinet behind him, where rested a likely looking wide-bottomed porcelain decanter and some up-turned glasses, before getting the hint.

Buy your own bloody drink, Alan scowled silently; that's what your Navy pay's for! *And* that remittance your brother gave you, so you could go a gentleman. Another sad shock for young Mountjoy when he'd first come aboard—that he'd *not* lodge in the great-cabins and share meals and wine with his "employer" after-hours. He berthed on the rancid, fetid orlop deck, with the surgeon's mate and midshipmen.

YOUNG, LEWRIE THOUGHT, once they'd gone. Thank God, 'cept for the few like Mountjoy, the fresh-caught landsmen, and the youngest of the ship's boys, we're mostly experienced. His proportion of seamen, ordinary or able, was higher than usual, thanks to generosity back in the Mediterranean. Recruiting had gone extremely well, too, and now he had enough strong backs among the landsmen to do the dumb-ox work of pulley-hauley. And a positive glut of ship's boys, who were young enough to learn the seaman's trade; quite unlike landsmen, who stayed at the rate for years, too old and set in their civilian ways to alter.

Hands and officers young enough, full of piss and vinegar—and ambition—to know what *could* be done. And not so old they'd turned mossy-backed old turtles, with their heads and legs drawn up in snappish old age, too frightened of departing from The Way Things Had Always Been Done, with a thousand excuses as to why a feat could *not* be accomplished.

"*Maiwee?*" Toulon the ram-kitten inquired from atop Alan's wine cabinet, as he poured himself a glass of rhenish. The catling'd been lurking up there in the shadows, wary of intruders into "his" territory. Arching and stretching, flexing sleepy claws as he craned his neck forward to touch noses, rub cheeks, and make lusty purring snorts of gap-mouthed adoration after a good nap.

Lewrie chucked him under his white chin, gave his white chops a thorough rub, then turned to head aft for the transom settee, to take his ease and sip his wine, where the opened sash-windows promised some fresh sea air. "Come on, Toulon," he coaxed. "Playtime!"

"*Mummer?*" Toulon grumbled as he padded his fore end down the face of the wine cabinet, his haunches still atop, readying for a leap. And announcing his stunt, as an acrobat in a raree show might shout "Hopa!" and clap his hands, to make the feat look more exciting.

Toulon sprang, a prodigious, steel-sinewed leap to the desk.

Unfortunately, the black-and-white catling landed on a sheet of folio paper atop that bee's-waxed and polished cherry surface. He and the paper skidded to starboard. And digging in his claws didn't help a bit! Laid over slightly "downhill" from horizontal, on the larboard tack, the silky surface became a greased slipway.

Toulon sat down on his haunches, as if that might help. Surely, sitting still meant *still*, right? Then, he sailed off the desktop into space. And a very perplexed, and forlorn Toulon, with a contrite and reverent "*Mowr?*", asked his cat gods just what the odds were he'd *not* come another cropper. Or how large a fool he was going to look in a few seconds.

There was a bit of midair scrambling, trying to *climb* the sheet of paper's front end as it collapsed beneath him and went sailing off on its own course of perversely cruel abandonment.

"*Urrff!*" he grunted as he landed, immediately slinking off to starboard, into the shadows where the brace of candles on the desk and the gently swinging pewter lanthorns overhead could not shed light on his humiliation.

"God, but you're *such* a bloody disaster!" Alan screeched with laughter, plunking down on the transom settee, too hugely amused to stand. Toulon was almost a yearling now, and still kitten-clumsy. And he'd been a most excruciatingly clumsy kitten to begin with, too!

Andrews his coxswain, and his cabin steward Aspinall, stuck their heads out for a second from the dining coach and small pantry. On the quarterdeck, the watch and the after-guard turned toward the open skylights over the great-cabins and marveled. What sort of a captain we got? they wondered. *That* wasn't a sound most associated with a sea officer!

"Come out of there, Toulon," Lewrie coaxed, after he'd calmed, and had a sip or two more of his wine. He got down on hands and knees in front of the pewlike sofa, a crude oak construct shackled to the starboard bulkhead between a pair of nine-pounders. Spindle posts on the back, and openings around the corners, held ties for bright damask cushions that Caroline had made for him. "Come on. 'Tis only your pride's hurt. I hope. Come out, poor puss. Towey?" Another thing Caroline had whipped together from scraps of colorful spun yarn; a rounded oval with ears and legs—Toulon's favorite plaything.

Two chatoyant yellow orbs regarded him from beneath the sofa, slowly blinking. But mostly slit in mortification. "*Meek?*" came a mournful little wren-peep. God, but he was so embarrassed!

Lewrie reached under to stroke him, to offer the plaything—but he was having none of that. Toulon folded his arms, tucked his front paws under his chest, and downturned his luxuriant whiskers.

"*Moi,*" he harrumphed testily, past somber jowls. Bugger off, you heartless bastard! 'Twasn't funny, Lewrie interpreted.

"Well, if you won't, you won't." Alan sighed, getting to his feet. He got down his plain undress coat, threw it on, and stalked forward.

"Yer supper be ready not ten minute from now, sir," Aspinall assured him quickly. "Yer cook come t'tell me." Aspinall was one of those unfortunate landsmen some regulating captain and surgeon of the press had passed, when they shouldn't have; a feeble-bodied city-bred footman, who'd lost his last employ. At least he knew enough about householdery to a gentleman for Lewrie to take him off the gangways, out of the waist, and apply his knowledge aft. Where he'd not rupture himself straining at braces and sheets. The lad was a slack, sunken-chested seventeen, ill-featured, but mannerly (mostly). At least, he had been, until he'd realized how grand his newfound stature was aboard a ship. A captain's servant ruled the roost over the stewards to lesser men.

"I'll be on deck, till then," Lewrie said, finishing his wine and setting the glass on the dampened tablecloth, which would keep most plates and such from slipping off in a moderate sea such as this evening's.

"I'll send yer . . . cox'n, t'fetch ya, sir," Aspinall suggested with lidded eyes, and a jerk of his head to Andrews, the West Indies free black who'd popped up like a jack-in-the-box a scant week before sailing to sign aboard.

"If you would come tell me, Andrews?" Lewrie said to his man directly, bypassing the servant, who most likely resented having a Negro give him orders.

"Aye, sah," Andrews allowed cheerfully, too experienced a man to take

notice of the jealousies of a boy; and a fresh-caught "newly" landsman, at
that. It was a huge joke, to him.

ALAN EMERGED ON the gun deck from the door to his quarters in the
substantial, but temporary, wood partitions. They'd come down in battle,
struck to the orlop, and his cabin would be stripped of all finery and
furnishings, to avoid the danger of splinters. A Marine private, one of the
watch who'd stand guard over his privacy 'round the clock, presented his
musket, and Lewrie touched the brim of his cocked hat in reply.

Up to the quarterdeck by the larboard, windward, ladder, to the further alarm of his watch-standers.

"Carry on," he called to them affably. "Just up for a breath of air," he
elaborated, as he paced to the windward mizzenmast stays. Lieutenant
Knolles and Mister Wheelock, the master's mate, shuffled down deck to
starboard, yielding the windward side to him, which was his by right,
alone, whenever he was on deck.

There was very little left of the sunset his paperwork had kept him
from relishing. Just a faint bricky trace of red and umber low on the
Western horizon, with towering banks of slag-gray clouds spread to either
side of *Jester*'s course, and but the slightest sullen primrose glade upon
the waves over which the ship's jib boom and bowsprit rose and fell. A
touch more wind on his cheek, perhaps a hatful, no more, and veering
forrud by no more than half a point from abeam. *Jester* rose and fell
more regularly, now, gently hobbyhorsing as the deeper water hinted the
long-set rollers of the Atlantic to come, after the chops of the Channel
closer inshore. England was an indistinct razor-thin ebony smudge to the
north. France was below the horizon, lost in the companionable darkness. It was almost late enough for the lamps forrud at the forecastle
belfry, by the watch, hour, and half-hour glasses and bell, and the large
taffrail lanthorns, to appear cheerful and strong. A few faint stars, mostly
astern above the lanthorns, were already out.

Lewrie paced slowly aft along the larboard bulwarks, skirting the slide-
carriages of the newly installed carronades. "Smashers"—eighteen-
pounders—they were, short, pestle-looking cylinders of guns that threw
heavy, solid iron shot, heavier than anything HMS *Jester* could ever
mount as deck artillery. Though they didn't shoot quite as far as long
guns, they dealt out horrific damage when they struck. And, so far (praise
Jesus) only the Royal Navy used them in any numbers. There were four
on *Jester*'s quarterdeck, and another pair forrud on the foc's'le, in lieu of

chase guns. Alan would have preferred two long six-pounders there, but the officials of the Ordnance Board at Gun Wharf had had only so much patience for the blandishments of a junior officer.

Lucky to keep the guns I *have*, Lewrie told himself, smiling in grim reverie. A full twenty guns made *Jester* a small frigate, under the new rating system, a post-captain's command; while an *eighteen*-gunned ship sloop was suitable to a newly promoted commander! They'd taken two away from him, with many "tsk-tsks" over his affrontery, to show up in a vessel armed beyond his rank.

British sloops, be they brig, schooner, ketch, or three-masted ship-rigged vessels, were allotted six-pounders, and that, by God, was that. Sixth-Rate frigates got nine- or twelve-pounders, 5th Rates carried twelves, or more lately, eighteen-pounders. The French, though (most sensibly, Alan thought), armed their equivalent *corvettes* with *les huit-livre canon*—eight-pounders. And the Frog Avoirdupois Livre was just a trifle heavier than the English Pound Weight, so his eight-pounders were the equal of a British nine-pounder. The shot was almost the same diameter, perhaps a quim-hair (about one twenty-fifth of an inch) smaller, allowing a tad more obturation, or "windage," between shot and bore diameter.

And what was that, about a cable less at extreme elevation, at range-to-random shot, where the odds of actually *hitting* anything, a mile-and-a-half off were pretty much By Guess and By God? *Half* a sea mile was considered long-range shooting, and most captains and gunners preferred point-blank, which was anything from one cable, right down to close broadsides, with the muzzles sticking almost through the enemy's gun ports—"close pistol shot"!

Had the officials insisted, it would have taken weeks more to outfit *Jester;* new six-pounders, a full eighteen of 'em, weren't just lying about, after all. Might not even be sufficient stock far up north near Scotland, where most of the foundries had relocated, now they'd gone to coke instead of charcoal for melting and casting pig iron. Wouldn't cost the Crown tuppence, sirs! *Bags* of Frog round shot aboard, sixty per gun *now*, and replacement nine-pounder English shot is a lot cheaper than an entire new set of artillery! Please, sirs! Pretty please, sirs? Can't swing idle for a *month*, sirs!

And, when they'd come, what would he have ended up with? Some of those new, lighter, and shorter Blomefield Pattern pieces, which he had heard had a distressing tendency to burst when charged with newfangled cylinder powder 'stead of puny old corned powder! No, there was only one thing he admired about Blomefields—that neat forged-on loop for the breeching ropes above the cascabel button. His old guns had breeching ropes eye-spliced *about* the button, while Blomefields let the ropes pass through ring bolts on the truck carriages, then through that loop, easing stress on the breeching if fired at extreme angles. They wouldn't snap their breeching and roll about like rampaging steers if pointed too far forrud or aft in the gun ports, or rip the end ring bolts in the bulwarks loose.

No, he'd have his nine-pounders, and God help the Frog who came within range, mistaking *Jester* for a quarterdecked ship sloop below the Rates, armed with mere popguns!

He spoke briefly with his surgeon, Mister Howse, that tall and lanky saturnine of the square, mournful face, who always looked as if he needed a shave, even right after shaving; and his surgeon's mate, LeGoff, who played the gingery terrier to Howse's rangy mastiff. No one had herniated yet; there were some sore muscles, but Howse held that horse liniment usually worked just as well on bipeds as it did for quadrupeds.

Midshipman Hyde with Knolles near the double-wheel. Knolles was midtwenties, blond-haired, and sun-bronzed. If some spark of relationship had arisen between him and his charge Sophie—and Alan had pressed 'em damn' hard together—there was no sign of it. Hyde . . . a year older than Mister Midshipman Clarence Spendlove, at sixteen, a seasoned lad, well-salted and daubed with his "ha'porth of tar" since he was nine. Hmm . . . good family, he'd learned, was Hyde. Talented, cheerful, able. A bit on his guard, being so new aboard, but the port admiral had recommended him highly, had lifted him out of a 3rd Rate seventy-four for more seasoning aboard *Jester* where he'd be one of two, instead of one among twenty-four middies. To do the port admiral a favor usually meant one in return; you scratch my protégé, I'll scratch yours.

"Yer pahdons, Cap'um," Andrews said at last, coming onto the quarterdeck. "But dot Aspinall say yer suppah jus' now come from de galley, pipin' hot, sah."

"Thankee, Andrews!" Lewrie brightened, as famished as a middie on short commons by then. "Toulon slunk out of hiding yet?"

"Well, sah, ah 'spect he's ovah 'is sulk," Andrews chuckled in a deep, soft voice. "An' when he caught a whiff o' po'k cracklin's, he come on out, sah. 'Twoz all me an' dot boy Aspinall could do, keepin' him off de table. Do ah go forrud an' tell ya cook ya be wantin' cawfee later, Cap'um, fo' dey douse de galley fires fo' de night?"

"No, no coffee tonight," Lewrie decided. There was a very good chance this wind would veer ahead during the Middle Watch, rousing him from bed. After all the excitement and tension, a good meal would put him under quickly, and he needed *some* sleep, beforehand. "You tell him to forget it, this evening, and turn in, the pair of you."

"Aye, sah. Thankee, Cap'um," Andrews replied.

"Enjoy the singsong, below-decks." Lewrie grimaced.

On the berth deck, where "pusser's glims" still burned on mess tables, the sounds of fiddle, fife, and tuning box could be heard, well into a droning, lugubriously sentimental, dirgelike song. Hands were singing along, some already in their hammocks hung from carline posts and overhead beams; linens, bolsters, and thin mattresses already full of softly swinging seamen, in the minutes before Lights Out.

"Ooh, Law', not dot'un, sah." Andrews shook his head in scorn. "Sailors, dey know de words t'hundred o' songs . . . but only know de one tune. Dot'un. Same'z it woz 'board ev'ry ship I been on, sah."

He and Andrews went back a long way, to the *Shrike* brig, and he had become Lewrie's coxswain briefly, before she'd paid off after the war ended. Now he was cox'n, again, in charge of Alan's gig and crew. Andrews had always been reticent about his past. In the West Indies, Lewrie'd been certain that Andrews in his youth had been a house slave, and a runaway. There were no lash scars on his back, he vaguely remembered, but . . . Andrews could read and write, even then, had skills enough to make ordinary seaman, and had been rated able before they'd paid off. Alan wasn't even sure that Andrews was his real name, but that was the one he was known by at the Admiralty, never a place to be picky about a volunteer seaman's antecedents.

His recent history had been merchant service, a summer in the Portugee fisheries off the Grand Banks, then a spell ashore as house servant and valet to a retired Liverpool merchant captain; but that fellow had passed over recently, and he'd lost his comfortable shore position. Now he was both cox'n and great-cabin factotum.

A "bright," Caroline had called him, after she'd met him, one of what she termed "the yard-Cuffies"; the by-blow of a white master or overseer on a mulatto or quadroon housemaid. Part white and part black, and pent like a storm petrel over both worlds, belonging to neither. Her North Carolina, slave-owning family experience, warned her, and Alan, against him, but he was an old shipmate. And a Navy man a lot longer than he'd been a fugitive, furtive slave.

"That tune?" Lewrie asked. He was not all that musical.

" 'Adm'll Hosier's Ghost,' sah!" Andrews snickered. "I t'ink ah teaches

de tune t' 'Ovah de Hill An' Far Away,' fo' we heah any *mo'* 'bout dot
dead mon's spook!"

TOULON WAS OVER his sulks, nothing hurt but his fierce feline pride. As
soon as he was seated at table, the cat was up his nose, wheedling and
begging, tail erect and quivering in gustatory anticipation.

So recent the break from shore, there was still fresh meat on the hoof
or paw, or on the roost, aboard, in the manger forrud. Hens, ducks,
geese, for fresh eggs, and a rare treat after Sunday divisions. For captain
and officers, alone, of course. Goat and kid for milk—or meat, if they did
not prosper at sea. A sow and piglets, a brace of ewes and four lambs.
There had been a yearling bullock, but he'd gone into the steep tubs in
four-pound cuts per eight-man mess, that afternoon, with tripes and
tongue and blood pudding, to boot. There were smoked or salted joints
hanging in gunroom pantries, captains' stores, everywhere one could find
a place to hang a hook. To stave off the day when everyone had to subsist
on salt beef or salt pork.

Alan dined on a fine pork broth, mixed with desiccated "portable" pea
soup; fresh loaf bread instead of hard and dry, soon to be weevily and
sour, ship's biscuit. A pair of small roast potatoes, piquant with some of
Caroline's herb vinegar. And a hefty pile of sliced roast pork, some with
the cracklings on; the most succulent cuts from a piglet shared with the
wardroom mess.

And, it was fine to dine alone, too, for once, after so many civilian, and
perilous, suppers with wife, ward, and children underfoot, sure to tip
something over at any moment. Calming, it was, too, to—for a few hours,
at least—have some privacy from the never-ceasing demands to be social
with his officers. In a few days or weeks, he'd begin a round-robin of
dining them in, a few at once, to be sociable. Once the rigidly demanded
isolation of command got too great.

There was a rather fine, smooth and dry Bordeaux, which Aspinall had
let breathe for an hour (and how the Portsmouth wine merchant got his
hands on such a wondrous French wine, he'd ask no questions!).

Fresh greens in a small salad to cleanse his palate for fresh Cheddar,
extra-fine sweet biscuits, and a smooth and heady Oporto. Gingersnaps,
the biscuits were, another of Caroline's touches, all lovingly packed.
Along with calf's-foot jelly; though Alan had no clue as to why—he
despised the stuff.

Toulon got his share, on the deck by Lewrie's chair. Cracklin's, pork, a sliver of cheese which he adored. A quarter of a gingersnap with a thin smear of fresh butter; good for his coat and teeth. For as long as butter remained wholesome, that is.

A LOLL ON the transom settee, with all lanthorns in the day-cabin extinguished. A sated Toulon stretched across his lap, being brushed softly, tail slowly curling in bliss. After nine p.m. now, on a sleeping ship, on an empty and dark ocean. All glims out, and the ship's corporal, an officious able seaman named Wilhoit, making his rounds with the midshipman of the watch, to see that all was in order and quiet, that no flame burned below-decks from lanthorn or candle.

Lewrie's gritty eyes fluttered, as he yawned aloud. So much tension, the last few weeks, so much last-minute folderol, the last few days and hours before sailing. Regaining his freedom.

And once back in the Mediterranean . . . once back with Hood, who had surely taken Corsica by siege, by now. First step, though, would be at Gibraltar, with dispatches for General O'Hara, the ancient "Cock of the Rock."

Where Phoebe Aretino was awaiting his return.

"Christ." Lewrie sighed to the companionable dark.

Best to end that, fast, he thought sadly. Face to face, that'd be best, I s'pose. Letter's so bloody cowardly an' cold. Well, I had my joy of her. Give her, what . . . a hundred pounds or so, to tide her over till she finds herself a new patron? Sounds about right. And . . . here on out, I've far too much on my plate, to spare time on diversion.

Even a petite and pretty diversion. He shrugged.

"Bedtime, Toulon," he announced in a yawny whisper.

HE UNDRESSED IN the dark of the sleeping coach, just abaft the chart space on the starboard side, a canvas and folding partition chamber. He pulled off his own boots, dropped his breeches, and tossed them over the top of a sea chest for Aspinall to stow away in the morning. His "man" had laid out a clean pair of slop trousers, which Alan preferred for undress wear at sea. Cheap, durable, and easy to part with once they'd mildewed, tanned, gotten stained with tar and slush . . . or simply wore out.

Fresh, virginal bed coverlet, painted and embroidered by Caroline's talented hands; fresh linen sheets, and pillow slips over puffy, never-used bolsters filled with home-farm goose down. The mattress in the bed box was from Anglesgreen, too; goose down packed top and bottom over a lamb's-wool batt center, sewed into a striped ticken cover.

The narrow hanging bed cot was slung at about waist level over the black-and-white painted checker of the canvas deck covering; slung fore-and-aft instead of the more-usual athwart-ship. An elegant form of hammock, really, braced by a rectangle of oak, with double layers of heavy storm canvas inside. Six feet long, it was, and a few inches more than three feet wide.

A bachelor's box, Alan snickered to himself as he rolled into it and set it swinging, as Toulon sat on the deck crying "*Maiwee?*" in a plaintive voice, as if he had to ask permission each and every evening, judging the best moment for his leap.

The little pest required a full ten minutes to satisfy, shoving his head under Lewrie's more-than-willing hands to be rubbed, purring and vibrating, nose-patting with soft paws, ear-snuffling as he kneaded the bolsters. He finally took his ease 'twixt torso and arm to the larboard side, paws braced against the canvas, with his back hard up against Alan's chest.

Damme no, not a bachelor's box. Lewrie grinned in the darkness, yawning so hard he thought he'd dislocate his jaw this time. 'Tis a *husband's* box. Narrow, and straight-laid.

His husband's box swayed to the easy roll and slow pitch of the ship as she snored her way across the deeps, loping for the open seas. And rocking her captain, his cat, and all the sleeping off-watch tars who put their trust in her, to a pacific rest.

CHAPTER

3

THE WINDS DID indeed come more and more westerly, as *Jester* came abeam of Plymouth on her slog down-Channel, veering bow-wards toward a close reach, then close-hauled, her second day of passage, forcing her to alter course nor'west, for she could not maintain a luff nearer than six points to the wind.

The old problem of leaving England; being driven shoreward by a brisk westerly, right up toward the *Lizard* or Torbay, or having to tack and beat sou'west toward the hostile coast of France, which was a rock-strewn horror in peacetime, and aswarm with warships now, from the French bases at Brest and St. Malo.

By ten of the second morning, *Jester* was near enough to Torbay to peek inside, with a long-glass from the top of the mainmast. No sign of Admiral Howe's fleet, though; the westernmost war anchorage was empty, which meant he was still at sea, somewhere out in the Atlantic. And so, one must suppose, were the French.

With a heavy sigh, Lewrie had been forced to come about south, and make that long board down toward France on the starboard tack; a day wasted, he thought, marching in place up and down, with no progress westward, if he wished to give the *Lizard* a wide berth.

But, near the start of the First Dog Watch at four p.m., the winds had begun to back southerly again, point at a time, and gain in strength. Near mid-Channel, Lewrie had summoned "All Hands" by five p.m., and brought her back to larboard tack, to make up lost ground. They continued backing, until, by the end of the First Dog at six, *Jester* was thrashing due west, close-hauled and flying over the wave tops like a tern.

32

Courses unreefed, tops'ls and royals full and straining, and the ship laid so hard-over on her starboard shoulder—where she'd heel so far and no farther—furrowing a wide bridal train of foam astern. She slashed the seas, the roar and wash of her passing, the irregular watery thudding of easily broken waves, and the hull's shudders at each foamy, curling lumping was a sailor's delight! A live, luff-flattening, coat-fluttering wind invaded every open mouth, filled every ear with tumult. It took four hands at the helm; Quartermaster Spenser, his Mate Tucker, and two able seamen trainees. Spoke by wary spoke, to weather or alee, with cries of "Meet her, easy now . . ." Grunts of dissatisfaction when she faltered an iota from fast, if they misjudged the infinitesimal variations in wind direction, the press of a curling roller against the windward bow, the slightest swing of the lighted compass needle in the binnacle cabinet. And sighs of ecstasy, the " 'At's th' way, lads! 'At's me darlin'!" when *Jester* rode up and over a roller met with a well-timed spoke to windward, luff maintained, the near-invisible commissioning pendant streaming and crackling at its tip, the lee edges of the main course and main tops'l still barrel-curved, without even a flickering roll of a single cupful of that invigorating wind lost.

And everyone on the quarterdeck rocking and riding on horsemen's legs, springing at the knee easy, like posting a gaited mount, smiles of pleasure, and wonder, on their faces. Duty-watch sailors, lookouts along the windward side, hooting and "whooing," ship's boys giggling those high-pitched, heart-in-your-throat, and heart-swelling shuddery laughs, as if they'd found a "pony" of guineas in their packet on Boxing Day. Off-watch sailors still on deck to savor this fleeting joy. Landsmen and young, first time at sea Marines staggering and reeling, whooping when a wave crest flung cold showers of spray above the bulwarks. Fiddle, fife, and tuning box from the foc's'le, near the galley and Copper Alley, speeding through a Dublin jig, the cook and his mate beating time on small pots.

"By *damn*, this is sailing!" Lewrie said aloud with pleasure, his voice lost in all the bustling noises. And Hyde and Spendlove, with the two boys first class in tow and tutelage, learning how to read the marks of a knot log in the dark, crying out, "Eleven knots, sir! Eleven, and a bit!"

There was bad weather in the Bay of Biscay, Lewrie was certain, some blow responsible for this that they'd soon meet, once they made a cautious offing into the Atlantic. It might be tarpaulin weather by noon of the next day. This could not last; night winds always waned a little after sundown—but at least they remained steady.

"Dead calm by morning, Mister Buchanon?"

" 'Tis my experience, sir," Buchanon opined reluctantly, "that a brisk sundown indeed makes for one o' two things—storm canvas an' three reefs by midnight, or . . . a spell o' calm an' drizzle by dawnin'. 'Twas another red sunset, ya did note, so . . ." He shrugged.

"And which would you put your guinea on, sir?" Lewrie smiled.

"I'd say this'll blow out in an hour'r two, sir," Buchanon said with a rueful wince, forced to have an opinion. After a *long* minute spent gnawing a corner of his lips, and much sniffing and probing at the skies with his nose. "Best we enjoy it, while we can. And f'r the mornin', well . . . a swing o' th' wind back toward west-sou'west. An' maybe drizzle, Captain. Smelt a *hint* o' fresh water on th' wind, I did. Rain, f'r certain, e'en with a red sunset, but . . ."

Buchanon lay his hands on the quarterdeck rails at the netting, feeling the shudderings, letting them transmit up his arms like some dowser witching for water.

"No counterwaves from a roiled sea?" Lewrie inquired to press him, or coach him. "No gales in the offing?"

"Nossir, didn't feel any."

"And no smell of storm rack, either," Lewrie went on, having done his own inhaling to sample the future. "No fresh-fish reek."

"Exactly, sir!" Buchanon answered, daring to essay his first tentative smile of agreement. "Grew up in the fisheries outa Blackpool, I did, sir, an' 'twas promisin' days we spent mendin' nets an' such, when th' granthers came back in early, not likin' th' smells, nor th' way th' waves felt on th' bottom o' their boats. An' they were almost always right."

"So," Lewrie said, going to the chart at the traverse board. "May we count on being headed, a bit, we stay on larboard tack, all tomorrow. Wind loses its strength, but stays *somewhere* round sou'-west, and we end up standing on west, nor'west for a day more. We miss the *Lizard*, gettin' this breeze when we were 'bout mid-Channel. And . . ."

A ruler laid from an educated guess of southing at sundown—west-nor'west—a thumbnail's crease along its edge, beyond Soundings, out into the wide trackless Atlantic.

"Well south of Land's End, and the Scillies," Alan concluded. "Enough sea room to weather them. If."

"Under th' horizon, sir." Buchanon nodded solemnly.

"Damme, Mister Buchanon, but I think we should stand on, 'bout a hundred leagues, at least," Lewrie told him, returning the ruler to the cabinet drawers. "Too soon a tack south 'cross Biscay, we'll run into something perverse down there, around the latitude of Nantes or so. A nor'wester that'd force us down toward the Spanish coast near Ferrol, and I don't wish to be embayed, and have to beat about and waste two days to weather Finisterre. We'll take all the westing this slant'll give us, before we alter course."

"If it holds, Cap'um," Buchanon cautioned automatically, "aye, if it holds."

"What the hell's that?" Lewrie snapped, of a sudden, disturbed by a tuneful noise. "You, there! Yes, you, sirs! Stop that noise!"

The first-class boys, gentlemen volunteers, were by the mizzen stays, up on the bulwarks and clinging to the inner face of the ropes, starry-eyed little new-comes, rapt in their first exhilarating beat to windward. Richard Josephs, he was only eight, a slight, cherub-faced minnikin. George Rydell was only a year older, a dark-haired pudding. They both turned to peer at him, eyes wide as frightened kittens, and aghast that they'd done something wrong.

"Which of you was *whistling* on deck, sirs?" Lewrie demanded of them, hands behind his back and scowling a hellish-black glare.

"Mmm . . . me, sir?" Little Josephs piped back shyly.

"Bosun's mate!" Lewrie howled. "Pass the word for the bosun's mate! And get down from there, the both of you. Mister Josephs, no one, *ever*, whistles 'board-ship, young sir. Never! It brings storm and winds. Dares the sea to get up!"

"I'm *sorry*, sir," Josephs quailed, folding up on himself like a bloom at sundown, and already weeping. "I didn't *know*, and . . ."

"Damn fool," Mister Buchanon spat. "Pray God, sir . . ."

Half his life in uniform, half his life at sea so far, and Alan, and Buchanon, knew why men should never tempt Neptune with cockiness.

"Aye, sir?" Cony said, knuckling his brow as he arrived on the quarter-deck.

"Josephs was whistling on deck, Mister Cony," Lewrie explained.

"Aye, sir," Cony rumbled deep in his chest, all his affability gone in an instant. "Half dozen, sir?"

"Aye, and then explain to both of 'em, so they never make such a cod's-head's mistake on my ship again, Mister Cony," Lewrie ordered. "Mister Hyde, you will see to it that Josephs is restricted to biscuit, cheese, and water, all day tomorrow, to drive this lesson home."

"Aye aye, sir," Hyde answered, smug with lore, and distaste for the error. There would be a raisin duff tomorrow at dinner, and that meant a larger portion for both himself and Spendlove.

"You, and Spendlove both," Lewrie snapped, "you're senior below in your mess. Kindly instruct these calf-heads more closely in ship lore, and the fleet's do's, and don'ts. Their future behavior, well . . . on your bottoms be it."

"Aye aye, sir!" Midshipman Hyde flushed, and gulped. Josephs's whiny mewlings rose above the wind-rush; that, and the sound of rope "starter" strokes, a half dozen, applied to his bottom, bent over the bosun's mate's knee instead of over a gun, to "kiss the gunner's daughter."

Josephs almost yelped like a whipped puppy at the last but one, forcing Cony to stop and shake him by the arm by which he restrained him. "Quiet, lad," he told him, almost gently. "Nothin' personal . . . but *real* seamen don't cry out. Else it'll be six more, see? Take the last'un like a man." And Josephs did, though in utter misery, as if everything in life had just betrayed and abandoned him. Which prompted Rydell to purse his lips and inhale.

"Don't!" Lewrie warned. "Find a new way to express yourself!"

"Oh!" Rydell all but swooned, half knocked off his feet by a further warning nudge from Mr. Hyde. "Oh God, sir . . . !"

"Half dozen d'livered, sir," Cony announced.

"Thankee, Mister Cony. I *trust* that'll be all," Alan told him sternly; though he could not quite resist a tug at the corner of his mouth, the constriction of one eyelid in a surreptitious wink. Which gesture was answered in kind, as Cony doffed his cocked hat.

From time immemorial, boys had been beaten to make them mind, or learn. Boys at sea, more than most, to drive their lessons home. It was a harsh world at sea, and it was better to be harsh right off, than watch the chubs get themselves maimed or killed, or hazard the ship, through inattention, ignorance, or skylarking. Spare the rod and spoil the child, the Good Book said, after all. And within one hour of reporting aboard his first ship, so long ago, Lewrie'd learned that simple Navy truth. Some days, his entire first year at sea, even as a half-ripe lad of seventeen, they'd been signal days when his own fundament hadn't felt a captain's, or a lieutenant's, wrath.

"You two do come wif me, now," Cony snarled, putting back on his fearsome bosun's face. "Th' more ya cry, th' less ya'll piss . . . n'r bleed, later. An' mind close t'wot I'm goin' t'tell ya . . ."

A faint, half-felt drumming against the larboard bows as the sloop of war faltered, as she met a wave instead of cocking her bows gently up and over. A hiss of spray and a cream of foam breaking on the catheads and the forrud gangway. And a disappointed sigh from Mister Spenser on the wheel. There was a grouse-wing beat aloft, a soft, suspiring whisper, as the luffs of fore and main square sails shivered a lazy furling down to the leeches. Headed!

"Damn 'at boy," Buchanon spat as he witnessed the wind's death.

"Damn' quick response from old Aeolus." Lewrie frowned, trying to be philosophical about it. Nothing *good* lasted forever, after all!

The tiller ropes about the wheel-drum creaked as Spenser and a trainee were forced to ease her off the wind as it faded, as the ship sloughed and sagged to a closer, almost weary companionship to waves and sea. The apparent direction of the wind had veered ahead almost half-a-point, for ships working close to weather made half their own apparent wind, backing the true wind slightly more abaft at speed.

"West-nor'west, half north'z close as she'll lay, sir," the quartermaster said, with the frustrated air of a man who'd still won small on his horse that placed, but had lost almost as much on the one he'd backed to win.

"West-nor'west, half north it is, then, Spenser. Full-and-by," Lewrie agreed, just as frustrated. He leaned into the orb of candlelight from the compass binnacle lanthorn. Both their faces were distinct in the growing gloom, as if separated from their bodies.

Still, Alan supposed, with a petulant grunt; we'll weather the Scillies, and Land's End. Few leagues closer inshore, but . . .

"Grand while it lasted, though, was it not, Mister Spenser?" Alan commented easily. "A glorious, dev'lish-fine afternoon's sail."

"Oh, aye . . . 'twoz, Cap'um," the older man replied, his eyes all aglow deep under a longtime sailor's cat's feet and gullied wrinkles. With the sound of a gammer's longing for a lost-lost youthful love, he ventured to comment further. "A right rare'un, sir. Damn 'at lad."

"Another cast of the log, if you please, Mister Hyde," Lewrie called aft, stepping into the gloom. Eight Bells chimed up forward; the end of the Second Dog, and the start of the Evening Watch. "Mr. Buchanon, you have the watch, I believe, sir?"

"Aye, sir. Send th' hands below, then?"

"Aye. Nothing more to savor tonight." Lewrie sighed, moving to the windward bulwarks.

"I'll call, should . . ." Buchanon began, then wrenched his mouth in a nervous twitch, to keep from speaking aloud a dread that should best remain unspoken. Aeolus, Poseidon, Erasmus, Neptune, Davy Jones . . . by whatever name sailors knew them, the pagan gods of the wild sea and wind had, like e'en the littlest pitchers, exceedingly big ears! And like mischievous and capricious children, could sometimes deliver up from their deeps what sailors said they feared most.

Uncanny, it was, though—whistling on deck usually fetched a surplus of wind, rather than the lack. Gales and storm that blew out canvas, split reefed and "quick-savered" sails from luff to leech in a twinkling, leaving nothing but braces and boltropes. Never a fade, though, never a dying away. Nor one so rapid.

Perhaps tomorrow, Lewrie fretted; comeuppance comes tomorrow!

"Sir, we now log eight and one-quarter knots," Hyde reported at last, sprinkled with spray and damp from the knot log's line.

"Thankee, Mister Hyde." Lewrie nodded, keeping his gaze ahead, toward the west. Aye, we had ourselves a rare old thrash to weather, he thought; nigh two hours at ten to eleven knots! That's at least twenty more sea miles made good, due west, till . . . damn that boy!

At sundown, winds usually faded, replaced by night winds that might not be so stout, but usually remained steady in both vigor and direction. *Clear* weather winds did, at least.

And pray Jesus, *that* holds true, he grimaced. Stays like this the rest of the night . . . fade around sunrise, of course, for a bit, but that's nine hours at eight knots—say another seventy or so to the good. And only half a point to loo'rd of the best course I can hope to make. *If* the wind didn't get up, and make us reef in. *If* we don't get headed! Comes westerly again tomorrow, we'll either fall afoul of Ushant down south, or Land's End or the Scillies up north!

He decided to do his further pondering over charts in his great-cabins, where he could worry and smolder in private.

"Good evening to you, Mister Buchanon," Alan said, touching the brim of his hat in salute. "I wish you joy of the evening, sir."

"And a peace . . . ahem! And a good night to you, too, sir."

Lewrie nodded firmly at Buchanon's sensible reticence, and his re-phrasing, then took himself to the larboard ladder to the gun deck.

Dispatches aboard, too valuable to lose, he mused; Frogs out in fleet strength . . . wind most like to die away to nothin', head us again . . . or come up by the bloody *barge load*, and . . .

Damn that boy!

CHAPTER

4

SURPRISINGLY, THE WINDS did no such thing, the third day upon passage. There was mist, to be sure, light sunrise winds that slatted sails for a while, but most cooperatively backing to the SW or SSW again. Clouds stayed low and cream-jug pale for most of the day. At the end of the Middle Watch, when the crew was summoned to scrub and sluice, then stand Dawn Quarters, there was a lot of dew, the mists riming everything with damp. Sunrise wasn't ominously red. The fog and mist dispersed, but never quite disappeared, limiting visibility to a scant four miles around *Jester*, even from the crosstrees. Noon sights were educated guesses of how high that diffuse, cloud-covered sun ball was, but the consensus of results on the quarterdeck, except for Mister Spendlove's, which placed them somewhere on the same latitude as Iceland, showed them weathering the Scillies and Land's End. And dead reckoning, and the record of the knot log, suggested a position *beyond* the Scillies— almost 100 nautical miles west of the *Lizard* since yesterday noon.

And, with the wind backing southerly, *Jester* could come back to due west again, though only at seven or so knots on a light, tantalizing wind, and stand even farther out into the Atlantic.

And the sea. It was almost calm, mashed flat by a humid, and rather pleasant warmth, glittering and rolling, folding and curling not over three to four feet, more mirrorlike, more oily and without ripples; though the long Atlantic rollers made themselves felt. The ship rose and fell slowly and grandly, lifted, her entire length, by the long period of the scend, instead of hobbyhorsing. When pitch she did, or roll, it was a slow, creaky procedure, quite predictable and almost pleasant for all but the lands-

39

men and new-come Marines, who "cast their accounts to Neptune" over the leeward rails. Faint wake astern, barely a bustle of disturbance down her flanks as water churned sudsy close aboard, and her forefoot cut clean and sure into the round-topped rollers, to part them with hardly any fuss at all.

Uncanny, Lewrie thought warily. Retribution's coming, sure as Fate. They're toyin' with us. Soon, it'll be roarin'. When we least expect it. Damme, I hate surprises!

Dawn of the fourth day was coolish and bracing, with a bit more life to the sea, the rollers now shorter-spaced and surging higher, in four- to five-foot swells. The wind backing even *more*, now all but out of the south! Toying with them, backing, then gusting up a touch, as it veered ahead a point or two. Yet still easily manageable winds.

Jester would luff up through the gentle gusts, driving close-hauled, and was able to maintain a base course of west-sou'west, and a half-hourly cast of the log showed a steady 7½ knots.

By noon sights, Alan was just about ready to start chewing his nails in fretful apprehension. And Mister Knolles and Mister Buchanon, two more who knew what whistling on deck could bring, stalked soft-footed about the quarterdeck as if the slightest misstep might bring the sky down on them like a tumbling house of cards!

"Sail Ho!" came a most unwelcome cry, from far aloft.

"Oh, Jesus!" Lewrie gawped in the middle of his fifth breakfast at sea, a forkful of treacly broken biscuit halfway to his mouth.

He was off and running, shrugging into his undress coat, cramming an old, unadorned hat on his head before the Marine sentry's musket butt hammered the deck without his cabins, and his leather-lunged announcement of "Mister Midshipman Spendlove, SAH!"

"Captain, sir," Spendlove began formally. "The first lieutenant's respects to you, and he bade me inform . . ."

"Yes, yes!" Lewrie snapped impatiently, preceding Spendlove to the quarterdeck. "Where away?" he demanded.

"*Two* sail!" came another shout from the topmast lookout.

"Sir," Knolles reported crisply, handing his captain his spyglass. "One sail on the larboard quarter, up to the nor'east, royals or t'gallants. Can't see her from the deck, yet. But, there's a second ship, sir . . . off the larboard beam, a touch southerly of us. Say, east-by-south to be her bearing? Just appeared moments ago, as these morning mists cleared. Royals *and* t'gallants, 'bove the horizon, sir."

"Thankee, Mister Knolles." Lewrie frowned. He took in the set of *Jester*'s sails, the strength of the wind that flailed the commissioning pendant. Even close-hauled, *Jester* was loafing along in light morning air. The sunrise cast of the knot log had shown only a touch over seven knots, and the wind felt no fresher than when he'd quit the quarterdeck to go below a half-hour earlier. "Be back, shortly," he said, slinging the telescope over his shoulder.

He climbed atop the larboard bulwarks, swung out around the mizzen stays, and began to ascend the mast, recalling how terrified he had been, the first time he'd been forced aloft, so long ago. All these years, and it still hadn't gotten any easier! He thought, surely, he would be senior enough, and like many post-captains too stout, to *have* to do this; could stay on deck and let the younger and spryer be his eyes. Except he knew himself for an impatient "hound," and wondered, just before essaying the futtock shrouds, if he could ever be content with second-hand information.

Most careful for a good handgrip and sure feet, puffing some, he got to the deadeyes of the fighting-top after a breathless dangle on the futtock shrouds, scaling the underface of the outward-leaning ropes and ratlines. Then on to the mizzenmast crosstrees, far up by the doublings of the topmast, to take a perch on the bracing slats.

The vessel off to the east wavered in his ocular as he embraced the topmast with one arm. Ship-rigged, he saw; three sets of yellow-tan ellipses—tops'ls, t'gallants, or royals visible, with her hull and course sails still below the horizon. Swiveling to the nor'east, he spotted the second. She was more broadside on, with three umber rectangles of sail peeking over the indistinct rim of the sea.

He returned his interest to the nearest ship. Had she changed her aspect to them? When he first espied her, he'd thought she'd been beam-reaching west-nor'west across the wind, her upper yards and sails fatter and wider. Now, they looked narrower, more edge-on, her masts beginning to overlap in his narrow view-piece.

"Altering course," he muttered sourly. "Comin' over to 'smoak us'. Discover what we are. Well, sufferin' Jesus!"

An infinitesimal gay splotch of color burst forth upon her upper yards, vivid bits of flapping cloth. She was making a signal, as she came about hard on the wind. But, to whom? he wondered. It was hard to make out— plain red square flag atop, what seemed like the Blue Peter next-below, a

yellow-white beneath that, and a fourth he couldn't make out. That, of a
certainty, wasn't a recognition signal in the Howe System *he* knew; nor
was it one of the private signals to identify one Royal Navy ship to another!

He turned back to the ship up in the nor'east. Sure enough, she was
replying. Making a single hoist of what he took to be a red square with a
white speck in the center. A one-flag signal—that could only be a reply to
an order. More like, an affirmative. And it was not a *British* "Yes"! And was
she turning, too, foreshortening the broadside view of her upper sails?
Also coming onto the wind? Merchantmen had no desire to speak each
other with flags. Nor be curious about strange vessels. A merchantman
sailing independently would shy from the sight of *any* other ship, even
were HMS *Victory* to heave up alongside with an invitation to dinner!

They had to be French!

A brace of frigates, he decided, out scouting in the van of the main
body of that fleet Howe had been seeking. And had just discovered a
weak and tasty treat!

"Deck, there!" he shouted. "Pipe 'All Hands'! Mister Knolles? Make
sail! Royals, t'gallants, and stays'ls!"

A LITTLE FASTER now, though heeled perhaps a bit too far hard-over, *Jester*
began to trundle along, adding another knot to her speed. To keep their
minds off it, and prepare them for the worst, Alan told his officers to
practice gun drill.

Five weeks in port, and not a shot fired! he lamented.

Port admirals didn't like the sound of guns going off in their harbors.
Bad for their digestions, he supposed; interrupts any naps they take. And
was a "waste" of good gunpowder that they'd have to replace, at Admiralty expense, before a ship sailed.

Jester had a good warrant gunner and mate in Bittfield and Mister
Crewe; her quarter-gunner was a Prussian named Rahl, who *claimed* that
he'd been one of Friedrich the Great's artillery masters. Cockerels and
Victorys, Agamemnons and a few others, were experienced. But except
for dry-firing, mostly running-in, loading, and running-out work with the
new-comes, his guns wouldn't be well-served. Not after the landsmen
and Marines, who would be forced to assist on the tackles, were deaf-
ened and quivered to a state of nerves by the first blasts. And half of that
had been instruction, employing only a single piece at a time, mostly
letting them watch, before trying them out at the least-skillful jobs.

There'd only been a week of dry-firing, using an entire broadside at once, and that wasn't nearly enough.

"Would you say this seems a bit familiar, sir?" Knolles said, after going below to change into clean clothing, and silk stockings and shirt, which were easier for the surgeon to draw out from wounds.

"It appears pretty much the way we *got Jester*, sir." Lewrie nodded, playing along in spirit with Knolles's humor. The officer was possessed of a very dry wit to begin with, and was purposefully japing, for the crew's benefit, to make them think that things were not quite as bad as they appeared.

"Damme, Mister Knolles," Alan said more loudly. Again, for the crew's ears. "Chased by two corvettes. Shot one to flinders, and took this'un! Do you think, sir, that the French'll oblige me a *second* time, and make me a post-captain, when we serve these, alike?"

He got the appreciative laugh he'd expected, though most of his inexperienced new men merely tittered nervously; and that only because the older hands had done so.

French frigates, he pondered, pacing aft to the taffrail for a peek. Longer on the waterlines, perhaps 120 feet, to his 100. They'd be at least a full knot faster. The one down to the nor'east was too far off, and with only a knot advantage, would take until sundown to catch him up. No, the main threat was the one to the east, now almost abeam. She'd cut the corner on *Jester*, sail a shorter course, with a half-a-knot to a *full* knot greater speed than her consort, because she wasn't beating to weather, but was sailing a point "free" on a damned close *reach*, to intercept off *Jester*'s larboard bows.

When she came up to shooting range, Lewrie decided, he'd have no choice but to wear off the wind himself, reach across the wind due west, to escape, *far* out into the Atlantic. Scouting frigates, that'd be most likely, he thought; out ahead of the French fleet's van division, looking for Howe's fleet, so they could steer their admiral into a massive battle. If *Jester* showed no sign of leading them to Howe's main body, they *might* break off their chase, he most fervently hoped; perhaps by sundown, at the latest?

"We're nigh on 350 miles out to sea," he mused; "350 miles west of Ushant *or* Land's End, for God's sake! What do they think I'm leadin' 'em *to*—the Happy Isles of the West?" he whispered.

And the weather . . . ! Alan felt like ordering "All Hands" up on the gangways to begin whistling, if it would stir up one more *pint* of wind. That remained steady from the SW or SSW, and none too strong. The morning was less humid than the day before, less dew and mist upon the decks at dawning. The clouds were higher and thinner, a first thin coat of whitewash brushed over cerulean blue, with many traceried gaps of open sky. Not superb sailing weather, but no sign of bad weather, of a certainty, which might bring a rising of the winds. For the Atlantic in early summer, it was almost warm and pleasant, too.

Just warm enough a day, as it progressed, to bring a stronger wind as the seas warmed. Or enough heat to stifle *any* winds, leaving all three warships boxing the compass on lying little zephyrs. And a longer and heavier French frigate might still coast through the dead spots, maintain her steerageway even in very light air, whereas the lighter, shorter ship would struggle and flag.

"Mister Knolles," Lewrie called out, coming back to the center of the quarterdeck. "We'll run in the starboard battery to loading position, and bowse the carriages to the deck ringbolts. Then, open the larboard gun ports and run out the larboard battery to firing position. That *should* shift enough weight to set her flatter on her keel."

"Aye aye, sir," Knolles responded. "Mister Bittfield?"

If *that* didn't work, next he'd try shifting all the round-shot into garlands on the larboard side, by hand, then crack the water casks and use the wash-deck pumps to "start" all that weight over the side, to lighten her. He'd heard of people jettisoning cumbersome cargo, even artillery, during a stern chase. Of course . . . most of the time, that'd been the heroic captains doing the chasing, not the chased. And the prize money afterward paid for all.

"It occurs t'me, sir . . ." Knolles began in a soft voice, minus his confident japery, and a tad shy of making a suggestion at all.

"Aye, Mister Knolles?" Alan rejoined with a smile.

"Well, Captain . . ." Knolles coughed into his fist nervously as he dared advise a senior officer. "Should we stand on, close-hauled . . . uhm . . ."

"Surely, our brief spell together, since Gibraltar, sir," Alan chuckled to put him at his ease, "and you're still afraid I'll *bite*? Ease her a point free, is that your thinking?"

"Aye, sir!" Knolles grinned shyly. "Spin the chase out. Make her work harder for her supper."

"An excellent idea, Mister Knolles. Very well, ease her. Wear us a point free, off the wind, so *Jester*'ll sail even flatter on her quick-work. So it takes yon Frog *another* hour to get within range-to-random shot. If you would be so kind, sir?"

"Aye aye, Captain," Knolles replied, turning to issue orders to brace-tenders, idlers, and helm, the forecastle men who tended the jib sheets and the bosun and his mate.

No way we'd *ever* outfoot her, and cross ahead, anyway, Lewrie told himself. She'll be up, even if she doesn't head-reach *farther* upwind of us, by dusk, for certain. With the wind gauge, and us to her lee.

Jester fell off from close-hauled to a fair wind, heading west-by-south, sometimes luffing up as the wind backed no more than half a point. She settled down with less heel to starboard, as the braces and jibs were eased a trifle, the yards swung around with the leading larboard yard-ends not quite so aligned fore-and-aft. Apparent wind eased, no longer keening through her rigging, softer on the ears, so conversations did not have to be shouted above the rushing.

"Hark'ee, sir!" Buchanon called, speaking for perhaps a second time in the last hour, as Three Bells of the Forenoon Watch chimed.

"Hmm?" Lewrie asked, wondering if there was something he had forgotten that he'd ordained to happen at half-past nine a.m.

"Thunder, sir," Buchanon oracled, sniffing at the wind with his large, crooked nose, like a fresh-awakened mastiff.

A squall line, that'd be a blessing, Alan wished; bags of rain and thunder, somewhere off to windward. Dive into it before the foe did, and tack away, leaving him to play "silly buggers" with himself.

"But, there's not a storm cloud in sight, Mister Buchanon," he was forced to say, after a long, and hopeful, search of the horizon.

"Thunder, sir," Buchanon insisted. "Hark'ee."

Lewrie went up to the windward rail, left the quarterdeck to amble forrud along the larboard gangway, to get away from the noise a ship makes, or a crew makes. Something . . . but what? Once more he raised his telescope, resting it on the foremast stays, this time.

Nope, nary a smudge upwind. The southern horizon was knife-edged, now that the mists and haze had cleared. Rolly, since waves made it, but . . . was there more cloud just looming over the sea, far down sou'west? Not squall-gray or blue-gray, but . . .

Damme if it *don't* sound like thunder, he enthused; off and away . . . but a roll of thunder, nonetheless. A faint sound that was *not* the wind's flutter about his head teased at his hearing.

Or was it a devoutly wished-for fantasy?

Again came something that *might* have been, if only . . .

"Bosun Porter, pipe the 'still'!" he snapped.

He'd served captains who did it; made their people work quiet, with pipes, halliard twitches and finger snaps as orders to the hands . . .

their slaves. After *Cockerel*, a ship run dead-silent would always strike him as Devilish-queer. He'd much prefer raucous caterwauling. At least that bespoke a crew with spirit! He'd made a vow he'd never be the sort of captain who demanded the "still." Yet, here he was . . .

Yes, it *was* thunder! Very far off, up-to-weather thunder, on the wind. "Thankee, Mister Porter, you may pipe the hands free, now," he said, with a grin on his face. And kept that grin plastered on—looking like the cat that lapped the cream—all the way aft past the curious sailors on the gangway or below at the guns in the waist. And thinking that perhaps he owed little Josephs a lapful of gingersnaps, for whistling up a saving storm! Thinking, too, that he owed Aeolus a debt, as well. The wind-god was an old slow-coach sometimes, in dealing retribution to cocksure sailors . . . but he got there, in the end!

"Mister Buchanon is right, gentlemen," he told the quarterdeck. "I heard thunder on the horizon. Under the horizon, to us, of yet, but . . . there is a faint smudge of *something* stormlike visible, up to weather. I'd admire we hardened up half-a-point to west-by-south, half south, so we reach it in time to befuddle yon Frog, and lose him in the squalls."

ONE HOUR MORE, standing on, on *Jester*'s fair wind, and the heat of the day increasing. She began to heel a tiny bit more to starboard as the wind freshened, even with her artillery run out to balance her.

It was piping up, at last! Not gusting, never approaching any blusters, but it was rising slowly, the nearer they sailed toward the single tumulus of cloud on the sou'west horizon. And beyond the main cloud mass, there appeared more mere suggestions of clouds, fuller and more substantial than the mare's tails aloft, seductively tantalizing in round cumulous detail.

Pristine white, those clouds, though, for such a din of thunder that came faintly, but more often, under the rush-keening of the wind. No black or blue-gray hazes of an advancing storm front, no trace of an expected towering thunderhead. Nor of the vast sweep of gloom, which should be swathing half the weather horizon. Nor the flickering sizzle of lightning, which accompanied all the faint thunder-growl.

Lewrie began to get a queasy feeling, though he masked it well, by pretending to take a nap in a wood-and-canvas deck chair with wide, well-spaced feet.

"Deck, there!" the foremast lookout finally hollered. "They be *tops'ls*, on th' 'orizon! Dead on th' bows!"

"How many tops'ls?" Lieutenant Knolles shouted back, with the aid of a brass speaking trumpet, as Alan pretended to "wake."

"Dozens, sir!" came the reply. "One point off th' larboard bow, t' *two* point off th' starb'rd!"

Lewrie arose and took a catlike stretch.

"Well, could be 'at grain convoy," Buchanon opined. "Hun'r'ds o' ships, I heard, Mister Knolles. Indiamen with New Orleans rice . . . more with corn an' wheat from th' Chesapeake. 'Ose *Ew*-nited States of America payin' 'eir debt t'France. *And*, makin' th' Devil's own profit, I'll warrant. As arse-o'er-tit'z France's farms an' markets are since their revolution, 'tis import 'r starve this summer. Why their Navy's out . . . t' p'rtect th' food, 'r the country goes under. Sounds like we found 'em, just'z ol' Admiral Howe lit into 'em, sir!"

"Somebody's lit into someone, Mister Buchanon," Lewrie agreed. Warily. There was too much thunder for ships of the line in General Chase of prizes. No convoy could ever make such a din, either.

"Perhaps we might gobble one up, Captain?" Knolles asked. He came of a good family, yes, but they weren't *that* rich, and prize money of his own would be more than welcome.

"I'm going aloft, again. Mister Knolles, might you lend me your glass?"

Forward this time, to scale the foremast, right up to the crosstrees to join the lookout, a spry young topman named Rushing.

"Mine arse on a bandbox!" Lewrie muttered, once he'd had his long look. "That's no grain convoy."

"Nossir, it ain't," Rushing agreed breezily.

" 'Bout twelve miles off, would you say, Rushing?"

"Ay, Cap'um. 'Bout that."

"Be up to them . . ." He pulled out his new watch. It was nearly gone eleven of the forenoon. An hour-and-a-half . . . two hours, and they would be up within spitting distance. Or shooting distance.

Without another word, Lewrie took hold of a standing backstay and clambered down it, legs locked and going hand-over-hand, like any topman. Hating every nutmeg-shrinking moment of it, of course, with nothing but oak to stop his fall from nearly 100 feet above the deck, should he slide too fast and burn his hands, or swing away and dangle by his fists alone.

Once on the quarterdeck again, he gathered his breath by taking another peek at the French frigate off to the east. Their closest pursuer was about five miles off, hull-up now, and driving hard. She had slowly gained on *Jester*, closing the distance between them, and, more importantly, crabbed up a'weather a touch, so she would still hold the wind gauge when they finally met.

"Hard on the wind, Mister Knolles," Lewrie ordered. "Lay her as close as she'll bear. Hoist every scrap of canvas, 'cept for stuns'ls. We've a race to win."

"Aye, sir," Knolles replied, before turning to issue orders.

"Sorry to disabuse you, Mister Buchanon," Lewrie told him with another forced grin, "but we haven't discovered their grain convoy, no. 'Tis their entire Biscay fleet, yonder. And ours. Having at each the other. *That's* the thunder we've been chasing all morning!"

"Wull, stap me, sir." Buchanon sighed, blanching a bit.

"Another hour or so, and we'll hear all the 'thunder' a man'd ever wish." Lewrie chuckled, genuinely amused this time. "Pass the word for Mister Giles!"

"Aye, sir?" the purser inquired from the midships hatchway.

"Mister Giles, I'd admire should you issue the midday meal as soon as we've completed bracing in and making more sail," Lewrie told him. "The rum issue, too. Today is a Banyan Day, is it not, sir?"

"Well, aye, sir . . ." Giles frowned.

"Little need for the galley fires, then."

On Banyan Days, the issue was cold victuals; small-beer, cheese, and biscuit, perhaps with the eternal pea soup, but no meat to be simmered in the steep-tubs.

"On the wind, sir," Knolles reported.

"Very good, Mister Knolles. Once the hands have eat, and drunk their cheer, we'll beat to quarters. Say, 'bout . . . half-past noon, or so? We've a sea battle before us. From a point off the larboard bow to two points to starboard, and we're going to have to tack around the short end, if the fleet that lies alee turns out to be hostile. Let us hope the Frogs are on the *far* side, holding the weather gauge. But, be ready for the worst," Lewrie explained to them all. "And, *must* we tack around to get inside the protection of our own liners, we're going to have to deal with this bastard frigate."

"Aye, sir." Knolles nodded grimly, plucking at his clean silk.

"Thunder, by Jesus!" Alan snorted. "Mine arse on a bandbox, Mister Buchanon. Mine arse on a bandbox!"

And laughed out loud as he strolled aft to study the frigate in his glass, leaving them all perplexed by such good cheer.

CHAPTER
5

HANDS AT QUARTERS, standing by their charged, shotted and now-primed artillery pieces, swaying as *Jester* rocked and rolled over the sea. Gun captains would fire them with modern flint-lock strikers in lieu of ancient slow-match linstocks; but slow-match sizzled slowly, wound 'round the mid-deck water tubs, just in case.

The French fleet, unfortunately for Lewrie, were the fighting ships that lay to leeward, those closest to him. There had to be at least thirty of them, it appeared, a ragged procession of proud line-of-battle ships— 74's, 80's, and larger, right up to massive three-decker flagships of 120 guns—in a tormented, shot-racked in-line-ahead formation that headed due west, stretching east-to-west across *Jester's* track for nearly three miles, like an oak and iron reef. It was no longer the tidy arrangement it had seemed as they'd approached; there were gaps between ships greater than the rigorously ordained half-a-cable separation. There were gaps aloft, too, where ships had lost topmasts and yards. Still, they doggedly plodded west, barring *Jester* a path as she beat close-hauled to weather, west-by-south.

Safety, unfortunately, lay on the *other* side of that bellowing reef of warships. Howe's thirty or so liners had gained the wind gauge and followed a parallel course to the French, lost in the foggy towers of gun smoke that rose from every ship.

Worse yet, there were even more French frigates to leeward of their battle line, to serve as aides to the combatants—as rescuers for those forced to break away, as occupiers aboard any British ship that was

49

forced to strike and be towed away as prize; and as signal repeaters, down in clear air, to relay their admiral's wishes.

And some of those repeating frigates toward the rear of that battle line had begun to show interest in the strange ship approaching them with no flag flying. The one that appeared to be pursued by one of their sisters! And the pursuing frigate . . .

Lewrie turned to have another look, no longer needing the telescope. She was up to them, within a mile or less, well within range-to-random shot. It had taken her awhile to recognize that *Jester* had hardened up to windward. She'd soldiered on, still sailing a point-free for about a quarter-hour, before going close-hauled to keep the wind gauge, herself. She'd lost *some* windward advantage, but . . .

There she lay, off the larboard side, nicely framed behind the mizzen stays, almost on a parallel course of west-by-south as a mate to *Jester*'s. Another ten minutes and Lewrie would face a hard choice of standing-on within range of the repeating frigates, perhaps the disengaged broadside guns of the French battle line, or fighting a larger, heavier-armed frigate that blocked her only chance to come about to starboard tack and jink around the stern of the French liners!

"A tack'd lay our head sou'east-by-east, Mister Buchanon?" Lewrie speculated aloud.

"Aye, sir. 'Bout that." Buchanon grunted. "Excuse me, Cap'um, but I'd not stand on five minutes more, on this tack, else we fetch too near th' Frog liners, an' have no wind alee of 'em, e'en for a reach to th' east t'sail around the last in line. A close shave e'en now, sir."

"Quite so, Mister Buchanon." Lewrie nodded, unconsciously rubbing his own raspy and unshaven chin at the mention. There'd been more to worry about this morning than his toilet. "Mister Hyde? Dig into the flag lockers, aft. I b'lieve Our Lords Commissioners issued some false flags? Find the Frog Tricolor."

"Aye, aye, sir!" The lad yelped, dashing off to search.

"A legitimate *ruse de guerre*." Lewrie shrugged to his officers. "Give a *few* minutes' confusion, perhaps."

"Aye, sir! Found it!" Hyde shrilled forward.

"Bend it on, Mister Hyde, and hoist it aloft," he ordered.

He was hoping that the French line-of-battle ships had just a tad too much on their plate, at the moment, to care one way or another, and the repeating frigates that could come about and intercept him would lose interest; just another corvette arriving with orders from Brest—some silly civilian nonsense from the landlubbers of the revolutionary Directory, or however they now styled themselves.

He raised his glass, as the French Tricolor was two-blocked high on the mizzenmast. What would that pursuing frigate do, now? he wondered. Wasted a whole morning, chasing some idiot who ignored his signals to fetch-to . . .

Come to think on't, Lewrie grinned, he never sent *me* a signal! Saw me as a chase, right from the start. And if we're both galloping for his fleet flagship like John Gilpin on a *good* horse . . . I *have* to be French, same as him. A body'd be daft as bats to get this close, else!

Three-quarters of a mile separation now, between *Jester* and her pursuer. Good gun range. *Damned* good gun range!

"Ah, sir . . . ?" Buchanon prompted uneasily.

"Aye, Mister Buchanon. Mister Knolles, stations for stays, sir! We will put the ship about on the starboard tack. And anyone who puts her in irons . . . I'll have his nutmegs off with a *damn'* dull knife!"

"Bosun Porter, hands to the braces! Hands to the sheets!" Lieutenant Knolles bellowed. "Ready to come about?"

A breathless minute of preparation, hands tailing on braces and sheets, laying paws on tacks, easing all but the last over-under turn around belaying pins and bitts.

"No more than half-a-point free to ease her around, Quartermaster!" Lewrie snapped. " 'Tis all the leeway we may spare." Ships were usually eased a full point off the wind, to gather an extra surge in speed to assure a clean tack.

"Helm alee!" Knolles screeched, at last.

Around she came, driving back up on the wind with a quarter-knot more speed, jib boom and bowsprit sweeping like a pointer across the embattled warships before her bows. Jibs and stays'ls fluttering and canvas popping like gunshots as *Jester* neared the eye of the wind, as sails lost their luffs—yards creaking and wood-ball parrels crying as they were swung around. For a heart-stopping moment, she slowed to a crawl, everything aloft aback and banging, before the fore-and-aft stays'ls and jibs *whooshed* across the deck to larboard as she took the wind fine on her starboard bows. The spanker over the quarterdeck and the royals and t'gallants rustled, flagged, then filled, with the hard crack of laundry airing on a line.

"Sou'east-by-east, Quartermaster!" Lewrie cried. "Meet her!"

The wheel spun, spokes blurring as they tried to catch up with her momentum, as she paid off half-a-point to the new lee in spite of their best efforts, as the hands braced hard on the gangways to make a proper spiral set aloft, royals more sharply angled to the wind than t'gallants, t'gallants more than tops'ls.

From his position at the new windward, starboard, rails, Lewrie espied their pursuing frigate, which now lay just a touch to the right of *Jester*'s bows. It would be a damned close-run thing, but sou'east-by-east would take her clear of the last struggling behemoth line-of-battle ship in the French line. And cross the frigate's stern, if she didn't alter course.

"Shit," he muttered, though, as the frigate opened fire!

It would be a bow-rake on *Jester* as the frigate crossed her T, employing every available gun in her starboard battery, while *Jester*'s two shorter-ranged carronades on the forecastle would be the only guns that could respond! Round-shot tearing through the curving bow timbers, frailer than her sides, rebounding and tearing down the complete length of her gun deck, and down her gangways!

He winced into his wool broadcloth coat, as if it might be some protection, flinching from the avalanche of screaming iron, the jagged metal shards, whirlwind cloud of wood splinters, and the sagging ruin of masts to come. Though feeling an urgent desire to fling himself to the deck, like a sensible person!

The air trembled and moaned above the general cannonade between the fleets, a very personally directed moaning and fluting, as fifteen or more twelve-pounder balls bored their way toward *Jester*. Before their Revolution, France had possessed the finest guns, the finest school of naval gunnery in the world, with a dedicated corps of lifelong professional artillerists. And frail little *Jester* was about to receive . . . !

Nothing, pretty much.

A ragged line of feathers erupted from the sea, to either side of her bows, as irregularly spaced as a London urchin's teeth. Great, and rather pretty, pillars of spray and foam leapt up where the round-shot struck the sea at first graze. More feathers abeam, or astern, as cannon balls caromed and bounded over the wave tops like a young lad's stone might skip across a duck pond. Lewrie was sure he heard one or two howl overhead like extremely fat and fatal bumblebees . . . but so high above the royals they didn't even spill an ounce of wind from frail canvas, or sever a single stay in passing!

"Well, damme!" he cried in befuddled exaltation. "Those poor buggers couldn't hit the ground, if they dropped stone-cold *dead*!"

A first broadside, usually the best-laid and pointed, at less than three-quarters of a mile . . . and they'd missed *completely*? Lewrie jeered. Now, stand for mine, you poxy clown!

"Mister Knolles, give us a point free! Mister Bittfield, the starboard battery . . . fire as you bear!" he shouted.

Up the fairly steep slant of the deck to windward, nine-pounders on their heavy truck carriages rumbled and growled, foot at a time, as the hands ran their pieces up to the ports and beyond, to point deadly black-painted hog muzzles at the foe. A tug on the side-tackles, or a lever with a crow iron for aiming. Fists raised in the air, from the foc's'le to far aft in the great-cabins beneath his feet, as the gun captains drew their flintlock lanyards taut and stood clear of their charges' recoil.

"On the uproll . . . *Fire!*" Lewrie howled, primed for vengeance.

The foc's'le eighteen-pounder carronade began it, with a deep bark of displeasure. Then, a stuttering series of roars rippled down the starboard side. Lewrie looked aft to Andrews, serving as captain to a quarterdeck carronade. He jerked his lanyard and the piece erupted a short, stabbing flame, and a corona of muzzle smoke. It snubbed to the rear on its slide-carriage, greased wood compressors smoking, too.

"We fired under the French flag, sir!" Knolles cautioned. It was a grave breach of etiquette, that. A *ruse de guerre* was accepted practice, right up to the moment of initiating combat.

"Get that Frog rag down, Mister Spendlove, and hoist our true colors!" Lewrie yelled, not caring much beyond witnessing the strike of his shot. "Swab out, and give 'em another, Mister Bittfield!"

Glorious!

Feathers of spray, close-aboard the French frigate; short, some of them, but grazing along at reduced speed for a solid hit on timber. The sort of low-velocity hits that smashed more hulls in than faster strikes, which might punch clean through. The frigate's sails, yards and masts quivering and twitching as guns fired from leeward, up that slant of the deck even with their quoins full-in, went high. Spanker holed dead-center, mizzen tops'l winging out free of its weather brace, and the main course ripped in half!

The frigate stood on, stolid in spite of her hurts. Cannon appeared in her ports again, and a second ragged, ill-spaced broadside erupted from her. With little more success than the last one! And then, she was forced to tack. She could stand-on on the larboard tack, sail up to her fellows, or she must come about to continue the fight.

Tack, or wear, Lewrie mused, even as his guns spoke again. To wear would put her even with *Jester*, well-astern after completing the twenty-four-point circle. No, she *must* tack, he decided, or throw her hand in as valueless. And that'll silence her guns, for a bit.

"Our ensign's aloft, now, sir," Spendlove told him.

"Very good, Mister Spendlove. One hopes the Frogs'll take our error as a *minor* slip in *punctilio.*"

"It appears they've worse things to worry about, at the moment, sir!" Midshipman Spendlove japed, pointing to the French battle line. Close as *Jester* had come to the fighting, they could now take gleeful note of British men-o'-war through the thick banks of powder fog, up almost yardarm to yardarm with the French, blazing away at pistol-shot range. "Oh, there she goes, sir . . . coming about!"

The frigate was presenting her stern to them, swinging up onto the eye of the wind, yards all a'cock-bill and canvas slatting.

"*Took* 'em long enough," Lewrie sneered. *Jester's* gunfire was splattering all about her as she slowed and turned. Sails caved in on themselves as they were punctured, to refill lank and disheveled, and Alan frowned as he thought he saw a round-shot strike her foremast's tops'l yard, spilling a wiggling speck or two loose. Two topmen who'd just fallen to their deaths on the hard oak below, or into the waters alongside, where they'd plunge deep before surfacing, to watch their ship sail on, uncaring, just before they drowned.

"Mister Knolles, harden up! Full-and-by!" Lewrie ordered, to put *Jester* back onto the wind, and wring out every foot of advantage above the frigate, which was visibly struggling to get around to her tack. The last French 74-gunned 3rd Rate at the tail of the enemy battle line was off *Jester's* starboard bows by then. Still with her offside gun ports closed, thank God! A minute or two more, and she would be too acutely angled to take *Jester* under fire—out of her gun arcs in the narrow ports. And that 74 was punch-drunk and reeling, her lower masts sprung and shivering to every new blow, ready to go by the board, any moment.

"Mister Spendlove, perhaps you might oblige me?" Alan inquired casually, in a moderate voice, as the gunners swabbed and loaded anew.

"Aye, sir?"

"Go aft and bend on this month's private signal to identify us," he suggested with a wink. "Once we get around to the *British* side of this battle, I'd not like to be shot to ribbons in error by some overeager repeating frigate."

"Aye, sir!" Spendlove chuckled.

The wind was dying away to nothing. Massive broadsides usually blasted air to stillness. And they were witness to one of the greatest sustained exchanges of massive firepower, even greater than any battle known so far in history. *Jester* was flagging once more, coasting along on her built-up momentum more than she was driving ahead close-hauled, hazed and half concealed in the sulphurous reeking mists that blew alee from that cannonading. The French frigate had come about to the starboard tack at last, but she was half-a-mile astern by then, though well up on *Jester's* starboard quarter.

"Mmm . . . Mister Ss . . . Spendlove's respects, sir," Boy First-Class Josephs almost hiccuped below Lewrie's waist. And shivering frightful, as if he'd quiver every bone from his body. Five days at sea—less than a month in the Navy, and he was already under fire, wondering what had ever possessed him to go a gentleman volunteer, or wish a naval career! And still half terrified of his own captain!

"Aye, Mister Josephs?"

"Pp . . . private signal aloft, sir, he bb . . . bade me tell you."

"Thankee, Mister Josephs," Lewrie replied, looking down at him intently, his father's heart softening. Sewallis was just as twitchy, just as miserable-looking, half the time. "Something to write home about, lad. To see a grand battle such as this'un. Perhaps the only one you'll ever see, your entire career! Now, d'ye understand why we start off harsh? So you end up the sort o' man'll *stand* such."

"I think so, sir," Josephs said with a gulp.

"Good lad," Lewrie said, rewarding him with a smile.

It was going to be Buchanon's "close shave," around the stern of that Frog 74, after all. Perhaps by no more than a quarter-mile. He could ease her off the wind a bit and parallel her, but the frigate on his starboard quarter was still pursuing, bulldog game.

"Broadside guns'll no longer bear, sir!" Bittfield shouted up from the waist. The nine-pounders were sharply angled astern in the ports. Any more, and they'd snap their breeching ropes, sure.

"Cease fire, Mister Bittfield! Mister Rahl? Supervise carronades on the quarterdeck. They have a greater arc of fire."

"Ja, zir!" Their emigrant Prussian barked, almost clicking his heels in glee to have some noisy toys to play with a bit longer.

And that frigate, Lewrie exulted to himself! She'll have to fall in almost astern of me, if she wishes to continue. She stays that high up on our quarter, we'll brush her off against the side of that last liner!

The frigate reopened fire, with her lighter forecastle chase guns. Five- or six-pound ball went sizzling across the quarterdeck.

"A little better shooting, at last," Knolles commented.

"They're not the skillful shots their fathers were," Lewrie agreed, with some relief.

"Bless me, sir," Knolles scoffed. "They're not the men they were two *years* ago!"

The starboard quarterdeck carronades belched fire, swathing them all in powder smoke for a period, before it was wafted away to the nor'east by the light winds, before *Jester* sailed past her own pall on the bruised air.

"*Hit*, I t'ink, *herr kapitan*! *Ja!*" Rahl delighted, watching heavy ball strike and raise a gout of splinters, dust, and oakum.

ON THEY STOOD, continuing their duel. The last French warship in the battle line was left astern, off *Jester*'s starboard quarter. A run of five minutes more would give her sea room enough to come about and resume her original course of west-sou'west, with the entire Royal Navy a protective fence between her and danger.

Gunners aft, and the after-guard, began to jeer, as the French frigate was forced to haul her wind to avoid a collision with that last, limping 3rd Rate.

"Frigate, sir!" Hyde pointed out. "One of *our* repeating frigates, four points off the starboard bows!"

"Acknowledging our private signal, sir!" Spendlove chimed in.

"Mister Knolles, you may secure from quarters, now," Alan said with a great sigh of success. "Safe in Mother's arms, from here on."

"French frigate is wearing about, sir."

Lewrie looked aft. Aye, she didn't have room in which to tack so she was swinging broadside on to *Jester*'s stern, presenting them her starboard side, to make the greater twenty-four-point circle off the wind to end up heading west, plodding along in company with the other vessels of her fleet. Deprived of her prey. Beaten.

"Better luck next time, you snail-eatin' bastard!" Alan bellowed in triumph, cupping his hands so his words might carry. Though he doubted a shout across half-a-mile would register on French ears, it was, after all, the smug, insulting victor's jeer—and thought—that counted!

Uh . . . sorry I did *that*, he told himself at once!

The frigate, outsailed then outshot, spent a last fit of Gallic pique upon *Jester*, rippling out one final, irregular broadside. A crash aft and below, as a ball scored at last, caving in the transom timbers abaft the stores rooms and officers' quarters, a great *thonk* as the ball continued to carom down the length of the empty berth deck. Glass shattered as another exploded the larboard quarter-galleries—both Lewrie's, and the gun-room's—toilets. Splashes and feathers to either beam around the stern, and a further hollow *thonk* and high whine as a ball ploughed a furrow down *Jester's* side.

And Josephs, up on the bulwarks, was beheaded.

One instant cheering and waving a fist in the air, the next he was flying, his small body flung almost amidships of the quarterdeck, minus his head, throat, and shoulders, which had been pulped into red mist by six pounds of wailing iron!

"My . . . *word!*" Lieutenant Knolles gasped, as his compatriot on the bulwarks, his mate Rydell, hopped down and began shrieking utter hor-ror, and terror. He'd escaped unscathed, though they'd been close enough to rub shoulders. Close enough, though, to be spattered with droplets of gore, brains, and bone chips!

"Surgeon's mate!" Lewrie shouted uselessly. "Lob-lolly boys!"

Whey-faced himself, but determined not to show it, nor allow this horror to demoralize his crew, he was forced by duty to cross to Rydell.

"Shut your mouth, Mister Rydell! Stop that noise!" he rasped. "Go below, if you wish to unman yourself. Lob-lolly boys? Get that . . . *that*, off the quarterdeck, at once!"

And turn his back, to deal with Duty.

"Oh, dear Jesus," LeGoff whispered as he came up from the cockpit on the orlop, the place of surgery during quarters. "Poor little chub!"

"Deal with it, Mister LeGoff," Knolles ordered coolly, after he was over his own funk. "Anyone else injured below, or aft?"

"No one, Mister Knolles, praise God," Lewrie heard LeGoff say to the first officer. "Here, you men. Scrap o' canvas. The carrying board. Take him below to the cockpit, and ready him for burial."

"Mister Buchanon," Lewrie inquired, his face a stony mask. "I believe we have enough sea room to return to larboard tack?"

"Aye, sir," the sailing master muttered, as shaken as anyone.

"Very well, then. Mister Knolles? Stations for Stays. Come about. New course, west-by-south, till we're well up to windward of our line-of-battle ships. Then we'll ease her due west, to parallel."

"Aye aye, sir," Knolles replied, happy to have something constructive to do. "Mister Porter? Stations for Stays!"

"Onliest one, sir," Buchanon continued, with a whimsical air.

"Hmm?" Lewrie grunted, still in pain, but curious about that tone in Buchanon's voice.

"Josephs, Cap'um. Onliest one e'en scratched!" Buchanon said more soberly, almost in a rueful awe. "We got our comeuppance from th' ol' mad buggers. An' 'ey took 'eir due from us. Th' gods o' th' sea, Cap'um. Th' ol' pagan gods o' winds an' seas, 'ey took 'im."

"Surely, Mister Buchanon, in this modern age . . ." Lewrie began to scoff, a little angered by such a heretical suggestion. Or, maybe a little angered at what he did not yet know. At himself, perhaps, for having the boy "started." For making his last days fearful.

"Me da', he was Welsh, Cap'um," Buchanon related. " 'Twas oft he tol' me 'bout 'em. Him an' th' granthers, all, sir, on th' stormy nights, with th' rain an' winds a'howlin' 'gainst th' shutters, 'r th' public house. Onliest folk still take note o' 'em'z sailormen, sir. Priests an' Church, 'ey drove 'em out, into th' wide, trackless seas. But 'at don't mean 'ey passed away, Cap'um. Oh no, not at all!"

"Ready about, Captain," Knolles intruded.

"Very well, Mister Knolles. Put the ship about," Lewrie said in response, mesmerized, and only half paying attention to his first.

"Helm's *alee*! Rise, foretack and sheets!"

"One 'ey named th' most, sir, 'at'd be Lir," Buchanon went on, paying only half attention himself, as *Jester* began to come about to the eye of the wind. "Don't know much 'bout th' ones crost th' seas, in th' heathen latitudes. Ones I read about in school, sir, 'em ol' Roman an' Greek sea gods, 'ey sounded like gennlemen ya could deal with, so long'z ya didn' cross 'em 'r 'eir boss Zeus. Sportin' sort o' gennlemen, who didn' mean much by it. But Lir, now, Cap'um. Ol' Irish an' Welsh sea god, one th' Scots dread, too, sir? Oh, he's a right bastard, sometimes. Jealous an' vengeful. Hard-hearted sort. A blood-drinker, some say. Nacky'un, too, Cap'um . . . smart'z paint. Th' sort who'll bide his time, 'til a body'd gone an' forgot what he done 'gainst 'im. But, he always takes his pound o' flesh, in th' end. He always gets his due, when ya least expect, an' hurts most."

And a hellish gobble more'n a *pound* of flesh, he took, Lewrie thought, trying to stifle an involuntary shiver of awe, himself, as he recalled the sight of that pitiful remaining husk. He turned his attention to his ship, away from this spectral higgledy-piggledy that Buchanon spoke of, this ancient superstitious folderol that he sounded as if he really *believed*! Buchanon, a man who'd dragged himself out of the fisheries, gone to sea in the fleet, come up on *science*, for God's sake! Astronomy, mathematics, the art of navigation, study of weather, charts . . . the sailing of a *ship*, which was man's greatest, most complex engine!

"Now, mains'l haul!" Knolles was crying, as *Jester* finished most of her tack, passing the eye of the wind, as braces dragged the sails aloft to the starboard side where they began to fill and draw.

"Um, this Lir . . ." Lewrie asked of Buchanon in a conspiratorial voice, eerily fascinated in spite of himself. "Sea god of the British Isles, in other words."

"Maybe all of 'em have 'eir own domain, Cap'um," Buchanon said softly. "Poseidon around th' Greek Isles an' Aegean . . . ol' Neptune, he has th' rest o' th' Mediterranean. Wherever Roman sailors went, sir? Lir, now . . . I'd expect he's got th' Channel, North Sea, all 'round th' British Isles, an' far down inta Biscay. Celts were 'ere, too, long ago. Down south o' Cape Finisterre we'll leave him, Cap'um. Now he has his revenge."

Lewrie shivered for real, in spite of his best intentions, as a cool zephyr of clearer air not shot to stillness crossed the deck. Almost an icy-cool zephyr, that raised his hackles and his nape-hairs as it passed. The sort of eldritch feeling Caroline sometimes called "having a rabbit run 'cross your grave," that unbidden spook-terror of the unknown, that harbinger of dire tidings.

"That far," Lewrie said, after clearing his throat.

"We should be fine, though, sir. His price'z paid, now. Lir's took th' mocker. Long'z 'ere isn't another, we can go in peace."

"Ahum," Lewrie commented, sealing his lips in a thin and wary line. "Ahum."

CHAPTER

6

"Toss yah oars," Andrews ordered as his captain's gaily painted gig came alongside *Queen Charlotte*, a venerable old three-decker; and the flagship of Admiral Earl Howe, better known as "Black Dick."

"Hook onta th' chains . . . boat yah oars!" Andrews snapped.

It was a hellish-long climb, up past an ornate lower gun-deck entry port as solid as an Inigo Jones house-front, to an upper gun-deck entry port, thence to the uppermost, on the gangways. Larboard side, though, Lewrie griped to himself; not the side of honor where subordinate commanders were usually received. *Jester's* position up to windward saw to that. And the proper side was probably shot half through, after a full morning of battle, he decided.

"Welcome aboard, sir," a lieutenant greeted him, with a minimum of fuss. "And you are, sir . . . ?"

"Alan Lewrie, of the *Jester* sloop," he replied. Short as the time had been between attaining safety behind that wooden wall of warships, and receiving a flag hoist for 'Captain Repair on Board,' with his number, he'd had a quick shave, and thrown on his dress coat and hat. Admiral Howe was a stickler for details. And he hadn't earned that sobriquet, "Black Dick," simply because he didn't often crack a smile, either! "Come aboard, as ordered, sir."

Perhaps it wouldn't have mattered, this once, since the strange lieutenant's white-lapeled coat, waistcoat, and breeches were stained gray with powder, and *Queen Charlotte* looked as if she'd been rather badly knocked about.

"Allow me to name myself, sir . . . Lieutenant Edward Codrington.

Welcome aboard, sir. If you'd come this way?" the young man said as he
gestured aft toward the poop. Lewrie followed him along the larboard
gangway to the quarterdeck. A rather tall and slim, and rather handsome
post-captain looked up as they passed. He wore a short tie-wig, no hat,
and was holding a white cloth against his head. Looking rather befuddled and forlorn, too, Lewrie noted, hoping his battle had gone well for
him, and that he wasn't looking so sunk in the "Blue-Devils," sitting on
an arms chest like a felon, for good reason.

"You are feeling better, I trust, Captain?" Codrington took the time to
inquire.

"Some better, aye, thankee, Mister Codrington," the man said, though
looking as pale as a cross-eyed corpse. "And you, sir?"

Codrington did the introductions, naming him to Capt. Sir Edward
Snape Douglas, *Queen Charlotte*'s commanding officer. Then, they were
off for the great-cabins under the poop deck, the admiral's quarters. That
grand space was being put back in order again, guns bowsed taut against
the bulwarks, furniture and partitions being restored by a procession of
seamen. "Took something on the noggin, d'ye see."

"Ahem . . ." Codrington said, clearing his throat. "Sir, I have the
captain of that sloop of war for you."

"Ah, good, good," a heavier-set post-captain said, leaving the desk
where he'd been rummaging through a stack of hastily ordered papers.
"Lewrie, hey?" He sniffed, after the introductions were once more done.
"Can't say as I've *heard* of you, sir. Well . . . no matter."

Sir Roger Curtis was Admiral Howe's captain of the fleet, suave and
slightly flesh-faced. Lewrie took an instant dislike to him, if for no other
than that very reason.

"And what fetched you to our little dance this morning, sir?" Curtis
asked. "Some dispatches from London for us, hey?"

"Dispatches for the Mediterranean, sir," Lewrie began to tell him, but
was interrupted by Admiral Howe's arrival from farther aft, beyond some
re-erected wood partitions.

Good Christ, Lewrie gasped, though in silence! "Black Dick"—with a
smile on his phyz? *That's* a new world's seventh wonder!

"Milord, Commander Lewrie here, off *Jester*—that ship sloop that
popped up like a jack-in-the-box—on passage for the Mediterranean
already, to Lord Hood, I s'pose. The perfect thing."

"Damme, do I know you, sir?" Howe inquired with a puzzled look.

"Lewrie, sir. You interviewed me, early spring of eighty-six, before
giving me *Alacrity* in the Bahamas, milord."

"Oh, my yes. That piratical business in the Far East." Howe sighed, squinching his mouth as if his dentures pained him. "*Telesto*, I seem to recall? Come to see the show, did ye, Commander Lewrie? A chair arrived yet? Damme . . ." Howe frowned, turning away before he could hear Alan's answer. Like a good sycophant, Sir Roger Curtis had a seat whistled up for the old fellow before one could say "knife!"

"Not quite my doing, milord," Lewrie smarmed, with his hat under his arm, once Howe had his chair. The battle seemed to have aged the old fellow dev'lish-hard. And he was sixty-nine, to begin with!

He quickly related his leaving Portsmouth five days earlier—the pursuit by French frigates, and his escape. Hoping the smoke had been too thick for anyone aboard *Queen Charlotte* to have seen him open fire upon the foe, still under false colors. Sadly, he'd assumed he was going to be chastised for it. Why *else* have him come aboard, when the decks were still reddened with casualties' blood, and the stench of gun smoke still lingered?

"Damme, Commander Lewrie," Howe almost wheezed with delight at the end of his narration. "A hellish well-managed affair. Wasn't to know, d'ye see . . . your gaining a command. But, from what I recall of our last *recontre*, you always were the plucky'un. Now, sir. During your passage, did you see any sign of Admiral Montagu? Gave him eight liners to escort a 'trade,' far as Finisterre. And he should have rejoined me, long since."

"Sorry, milord, but we neither spoke nor saw any English ships of war since sailing," Lewrie had to tell him. "Had a bad slant, the second day, sir." He dared to continue to, to "prose on" to a senior officer who hadn't asked yet. "Almost into Torbay, and nary a sign of him did I see, sir."

"Well, we *did* manage quite well, without Admiral Montagu, sir," Curtis said, sounding very smarmy himself. Boot-lickin' toady-ish, to Lewrie's lights. As a fellow who'd always known how to toady to those above him, Lewrie could appreciate a good performance. And did.

"Forgive me for being remiss about doing so, milord, but . . ." Alan could not resist interrupting, "allow me to extend to you congratulations 'pon your *splendid* victory this morning."

"Damme, Lewrie, we laid into 'em, aye!" Howe barked with a tiny yelp of rare amusement. "Twenty-five of us. Lost the use of *Audacious* early on, the first day—and Montagu already off with eight. Almost equal in strength to my opposite number, Admiral Villaret-Joyeuse, I'm told he's called. Four days of sparring with him, daring him to fight toe-to-toe. Him hanging up to windward of me, down south? Nettling him? Cost

him the use of four ships or better, he had to send back to Brest under-
tow. Knocked three about . . . was that yesterday, Curtis?"

"Two days ago, milord," Curtis supplied, all but wringing his hands in
concern for his chief's health. Howe looked exhausted, dark circles under
his eyes, and his face-flesh so worn down it appeared to hang in tatters.
"Cut off his rear, two days ago, sir, that's when we isolated those three,
and shot them to rags."

"Aye, yes." Howe nodded; almost nodding *off*! With a jerk, he was
upright again, once again enthused. "Forced him to wear about, sir! Took
the weather gauge from him, then. And borrowed a page out of Rodney's
book, at the Saintes. He lies to my lee, he'd imagine I must come down
upon him, while he shoots high, damaging rigging, as the French are
wont to do. I become too threatening, sir, he always has the lee advantage of hauling his wind and retiring in good order. But, sir! But, Commander Lewrie, our Villaret-Joyeuse was not ready for us to close with
him direct, bows-on to him, then lask up alongside and lock yardarms.
Signal I flew, sir . . . 'Closer Action' . . ."

"Though not *all* followed your instructions, milord . . ." Curtis said
with a sad, begrudging moue. And Lewrie suddenly felt sorry for whichever captain *hadn't* gotten in pistol-shot range!

"Seven, Commander Lewrie!" Howe exulted, getting to his feet to
cramp about wearily. Perhaps his shoes pinched him sore, Lewrie wondered. "Six taken as prize . . . one a total loss. Four more, and one of
those a three-decker, mind! Four more battered so badly they might
spend the next year, entire, in graving docks. Oh, aye, 'twas a splendid
day, indeed, sir! Perhaps my *last* service to the King . . ."

"Oh, sir, surely not, why . . ." Curtis toadied some more.

"Damme, Curtis, I'm ancient," Howe countered petulantly. "I should
be ashore, and allow some younger, fitter man a sea command. So, you
are off to Admiral Hood, are you, Lewrie?"

"Aye, milord. Gibraltar first, then Corsica."

"Then we shan't keep you but the one hour more. Sir Roger will have
dispatches for you, to carry on for me."

"I would be *most* honored, milord," Lewrie replied firmly, all but
laying his hat over his heart and making a "leg" to the old man.

"Your clerk has a fair hand, sir?" Curtis inquired.

"Aye, sir."

"Then I shall deliver to you a single copy, and your clerk . . . and
anyone else with a fair hand, may reproduce it while you're on-passage,"
Curtis decided. "It is vital. It is urgent . . . goes without sayin' . . ."

Smirky little smile and a chuckle. "But hardly a national secret. Not after a ship gets word to London."

"One more thing, Commander Lewrie," Howe interjected, coming back to the desk after a fruitless search for something to drink. A wine-glass was in his hand, from his re-erected pantry, though there was no sign as yet of his wine cabinet. "Sir Roger, an order for Admiral Montagu, directing him to place his squadron off Brest, denying the French re-entry. Explain to him that my ships . . ."

"Your most *able* ships, at least, sir . . ." Sir Roger suggested as he whistled for the flag lieutenant, who should be doing the scribbling for his betters. "And captains," he muttered *sotto voce*.

"Uhmph," Howe grunted, with a sour, dyspeptic expression, one more time reminding Lewrie of just how much "Black Dick" really *did* resemble the Rebel, George Washington, with an attack of gas! ". . . that until the fleet is fully found again, *he* must keep them from reaching the French coast. And that I will bring the main body along, as soon as we're able. Should he have taken prizes from the grain convoy . . . made contact with it at *all* . . . he is to send them into English ports under prize crews, without escort. Further, it is my appreciation the French, having suffered severe damage aboard those ships that retired our recent action, will be shaping course for Brest or L'orient, and quite possibly will be unable to make any reasonable or spirited resistance to any action he should undertake. Do you have that, Roger?"

"I do, milord. In essence," Sir Roger Curtis replied, making a few hasty scribbles of his own, and seeming to resent it.

"Lewrie, I cannot delay you 'making the best of your way' with dispatches, but . . . *should* you sight Admiral Montagu's squadron, you are to break your passage and speak him . . . deliver my orders to him."

"I will, milord. But . . . what if I should sight their grain convoy?" Alan asked. "Should I break passage and attempt to inform anyone?"

"No," Howe decided, after a long, mazy yawn and a period of weary reflection. "You carry on, with dispatches. I will use our attached frigates for scouting."

"And we rather doubt their convoy is actually close enough to even Mid-Atlantic, as of yet, Lewrie," Curtis added. "And *most* certainly, will *not* be taking a southerly track anywhere near your course."

"I see, Sir Roger," Alan replied, much eased that he'd not be swanning about for days or weeks, in a fruitless search. "Very well, then, milord. Should I stay aboard *Queen Charlotte*, to await orders, or go back aboard *Jester*? I am completely at your convenience, sir."

"No, best let Mister Codrington fetch them to you," Admiral Howe decided, after another stupendous yawn, and taking his chair once more. "I fear our hospitality, at the moment . . . given the circumstances . . . is none of the best, after all."

"I'll take my leave then, sir? Milord Howe? Sir Roger?" Alan said, beginning to bow his way out. "My congratulations once again, on this victory . . . a *glorious* way to usher in the summer."

"A *most* glorious first day of June, Commander Lewrie, aye!" Sir Roger Curtis brightened, making a little note to himself that he stuck in a side pocket of his "iron-bound" dress captain's coat.

"Sorry we could not make you more welcome, Commander Lewrie," Lieutenant Codrington said, once they'd gained the gangway. "After your actions, as well, in escaping those frigates, and shaving their battle line, well . . . ! There *should* have been a bottle in it, at least!"

"I quite understand, sir," Lewrie chuckled in mock rue. "I'm quite satisfied the fleet was here, to rescue *me*, as it were. Uhm . . . when you come aboard, Lieutenant Codrington? The fleet will be off for home, soon?"

"I doubt that, Commander," Codrington told him. "Still all the Frog ships that got away to deal with. A letter to send?"

"Aye," Alan answered. "A letter of condolence to the parents of a lad who was killed this morning."

"I apologize, sir, I didn't know . . ."

"None needed, sir," Alan allowed. "I'd hate for them to think he's still, well . . ."

"I'm *quite* certain Captain Curtis will have a frigate sailing for England with our good tidings, Commander Lewrie." Lieutenant Codrington scowled. "*Dashing*, really—sails set 'all to the royals.' When I fetch you the documents, you may rest assured your letter to the lad's parents will be aboard that frigate. My word on't."

"My heartfelt thanks to you then, sir," Lewrie said as they shook hands on the agreement.

"Ahoy, th' boat party, below! Make ready!" A petty officer shouted down. "Side-party . . . uhmm. Sorry, Mr. Codrington, but . . ."

"Do make no fuss over me," Alan offered. Most graciously, and modestly, he thought. "You've better things to do, at the moment, I'm sure, than take men away from repairs. Or seeing to their mates."

"Oh, thankee, sir!" The petty officer beamed in approval.

"An hour, no more, sir," Codrington promised, casting an envious eye over Lewrie's shoulder to the beautifully formed sloop of war that rode fetched-to, two cables off.

CHAPTER
7

"SHIP'S COMP'NY . . . OFF hats," Bosun Porter ordered, speaking in a throaty rasp, though one almost soft and reverent, for once, as the ship lay once more fetched-to, just at sunset.

Once free of Howe's fleet, just after sailing them under the horizon, the winds had come more westerly, more like what was expected in the Bay of Biscay, and *Jester*, on starboard tack, had loped nearly forty-five miles farther, by dusk. Now she lay cocked up to weather, some sails full of drive, others laid all a'back to snub her motionless.

T'gallant yards a-cock-bill, though, to signify a death, and a burying— lift-lines purposely put out of trim to speak grief.

The entry port on the starboard gangway to weather was open, and a party stood by with the canvas-shrouded corpse on a long eight-man mess-table board. The small hump beneath the Red Ensign seemed too small to bother with.

How much room did a mere boy take, Alan wondered; short before— shorter, now? There'd been little to find of his head and shoulders but scoops of offal. Josephs's body looked arsey-varsey; the two round-shot at his feet more headlike. Heretical it might be, but Lewrie had the thought anyway, as he opened the prayer book to the ribanded page . . . custom said the sailmaker took a final stitch through the nose of those dis-charged-dead, to assure the crew that the departed was truly gone over. Now, if there *wasn't* a nose, or a head . . . ?

He shook himself, to silence such fell musings. The light of a spectacu-lar sunset was fast fading. He had to hurry.

"O God, whose beloved Son didst take little children into His arms and bless them; Give us Grace, we beseech Thee, to entrust this child, Richard Josephs . . . gentleman volunteer . . . to Thy never-failing Care and Love . . ." he intoned from the prayer book. And followed its suggestion that, for the interment of a child, Lamentations 3:31–33 was particularly apt. ". . . for He doth not afflict willingly, nor grieve the children of men . . ."

There followed Psalm 130, tried and trusted by sailors since time immemorial. Most of them knew it, and could recite it softly, with the older men leading:

> *Out of the Deep have I called unto thee, O Lord;*
> *Lord, hear my voice,*
> *O let thine ears consider well,*
> *the voice of my complaint . . .*

And it got especially tearful, and Lewrie could hear rough tars beginning to weep, when they got to

> *. . . My soul fleeth unto the Lord before the*
> *morning watch; I say, before the morning watch.*

A lesson from the New Testament, the equally familiar 23rd Psalm, and then, since they had no clergy aboard to celebrate the Eucharist, or speak a homily, Lewrie skipped ahead to the Committal.

"In sure and certain hope of the resurrection to eternal life, through our Lord Jesus Christ, we commend to Almighty God our shipmate Richard Josephs, and we commit his body to the deeps . . . earth to earth, ashes to ashes, dust to dust. The Lord bless him and keep him, the Lord make His face to shine upon him and be gracious unto him, the Lord lift up His countenance upon him, and give him peace. Amen."

There was a dry swishing noise as the mess table was upended, as the Red Ensign collapsed, followed by a splash alongside. Josephs was making an end to his first and only passage, sped by the weight of combative iron to abyssal depths, where, it was hoped, there was no corruption, until the Day of Resurrection.

Thank God, he knew it by heart, for he could no longer read the text of the prayer book. His eyes were just as full of tears. Damme, only a year older'n Sewallis, he thought! As he, and his crew, began to chant the Lord's Prayer. Even as the westerly huffed impatiently over the gangway, fluttering the pages of both prayer book and Bible, as ratlines quivered and shook, and an eldritch wailing keened aloft in the rigging. And ghostly wind-mutters spoke in the shrouds.

". . . for ever and ever, *Amen*," he concluded.

"Saints presarve us!" an Irish Catholic seamen whimpered, and a number of the burial party on the gangway crossed themselves, muttering like sentiments. There was a surge forward to the bulwarks.

" 'E's come!" An ancient-looking member of the sail-maker's crew swore. " 'E's come fr 'im!" he declared.

Lewrie stepped to the starboard bulwarks and peered over the side, and once more, his hackles and nape-hairs went up. Heart rose in his throat, stomach chilled in icy terror, and his breath stopped, faint!

There were seals in the water, close-aboard, cavorting about; their wine-bottle bodies swirling half submerged, round in a circle below the entry port where little Josephs had splashed!

Sweet Jesus, save us, Lewrie gibbered to himself!

A seal's head broke water, about ten yards off to windward, a sleek, bewhiskered hound's head, with wide-open, gentle puppy eyes.

Lir, Lewrie gawped! Seals, this far out to sea, why *else*'d . . . !

More heads appearing, in a pod as they back-paddled, gazing up at the sailors along the rail, as more and more left off their circle to join them, until the entire pack was motionless. Just breathing and staring! Bobbing on the slightly restless sea, letting wrinkly wind-stroked waves break over them as the sea got up.

"Seals, not sharks, Cap'um," Mister Buchanon whispered harshly near his ear, which made Lewrie like to jump right out of his skin! "*You* be th' one t'tell 'em, sir. 'Tis *seals*, come fr him. You'll see. They won't be afeard no more, when 'ey hear 'at."

"Calmly, lads!" Lewrie called out, still skittery with fear of the unknown, himself. " 'Twasn't sharks that have come to . . . take him. 'Twas *seals*! Look at 'em. Just playful seals!"

"Aye, 'tis a *selkie*, th' tyke's t' be!" the Irish sailor said, with a note of gladness, and pleasure in his voice. And several more West Country men agreed aloud, still crossing themselves cautiously, but sounding almost crooning, now, as if a wrong had been righted.

"Goo'bye, lad!" one called down to the depths. "Goo'bye, boy! 'Twill be playin' t' yer heart's content, ye'll be doin', now on 'til foriver!"

Christ, what sort of madness *is* this, what heresy have I countenanced? Lewrie wondered. Though his hands were calmer, easier, and no longer terrified—most of 'em, anyway, he thought; noting how a landsman or new-come was being told the Real Facts of Life by the old and experienced "sea-daddies."

"Ye selkies . . ." the old sail-maker's assistant chortled. "Poor chub'z a good lad, 'twoz Josephs. See ye take th' best o' keer o' him, hear me? An' . . ." More fresh tears ran down his aged cheeks. "An' when it come me own time, pray Jesus an' all th' saints, ye come f'r *me*, when I go o'er th' side. God pity ye . . . an' God love ye."

One by one, the seals' heads submerged, into a swirl of barely disturbed water, until only the oldest and largest was left, blinking incredibly huge and soft brown eyes at them. Why he did so, Alan had not a clue, but . . . he waved to him. The seal seemed to nod, as a sea broke over him, and came up blinking once more, his huge gentle eyes swept clear of saltwater tears, Lewrie could conjure, with droplets of sympathy bedewing his mustaches.

And then he was gone.

As if he'd never been, he submerged, making not even the tiniest ripple on the waters; he sank out of sight, and he was gone. And Alan Lewrie shivered like a wet dog, having to grip the bulwarks' oak to keep a grip on his sanity. Shivering at the revealed presence of a sea god far older than Jesus!

"Christ!" was all he could mutter in icy awe, as he came back to his senses. And wishing to be far away from that hoary phantasm.

"Ahum," he continued, "Mister Knolles? Hands to the braces . . . put us back on the wind, and get us underway."

"Aye aye, sir," Knolles replied from the quarterdeck astern.

Bible and prayer book gathered from the deck where he'd dropped them, bent pages reverently smoothed out. That took a few welcome and contemplative moments. Hat back firmly on his head. Back to his place along the weather bulwarks of the quarterdeck, where he could pace, as a symbol of authority . . . Christ, as a symbol of *Reason!* . . . again.

"Mister Buchanon," he had to ask, though, drawing the sailing master to his side, where they could talk confidentially. "What are they, the what-you-call-'ems . . . selkies?"

" 'Ere's a legend, Cap'um," Buchanon told him, " 'at long, long ago, 'twas a battle comin' 'twixt Good an' Evil, an' Lir, a as one o' ol' gods, come t'this fishin' village, lookin' for help 'gainst Evil. Now th' villagers cried off, d'ye see, sir. Said 'ey's too poor, 'ey didn't know a thing 'bout fightin', nor weapons. 'Eir men go away t' fight, 'eir wimmen'n babes'd starve. So Lir—so me da' tol' me—put 'is *cess* on 'em all. Said he'd come again, oncet th' battle woz won. Good did beat Evil. Never for very long, though . . . an' ain't *that* just th' way of it, sir? Well, ol' Lir come back t'at village, 'bout th' time 'ey'd all forgot, an' laid his curse. He turned 'em into selkies, Cap'um. Seals with human souls, sir, who remembered livin' ashore, an' how good 'twoz. Drove 'em inta th' sea, weepin' an' wailin', where 'ey'd bawl all 'eir live-long days."

"Doesn't sound like a good god, to me, to punish so," Lewrie sniffed in disapproval. Of action, tale, or truth, he didn't know.

"Ol' Testament's full o' such, though, sir," Buchanon countered wryly. "But, here's the cruelest part o' Lir's curse. After a century'r two, his *cess* seemed t' sputter out. One at a time, 'ey swim ashore on some rookery beach, an' woke up *people*, again, Cap'um! Thought 'ey'd *paid* for 'eir sins, at last, an' woz free. But, oh no!"

"Don't tell me they got so used to being seals, that . . ." he kenned with a wry grimace. "They began to ache for the sea?"

"Aye, sir, 'at 'ey did." Buchanon chuckled. "Fell in love an' wed, had babes an' houses, an' lives worth livin'. But then, some night, sir . . . when the wind's blowin' soft off th' sea, an' th' moon is shinin' soft an' pretty, 'ey gets t' starin' at it, walkin' th' beaches night after night, listenin' t'th' others out there, callin' to 'em . . . ? Comes a time, sir, 'ey can't resist no more. Strip off 'eir clothes, an' swim out, with no lookin' back, an' turn back inta seals, 'ey do, Cap'um! Have a high old time o' it, for a while, back with 'eir ol' friends in th' sea, as selkies again."

"And then that gets old, and they remember being people, and their loved ones ashore?" Lewrie shivered.

"Doomed t'go through th' whole pain, over an' over, again . . . 'til th' end o' Time, Cap'um," Buchanon intoned, as sure of his lore as he was of the next sunrise. "But, 'tis said, sir . . . 'ere's times 'ey come *back* ashore, t'fetch 'eir gits. Selkie makes a babe, he's half selkie, himself, then. An' *he* can't resist wadin' out some night, neither, when his da' or ma does. No matter whose heart it breaks. 'Twaz a heavy curse Lir laid on 'em, sir. A heartless bugger, he."

"No, Mister Buchanon," Lewrie protested. Or felt that he had to, as a rational man. As *some* sort of a Christian. "Lir sent the seals—selkies—to take Josephs? That'd be robbing God of that lad's immortal soul! That'd keep him from Salvation!"

"Th' lad'z from Bristol, sir," Buchanon explained, shaking his head, utterly convinced of his rightness, no matter that he was speaking an ancient pagan heresy. "Little Josephs might o' been a selkie t'begin with, livin' 'at close t'th' sea, from a seafarin' fam'ly? I seen, or heard, o' such before, Cap'um, back home when I'z a lad. A spell as a seal . . . Lir didn't rob God. Jus' *borrowed* Josephs's soul, for a piece. More like, th' lad'll appear in 'is world again, might be a foundlin', an' grow up t'be a sailor. Maybe one with a better run o' luck, th' next time, an' a longer life. After he pays off whatever sin he done in his ol' life afore, sir . . . *then*, he'll go t'his true reward. B'sides, sir . . . 'ere's more myst'ries in 'is here world'n we can shake a stick at. An' we just *saw* one, sir, and 'at's a fact! All folk can do sometimes is be left t'wonder."

"Amen to that," Lewrie said automatically, looking astern at their wake, a gray specter, only darkly sunset-tinted upon the foam. Wondering if it *would* be a wonder—or a sign of a further curse from Lir!—to espy another seal. "Well, then. Ahum! Thankee, Mister Buchanon. That'll be all for now. Do carry on."

"Aye aye, sir," the sailing master replied, doffing his hat in salute as he wandered over to the hands by the wheel, as Seven Bells of the Second Dog were struck up forward.

LEWRIE WENT BELOW to his cabins for his supper, stowing Bible and prayer book in the shelf above the chart table on the way.

"Yer rhenish, sir?" Aspinall inquired, cleaning his hands on the fresh white apron he wore. "A glass o' claret tonight, then?"

"Brandy, Aspinall," Lewrie decided grimly. "Big'un!"

"Aye, sir. Best for what ails ya, says I," Aspinall rambled on cheerily, as he poured three fingers-worth into a snifter. "Sad it is, sir. That little tyke? But, a stout measure o' something always bucks a body right up, sir."

Toulon came slinking out of hiding, into the cheery light from the overhead lanthorns, wailing a welcoming "Maa-ahh-*warr*!" with even more urgency and enthusiasm than he usually showed. And that was not insubstantial, to begin with. Greeting his master (as much as cats may be said to *have* the concept of master down pat) with a desperate show of affection. Or a desperate need of it, himself.

Never known to be a particularly doting tribe, except when it suited them, still . . . Toulon seemed to empathize as he climbed Alan's chest, patted and kneaded furiously, and reclined on his shirtfront finally, little head butting under Alan's chin, licking and purring in remarkable, commiserating ardor.

"You feel it, too, Toulon?" Lewrie asked softly. "Scare you, too?"

"*Maiwee?*" was the ram-kitten's shuddery reply, as he turned himself boneless, to flatten his body even closer.

"Scared the Devil out of *me*, let me tell you," Lewrie confided to his creature. He stroked Toulon down from forehead to tail-tip, in thankfulness that there was somebody there to give him comfort at least. "Was it even real, puss? Did it really happen like I think it did? God!"

Should it ever come my time, Alan thought, cringing at the very idea; that's *one* way to escape the Devil and his fires. A back gate for the damned—become a selkie!

"Wouldn't do you a bit of good, would it, Toulon?" Lewrie told the ram-cat. "Can't abide your sponge-down now, much less a swim."

"*Moi*," the cat sang under his jaw, paws working as he slinked higher toward his collars.

"Christ, what use is a selkie who can't swim?" Lewrie snorted, forcing himself to chuckle. Like most good English seamen, he could not swim a single lick. If a ship went down, most of them said that trying to swim only prolonged the inevitable. Or saved one just long enough to be eaten by something, right after one got one's hopes up, and . . .

"Damme!" Lewrie sighed, taking another refreshing draught of his brandy, shoving another fey feeling away.

Poor little Josephs, he pondered, instead; barely got his sea legs, and bam! Maybe it *is* best, that . . . that Lir took him? Just for a bit, say. Chub might be happy to be a seal, for a while. Happier'n he was 'board *this* ship, at any rate!

A lad about Sewallis's age and size, Lewrie mourned with infinite regret; dreams shattered, terrified—started!—heartbroken, then dead, long 'fore his time!

There came the faint sound of a fiddle tune from the gun deck. Slow, lugubrious, and atonal, like what Captain Ayscough aboard *Telesto* had delightedly told him was the "great music" played on bagpipes.

But this was one he recognized—the funeral song played for Stuart hopes, and the dead of Culloden, after the '45: "The Flowers of the Forest." His eyes pricked with remorseful tears. He thought, for an instant, of ordering the fiddler to cease, but . . .

Toulon climbed to his shoulder, to snuffle at his ear. Lewrie felt him stiffen, heard him chitter, as he did at the sight of a seabird. Claws dug into his shoulder, and the little ram-kitten's tail, which lashed before his nose, bottled up to double-size. He made his chatter again! A seabird, *this* late in the evening? he wondered.

Or a selkie in their wake!

"I'll not look!" he whispered, keeping his gaze firmly ahead, and taking another deep draught of brandy. "I *don't* want to know!"

And he didn't, though Toulon continued to knead and shiver his little chops, quavering, and would not get down. And lashing his tiny tail, thick as a pistol swab brush, in a frenzy. Lewrie did turn his head just enough to see Toulon's neck, his whole body, straining aft, intent as only a cat may be intent, upon *something* astern, almost as if in yearning . . . or silent, beastly communion.

"Rot!" Lewrie muttered harshly. "Rot, I say! *Has* to be!"

"*Muwuhh?*" Toulon said at last, sounding disappointed, as his body lost its lock-spring tension. Then, he was amenable to a rub on his flank, to turn (clumsily) and drop down to Alan's lap to knead a new nest. And rasp his rough little tongue on Alan's hand.

Purring like anything.

BOOK II

Anceps aestus incertiam rapit;
ut saeva rapidi bella cum venti gerunt
utrimque fluctus maria discordes agunt
dubiumque fervet pelagus haut aliter meum
cor fluctuator.

A double tide tosses me, uncertain of my course; as
when a rushing tide wages mad warfare, and from
both sides conflicting floods lash the seas and the
fluctuating waters boil, even so is my heart tossed.

MEDEA Book II, 939–944
Lucius Annaeus Seneca

CHAPTER
1

A QUICK INVENTORY, a circular course for his jittery right hand along his uniform. Cuffs shot, waistcoat tugged straight, hat set on just so. Wash-leather purse full of guineas still safe, and, a blank note-of-hand snugly ensconced in a coat pocket . . . well, then.

A deep, spine-straightening breath before he rapped on the door. As he waited for someone within to answer, Lewrie experimented with a range of expressions on his face. Smile? No. Frown? That wouldn't do, either. Something in-between, perhaps? Though he suspected that "something in-between" would resemble a gas attack, or a pair of too-tight shoes. He was striving hellish hard for Ambivalent!

And why the Devil'd she remove herself to *this* set o' rooms? he asked himself with a quick, fleeting scowl; her old'uns were nice enough, and not *that* dear. She have a comedown, 'spite of the money I left her? Waste it all on fripperies, or gamblin' . . . ?

"Yessir?" A mob-capped oldish maidservant inquired of him as the door opened with a rusty creak, at last.

"Commander Alan Lewrie . . ." he flummoxed out, not sure exactly what sort of expression his phyz wore, then. "Come to call upon Made-moiselle Phoebe Aretino. Is she in?"

"God be praised, sir!" The square old crone cried in delight, clapping her hands together, and raising enough noise to wake the entire neigh-borhood. "You're her Navy fella, come back at last! Come you in, sir! Come you *in*! Let me take your hat, Commander Lewrie . . . have a cane, an' . . . no? *Mistress!*"

She bawled that with the door standing wide open. Cartmen and vendors were stopped dead in their tracks in the narrow, steep little street that straggled uphill from the Old Moles. A curate and his wife out for an invigorating uphill stroll, both clad in old rusty-black dominee ditto, were frowning heavily as Lewrie sought some way short of strangulation to stifle the old mort's bellows.

"Mistress Phoebe!" the woman halloed upstairs. " 'Tis Commander Lewrie! He's come, ma'am! Hurry!"

At least he could use his foot to slam that heavy old door, to keep their reunion somewhat private, as a delighted shriek came from above, quickly followed by the patter of petite feet on the carpet and floorboards and stairs. Lewrie's lips twitched as he attempted to regain the composure of his face anew. And trying to recall just exactly which demeanor he'd thought most suitable.

"Alain!" Phoebe cried breathlessly—almost brokenly, as she appeared on the tiny middle landing of the narrow pair of stairs. Her brown eyes were fawn-huge and lambent, as if suddenly aswim with tears of joy, and her cheeks flush with emotion.

Oh, damme, Lewrie thought with a shudder, a definite lurching in his chest, and an instant, tumbledy flood of warmth; why the Devil she have to look *that* handsome! That young and . . . !

He went to raise his right hand, as if to doff the hat he didn't wear to her in genteel salute, but it got no higher than his midchest, appearing to her as an invitation, before she dashed down the stairs to fling herself upon him with such a fierce ardor that he was almost driven backward, off his heels, to the floor.

He rocked one heel backward to balance, put his arms about her to hold her up, savoring all over again just how tiny, how petite and perfectly formed Phoebe Aretino was. With her arms about his neck and most happily dangling, with her heels far off the floor, showering his face, his neck, his eyes, with a positive deluge of kisses, whispering betwixt each some French, some English endearments, and declarations of how much she had ached for the sight of him.

To support her, of course . . . doin' the gentlemanly thing, Lewrie swore to himself! . . . he was forced to place his hands under her bottom. Touch her small, spare, incredibly soft . . . !

"Phoebe . . ." he whimpered. He'd meant to growl, to caution her about the maid, whose presence Phoebe was blissfully ignoring. Meant to greet her pleasantly, in point of fact. *Merely* pleasantly, but . . . Their lips met, open and inviting, coffee-hot and musky, already, as she, still oblivious to the cronish maidservant, lifted her ever so slim thighs and wrapped them around his waist!

"Phoebe . . . ?" he essayed again.

Well damme, he thought, in a hopeless muddle! Meant that'un to be japing . . . cajole her down! But it had come out throaty, caressing.

He evidently had called upon her just about the time she'd arisen from bed, or just after her morning ablutions. Phoebe hadn't taken time to throw on a morning gown in which visitors could be decently received— only a spiderweb-thin silk dressing robe. No corsets, stays, or underpinnings, no chemise, nothing even a *bit* cumbrous came between his hands, which were now beginning to rove her back and bottom fondly, and her tender young flesh, but that dressing robe.

Damp ringlets of lustrous dark brown hair toyed about his face and collars—rich, sultrily Italian, Mediterranean, exotic and dark-as-coffee hair.

"So long, Alain, *mon cerf formidable!*" she crooned in his ear, a tiny, breathless huskiness to her usually small voice. "Mont' an' mont', you be away, an' on'y ze une lettre! *Mon coeur*, ah mees you *si très beaucoup!*"

"Phoebe!" He sighed, chuckling with uncontrollable, undeniable delight, by then, as he dipped his head to kiss her throat, the soft flesh under her chin, her slim neck below her ears.

Knew this'd happen, he chid himself; *knew* it! But not anywhere near as harshly as he might. God help me, but . . . !

Nature had her way with him, by then. Unbidden, in spite of a whole host of good intentions, the fork of his breeches felt nigh to bursting with a raging tumescence which he swore could serve as taffrail flagstaff in a full gale! He took a clumsy step toward those first set of stairs, felt her shift against him, meaning to keep his balance under such a tempting, alluring, top-heavy cargo . . . and he was lost. Again.

"*Ma cherie*," he muttered, "*ma petit biche. Ma chou!*"

"Oh, Alain, 'urry!" she teased, glancing upward. "*Mon amour!*"

Well, he thought, not a *touch* rueful; s'pose we have to get reacquainted first. In for the penny, in for the pound, an' all that!

THEY'D NOT QUITE attained real privacy, not that first reunion. A trail of his shoes, sword and belt, neck-stock and coat littered up the second flight attested to that. Waistcoat gone, long-tail shirt and breeches open, he'd played horsey to her hunter, and trotted her to the tiny upper landing, into her bedchambers, and all about the room. Laughing all the while,

crying "Yoicks, Tallyho!" and making bugle calls through his nostrils.
"Trot! Canter! Draw sabers and . . . sound the Charge!" As he recalled
from seeing the local Yeoman Cavalry practice their drill back in Anglesgreen. Spitted upon him, Phoebe had shrieked aloud, open windows to
the street bedamned . . . and more than once, too, he smugly congrat-
ulated himself . . . before they'd collapsed exhausted across her high
bedstead, in shuddery giggles of delight, tears of ecstasy, and much-
needful pantings.

A quarter-hour of kisses, caresses, strokes of dearly remembered skin.
A quarter-hour of endearments, of pledges of heartbreak over the long
separation, many sighs and shudders, and rolling about, twine and
countertwine, stoking the coals with kisses becoming more and more
intimate and giving. . . .

Looking up at her, rough sailor's hands on her slim, swansdown hips as
she bestrode him, rocking and riding bold as a plumed lancer . . . riding Saint George with her head thrown back and her carefully coiffed
hair come down in sweaty "*à la victime*" ringlets. Incredibly slim arms,
her waif-slim waist, and taut little belly . . . Phoebe's small breasts in
his eyes, large dark areoli and pouty little nipples mesmerizing him all
over again, bedewed with perspiration as she flung herself, thrusted to
meet him. So tiny, she was, so gamin and light, so completely engrasping
and enfolding about him! So utterly kittenish, yet minxlike and en-
thralling! And so strong, her slim little fingers, on his shoulders as she
leaned forward, face crumpled, tears flowing, breath rasping harsh and
insistent between her moans and cries.

He slid his hands up to surround her breasts and she leaned in to
support herself, eyes flying wide open as she began to smile, expectantly,
speared to the utter depths of her heart, of her soul, in one more of a
series of "the little deaths." As his own release built to more than he
could stand without bellowing like a steer, not a moment more could he
wait, withhold himself, delay his pleasuring in hopes it might help her
attain hers! Hard and greedy now, niceties bedamned, and Phoebe took
his hands in hers, crushed sword-bruted, rope-bruted palms into her
tenderest flesh. Twined fingers and keened aloud, a victory paean that
went on and on, rising falsetto in time to their every shift and judder,
until at last . . .

She screamed a weak, thin scream, twined fingers tighter, and leaned
back, trusting him to keep her from falling, as his own head exploded, as
he departed his life for a maelstrom of colored stars, tumbling down a
cannon's barrel into the swirling sparks and flame points of eruption.

Exploding upward, delirious and aswim, reeling and rolling in a fever-dream, feeling her grip him, grip him, grip him and spasm, as their senses tumbled around the cosmos.

Utterly ruined, when he came back to his life, a few moments later, chest heaving for air. Utterly spent, as she sat back erect, then dropped, shuddering and gasping, atop him. Her soft, gentle breath gusting now, across his shoulder. Damp ringlets clinging to both their faces. Surprisingly strong little hands and arms about his neck. Yet such an utterly soft, sweet, and spent kiss did she give him in reward, her full, sweet lips brushing his so lightly, and curling upward in a smile.

He put his arms about her slim back, stroked her damp flesh from shoulders to buttocks, then encircled her and squeezed possessively, inhaling deep for his wind, and taking in every subtle nuance of cologne, scented soap, perspiration, sweet hair, and lovemaking, as if to fill his lungs with her forever.

"*Je t'adore*, Alain," she told him, her voice tiny, and barely audible, even with her lips near his ear. "Afterr aw' zees time . . . you are 'ere, encore! *Je t'adore, mon coeur. Mon chou fantastique.*"

"Missed you, too." Alan sighed, giving her another squeezing hug and feeling a shoulder-rolling shudder go right down to his toes as he did so. "You, *I* adore, *aussi, ma chou. Je t'adore . . . très beaucoup!*"

Damme to hell, but . . . he sighed to himself, biting his lip but with his hands gently caressing her in spite of all; I said it, both ways—Frog *and* English. Damme to hell, but it's *true!*

"*Je t'adore, ma belle amour. Je t'adore,*" he whispered. In for the penny, in for the pound, indeed. But it felt so good to be back!

CHAPTER
2

"Ahoy, the boat!" Midshipman Spendlove called to the heavy hired cutter, as it neared them, oars dipping in liquid gold water in an amber-tinted Mediterranean twilight.

"*Jester!*" came the return hail, from their captain himself.

"Must be in a hurry, not to've sent off for his gig," Hyde opined by his side, on the starboard gangway.

"Thought we'd have been up-anchor, and away, hours ago," Mister Midshipman Spendlove rejoined. Though he had already speculated on why the captain had sent his gig back to the ship, just after he had gotten to Gibraltar's Old Mole landing, a heavy bundle of dispatches in a canvas-wrapped case under his arm. And then he hadn't returned since noon? And Midshipman Clarence Spendlove, from previous service, knew what tempting lure still lurked at Gibraltar, to ensnare the captain . . . just like Dido from his Latin texts. Dido and . . . *whatever* his name was! Imprudent reality made his slim erudition flee his head.

"Mine arse on a bandbox," Spendlove muttered *sotto voce*, emulating his commanding officer, once he had a gander at the cutter's contents. "Mister Rydell, midshipman of the watch's duty to Mister Knolles, and inform him the captain's returning aboard. Run, boy! Mister Cony? Bosun o' the watch, there! Side-party, man the gangway!"

Spithead nightingales shrilled, Marine Sergeant Boothby and the first officer, Mister Knolles, presented swords. Marines stamped their feet and slapped walnut musket stocks in salute, as the top of their captain's hat loomed over the lip of the entry port. Crewmen of the watch, and most of the off-duty watch idling on deck, doffed hats, to pay homage.

Homage that was returned, by the doff of a gold-laced cocked hat, on Lewrie's part, once he'd attained the security of the upper oaken gangway deck.

"Mister Knolles, I . . ." Lewrie began hesitantly, quite unlike his usual demeanor.

"Aye, sir?" Knolles prompted, wondering why his frank and open commanding officer could not quite match glances with him, of a sudden.

"Bosun's chair, over the side, to the boat, Mister Knolles." The captain grunted. "And a working-party. Blackwall hitch on the main-yard stay-tackle, to fetch dunnage aboard."

"Aye, aye, sir," Knolles replied. "Mister Cony? Rig a bosun's chair. And a cargo stay-tackle hoist."

"Dismiss the side-party, Mister Knolles," Lewrie ordered, turning to peer over the side, arms spread wide on the bulwarks. "We're not receiving officers."

Ralph Knolles raised an eyebrow, stepped to the side, surreptitiously, and cast a single furtive glance over. Their lone passenger was a woman! A most beautiful young . . . lady? Knolles frowned. Oh, he gasped in recognition. Last time we were at Gibraltar, the captain . . . they *said* he had a doxy ashore, but . . .

Hell's bells, Knolles thought, with a weary sigh, before turning to supervise the working party. It was no concern of his, really, what his captain did, whom he entertained aft on-passage. Knolles had served in ships with a captain's entire family aboard, had been aboard a 3rd Rate in which every warrant, division, or department head had his "wife" and kiddies along! The solitary, celibate seafaring life was a convenient fiction, for the most part—mostly for the benefit of the true wives and families left ashore—! But, he never thought Commander Lewrie'd be . . . !

No, probably *not* a lady, Knolles sniffed in prim dismissal; an affair . . . most definitely an *affair*! . . . he had no business in.

YOU DAMN' FOOL, Lewrie chided himself; you damn' fool! His face felt flush, and his clothing chafed him, itchy and sore. Or, perhaps, his very skin, he thought. Yet, he stood atremble with more concern for Phoebe's safety than for his repute, as she was hoisted aboard.

He'd really *meant* to end their relationship, had taken a fair amount of solid coin, and a note-of-hand upon his shore agent, then his London bank, to cushion her dismissal from his life. So short a time, though, in her bewitching presence, and he was as will-less as a drunken gambler.

"Zat ees *effroyable*," Phoebe peeped, once free of the slings of the bosun's chair, a high color to her own cheeks, but with glitter to her eyes. "*Mais . . . ees très émotionnant!*" With a giggle of fading delight, she slipped an arm through his.

"Ahum . . . Mister Knolles, allow me to name to you, Mademoiselle Phoebe Aretino," Lewrie stammered over the social graces. "She will be sailing with us. Mademoiselle is *from* Corsica, originally, so . . ."

"Mademoiselle Aretino," Knolles said, doffing his hat, and making a "leg" in reply to her graceful curtsy. Though his expression was hellish-bland.

"Lieutenant . . . Knolles, *enchanté, m'sieur*," Phoebe rejoined, with her best formal manner. "Ah, *M'sieur* Spen'loove! *Bonjour, encore!* You are-ah well?" she cried, as she spotted a familiar face.

"Ma'am," Spendlove greeted, blushing. "Aye. Well, uhm . . ."

"An' *m'sieur* . . . Lapin? *Non* . . . *pardon, merci merde alors* . . ." Phoebe stumbled. "*M'sieur* Cony! Ze gran' 'ero weez ze . . . grenades?"

"Aye, ma'am," Cony said, preening, " 'twaz grenadoes, we used. Good o' ya t'remember, ma'am."

"Well, hmm . . ." Lewrie flummoxed, once the many introductions were done among the quarterdeck people, who had crowded forward, after word had gone around that a vision had descended from heaven. And that the captain had a doxy! Alan felt as a pilfering thief might, forced to run a gantlet of his mess-deck victims, and their starters or rope ends. "Cony, do you be so good as to see uhm . . . Mistress Aretino's . . . dunnage, aft? Mister Knolles, I note the wind'll serve, just. We've an hour till full dark. We could be standing out, around Europa Point, by then. Pipe the hands to Stations for Weighing Anchor, and prepare us for getting underway."

"Aye aye, sir," Knolles replied, just as glad as Lewrie to escape into something more mundane and maritime.

"I'll see Mistress Aretino aft, and get her somewhat settled," Lewrie promised, "then rejoin you. Carry on, till then, sir."

✣   ✣   ✣

"BUT, ISN'T HE married?" Midshipman Hyde queried in a whisper.

"Aye, but . . ." Spendlove griped, just as softly. "Met her at Toulon. Used to be . . . enamored, I s'pose you could call it, of our Lieutenant Scott, but he passed over when we were sunk. Didn't have anyone else to turn to, around the time of the evacuation, so . . ."

"Oh, like the Vicomtesse de Maubeuge?" Hyde said, his tongue firmly in cheek. "I must say, Clarence . . . at least the captain has grand taste, when it comes to women. Wives *and* doxies, hmm?"

"MY *WORD,* CONY!" Knolles grumbled. "My bloody *oath!* So she is, well . . . *was* Scott's paramour, first? Now, our captain's?"

"Aye, sir," Cony said with a faint scowl of worry. "A sweet l'il thing, though." He'd known Lewrie's amatory appetites for years; shared 'em, in point of fact. Reveled in 'em, truth to tell! Going to sea, becoming Lewrie's "man" so long ago, had opened his eyes to life, broadened his horizons far beyond that bucolic innocence he'd known as a rustic Gloucestershire "chaw-bacon," with thatch sticking from out his ears. What enthusiasm he had for his new status as the Proper Married Man, he owed to the Lewries' fondness for each other.

And what enthusiasm he had for Maggie had been born abed with her. How else was there a Little Will in swaddlings, now, if not for prenuptial passion? Being a practical, commonsensical sort, Bosun's Mate Will Cony knew from long experience that sailors will usually be sailors, far from home, with months between letters or news. Maggie almost kenned that, as any seaman's wife should. As they said on the lower decks . . . "shouldn'ta joined, if ya can't take a joke!"

Still, he'd always believed that Lewrie would be more discreet than that. He'd even spoken disparagingly of officers who carried a mort to sea, parading before the love-starved, lust-surly "people" what they could not have. If the little sauce-pot had *that* much influence on him, though . . .

"She is, that!" Knolles commented, rather wistfully. "Well . . . Mister Cony. Ahem. Carry on."

"Aye, sir." Cony chuckled, knuckling his forehead in salute, knowing he'd been dismissed. Knowing that Knolles had said too much to an inferior, and was seething inside for being so open.

"Dot de guhl th' cap'um woz s'sweet on, Will?" Andrews asked, once Knolles had walked away. "De one ya tol' me 'bout?"

"Aye, that she be. 'Ope she don't spell trouble. For him, or us." Cony shrugged.

"Law, Will!" Andrews guffawed, his teeth brilliant against the dusk of his skin. "It be th' same'zit always woz, bock in de Wes' Indies, durin' de 'Merican War. Jus' a whiff o' quim, not de whole garden. Cap'um, he lose his head ovah de ladies, now'n 'gain. But, he nevah lose it fo' long!"

"Mister Cony, make 'em hop to *it*!" Midshipman Hyde called to them, snappish and still fretful. And more than a little scandalized.

"Aye, Mister Hyde. Hoppin', this instant," Cony answered as he withdrew his bosun's pipe from a chest pocket of his waistcoat by its ornately plaited lanyard. "Messenger, aft t'th' capstan-head!"

"You, too, Andrews," Hyde added.

"On me way, t'de quawtah-deck, yassuh, Mistah Hyde, uhuhh!" the coxswain replied, falling back on a West Indies slave patois in subtle mockery, to rejoin the hands of the after-guard, who would tend sheets, halliards, lifts, and jears on the mizzenmast. "Right, lads. Tail on, weaklin's. De strong men'z walkin' de capstan *fo'* ya."

"Canne do 'at, Cox," a landsman asked, perplexed. "Jus' 'ave 'isself a lady, all t' 'is own? Any why cain't we, I asks ya . . ."

" 'Cause he be de cap'um, an' you *ain't*, Cousins!" Andrews told the fresh-caught lubber, steering him away from a standing back-stay to his proper post on the mizzen tops'l jears. "Law, ye be so dumb, I lay odds ya thought dey call 'im de 'Ram-Cat' jus' 'cause he be fond o' de kitties, didn' ya, Cousins? Haw haw!"

ONCE AT SEA, Lewrie quit the deck, after *Jester* was well clear of Europa Point, and reaching easterly on a beam wind, the galley funnel fuming once more to simmer up a late supper.

Aspinall took his hat to hang up, as Lewrie hesitantly went aft to his day-cabin, suddenly feeling like an intruder in a strange salon.

There was a slanging match going on, with much hissing, spitting, and a noticeable nimbus of stress-shed fur, as the litter mates, Toulon and Phoebe's kitten—now half-grown to an almost calico white-and-tan—got "reacquainted." Toulon on the desktop, pawing the wine cabinet in threat, as her cat cowered atop it, looking over the edge, hunkered up and snarling, trilling deep in her throat between nervous chop-licking.

"Take no guff off the ladies, Toulon—that's the way," Alan muttered as he opened the cabinet doors to pour his own drink.

"Sorry, sir, but I wasn't goin' nowhere near 'em, long as they're in a snit," Aspinall apologized.

"No problem, Aspinall," Lewrie told him, tipping himself a glass of hock. "And what's your name, little girl? Whatever did your mistress name you? 'Spit'? 'Whurdrdrdr,' did ye say?" he yodeled.

A traveling case thumped to the deck, in the sleeping coach. A bustle of domesticity, accompanied by a pleased humming tune, sometimes breaking into a soft, half-conscious "la-la'ing."

Good Christ, but I'm *such* a fool! Lewrie told himself, perhaps for the hundredth time since midmorning. Well, 'tis only till Corsica . . . bags of time to 'wean' both of us, after.

The military authorities at Gibraltar had been gloating merry about Admiral Lord Hood's siege-work, there. The main harbor, San Fiorenzo, had fallen early on, and just recently, the city of Bastia had come into British, or Coalition, possession. Now the French were isolated, hanging on by their fingernails at the extreme northern end of the island, in Calvi. The coastline was so well guarded by Royal Navy ships that a fishing smack couldn't sneak in with supplies, or reinforcements; neither could the French hope for a piecemeal evacuation over several nights.

And, to discomfit the Frogs even further, the fleet they'd put together from scattered units in the Mediterranean—or brought back into commission after the Coalition had failed to burn them when they had evacuated Toulon the previous Christmas!—had been countered at sea, rather deuced well! Hood had sailed away from the siege to meet Rear Admiral Comte Martin, and had snaffled the dismal bastard into a sack, in the Golfe Jouan east of Cannes, where he was now embayed and most effectively blockaded; of absolutely no use to the desperate Republican army at Calvi . . . or anyone else, pretty much.

Toulon interrupted Lewrie's musings, breaking off his own sort of "siege-work" to rub and purr, and meow for attention, which he got at once. Looking up and sneering a lofty "so there, see?" at the cat atop the wine cabinet.

"Only the few days, Toulon," Lewrie promised him. "*Oww!*"

Piqued, perhaps, Phoebe's calico had taken a defensive swat at him, and had connected on his right ear!

"Oh, *merde alors*," Phoebe cooed, exiting the sleeping coach in a lacy flutter of feminine finery. "Joliette, elle est ze *méchanceté*, ees 'naughty,' *oui?* . . . ze *très* naughty *jeune fille.* I am sorry, *mais* she ees protec', uhm . . . ?"

"It's *my* wine she's protecting," he groused, placing a handkerchief to his ear. Damme, he carped to himself; the bitch'z drawn blood!

"Oh, Alain!" Phoebe comforted, taking the handkerchief, and dipping it in his hock, to dab at his ear. "I kees, an' mak' . . . uhm . . . a *meilleur? Ah, better? Merci.* My Englis', ees . . . better, *mais* . . . *n'est-ce pas?* I kees an' mak' eet better, hein?" she cajoled, swishing her hips and gazing up at him with mischievous, impish eyes.

"Après souper, peut-être," he japed in return, any qualms in his head evaporating in another instant.

"Certainment, mon chou," she replied, with a promising grin. And retrieving her cat, Joliette, and keeping his wineglass, to sashay off astern to the crude sofa to sit and stroke her beast down. He poured himself another, and joined her.

Along the way, he got a peek into the sleeping coach, to find that her pitiful collection of luggage he recalled from Toulon before the evacuation had grown considerably. There were now two full portmanteau chests, brimming with yard goods. Not only dresses, but bed linens, coverlets, the wink of pewter. There were unopened crates that had rattled as they'd come aboard—glassware and plates.

"I was surprised, your removing," he began.

"Oh, Alain, to 'ave ze proper establissement *pour vous,* I mus' buy ze many s'ings!" she explained, looking as if she would be eager to jump to her feet, dash into the sleeping coach, and display all her new possessions like a birthday child. "To take ze suite, wiz furnishings, uhm . . . ze chair, ze tables, ze bed, *oui. Mais,* ees ver' empty? So I change rooms, for save you' monnai. An' I buy zose nice s'ings zat mak' eet . . . familial? More homey? Zo when you are ashore, wiz me, you are non asham-ed."

"Aha," he said noncommittally. It sounded hellish close to hopes of "familial," domestic bliss; last year's wren hatchling making a first nest of her own.

'Least I'm fortunate, he thought, taking a cool sip of his hock: don't know why, but all my girls have been the economical sort. Never a spendthrift in the lot! Knock wood!

Phoebe shrugged, turning pensive.

"D'avant, w'en I am leetle girl . . ." She sighed. "Papa an' Maman are *très pauvre* . . . ver' poor. 'E ees ze soap-maker? Maman 'elp eem . . . or wash ze laundry for ozzers. Sometime ze *domestique* . . . for ze rich?

Ver' poor. 'Ave nozzing. I go wiz 'er, sometime . . . I see what ozzers 'ave, an' I wan' zat *pour moi*. For Papa an' Maman, *aussi*."

She put out a hand to him, to draw him to sit by her side more closely on the sofa, as she tried to explain her life.

"Papa, *'e nous a quittes*, w'en I am *seize*, uhm . . . sixteen? An' Maman ees weak, ver' sick sometime, so I tak' 'er place, an' work as ze *domestique*. At firs', in Bastia, w'ere we live. Zen I go Toulon," Phoebe told him, almost sadly, slipping an arm through his, turning to face him. "*Oui*, I become *putain* . . . ze petite whore. *Domestiques* wiz pretty . . . 'oo *are* pretty, hmm . . . eet 'appens, *n'est-ce pas*? *C'est dommage, mais* . . . ? 'Ave ze *belle vetements*, ze beautiful gowns, go to ze dances . . . ride een ze fine coach? *Mais*, come 'ome to ze rooms zat I on'y rent. Ver' impersonnel, wiz nozzing of mine? Oh, Alain, 'ow ver' much I wan' ze 'ome of my own, someday! Furniture *I* prefer, non w'ot come wiz rent. Forgeev, *plais, mais* . . ."

She ducked her head.

"I take ze smaller rooms to save *monnaie, oui*. Non jus' for you' sake. For *moi*. Zo I 'ave *monnaie* for to buy preety s'ings for . . . for zat someday, *comprendre*? Zo someday, I weel *be* somebody."

"If you needed more, Phoebe . . ." He chuckled.

"Non," she insisted, with a somber cast to her features, perhaps for the first time in his experience of her. "You, I adore, Alain, *mon coeur*. Anozzer man, per'aps 'e 'ave more monnai, can mak' me to be ze somebody at once, *mais* . . . *j'm'en fous*! Wiz *you*, I am 'appy! Eef eet tak' time for to be ze grande lady, *c'est dommage*. I be mistress to one man, on'y. *Vous*! Non more putain. We mak' each ozzer 'appy, an' I wait for you to sail 'ome to me. W'ere I mak' you ze domicile, uhm . . . *intimé et agréable* . . . 'ow you say?"

"Pleasant and cozy." He grinned.

"*Oui*, pleasan' an' . . . cozy!" Phoebe giggled, rewarding his abbreviated English lesson with a chaste little kiss, and settling down on his side, her head on his shoulder, cooing with delight. "*Mon Dieu*, I am so *beaucoup* 'appy you 'ave return-ed, Alain! I mees you so much, I *ache* for to be 'appy an' content, again. To be wiz ze on'y man 'oo . . . *care* for me. 'Oo tak' si . . . *such* good care of me! I weel non be expensive, you weel see! *Parce que* . . . be-cause, I love you so much."

"A quiet, *little* place, then," he inquired hopefully. Though coin did "chink" about in his head. How much might that "quiet, little place" cost? There'd be furniture, paintings, servants' wages . . . And quiet, secure lodgings meant good neighborhoods, far removed from the com-

mercial quarter; a coach-and-four might be necessary! The need for
china, silver plate, cutlery, lanthorns, and candle stands, *beeswax* candles
by the gross. Drapers and paperers in and out with even more
costly . . . ! He took a fortifying sip of wine.

"Nozzing *grande, mon chou*," she reassured him, though, half lost in
fantasies of domestic perfection. "I non need ze *palace*, hein? Une leetle
appartement, wiz balcony. We go to San Fiorenzo? *Bon.* So ver' steep ze
hills, *mais* . . . non ze *rent*, Alain! Balcony wiz view of ocean. Zo I
watch fo' you' *navire* . . . you' ship. *Une domestique*, on'y, 'oo eez live
zere wiz me . . . *une* 'oo come for day, to cook an' clean. Corsica . . .
ees ver' poor. *Une peu monnaie* go ze long way, zere, you will see, I
promesse. An' zo many *émigrés royalistes* go zere. You remember, w'en
we leave Toulon, zey tak' away zere good s'ings? 'Ave *non monnaie*, now.
Zey will be sell zose preety s'ings, *bon marché*. Zat ees ze 'cheap'!"

Alan turned to peer at her. For such a sweet, seemingly guileless
young fairy girl, Phoebe had suddenly sounded as calculating and pinchpenny, as grasping as a Haymarket horse trader!

"Be grow up poor as *moi*, Alain, *mon chou*." She chuckled, in answer
to his puzzled expression, with a wry tip of her glass in salute to her past.
"You fin' 'ow to shop for bargain!"

The thought *did* cross his mind (it must be said), even as he was
placing a supportive and comforting arm about her shoulders, that there
was *still* time to cry off their cozy arrangement. He could give her fifty
pounds in coin—the Devil with his note-of-hand! Fifty pounds would be
more than enough to support her for months, if Corsican living was as
cheap as she described it. Certainly, it would be cheaper than establish-
ing an entire new household, with all the requisite furnishings.

Damme, he thought wryly, I know sailors're said to have a *wife* in
every port. But nobody said a bloody thing 'bout whole *houses*!

"Trus' *moi*, Alain," she whispered, her soft breath close, and promising, near his ear. "As I trus' you, wiz my 'hole 'eart."

Well, *that* did it!

I *do* have a fair lot o' prize money, he relented, anew. Maybe it won't
be as cheap as it was in Toulon, or aboard *Radical* after the evacuation.
God, that didn't cost tuppence, really. And the Navy'd paid most of it,
didn't they?

They looked into each other's eyes, fond smiles threatening to break
out on each other's lips. Eyes crinkling in remembered delights.

That, too, did it!

Right, so she'd had a hard life, he told himself. She was so lost and alone, in a harsh world. Should he spurn her, she'd find a new patron, of course . . . that was the lot of penniless but beautiful young girls, with no family connections, or power to resist. That was the way of the world! If needs must, Phoebe might return to being a courtesan for a dozen, a hundred other men, to make her way. What was it his brother-in-law Burgess Chiswick had said, when they were besieged at Yorktown? A North Carolina folk colloquialism? "Hard times'd make a rat eat red onions!"

She'd hate doing so, of course. Phoebe had abandoned that life to take up with poor Lieutenant Scott, as her only lover—she his only—not because Barnaby had been any *sort* of decent toward her, really, or kept her in *any* sort of style, but because she didn't want to tumble any farther down that maelstrom spiral to ruin and oblivion that was the lot of most whores, no matter how pretty or clever.

Aye, Phoebe might be a little "Captain Sharp" when it came to finding a bargain, of wheedling for any edge that might guarantee her another week of safety and security. In that, she might be as grasping as the boldest, most raddled dockside "mutton," as cunning and sly, and rapacious, as a starving fox by the hen-yard fence. But Phoebe hadn't yet grown talons and teeth. Or armored herself against exploitable emotions. She was still vulnerable, and *somewhat* open.

For the sham, the semblance of true love and affection, Phoebe would offer him . . . dammit, *any* man who was halfway kind to her! . . . all that she possessed. So she'd never have to surrender herself to servitude in some filthy knocking-shop. So she could think of herself as something more than an easily expendable commodity.

So she could cling to that longed-for, sometime in the misty future, that "Happy Isles of the West" fantasy of hers that she could rise. That she *could* be somebody fine before she lost her beauty and it was too late to escape her lot, or her poverty-stricken childhood.

Not much of a sham at all, really, Alan told himself as he gave her a gentle kiss on her forehead. God help me, I really *am* fond of her! Can't ever offer her what she most like wishes of me, but . . . even if I'm a halfway port on her passage, the voyage'll be great fun. She's fond enough of me, certainly. And trusting. Rather simple and trusting, when you come right down to it. God help me, again . . . but *I'll* not be the one to turn my back on her. I'll *not* throw her back into the sordid stew she's worked so hard to flee!

"I do trust you, Phoebe," he told her at last. And giving her a supportive hug. "I won't let you down. Do my best by you, hmm?"

"You' bes' eez formidable, *mon amour*." She chuckled, shuddering a little with emotion, with perhaps a girlish, childish-pleased trill to her insides. And, perhaps, with some measure of relief, he imagined. "I am you's, alone. Oh, Alain, you mak' me *so* 'appy!"

Right then he sighed, lost in their mutual embrace; if she makes a fool of me, after all, well . . . I went into it with mine eyes wide open. And, 'least . . . I'm a well-off fool. She means half what she says, 'bout bein' a careful buyer . . . 'bout bein' faithful to me, well. 'Tis a folly I can almost afford!

CHAPTER
3

"So you never actually saw nor spoke Admiral Montagu's ships, Lewrie?" Admiral Lord Hood inquired, rather offhandedly, to Alan's lights.

"No, milord," he replied. "A return voyage from Finisterre might have taken him inshore of me, if he'd planned to peek in at any of the French Biscay harbors, or pass close to Ushant."

"Damn' good work, though, on old 'Black Dick's' part." Hood smiled thinly for a moment. "At least, his Villaret-Joyeuse wished an action. Unlike my opponent, Martin. Well . . . fewer French liners to return to Brest, the fewer they have to send to reinforce against us."

Hood seemed preoccupied. A tall sheaf of reports, orders, and fair copies of dispatches mounded upon his desk, and a flag lieutenant and a brace of midshipmen and clerks trundled back and forth with more. And, he'd aged, too. Like Admiral Howe, he appeared worn down by care, far more than he'd looked when Lewrie had last spoken to him back in March. And aren't he and Howe *both* almost seventy?

"And fewer officers and seamen who know what they're about, milord," Lewrie offered with a smile. Hood seemed, though, as if he had not heard the comment, so Lewrie blundered on. "Cut the heads off all their senior officers, or turned them into *émigrés*. Made captains out of bosun's mates. Command by committee, I've heard tell, bad as any Yankee Doodle privateersman during the . . ."

"Hmm? Aye," Hood said with a nod, though handing his clerk a freshly signed document for sanding, folding, and delivering. Sounding as if his comment had been directed at the clerk, not Lewrie.

How many times I know better than to rattle on, and yet . . . !, he chided himself, trying to find a graceful exit line.

"What do you draw, Lewrie?" Hood asked, though already intent upon a new document, which intent furrowed his brows dev'lish gloomy.

"Uhm . . . two fathom, milord."

"Ah." Hood nodded distantly. "Good. That'll be useful. Well."

"Should that be all you require of me, milord, I'll not take a moment more of your time," Lewrie offered his major patron. Trying most earnestly to not offend his commander-in-chief, who could make, or break, any officer's career in an eye-blink. And, Hood had done so before, sometimes over what others might consider to be mere trifles!

"Orders for *Jester* will be forthcoming, Lewrie," Hood told him, with a brief but dismissive grin. "Make good any lacks . . . firewood and water, an' such . . ." Then Hood turned dour, and away.

"Aye, milord. Thankee for receiving me, sir," Lewrie replied, backing toward the door in the day-cabin partitions.

NEVER KNOW WHAT that man's thinking, he griped, once he was out in the clear; never know whom you're dealing with, one day to the next! S'pose I got off fortunate, at that. And got at least *one* welcoming glass o' claret off him! It didn't matter whether Admiral Lord Hood liked you or not; he could be uncommon gracious in the forenoon, then tear a strip off your arse, for all the world to hear, by the First Dog Watch!

Well, Lewrie had already made arrangements for supplies, with the captain of the fleet, and Mister Giles was off to old HMS *Inflexible*, the fleet storeship with a working-party, to secure fresh livestock and salt rations, to top off what little they had already consumed on-passage. The ship was in good hands, safely anchored in four fathoms of water, "as snug as a bug in a rug," surrounded by larger frigates and 3rd Rate line-of-battle ships.

Phoebe had the right of it, he noted—San Fiorenzo was steep-hilled, a wide and sheltered bay on Corsica's northwestern tip just west of, and below, now-taken Bastia; and about twenty or so miles east of now-besieged Calvi. San Fiorenzo itself wasn't much of a town, a small and drowsy place before the arrival of the fleet, and the Army, who were now busy farther west. Dusty, rocky, and sere, the color of old canvas, it was; roadways, buildings, soil, and hillsides, and many sheltering walls separating tiny farm fields or olive groves, grazings or residences all of a rocky pale-tan piece, but for the dull-red tile rooves, in ancient Roman fashion.

What greenery there was consisted of hardy wind-sculpted trees, gorse-like pines, as matted and tangled as dogwoods or coastal capeland oaklets, as tightly kinked as the hair on a terrier's back, and that mostly a muted, well-dusted dark olive, even in the verdant month of June. Phoebe had said the forests were called the "maquis," where only the toughest trees could survive.

And San Fiorenzo was hot, even for mid-June. Sitting in the stern sheets of his gig, being rowed back to *Jester* from the flagship, HMS *Victory*, where one might expect motion to create a cooling breeze, it was beyond balmy warmth. Quite frankly, it was as hot as the hinges of hell! And as stifling and humid as Calcutta on a bad day before the monsoons.

Orders, he mused; upon Admiral Hood's promise, and his inquiry as to *Jester*'s draught. Whenever senior officers had asked that before, it had meant service very close inshore, feeling his way through unfamiliar waters by lead-line and guess. And soon, he thought. If Admiral Goodall's blockade of the French fleet in Golfe Jouan was to continue, he'd need scouting vessels to warn of reinforcement or any attempt at resupply by sea. Roads ashore, anywhere in the Mediterranean were so horrid, Hood had intimated, that coasting merchantmen were the fastest and surest conveyors of civilian, or military, commerce. The local road to Calvi was little better than a goat track that wound a serpent's dance over every hillock and ridge. Coalition troops were better supplied from the sea, as well.

There was the blockade of Calvi, too; to sink, take, or burn any local vessels, no matter how small or unimportant, which could deliver even a single cask of water to the Frogs.

Shore service? He rather doubted it, and made an audible sniff of dismissal. Hood already had idled many line-of-battle ships, crews of seamen and Marines sent ashore to help the Army, to man-haul, then man, the heavy lower-deck guns to serve as siege artillery. To strip *Jester* of even two-dozen hands would leave her useless, swinging around her anchor, just as idly ineffective as any of those decimated liners.

And, after his most recent bitter spell of shore duty at Toulon, Lewrie would gladly have run on his elbows to Calvi and back, with his thumbs up his arse, before being forced to spend a single day playing at soldiers!

Out to sea, within the week, he suspected; and with more than a little joy in the doing, too. Perhaps a long, independent cruise, far removed from pettifogging admirals, commodores, and fleet captains, or any of their pestiferous interferences.

Far removed from Phoebe, too; for a time, at any rate. Sweet though

she was, as heady and passionate though their *rencontre* had been . . .
he was aflutter to be out and doing. And, be far removed from whatever
horrendous expenses he was certain his heady, passionate, and sweet
relationship was going to end up costing him!

Cost him, perhaps, that very afternoon, he gloomed to himself. Orders
surely couldn't come *that* quickly, but . . . from what little he had seen
of San Fiorenzo from shipboard, and as bustling as the Army traffic and
many uniforms in the streets, the prospects of discovering suitable lodgings looked pretty damn' dismal. He'd have to get Phoebe settled that
very day. There might not be time afterward.

And get her off my ship, instanter, he concluded, frowning just a trifle
more, as he looked past Andrews's shoulder to gaze upon *Jester* at her
anchorage. Gaze almost jealously.

Swore I'd never carry a wench aboard—to myself, too!—and just look
what I've gone and done. Caroline to the Bahamas and back, well . . .
that was proper doin's, takin' the wife along. But Caroline went ashore,
and *stayed* there, when it came time to set out on King's business!
Should have stuck her 'board a packet, *paid* her passage to Corsica, 'stead
of . . . well. What's done's, done.

'Sides, Toulon can't abide that Joliette of hers, and . . .

And, dammit, they're my great-cabins! And I want 'em back!

CHAPTER

4

HAPPILY, THE FIRST place was the perfect place; a walled house halfway up a straggling cobbled street from the waterfront. From the outside, it had seemed a blank-faced enigma, a warehouse, perhaps, on a corner, about five streets up and back. Only the propped-out wood shutters of the upper-floor windows revealed it to be a residence. A heavy iron-bound wooden gate in the outer wall, which towered almost nine feet above the street, was the only break in the lower level's fortresslike exterior on the cross street. As was a narrower iron-strapped doorway that faced the uphill street the only entrance upon that side; a doorway, they discovered later, which was the kitchen and servants' entrance.

Upon entering the larger gateway, though, they'd been delighted to find a miniature Eden. There was a small courtyard, sheltered from the harsh sunlight by an expansive wood-slat pergola, adrip with ivies or climbing, flowering vines. The courtyard was ringed with planters full of flowering bushes; round, amphoraelike planters, tropical and adobe-colored, or pale stone rectangular box planters. There was the luxury of a fountain and pool in the middle—tiny but refreshing—as a cherubic winged Pan poured an endless plashing trickle of water from a tipped jar. There were patches of carefully tended grass, verdantly green and tender, compared to the harshness outside. Though most of the court-yard was sandy soil over which square paving stones had been laid.

There was a door off the courtyard to the kitchens, a covered walkway wide enough to shelter a small table and two chairs whenever the residents felt like breakfasting *en famille*, and a larger round stone table with curved stone benches near the street-side wall, to seat a larger party.

Off the courtyard on the house side, there was a pair of tall glazed windows, and shutter panels, a wide doorway that led into the parlor. There was a proper dining room behind that, just off that kitchen. Pantry, stillroom, butler's closets, and a "jakes" completed the downstairs. A rather larger than necessary "necessary," he noted with amusement, which also held the splendor of a large copper hip bath. Perhaps that "necessary closet" had once been a first-floor bedchamber, he thought; though one done all of stone, which he deemed rather an odd choice. And with a trough set into the floor for outflow of effluents and used bathwater that looked intentional.

The agent, a wary old tub of a puffing, panting *padrone*, done up in velvet and satin finery—as unctuously leering and "Beau-Trap" as a Covent Garden pimp—had insisted upon cash payments, and only in gold, preferably.

"What's he sayin', now, hey?" Lewrie had asked, over and over again, as their negotiations proceeded; and those, mostly in extremely rapid French, far too fast for Lewrie to follow, or in Italian, which was another of the world's languages he most definitely lacked. She did all the negotiating, switching easily from French to Italian, then an aside, now and again, in fractured English. Which had become even more tortuous and fractured as the afternoon drew on, as Phoebe's brow furrowed in frustration. Now and again, too, there were shouts, some hand gestures more easily understood by Mediterranean peoples.

"Ah, *billioni*!" the well-larded agent had once exclaimed, in a worse-than-usual snit, "Poo!", he'd pretended to spit upon the tile floor of the parlor.

"Alain, ve 'ave arriv-ed on ze price," Phoebe had then informed him. "'E tak' no less zan ze five *doppia* per mont', ze feelt'y peeg!" For emphasis, *she* had then pretended to spit upon the floor. *And* put her thumbnail to her teeth and flicked her hand at him for good measure!

"Billion?" he'd been forced to ask rather tremulously. Wait half a minute, he'd thought in alarm. There's people invested with "John Company" in the Far East, some're said to be worth a *million* pounds, by now! I ain't *buyin'* the whole damn' island, just payin' rent on a single house, by God, I ain't!

"Eez *pauvre* silver coin, Alain, non to be worry, *mon coeur*?"

There had followed a bewildering tirade, from both sides, it must be admitted, as to the relative merits of *florins, zecchinos, scudos*, and *doppia*, in comparison to the value of *livres, liri*, and the *ducat*. Savoian *lira*, versus the Papal States, or the Kingdom of the Two Sicilies. Where Alan had learned (whether he'd really wished to or not!) 12 *denieri* made one *soldi*, 20 *soldi* made one *lira*, or 6 *lira* equaled 1 *scudo*. But, as good Catholics, should they obey the Pope's decrees that 30 *baiocchi* made 6 *grossi*, or 3 *guilio*, or one *testone*, and 100 *baiocchi* equaled a *scudo*? Or, more closely attuned to English measure (perhaps!) 6 Sicilian *cavalli* made 1 *tornasi*, and 240 *tornesi* equalled 12 *carlinis*, or 1 *piastre*. No, no, "*piastre*, zat eez trop 'igh," Alan dimly recalled her stating. Although 200 *tornesi*, which was only one ducat, *would* be preferable.

In good, undebased silver, now, most definitely *not billioni*! "Ah, *magnifico*!" the agent had declared, kissing his fingertips and thence, the very air. But, the *piastre*, the *tallero*, the *scudo*, the *royal, crown, ecu* and *peso*—the last two the tried-and-true French pre-Revolutionary *Ecu*, or the ancient Spanish Piece of Eight—they were understandable. Somewhat. And the mention of the sum "Crown" at least penetrated Lewrie's fog. Though they all weighed different amounts of silver, at least he knew what a bloody Crown was worth!

"Let me see if I have this straight, so far," Alan had stated, after what had seemed a full hour of haggling. "The greedy bastard *is* aware we aren't *buyin'* the damn' place lock, stock, and barrel, isn't he?"

"*Oui*, Alain," Phoebe had replied, a tad huffy and exasperated. "I s'ink," she had been forced to admit, kitten-shyly.

"Right, then. We're makin' progress, damme if we ain't!" he'd cried, with a huge sigh of relief. "So, just how many good, English shillings make one of his bloody *ducats*? The ones he keeps rantin' on about?"

"Uhm ze *doppia*, zat ecs dcu . . . two *ducat*, so . . ." she told him.

"And the *ducat*'d be . . . ?" he'd prompted, with a surly purr.

"Een silver?" she'd puzzled, followed by a rapid ticking off on her lace-gloved fingers, and much muttering under her breath.

"That'd be a grand place to start," he'd muttered under his *own* breath, as she'd done her current exchange rates.

And trust a retired whore to know her sums, to the ha'pence, he'd told himself.

"Mmm, *une ducat*, zat ees twelve shillings, Alain, *mon chou*."

"Aha! Now, we're getting somewhere!" He'd beamed. "Let me see one of them."

The fubsy agent had produced a *ducat*, from a floridly embroidered silk poke. It weighed next to nothing, a wafer-thin, and almost bendable gold coin little larger round than a silver sixpence.

"So, ten *ducats* . . . that'd be 120 shillings the month, or six English pounds, hmm." Lewrie had pondered. He'd extracted his purse, weighing it on his other palm, heavy and promising, toying with it to make the gold one and two guinea pieces inside rustle and chink. The agent had swallowed heavily, eyes darting in a fever of greed. Or in fear that his *ducat* might be conjured away, if he didn't keep his eye glued to it!

"Two two-guinea pieces, in gold, sir," Lewrie had offered, as he lay them out on his palm next to the *ducat*, which shrank in comparison to the size of a tea saucer next to the dinner-plate appearance of the two-guinea's breadth, and most importantly, its thickness! "I will offer four guineas the month, and not a pence more. That's worth eighty-four shillings, or seven of his damn' *ducats*. Or, you tell him, Phoebe, that when the *troop* convoy arrives, with *thousands* more English soldiers in need of billets, well . . . we may commandeer *any* house that isn't *already* rented, d'ye see? For *nothing*, tell him?"

It amounted to £50/8/0, he'd thought smugly; a bargain. *If* the damn' fool will just realize it! Markets not a stone's throw off, down to the waterfront, or a short block uphill and one over, to that plaza we saw, and all the market stalls. No need for a carriage, after all, or even the keep of a single horse! Furnished, mostly; a tad tawdry, at present. Two bed-chambers above-stairs, both with balconies and ocean views, rather good bedsteads an' such. His price would have been £72, and that'd be a trifle steep, even for a decent set of London rooms!

Expostulating that he'd been gored, diddled, raped, the agent had at last acceded, and the place was theirs; *if* they'd pay the year in advance! Feeling just as gored, Lewrie had been forced to accede on his part, as well. Knowing that as long as the French had a Navy in-being, in Golfe Jouan or Toulon, that could threaten their hold on Corsica, or the sea-lanes across the Ligurian and Tyrrhenian seas to Genoa, Porto Especia, Rome, or Naples, he'd most like be based out of San Fiorenzo far longer than that.

Half that ponderous purse of his disappeared into the agent's poke, with a further stipulation that he'd remove any items of furnishings they didn't need, or wished to replace; thus lowering the rent somewhat, later on. That had required another spitting, hissing catfight to negotiate, but in the end it was done, to the begrudging dissatisfaction of both parties.

Phoebe had received the heavy ring of keys from him, had hugged them to her bosom, and had skipped and danced around her new parlor in great delight, after the agent had taken his leave.

"Alain . . . eez so . . . !" She'd sighed at last, coming to him and flinging her arms about him, crooning as he lifted her off her feet to eye level. "Eez non ze *appartement* no more . . . eez ze 'ouse *grande, si belle*! Eez non ze . . . shabby? Solid an' secure! An' I mak' eet even nicer, soon! *Merci, mon amour.* Oh, *merci si très beaucoup*!"

And there had been tears of joy in her eyes, to be so settled, at long last. Her lips had trembled against his as she kissed him so warmly. And her little shoulders had shaken in grateful emotion.

"We mus' 'urry, Alain!" she'd declared finally. "We can 'ave mov-ed een, *avant coucher de soleil*, uhm . . . before sundown? Non cook, we 'ave, t'night, *mais* . . . we fin' ze café, an' *zen*, een our own bed, I tell you 'ow *ver'* much I love you for . . . ! Non, I *show* you . . . 'ow much I am thanking you, *mon chou*!"

THEY'D LEFT PHOEBE'S chests and luggage at a waterfront *osteria*, a tavern/ lodging house, in the care of an elderly couple, who had made much of Phoebe's arrival in their midst. Lewrie was arranging a burro and cart, and Phoebe was chatting away, gay as a magpie, with her fellow country- men, and stroking Joliette, who was daintily lapping at some goat milk, when Midshipman Spendlove arrived, with a packet under his arm, sweating heavily.

"Sir!" Spendlove announced, doffing his hat. "Thank God you're here, sir. Else I'd have had nary a clue as to where in the town . . ."

"Trouble aboard, Mister Spendlove?" Lewrie barked, breaking off his negotiations with the carter.

"No, sir." Spendlove took the time to smile. "*Orders*, sir! Come aboard not a quarter-hour past."

"Mmm, good." Lewrie sighed in relief. "That was quick work, I must say. I didn't . . . Mister Spendlove. These have been *opened*," he rasped, turning stern and surly in an instant.

"Not my doing, sir," Spendlove assured him with some heat. "Nor the first lieutenant's. Uhm . . . your clerk, Mister Mountjoy, he, ahh . . ."

"Mountjoy?" Lewrie snapped.

"Said he thought they were normal correspondence, sir, that he . . . as your *assistant*, should read first, so . . ." Spendlove shrugged. Not in defense of the captain's clerk, no. By the tone of his voice, even a lowly midshipman could express a tiny bit of exasperation, or disgust, with a "new-come" who knew so little. Or could not seem to learn.

"Damn fool!" Lewrie growled. Ship's orders were addressed for cap- tains only, for their eyes only. "Not *you*, Mister Spendlove. Pardon the comment, sir. No one else aboard has read them, yet?"

"No, sir!" Spendlove strenuously denied. "Mister Hyde was at the gangway to receive them, and took 'em aft, still sealed, to your quarters. We informed Mister Knolles, of course, and he thought it best if you saw them straightaway, so I readied a boat, to fetch you, Captain. But, were they urgent, Mister Knolles then thought tŏ send them on, so he went aft, to get 'em, and he asked of them from Mister Mountjoy, well . . ."

"My 'assistant'!" Lewrie hooted sourly. "My God, that's rich!"

But, as long as he had them, he might as well read them, so he stepped away for a tiny shred of privacy. When he discovered:

You are directed to ready your vessel for sea, and, at your earliest convenience, the wind being obliging, proceed to the port of Leghorn, upon the Italian mainland, carrying with you the assistant surgeon of the fleet, his appurtenances, and monies, for the purchase of a quantity of onions and thirty to forty pipes of wine from the Tuscan authorities; to store aboard as expeditiously as possible the aforesaid, upon affirmation by the assistant surgeon of the fleet as to the antiscorbutic properties, then to proceed afterward to San Fiorenzo Bay with the onions and wine . . ."

"And just what do you draw, Lewrie, hey?" he muttered, half amused. "Jesus Christ!" There went all his previous speculation on hopes of neck-or-nothing sea service. Amazing, really, what fickle Dame Reality actually had up her sleeve!

He folded them and stuck them into an inner coat pocket.

"Very well, Mister Spendlove. Go back aboard, and deliver my utmost respects to Mister Knolles and the sailing master. They are to ready the ship for sea. Tell Aspinall we'll have a single piece of 'live-lumber' aft, in the great-cabins, with some dunnage of his to store away in my personal lazarette. Have 'Chips' run him up a bed cot. And warn my cook he'll be 'sizzling' for two, this evening."

San Fiorenzo Bay was a mirror. There wasn't a breath of wind, and every commissioning pendant, every sail freed of its gaskets and let hung to prevent mildew, were as slack as a hangman's noose, still and flaccid. There'd be no departure this evening. Perhaps the morning might bring up enough wind to work out of harbor on. Or, they'd lower the ship's boats and row her out, in tow, to a sea breeze. He'd have about an hour, no more, to settle Phoebe, leave her some coin for incidentals, but would have to forego her expressions of "gratitude."

Before he could inform her of that sad fact, though, he espied a Navy officer at the dockside, one familiar to him, about to mount a horse.

"Captain Nelson?" he called, walking down to the pier-front, to re-make his acquaintance.

"Ah, Commander Lewrie!" the little minnikin of a post-captain cried jovially, once he'd gotten his "seat." "Saw your *Jester* lying at anchor, on my way out to *Victory*. Just come in. And with such a wondrous packet of news, too, about Admiral Howe's splendid victory! How I wish I'd but been there to take part, but . . . And how do you do, sir?"

"Main-well, and thank you for recalling me, sir," Lewrie said, doffing his hat. "And thank you again for the permanent loan of men off your *Agamemnon*. They eased our passage home wondrous well. Form the very backbone of my new crew. I can't express how indebted I am to you for your generosity, short-handed though you were at the time."

God, what a complete toadying wretch you are, Lewrie, he chided himself; must be instinctive! Nelson's just another captain, not an admiral whose back you have to 'piss down' for favors!

"And you are well yourself, sir?" Alan asked, as a party of seamen trudged by in a dust-raising shamble, loaded down with sacks like so many draught animals.

"In splendid fettle, sir," Nelson assured him. "Been on shore service, over toward Calvi, d'ye see. As long as the French Navy is blockaded, there's the seat of the action. There's the very cockpit! A chance for action, great doings!"

Capt. Horatio Nelson was such a thin and nervous whippet of a fellow, so lean and wee to begin with, well . . . Lewrie thought his duty ashore had sweated him down. He didn't *look* in splendid fettle, really. Haggard as a dog's dinner, in point of fact.

"Why, were I half sunk with the flux, the opportunity for action against our foes would revive me from my very deathbed, sir," Nelson assured him firmly, speaking a trifle louder, for the benefit, Lewrie imagined, of those trudging, plodding sailors, and the general audience at dockside.

Always did have a touch o' Drury Lane theatrics in him, Lewrie re-called, smiling in reverie.

"You should *see* what British tars can accomplish, Lewrie," he "emoted," regaining that infectious enthusiasm for a chance to get him-self blown to bits, or knighted—whichever came first. "You simply must ride up and visit us, should you have the chance. Erecting batteries, man-hauling guns over hill and dale, digging trenches and parallels . . . ah, here's Captain Fremantle! Another of our stalwarts."

Taller, lankier, and mastiff-dour, was Capt. Thomas Fremantle, whose sole response to Nelson's introduction was a nod and a grunt.

". . . shelling the Frogs night and day, storming their positions to keep monsieur on the hop," Nelson rattled on. "Minding shot around their own ears no more than peas, I tell you, Lewrie! Been at it ever since the first days of the siege of Bastia. Well, Captain Fremantle *might* mind shot and shell, after our little . . . 'incident,' hey?"

"Uhm," interjected that worthy, shifting in his saddle rather uncomfortably.

"The Frogs got the range of us, at Bastia," Nelson reminisced gaily, "and literally blew us off a hillside. Right down off the side of the path. Showers of earth, gravel, and dust. Fremantle was sore hurt."

"Tore a good pair o' breeches," Fremantle grunted laconically.

"Now he swears he'll not walk within a musket shot of me, sir." Nelson chuckled. "I attract too much attention from their gunners!"

Sounds like Fremantle is smarter than he looks, Alan thought.

"Should I do come visit, sir," Lewrie said with an agreeable chuckle of his own, "I'd hope for better horses than these for the journey."

While all the while swearing that it would take a battalion of gaolers to drag him *anywhere* near Calvi's trenches. Or Nelson's side.

"Spavined wretches, are they not, sir?" Nelson shrugged, even as he patted his ill-featured mare's neck. "A poor prad, but mine own, to quote the Bard. And, well . . . Father's a churchman, and our glebe didn't run to blooded hunters. Then I, away to sea at such a young age . . . I must confess I am nowhere near as confident upon this horse as I am upon my quarterdeck. This idle waiting, and swinging around the anchors . . . I quite envy you, sir, your freedom of a smaller ship. Out at sea, our proper place . . . anything exciting by way of orders for you yet, Lewrie?"

"Onions, sir." Lewrie sighed. "Onions and wine. I'm off for Leghorn at first light, pray God the wind returns, to purchase onions to prevent the scurvy."

"Oh, poor fellow." Nelson seemed to commiserate for a single sober moment, though he perked up rather quickly, not a second after. "Still, your turn will come, sir, be confident of it. Once Calvi is ours, we'll all be free to seek out our foes, and win such glory as even a Hawke, Anson, or Drake might envy!"

Lewrie continued to smile, though he did raise one rather dubious brow. Fremantle, though, who'd been slouching like a sack of onions in his saddle, sat up a bit straighter, got a light upon his dull visage, as if he'd just been Saved, and was leaving Church with his Life Amended. Uncanny, how this wee fellow Nelson could inspirit people! "Well, sirs, if you must ride as far as Calvi before dark, I won't keep you a second longer. And the best of fortune go with you, sirs. Captain Nelson, Captain Fremantle . . . I'll save you a sack of my very best . . . mmm, produce, sirs," he could not help saying with a deprecatory smirk. "My word on't."

"Likewise, good fortune attend your voyage, sir, and I *would* be much obliged for something more savory than 'Army' rations. For the men, d'ye see." Nelson beamed. "Godspeed, Commander Lewrie!"

He kneed his spindly mare into motion, to clatter off to join a procession of heavily laden mules, heavily laden sailors, and top-heavy two-wheeled carts crammed with ammunition.

Damme, I just promised to deliver them onions! Lewrie shuddered. Now I'll *have* to ride up there, once I'm back. Within speakin' distance of Nelson, and let's hope the Frog gunners're sleepin'!

Wherever that firebrand went there was blood and mayhem. And the Devil's own amount of shot and shell involved in a Nelson "outing." Forever thrusting himself forward, all that Death or Glory twaddle . . . and Alan suspected the little minnikin actually *believed* what he was forever saying.

Still . . . he could almost essay a feeling of . . . dare he call it jealousy? . . . to be left out. Grubbing about in trenches, plagued with insects, flinging oneself flat whenever a shell howled over. Well, an officer could *wish* to fling himself flat, but had to stand and take it, like a dumb ox. To inspire courage, so please you! Sleeping rough as a gypsy . . . well, perhaps not. Alan wished to make his name, and his ship's name, at sea, where sailors belonged. Not playing greengrocer, certainly, but . . .

He felt a hellish snit coming on. Sent off to be a carter for the fleet, 'stead of a fighting cruise. Deprived of Phoebe's charms—that he'd by God paid damn' *dear* for!—not even one evening with her in their new "house." The prospects of a damn' dull supper, with a "sawbones" for company; they were usually horrid drinkers, and just how much of his wine cabinet would be left to him by the time *Jester* returned to San Fiorenzo Bay? he wondered.

It all put Lewrie in a Dev'lish black fettle.

Mayhem? Well, God help Mountjoy, when he got back aboard. A chance to shout, to rant and scream at someone, to vent all his frustrations . . . it sounded *damned* pleasant, of a sudden!

Book III

Ego, dum cremandis trabibus accrescit rogus,
sacro regentum maria votivo colam.

Now while the pyre feeds on the burning beams,
with promised gifts will I worship Him who rules
the sea.

Hercules Furens 514–15
Lucius Annaeus Seneca

CHAPTER

1

Now *this* is more like it, Lewrie told himself, fidgetting, but with pride, as he stood foursquare on his quarterdeck, with his hands clasped together in the small of his back. Rocking and swaying on the balls of his feet, easy, as *Jester* tore through the waters, gun ports open, and artillery run out.

It was a rare day, no error, a brilliant, glittering morning of bright-water winds, whitecaps and horses, the sea heaving and chopping in short, close-spaced waves, and the sirocco up from the south was a force one could almost lean into, a stout, clear-weather quarter-gale, deafening in his ears. A hat-snatcher of a wind into which HMS *Jester* pounded close-hauled, in pursuit of prey.

A clumsy old Provence bilander already lay far astern, a prize easily snatched up from the clutch of odd vessels assembled in convoy. No matter that she'd sported a massive lateen mains'l on her after, or main-mast, the compromise of her foremast crossed with course, tops'l, and t'gallant yards, had made her slow to windward. Taken with but one warning shot fired cross her bows, and a long ten minutes of nail-biting frustration as a boat was gotten down, and a prize crew under Wheelock, the master's mate, rowed over to secure her. Then *Jester* was off once more, lumping and drumming into wind, spray flying high to either beam, with a bone in her teeth.

They'd spotted the convoy at dawn, on east-to-west patrol sixty miles north of Corsica; a gaggle of tartanes, bilanders and poleacres to their south. Lying-to, hardly moving, as if awaiting the coming of dusk before closing the coast in the wee hours, when they might stand a chance of sneaking past other patrol ships. Immediately, *Jester* had hardened up, beat to quarters, and taken off in pursuit. Now the motley collection of ships had become what were termed "Chases."

The nearest Chase, Mister Buchanon informed them, was a tartane, a single-masted coastal trading vessel with a fore-and-aft lateen mains'l and a bowsprit that allowed her to set jibs and stays'ls to go closer to the True Wind than *Jester* could ever hope to. She might have made an escape, outpointing them, if she'd been longer, or been less heavily laden. She merely ploughed along, burying her bows whenever she met the rolling chops, and flinging clouds of spray and foam over herself, as if trying to hide in it.

"Starboard foc's'le carronade!" Lewrie shouted to the gun deck. "One shot across her bows!" They'd overhauled her rapidly, striding up to within half a cable—120 yards—of her larboard side, as she labored to flee.

A sharp bark, a quickly dissipated bloom of smoke, sulfurously bitter and smelling of rotten eggs as it whipped past the quarterdeck, and then a great splash and pillar of spray as the ball struck short and a little to the right of "across her bows." *Under* them, was more like it. The eighteen-pounder round-shot, five inches and four parts across, caromed up from first graze like a goosed dolphin, smashed into the underside of the hapless tartane's bows, shattering the jib boom and bowsprit, amputating it just beyond the cutwater!

"*Sofort! Ja!*" Quarter-gunner Rahl could be heard to exult as he saw the results of his handiwork. "*Genau!*" Exactly!

Without jibs to balance her helm, she sagged alee, veering away to starboard under the press of that great lateen sail and yard, showing her weeded quick-work as she heeled precipitously.

"Helm a'weather, Quartermaster! Ease us a point free!" Lewrie snapped, so *Jester* would surge up even with her, still on her larboard quarter, showing her there would be no escape. "Number one gun, ready!"

He waited until she rolled more upright, so he wouldn't lose her by putting a ball through her hull, too far below the waterline to be repaired. "No more warning shots, Mister Crewe. Show her we mean it."

A quick fiddle with the quoin for elevation, a tug on the side tackles, then the crew scrambling back from the line of recoil. *Bang!* the nine-pounder erupted. At 100 yards, the ball's strike was immediate, a crash of timbers, the *squawk!* of rivened wood as a star-shaped hole three feet across was blasted into her side, just before her mast, and the tartane shook and rolled alee once more to the impact. Then, down came her long lateen yard, crashing to the deck as halliards were cut, instead of handed. Eight or nine men—perhaps her entire crew—appeared at the rails, hands flailing, arms raised in prayerlike pleading, and jabbering away fit to bust in French!

"Mister Hyde, she's your prize, sir," Lewrie crowed. "Mister Tucker the quartermaster's mate, and six hands to go with you. Hoist what sail you may, once you've secured her crew, and follow along aft of us as best you're able. Take the jolly boat. *Move* yourself, sir! Mister Knolles, fetch us to, to lower away the boat."

Two prizes, already, and it had barely gone eight, he exulted. Why, we might take *all* of 'em, by the end of the forenoon! And not a single other sail in sight to share with! Any other British warship, with even her royals 'bove the horizon, "in sight" at the time that a prize surrendered, shared in the prize money adjudged by an Admiralty Court. This morning, Lewrie was feeling particularly greedy. Hungry for more than his breakfast!

'Sides, there's my bloody expenses to make good, he sighed, as the jolly boat was swung high off the cross-deck beams that spanned *Jester*'s waist from gangway to gangway, even before she came to a full halt in a welter of foam and a calamitously windy din from aloft.

"Come on, come on, damn yer eyes!" he muttered under his breath at how long it was taking. Take in fore and main courses, so they'd not be torn; topmen aloft to trice up yard tackles with clew jiggers, hook on burton purchases from the tops to the yardarms, jump a triatic stay between the stay-tackle pendants, and send the falls to the deck; lift the jolly boat off the cross-deck beams that spanned the waist, with stay tackles; swing her outboard with the yard tackles, and six guy lines for preventers; then lower away together. Then, even before the boat crew was down overside, take in all the hoisting gear, which was in the way aloft, ungasket the course-sails and clew them full of air once more . . . !

His own gig was away to the bilander, with Andrews in charge of it. Now the jolly boat. There was only the one twenty-six-foot cutter left, which took eight hands to row, and one to steer. Only one more prize taken, before he ran out of conveyances for prize crews? he groaned. Surely, not!

"Cony!" He decided. "Half a cable's worth of messenger line to the jolly boat, as a painter. Once she's alongside the prize and empty, walk the painter aft and use it as a towline. We'll keep her with us!"

* * *

WHAT SEEMED AN hour later, they were off again, this time chasing what looked like an Egyptian dhow; high-pooped, two masts with lateen sails, a sweet curve to her sheerline, almost saucy—almost too cute to frighten. But a prize was a prize. Like the tartane, she was too short on the waterline to make any speed.

But beyond . . . !

Spreading out now, hauling their wind to escape individually, all order gone, were three rather substantial, and rewarding-looking ships. One, the nearest, heading sou'west, and another pair farther off bearing sou'east, still almost in company, dodging away with the boisterous wind abeam. Three-masted poleacres, with lateen rigs upon their fore and mizzenmasts to take the place of spankers or jibs, but oddly, and downright gruesomely, square-rigged on their much taller mainmasts, with courses, tops'ls and t'gallants towering over their decks, as bastardly appearing as "hermaphrodite" brigs!

They fetched the dhow-looking coaster up to their starboard side in a brief quarter-hour. Up close, she was scarred, weathered, faded, and neglected, as stained and dull as an old dishcloth. She labored within close musket shot, about fifty yards off, her few crewmen stock-still and hangdog at the rails. No warning shot was even required!

Down came her lateen yards, collapsing those triangular ellipses to her decks, and *Jester* fetched-to once more. The jolly boat was led around to the entry port by its towline, and Midshipman Spendlove, with Quartermaster Spenser and six seamen, rowed over to take charge of her; the jolly boat hauled back to *Jester* afterward for further use.

"Hardly seems worth the effort, Captain," Lieutenant Knolles remarked, laughing in scornful appraisal. "A dowdy old tub, she is."

"Well, let's hope she's a decent cargo aboard, to pay for our efforts, Mister Knolles." Lewrie shrugged. "Mains'l haul, and let's be going."

NOW THEIR PROBLEM was that of a single staghound that had come across an entire herd of deer—which to pursue next. The nearest to them was running due west by then, about two miles off. The other two poleacres had fallen off the wind to east-sou'east, were closer together, but had at least another mile lead on *Jester* before she got back to full speed of nearly eleven knots.

"Mister Buchanon?" Lewrie called to his sailing master.

"Aye, sir?"

"Those two masters yonder know something we don't, sir? Current around the east'rd of Corsica?" Lewrie inquired. "Seems silly, to run east-sou'east, closer to the Bastia peninsula."

"North-set current, Cap'um, aye," Buchanon agreed, pointing to a chart. "Runs up past Cape Corse, 'tween 'ere an' th' Isle of Capraia . . . an' in shallower water, too. Nought t'dread, 'tis deep enough even for a 1st Rate, but . . . do they get into its . . . fan, I s'pose, an' with this southerly wind, 'ey'll fly like a pair o' pigeons. One an' a half, mayhap two knots, more, 'ey'd gain."

"*If* they may weather Cape Corse!" Lewrie intuited, at once. The poleacres had run far enough south, within forty or so miles of Corsica, that flight in that direction could come to an end, hemmed in by bluffs and shoals. If they stayed somewhat on the wind, as they still were.

"Sir, starboard Chase is altering course!" Knolles cried out to warn them.

Inexplicably, the nearest poleacre had come about to the starboard tack, as if suicidally intent upon making Calvi, after all, and arriving in late afternoon—broad daylight! Even as close-hauled as she lay to the eyes of the wind, she'd cross ahead of *Jester*'s present course. Or, their courses would meet, like the two upright legs of a triangle, and *Jester*, of course, would shoot her to rags, and then take her.

"Mister Knolles, ready about! Stations for Stays!" Lewrie said with a wry smile. "We'll come to starboard tack. Make our new course east by south."

"Aye aye, sir," Knolles replied automatically, though sounding quizzical. "Mister Porter, pipe hands to Stations for Stays. Ready to come about!"

"Only a purblind fool'd come about like 'at, Cap'um," Buchanon opined. "Meanin' *her*, yonder, sir, d'ye understand, no disrespect . . ."

"My thoughts, exactly, Mister Buchanon," Lewrie agreed with a soft laugh. "Remind you of a mother goose, leading the stoat away from her hatchlings?"

"Flaggin' th' broken wing, aye, Cap'um."

"That pair to the east'rd, they're hoping to get away. This'un might be their leader. A merchant poleacre, yes. But perhaps carrying a French naval officer aboard. As short of ships as they are, it might even be a well-*armed* poleacre, servin' as escort. It'd be a criminal waste to send these poor vessels out to resupply Calvi without at least *one* warship. I'll wager that pair has the valuable cargo."

"Ready about, sir," Knolles reported.

"Very well, Mister Knolles. Tack the ship about."

HALF AN HOUR on starboard tack, floating almost without visible effort, now, across the seas, on a close reach with the winds nearly on her beam. Striding closer and closer to those two poleacres, who were forced by her presence, and the threat of the so-far unseen Cape Corse to haul their wind even farther, steer due east to try and beat *Jester* to that underwater river of current that would speed them back up north to the French Riviera coast, where they'd come from.

"Sail Ho!" came a cry from the foremast lookout, Rushing. "*Two* point off th' *starb'rd* bows!"

Lewrie twitched, almost began a quick dash to the shrouds to take a peek for himself, but checked his motion. It looked like an upright stumble, which made him blush in chagrin; chiding himself for appearing to start at the slightest omen, like a goose-girl!

"Two points to weather, that'd be . . ." he said, instead, stalking to the chart, trying to seem deliberate, this time. "Down near the Cape, I believe, Mister Buchanon?"

"Aye, sir. Inshore o' Cape Corse, west o' it, do we see her with her royals'r t'gallants 'bove th' horizon," Buchanon agreed.

"Show me the Frog with any sense at all, who'd venture into San Fiorenzo Bay or its approaches by herself." Lewrie frowned. "Surely, this new-come's bound to be one of ours."

"Oh, bad luck, sir," Knolles groaned. "Another man o' war to go shares with, should we take these last two."

"Well, they haven't a hope of our bilander, the tartane, or our dhow, at any rate, Mister Knolles. They weren't in sight when we took *those!*" Lewrie said, striving for a *less* than greedy pose, himself.

"There is that, sir." Knolles shrugged.

"Signal, sir!" Rushing shouted down to them from far forward. "*White* Ensign to the *main*mast truck! *Number* pennants! Four . . . Six . . . Repeater! . . . Nine . . . Fifteen, sir!"

With both midshipmen, who normally were in charge of the signal flag lockers, away on prizes, it fell to Lewrie himself to delve into the binnacle cabinet drawers for the latest code combinations.

"Ah, hum . . . right, then," he concluded, after a long moment's fumbling over a loose sheaf of wrinkled papers that threatened to go overside with the wind. "This month's recognition code, to the tee, gentlemen. She's one of ours. Mister Knolles? Do you have the White Ensign hoisted to the mainmast truck, and reply . . . uhm . . . Fifteen . . . Twenty-Two . . . Three . . . Repeater . . . Four. Got that?"

"Aye aye, sir," Knolles called back, snapping his fingers at a man of the after-guard, one of those literate "strikers" who assisted on the taffrails as a signalman.

Barely had that been bent on and hoisted high on the weather side of the mizzenmast, where it could be more easily read, than the newly arrived ship up to the sou'east hauled down her original hoist, and up went another one identifying her. Then a third; this one, orders.

"Pursue . . . Chase . . . More closely . . ." Lewrie translated, as the numerals were read off to him. Feeling like a half-wit midshipman all over again, at how long it was taking him, compared to the fluency of his inferiors. And with every eye on the quarterdeck upon him, too! "To Loo'rd!" he completed, puffing out his cheeks in frustration.

Well, o' *course*, he thought with a silent grunt; that recognition code had told him that the other ship was a 6th-Rate frigate, HMS *Ariadne*, twenty guns. A proper, post-captain's command, a man senior to him. Two guns, all the diff'rence in the world! Alan griped. She wished *Jester* to haul her wind, sail a touch north of due east, cutting off any hopes the poleacres might have of simply turning and running to the north . . . or of gaining their saving current before *Ariadne* had come to grips with them.

"Haul our wind, Mister Knolles," Lewrie snapped. "Give us two points free, to east by north. And, topmen aloft, to set royals."

"Aye, sir."

Ariadne, Alan sighed; a brand-spanking new ship of war! My old 'un must've sunk at her moorings in English Harbor, at last. His very first ship had been HMS *Ariadne*, then a tired and worn old sixty-four-gunner of the 3rd Rate. Condemned after his very first action in the West Indies, too, for "hogging" at bow and stern, her back most likely broken, she'd become a guard ship, receiving ship, later just a useless hulk without a single gun, stripped down aloft to her fighting tops and gant lines.

Captain cashiered for her loss, first lieutenant court-martialed with him; fourth and fifth killed, third lieutenant convicted of cowardice . . . oh, she'd been a miserable old hag, even before then, and a terrible place for a seventeen-year-old to begin a naval career. Autumn of 1780, it was . . .

Damme, I'm gettin' bloody *ancient*! he thought.

He took a deep breath, clapped his hands together, and paced to the lee bulwarks with a telescope, to shrug off just how far back, in the antedeluvian age, he'd really gotten his "ha'porth of tar"!

There was their bilander, pacing along about ESE, four or five miles alee and off the larboard quarter. Nearer in to them was their tartane, only a mile astern, but three miles alee. And Spendlove and his dhow— or whatever else one might call it!—was, of course, the poor third, behind them all, even though she'd been the last, nearest, taken. A clumsy, udder-swinging old cow to begin with, and now directed by English tars, who'd never even clapped *eyes* on her like, before, much less tried to handle her lateen rig to best efficiency.

And the poleacre that had tried to decoy them away from her two consorts was . . .

"Christ, shat on a biscuit!"

She'd hauled her wind, worn about to run with the wind large on her starboard quarter, and was not three miles astern of *Jester* at that very moment, crossing from starboard to larboard quarter. Steering on what he took to be a course of nor'east by east. The bugger was after the prize vessels, bold as a dog in a doublet!

"Mister Knolles, new course . . . nor'east!" Lewrie shouted. "And bend on a signal to our prizes . . . Make All Sail. And add 'Imperative' to that! Uhm . . . they are to . . ."

What the Devil was the clearest signal, he fumed, running through a combination of orders. Damme, yes! "Order them to 'Take Station to Weather' of us!"

Half-past ten o'clock of the Forenoon Watch, by then, the winds beginning to abate, beaten into sullen submission by the oppressive and sultry heat of a Mediterranean July. Last summer around Toulon had been a coolish fluke of nature, all that rain and nippish cold. Here in the Ligurian Sea, summer winds were fickle, at best, a morning's gale blown out and hammered to compass-boxing zephyrs by midday. Just what they needed least, Lewrie thought. And hellish bad timin', too!

"Deck, there!" Rushing called from the foremast. "*Ariadne* is sending . . . 'Interrogative'!"

"Almost polite of him, consid'rin'," Lewrie said with a grimace. What that full-of-ginger post-captain yonder had really asked was, "Just what the Devil you think you're *playing* at, you damn' fool!"

He raised his telescope once more to study his laboring prize ships. Yes, they'd begun to make more sail, to alter course harder on the wind to get closer to *Jester's* protective artillery. Even Mister Spendlove's weary old dhow-thing-gummy had sprouted a mustache of foam under her bows. Not much of one, admittedly, but it was there. Lash the fore-ends of the lateen yards low to the center of the decks, and haul them fore-and-aft by brute force, though . . . she simply *must* sail better to windward, like a gaff-rigged cutter or sloop.

"Sir?" Knolles prompted at his elbow, his voice soft and confidential. "What reply do we send *Ariadne*?"

"The only one she'll understand, I s'pose, Mister Knolles," Alan snickered, with a lift of his eyebrows. "Bend on good old Number One."

Admiral Howe's revisions to the code flags always put the most important message, the one that alerted warship captains to the prime reason for existence, at the very top of the list, and, in an easily understandable single-pennant hoist.

Number One of the Howe System was, *"Enemy in Sight!"*

CHAPTER
2

"MISTER KNOLLES, IS there a code flag for 'Suggestion'?" Alan inquired, once *Jester* had worn off the wind, and had begun to run alee toward her struggling prize vessels.

"Uhm . . . there's 'Submit,' sir," Knolles answered.

"And I s'pose that's a picture of a man tugging his forelock?" Lewrie posed, tongue-in-cheek.

"Groveling most humbly, as well, I should imagine, Captain," his first lieutenant replied with a bright grin.

"Make to *Ariadne*, then . . . most *humbly*, mind . . ." Lewrie ordered, "Submit—her number—Pursue Chases—uhm, Closer Action? He might make *some* sense of that. Followed by . . . Our number— Closer Action—Chase to Leeward. No sense losing those two poleacres, to deal with a single armed ship. *Jester* can handle this'un, by herself."

"Aye aye, sir," Knolles agreed, full of pride in their ship.

"Besides," Lewrie continued. "Damme if I'll make that fellow a richer man, at the expense of our people's freedom. I'll not lose 'em, when we've come this far together."

FARTHER OFF THE wind, then, running almost "both-sheets-aft," on a landsman's breeze, due north; *Jester* passed the first of their prizes and put herself between the overly aggressive French poleacre and their tartane. The strange-acting Frenchman hardened up on the wind, as well, coming more nor'easterly, to meet them, ignoring the bilander and dhow.

118

"Mister Bittfield, we'll engage with the larboard battery," Alan told his master gunner. "Porter! Be ready to brail up the main course. Chain-slings on the yards, now, and lay out the boarding nettings!"

At least eighteen prime hands gone, Lewrie fretted; gunners, and tacklemen, rammers and loaders, off on the prizes. This short of a voyage from Toulon to Corsica, the Frog'll most like have no need to worry 'bout victualing a large crew. He's liable to have a hundred men or more, aboard that damn' thing. Like a Breton *chasse-marée* privateersman. *Two* hundred, more like!, he thought, with a wary sniff. We have to stand off, so he doesn't board *us*. But blow the living hell out of him! Lewrie thought a full cable's range would be cautious.

Both so eager for combat, the two ships closed each other rapidly. The range fell off to barely five cables—half a nautical mile—and Alan sorely regretted not having six-pounder chase guns up forrud on the forecastle, with which he could open the affair. He raised his telescope to scan the poleacre.

Indeed, she swarmed with seamen, as thickly clustered as a pack of cockroaches around a butter tub. At least his estimated 200 men, aboard a ship little larger than a merchant brig. 'Bout 85 feet, on her waterline? he pondered. Flush-decked, almost—gun deck and weather deck the same, with only a slightly raised quarterdeck astern. How many guns could she carry—and how heavy a battery could such a small ship bear? he wondered.

There! Gun ports coming open.

"Ready, Mister Bittfield?" he called in warning. "Make your first broadside count, sir! Full battery firing . . . on the uproll!"

"Ready, sir!" Bittfield shouted back. "On the uproll . . . wait for it! . . . Fire!"

Almost as one, they opened upon each other; the poleacre disappearing behind a cloud of spent powder smoke, gushing from bow-to-stern as if she'd just blown up! And *Jester*, poised atop the scend, a stable gun platform for a breathless second or two without rolling, hammering and shuddering at the violence of her own broadside's eruption.

Then shaking and quaking, as round-shot hit her, almost flinching as thick iron ball droned or screeched past in near-misses! Spray flung high from strikes that landed short, wetting down her gunners and brace-tenders!

Seven guns, at least, Lewrie thought, coughing on niters as the smoke-pall from *Jester*'s broadside ragged away to leeward, creating a sour fog-bank just yards alee, through which he could barely make out their foe.

And a *heavy* seven guns, he frowned in perplexity, seeing the quick damage done to *Jester*'s larboard side. The twenty-six-foot cutter on the cross-waist beams had been shattered. There were hammocks and thin, rolled-up mattresses scattered like so many fishing worms about the gangway bulwarks. Bulwarks that had been caved in, in places, by the impact of heavy shot! There were men down, lying still; men, too, who shrieked in sudden terror, writhing frantically over their wounds!

"Again, Mister Bittfield! Quickly!" Lewrie shouted. Quicker to load and fire, the quarterdeck carronades behind him were coughing thunderously. Followed by the pleasing sound of French timbers being penetrated with booming *thonks* and *rawrkks*! No hastily converted merchantman, no matter how billeted in-board with reinforcing baulks, had a chance against the weight of eighteen-pounder iron!

A second broadside, still controlled, but a little more ragged this time, spat from *Jester*'s larboard guns. Aiming was perhaps more a hoped-for thing, though; blazing away through a bitter haze, firing into a thicker bank of smoke, now only four cables off.

"Tricolor, sir!" Buchanon pointed out. "French national ship, no error! Damme! She's comin' hard on th' wind! Clewin' *up*, sir!"

Out of that fog-bank came the thrusting jib boom and bowsprit of the poleacre, her anchor catheads jutting through the haze. That taller mainmast bore topmen aloft, taking in her tops'l and t'gallant sails, clewing them up to the yards by sloppy "Spanish Reefs"! Using her weatherly fore-and-aft lateen sails to keep drive on her!

"Christ!" Lewrie gasped, appalled by his stupidity. She would claw up abeam the wind, cross his stern and rake *Jester* at close range!

"Quartermaster, helm hard alee!" he cried, trying not to sound panicky, as *Jester* trundled on north, with the poleacre slipping astern on her, moving from afore the main chains to afore the mizzen chains in the blink of an eye. Shorthanded, he could not man his starboard guns in time. He *must* keep the larboard battery engaged! And round *Jester* up abeam the wind on the opposite tack, to keep her thicker side wood facing those unexpectedly heavy guns, instead of her frail transom!

"Mister Knolles, scandalize her, every square sail!" Alan said in a rush. "Waisters, bend on main and mizzen stays'ls! Bow-rake her now, Bittfield, while we have the chance!"

A bloom of smoke from the French poleacre's bow, from her forecastle. A *damn'* heavy chase gun, its report deeper-bellied than a six-pounder, as ominously loud, even upwind of her for the moment, as any twenty-four-pounder gun aboard a 3rd Rate! A tremendous pillar of spray, which leaped into being close-aboard. *Jester* feeling almost wrenched off her course by the slamming impact! A *damn'* heavy gun, of some kind!

"*Carronade*, Mister Lewrie!" Cony screeched from the gangways, reverting to his old form of address to him. "Th' buggers got a carronade'r two, yonder, sir!"

The French warship was blotted out of sight by the blossoms of gun smoke as Bittfield got off his broadside. A ragged effort, starting amidships of the waist, and stuttering left or right from there, or from the far ends to the center, the gunners half blinded and pulling their lanyards as quick as their sweating crews could stand clear.

Jib boom tip, poking through the sudden pall, abaft the mizzen stays! *Jester* heeling hard to starboard, as her wheel was forced hard-over. Square-rig canvas aloft shivering and flapping.

"Carronades!" Lewrie screeched. "Load with canister . . . grapeshot! Mister Rahl, hear me? Clear her decks with canister! And her quarterdeck, when we're close-aboard! Ease your helm, Quartermaster. Steer due west, as best you're able."

"Aye aye, zir!" Brauer, the Hamburg seaman replied crisply.

Jester had just worn from one tack to the other, off the wind, everything crying and screaming aloft, as out of order, and confusing as a rioting mob, yards cocked any-old-how, some tops'ls and t'gallants aback against the masts, others flapping useless.

Aye, canister, Lewrie thought grimly! *Murder* that bastard over there who outsmarted me! Powder monkeys staggered under the weight of the canister tins come up from the lower deck shot-lockers as the guns on the quarterdeck were loaded.

"Ready, larboard, Mister Bittfield! At 'close pistol shot'! Fire as you bear!" he cautioned. "She's coming up, fast!"

And did his foe have men enough to man *both* his own batteries, Lewrie gulped with a sudden cringing, in a throat gone bone-dry from shock, and excitement? And, did that Frenchman have his own artillery loaded with canister and grape, to return the favor? If he was smart he did. And this'un was bloody clever!

"Christ." Alan sighed as the poleacre loomed up, as if sailing through a parting in a stage curtain. Not sixty yards off, larboard to face the poleacre's larboard. Gunners and sailors lined her bulwarks, French Marine Infantry with muskets leveled. Her antiboarding nets were down, and her guns were run out in-battery; at least one carronade on her foredeck to fear, Lewrie saw. Another aft on what passed for a quarterdeck. And five long guns amidships, upon that flush spar/gun deck; Frog eight-pounders, thank God, no heavier than his.

"*Feuer!*" Quarter-gunner Rahl shouted up forrud, and the larboard eighteen-pounder carronade lit off with a deafening roar.

"Fire as you bear!" Mister Bittfield screamed, as soon as the first larboard gun could bear in its port, and the long guns began to bark like ferocious guard dogs.

Out of my hands, now, Lewrie groaned to himself, heaving a philosophical shrug; our weight of iron prevails . . . or theirs does. Sweet Jesus, just a little help, here, he prayed. Let 'em *not* have thought to load with grape or canister!

Jester bucked and trembled like a first-saddled colt as her guns, the enemy's guns, filled the short space between the racing hulls with hot gushes of gray-tan smoke, as both ships screamed in agony as heavy iron took them in their vitals!

Lewrie could barely see enemy sailors at her rails, being tossed aside; bulwark timbers flying, bodies flying, hear the stupendous boomings of guns fired straight into his face. Oak screamed, masts cried, short stabbing blooms of pink fire lilies and swarms of amber-reddish sparks swirled spent as dazed lightning bugs in the smoke wall! Quick splinters of wood flew from *Jester*'s wounds, flicking past, whickering and fluting, a giant's toothpicks, their sharp edges hungry for flesh!

The high, terrier-yip blasts of swivel guns at the rails, which spewed loose bags of pistol shot and langridge—scrap-iron bits—at the French. And then the blessed *barrooming*! of the quarterdeck carronades, as the enemy command staff came abeam!

Lewrie shut his eyes, staring directly down the barrel of *their* quarterdeck carronade the instant before the sight of his own death was blotted out, and he was staggered almost off his feet by the noise and the shock waves. Another shock wave, which made his heart flutter and pause, the breath stop in his chest! Turned half sidewise, and hammered to his knees for real, this time, as a round-shot passed within a few feet of him, howling over the quarterdeck, ululating off into the distance like an irate eagle robbed of its prey at the last moment!

"Jesus, sir, ya hurt, sir?" his cabin steward whimpered, coming to his side with a box of pistols. Aspinall was shaking like a sodden hound might just after leaving a stream, terror-tears streaking, lower lip blubbering.

"Don't think so, Aspinall." Alan grimaced, as if in real pain, feeling himself over quickly. "But thankee for askin'. Bloody hell, what're *you* doing on deck?" Aspinall's post during quarters was down on the orlop,

to assist "Chips," Ship's Carpenter Mister Rees, as a dumb carrier and
fetcher should any repairs be necessary.

"B . . . bosun's mate, sir," Aspinall wailed, his teeth chattering so
badly he could barely avoid biting his tongue. "Mister Cony, he tol' me
t'fetch ya yer pistols, sir. Said 'e thought ya'd be needin' 'em, so I did, an'
. . . kin I go *below*, agin, Captain, sir? Now ya have 'em, like?"

"Aye, with my gratitude, Aspinall, me lad. Just help me to my feet,
first. Mister Knolles?"

"Aye, sir?" the first lieutenant rasped back, his throat raw with gun
smoke, and his hat gone somewhere on its own.

"Helm down, sir!" Lewrie ordered, once he'd gotten erect. "A tack,
cross the wind, and keep the wind gauge 'bove that bastard! My telescope."

So close, one bloody instant; so far apart the next. The Frog poleacre
had fallen off the wind, was running large to the nor'east—minus her
mizzenmast and lateen spanker. In the round ocular, Lewrie saw she'd
been beaten to a pulp by that broadside, fired so close they could have
spit at each other. Her larboard side was bashed in, with several large
punctures below her gun ports, and about a third of her bulwarks had
been torn away, merging two gun ports into one long tear. Larboard
mainmast stays were sagging loose, the chain platforms, and the deadeye
blocks that tensioned those shrouds savaged! And on her quarterdeck!
That mob on her stern, her officers and after-guard, were gone! Barely
half a dozen figures could be seen moving about, mostly throwing themselves on the abandoned helm. Topmen were sheeting home her main
course and tops'l, not trusting the upper t'gallant mast with the pressure
of canvas, her foremast lateen sail swung almost athwartship. Trimmed
for a run!

" 'Ware, below!" Bosun Porter shouted, as *Jester* swung up close to the
wind. There was a rending screech of pine as top-hamper ripped, as
Jester's own royal and t'gallant topmasts sagged backward, shedding
blocks and rigging. Crosstree slats snapped like twigs, freeing tension on
shrouds, and the entire mess slowly inclined farther astern, until everything above the crosstrees sagged back into the mainmast stays, and hung
up on the main t'gallant yard, tangling stays'ls and halliards, jears, and
lift-lines, into a rat's nest!

"In der irons, Herr Kapitan!" Brauer reported from the wheel, as
Jester poised in the very teeth of the wind, and stalled, unable to complete her tack and slowing to a crawl.

"Secure from quarters. Porter, Cony! Secure what you can, till she pays off," Lewrie ordered. However much a draw the battle had been, it was now over. It would be long minutes before *Jester* could fall off to either beam, even more a long half hour to clear away all the raffle and take up pursuit once more. By which time that poleacre would have sailed herself almost hull-under for Toulon or Hyeres Bay. Beaten, at everything she'd tried; ignored when she'd attempted to lure them away, useless when charged with protecting her convoy. And, shot to ribbons when she'd tried to retake the prizes, denied even that crumb of comfort. Still, she would escape them. Lewrie devoutly hoped he'd slain her captain. Had it become a real broadside-to-broadside slugging, he wasn't sure he might have won, after all, unless that bugger had died.

Aye, he hoped that poleacre's commanding officer had been shot to a blood pudding, by a cloud of canister! Should he live to fight another day . . . there was a *damn'* dangerous Frenchman on the loose, a one too clever for anyone's good. A one too dangerous to live!

"Two dead, outright, sir," Surgeon Mister Howse related grumpily, still streaked with splotches of blood on his butcher's apron. "One more to pass, by sunset, if God's good to him. Nine injured."

"I see." Lewrie nodded, almost numb, still shaken by how brief, yet how savage, the engagement had been. "Those injured, uhm . . ."

"Two, Captain." Howse scowled, a bite to his voice, as if war's mayhem was Lewrie's fault, and the "butcher's bill" the captain's debt. "Amputees, to be discharged. Both Marines. T'other seven, well . . . few weeks to mend, light duties after. Assuming suppuration does not take them. I have their names. For your clerk."

Howse offered a quick-scribbled list, almost official-looking . . . but the red "wax" seals were his gory thumb and fingerprints.

"Thankee, Mister Howse," Lewrie replied, gingerly accepting it and passing it to Knolles at once. "Adjust the watch-and-quarter bills accordingly, Mister Knolles. I'll go below, to the surgery, for a moment . . ."

"Aye, sir, but . . ." Knolles answered. "Uhm, as to the foremast. You said you wished to oversee . . . ?"

"Aye, right with you, then," Lewrie harrumphed. There was little more to do, for the short run, than to strike all that damaged top-hamper off the foremast, right down to the fighting top. The mainmast, too, had lost its royal and t'gallant topmasts and spars. A spare foremast tops'l pole stood, quickly doubled to the lower foremast cap, so they could raise jibs to work her to windward, into shelter. And the hands to see to, to visit the wounded, tell them their suffering was . . .

" 'Scuse me, Cap'um," Bosun Porter intruded, doffing his hat to him. "But th' hands from th' prize crews you recalled is come aboard."

"Aye, Mister Porter," Lewrie all but snarled. "Do you and Cony tend to alloting them work. With Mister Knolles, and his damn' *list!*"

"Aye aye, sir." Porter nodded, almost scraping his feet as he backed away from his captain's foul mood.

Damme, so much for being a lucky ship, Lewrie mourned in silence. Everything going so bloody good, so far, the crew shaken down and main-well content. *Proud* of her; and now this! Should have been a day to celebrate, taking three prizes, and sharing in another two, then . . .

He hoped they weren't as dispirited as *he* felt, right then. He heaved another bitter sigh, and started forward to judge their jury-rig repairs on the foremast.

"Sir!" Spendlove cried, as he came back inboard on the larboard gangway. "Sir?"

Another damned interruption! "*What*, Mister Spendlove?"

"Sorry, sir, but . . . this fellow . . . master of that dhow-thing-gummy?" Spendlove said, gesturing to a civilian he'd fetched along with him in a borrowed longboat. "Spot of bother, sir. Says he's Genoese, and he has papers and manifests you must see, sir. At least, that's what I've gathered so far, sir. Speaks damn-all French or English, a word or two, and I've no Italian, so . . ."

"Mister Spendlove, this is hardly the time." Lewrie glowered at him. "He was caught for fair, sailing in-convoy with French ships, and with French escort. Admiralty Prize Court's the place for him."

"Well, sir, he *claims* neutrality, and all . . ." Spendlove allowed, one more member of the crew suddenly wary of his captain's wrath.

"If I may, sir?" Mister Mountjoy offered, of a sudden, popping up like a jack-in-the-box from their offhand side. Whether Lewrie knew it or not, Mountjoy had been dogging his footsteps, making hasty notes and juggling (fumbling, more like!) a sheaf of record documents, such as the forms for "Backstays Shifted During the Course of the Commission." And pestering one and all with questions to inscribe upon those forms— as if that made everything tidy!

"*What*, Mister Mountjoy?" Lewrie demanded impatiently of him, as well.

"Mister Spendlove's concerns, sir," his clerk said with an apologetic purr. "Why I was so pleased to take the position under you, Captain . . . to the Mediterranean, and all?"

"Bloody . . ." Lewrie huffed, ready to explode at the nearest target to hand, the very next pestiferous . . . !

"I've a good ear for languages, sir," Mountjoy hastened to explain, backing up a few half steps. "The Romance tongues were my particular forté. A hobby, at school—languages? French, Italian, Portuguese, Spanish . . . ? Should I converse with this merchant captain for you, sir? That's what I meant. Begging your pardon, sir."

"Ah." Lewrie sighed, deflating once more, and unable to fume at such a whey-faced tom-noddy, with such a sheepish expression. He had already delivered one prime rant, over the opened orders, weeks before, and Mountjoy had been as shy and missish about him as a dormouse in a roomful of ram-cats, ever since. "Aye, deal with him, Mister Mountjoy . . . practice your skills. Make him no promises, mind. Think of it as an exercise before the bench, perhaps. And him a debtor."

"I will, sir."

With that, Lewrie went forrud, with Knolles and Cony, Mister Rees the carpenter and his crew, to complete what at-sea repairs they might. By dusk, they could be anchored in San Fiorenzo Bay, begging supplies from HMS *Inflexible* for permanent repairs.

"Looks a whole lot worse'n h'it really is, sir," Cony told him confidentially, after they'd descended the newly rove larboard foremast stays from the fighting top. "Larboard cathead's shivered, we'll need a new'un. Frame'r two busted, carline posts broke . . . and scantlin's on the larboard side stove in, o' course, but that'd be 'bove th' gunnels, Mister Lewrie, sir, an' nothin' permanent like, 'less'n there's no oak plankin' 'r baulks t'be had."

"Well, it feels damn' bad, Cony," Lewrie confessed to him.

"Aye, sir, that h'it does," his longtime confidant agreed with a sad shrug, "but we give a whole lot worse'n we got. Them Frogs woz bein' blown high'z their own main yard, last I seen of 'em. Heads an' arms, an' all. One second they woz thicker'n fleas on th' bulwarks . . . th' next, twoz clean'z a tavern counter at op'nin' time. Weren't all that much fun, I'll lay ya, sir—t'be on th' *receivin'* end o' carronades f'r th' first time, but we beat 'em, sir. Beat 'em bad."

"And the lads . . . ?" Lewrie asked, chary of Cony's optimism.

"Lord, sir!" Cony grinned. "They got eyes, too, Mister Lewrie. An' sense 'nough t'know that we got off easy, compared t'th' Monsoors. And, uhm, sir . . . well. Five prizes, alt'gither, took afore Noon Sights, sir.

And th' share-out'll be better f'r them wot lived, sir. Take yerself a gander, sir. Give an ear to 'em. This ain't no beat crew, not by a long shot, Mister Lewrie. They're a *lucky* crew, they thinks. With a lucky captain. *Jester* got blessed, back in th' Bay o' Biscay. Seal, 'e spoke t'ya, Mister Lewrie, after 'e come f'r little Josephs. We're still a *lucky* ship."

"Dear Lord, they believe . . . ?" Lewrie sighed. He'd say no more about it. If Cony was right, and as a damned good seaman and boatswain he usually was—as a decent and caring person who usually knew more, and had more sense than his superiors—then he still had a crew who would be willing to dare. A crew who'd be willing to toe-up and fight once more, in future. At that moment, he didn't care *what* the "people" believed was responsible; if they wished to sing praises to Mahomet or Pitt the Elder, he couldn't have cared less. And, if they wished to hold to the belief that a pagan sea god had come to them and blessed *Jester* as one of his chosen, blessed "Ram-Cat" Lewrie as a captain they should follow, then so be it! Lucky ships were made of even *more* insubstantial moon wash than that. And lucky ships triumphed, in spite of all!

"Signal from *Ariadne*, sir!"

"Uhm. What now, then?" Lewrie asked, feeling relieved of his foul, guilty mood, though still burdened by the deaths and injuries of those who had taken their King's shillings, and blindly allowed him to lead them to such a slaughter.

"Do You Require Assistance? Then . . . Submit . . . Remain on Station." The signalman striker read off slowly, bawling his translation from far aft. "His Number . . . Escort Prizes . . . Into Harbor, sir!"

"Be damned if he will," Lewrie snarled. "Make . . . Negative, to his question of assistance. Then . . . *Our* Number . . . Escort Prizes into Harbor! And add . . . 'Require Repairs.' The greedy bastard!"

Lewrie went aft, while the signal pennants soared aloft, sour again as he contemplated what a report *Ariadne*'s captain might write. She'd taken the pair of poleacres without a scratch, and had run down to *Jester* long after the French warship had sailed out of gun range. She'd made a halfhearted attempt at pursuit, but had broken it off after half an hour, and beat back to *Jester* and her huddled prizes.

Report, Lewrie thought. I'd best be writing something myself, and get Hood's ear first. Why, there's no telling what *Ariadne* could claim he did to recover the first three prizes—and share in the lot!

"Mister Knolles, Mister Buchanon, let us get a way on her," Alan decided. "Best course to San Fiorenzo. Make sail, conformable to the weather."

"Aye aye, sir," Knolles agreed.

"Ah, Captain, sir?" Mountjoy harrumphed shyly, once Lewrie was back on the quarterdeck.

"Aye, Mister Mountjoy. Our Genoese?"

"Yes, sir. A most specious case, sir," Mountjoy said fussily. "His papers, uhm . . . what any court might construe as highly . . . colorable? Then, there is Mister Spendlove's hasty inventory, as to what she carried, as opposed to what is listed in her manifest, do you see . . . water, wine, flour, and biscuit, uhm . . . rice, dry pasta . . . outwardly it might *seem* innocent. But there is the matter of powder, flints . . . boots, premade cartouches and pouches . . . all bound in cases bearing French markings. Most conveniently *not* listed as cargo, sir," his clerk concluded, preening a bit, now that his legal, and linguistic skills had been of some use at last.

"So his ship and his cargo are certain to be condemned in Prize Court, aye," Lewrie surmised. "Well fine, then, Mister Mountjoy. A fair morning's work, sir."

"There is uhm . . . well, sir?" Mountjoy rejoined. "As I stated, I was a scholar of languages. Our recent foe, sir, was called *Fléche, Signore Capitano* Guardino rather grumpily informed me."

That worthy, at the mention of his name, drew himself up to his full height, which wasn't much worth mentioning, and tucked his voluminous coat over his greasy, straining waistcoat.

"A most interesting regional dialect, sir, the Genoese," Thomas Mountjoy happily digressed. "So quite unlike that Neapolitan Italian that I first heard . . ."

"Anything *else*, Mister Mountjoy?" Lewrie pressed, sensing that there was. And unwilling to waste half the rest of the day letting his clerk maunder and prose.

"Uhm, that her captain . . . *Fléche's* captain, that is . . . was named Michaud. *Signore* Guardino refers to him in rather a hostile manner, so I intuit, sir. A perfect Tartar, altogether. The *signore capitano* did express the wish that you blew him back to Hades, where he came from, I believe were his exact words, sir? Or at least made him as hideous as his superior, who is, in the *capitano's* mind, Satan himself, had he to choose betwixt the two. A cheese-parer, a miser, he called him, *and* a fiend, sir . . . this Brutto Faccia. Or, Le Hideux. He derogates him in Genoese, *and* French, with equal ease, sir."

"Both of which *mean*, sir . . . ?"

"In Italian, sir . . . that is to say, 'Ugly Face.' 'The Hideous,' is the

French vernacular. *Signore* Guardino's ship was lying at Toulon, sir, and was, he protested, *dragooned* into French service. Such excuse for his participation, he believes most strongly . . ."

"Won't do him a damned bit of good," Lewrie said, smirking.

"Well, sir. 'Le Hideux' is some new senior officer, just come down from Paris, so *Signore* Guardino related to me, sir . . . to command their convoys, and arrange escorts," Mountjoy related with a confidential air. "And to, uhm . . . *inspire* loyalty and enthusiasm in those officers and men under him. Brought his own guillotine, so 'tis said, sir," Mountjoy concluded with a shivery, theatrical shrug.

"Then, Mister Mountjoy, do let us wish that Captain Michaud, have we not *already* knackered his arse," Lewrie said with a grin over hearing the first bit of news that could possibly be considered cheery, "his loss of this convoy will encourage his 'Hideous' superior to harvest his head! Very well, Mister Mountjoy. Well done."

"Er . . . thank you, sir," Mountjoy replied, nearly stunned to be complimented.

"Do you see Mister Knolles. He'll have work for you. And when he's done, there's a fair copy of my report to be produced for Admiral Hood."

"Oh," Mountjoy said, dashed at the prospect of another slew of correspondence. "Very well, sir."

Damme, I just *hope* the bastard gets the guillotine, Lewrie sighed to himself; this Michaud was just too clever by half! We'll have a much safer, and quieter, time of it, with him toasting on Satan's coals!

Commander Alan Lewrie, RN, surveyed his ship, peering forward at the truncated main and foremasts, the untidy, unbalanced jury-rigged display of low-angled forestays that bore spare canvas jibs, of masts spreading nothing cross-yarded above the tops'ls. The sailmaker, Mister Paschal, and his crew had taken half the foredeck for their work area, and were busily stitching and patching. No, *Jester* wouldn't *dash* into harbor in triumph; she'd *limp*, no faster than the odd clutch of prize vessels she would escort! It would be near the end of the Day Watch, the beginning of the First Dog, before she dropped anchor.

Time, and enough, to go below and visit the wounded first. See that fellow who was sure to pass over before then, if Howse was correct in his assessment . . . and think of something to say to him.

The report could be done later, after all. Delivered verbatim, in Hood's presence, really, with a written account to follow. Perhaps a rough draft in hand, should he *dictate* it to Mountjoy . . . ?

And in the waist, along the ravaged larboard gangway, Marines in slop clothing, and sailors, toiled. Sluicing and holystoning away the blood-stains. Hammering and driving what spare lumber they carried in car-penter's and bosun's stores, to the music of the fiddler and fifer. Not the dirge he expected—they labored to the easy-paced lilts of "The Derry Hornpipe." Soft-joshing each other, faint smiles and some bleak chuck-ling, now and again. A subdued and fairly somber crew, aye, he thought; but not a broken one.

HMS *Jester* was still a useful instrument of war.

CHAPTER

3

"AND," LEWRIE DICTATED to Mountjoy, who was scribbling away as fast as he could to get a rough draft, "at *no* time were the three previous captured prize vessels *ever* actively threatened with recapture . . . as HMS *Ariadne*'s captain suggests in his report. Therefore, sirs, his claims upon them are . . . damme, Mountjoy, what's a good *legal* word for horse turds?"

"I should think 'nugatory' would suit, sir," Mountjoy allowed with a brief grin. "Of little or no consequence."

"Right, then," Lewrie exulted, mopping his sweaty brow with a handkerchief, almost stifling in the great-cabin's enclosed warmth . . . and "exercised" with sullen ill-humor, to boot. "Therefore *Ariadne*'s claim of shares in the aforesaid three vessels, taken solely by *Jester* long before her arrival . . . on the horizon, mind! . . . are nugatory, and totally without merit."

"Same thing, really, Captain," Mountjoy said dubiously.

"Wrap it in ribbons, plate it in gilt and shit . . . you read the law, you know the catchphrases." Lewrie snorted impatiently. "Hold him to the coals, and paint him the greedy fool. Trot out your really big guns and hull him, Mr. Mountjoy. The Prize Court's bought every one of them, and their cargoes, and the settlement's been adjudged at nearly £30,000. And the lion's share should be ours. *Ariadne* didn't even get a scratch. Aye, add this . . . or something like it—couch it however you will— *Jester* fought the French national ship, and by her valiant duty reaped the higher *honors*, the greater glory, so . . . ."

"To the victor belong the spoils, sir? Something like that?"

"Capital!" Lewrie rejoiced. "I'll leave the rest to you, you know the form by now for closure in Navalese. Have it, and a copy, in hand for my signature by tomorrow morning . . . just into the forenoon."

"Yes, sir," Mountjoy assured him. "I meant to say, 'aye aye, sir.' Sorry."

"Very well, Mister Mountjoy, that should be all. Aspinall?"

"Aye, sir?"

"I'll have that fresh shirt and stock now, for shore."

"INSUFFERABLE DAMN' PINCHPENNY," Lewrie still fumed, even as he made his way uphill to his town house, sweating that fresh shirt and stock, his waistcoat and breeches, to a pearl-gray rather than white. San Fiorenzo Bay had turned into a roasting pan, the last month or so. Aboard ship, one might snatch a cooling draught of air under awnings, or down a ventilator chute made from a topmast stays'l, but ashore . . . ! The town had grown in size, had spread out along the strand and up over the scraggly hills on either hand, in the blink of an eye. But, a tent city, mostly—for the sick and wounded from the siege of Calvi. More sick than wounded, though. Illness that accompanied a land force slew even more than shot or shell.

That tumbledown *osteria* at the waterfront, that sprawling, and sleepy little tavern, had become a fresh-painted wonder; had added some patios, tables, and benches, almost doubling in size. The owners bowed to him as he passed, saluting him in the local dialect, as if he were their feudal liege. *Osteria Paoli*, their large new signboard boasted, replete with a crude portrait of the Corsican patriot leader. British officers (officers *only*, Lewrie noted!) were its principal patrons who almost filled every seat and table. Them, and their doxies.

" 'Least someone's profiting." Lewrie scowled, begrudging. Soon as the Prize Court had released their judgment, the month before, he'd fought a running battle to keep what he'd captured. Off at sea again, taking another pair of prizes in the meantime—large poleacres, this time. Burning or scuttling at least half-a-dozen more for which he'd been unable to supply prize crews . . . those new captures were all his. But every return to San Fiorenzo had brought new obfuscations about the convoy! And the share-out of prize money. Admiral Hood and his flag captain, his small staff, had already been awarded their eighth, while both *Jester* and *Ariadne* were still waiting for their portions. And Lewrie's two-eighths represented nearly £4,500! He suspected the agents and commissioners of the Prize Court were having an enjoyable time, just living off the interest, and their "take" for performing their duties—and those badly. "Probably spinning this out, damn' near till next Epiphany, so they can play with the . . . *hullo*?" He had groused under his breath, suddenly stopped short at the corner, having seen his and Phoebe's town house. "What the *Devil* . . . ?"

There were *two* fashionable carriages, coach-and-fours, along the curbing, equipages that gleamed in the sun. Teams of decent-looking horses flicked their tails and manes against the ubiquitous flies, and liveried coaches and postilion boys did their duties as their masters prepared to depart. Richly clad civilians, done up in gowns or suits that wouldn't have looked out of place on The Strand, back in London!

And another brace of dray wagons along the side street, laden with heaped picture frames, paintings, chairs, and tables. Had Phoebe moved again, taken cheaper lodgings, been forced to . . . ? No, they'd paid the year in advance. Or had she *left* him? he shivered.

He crossed the street, ready to lash out at somebody . . . anybody! But was greeted most jovially, in French or Italian; most of which he couldn't follow, but did get some gist from, something to do with being affiliated with "la contessa," or "vicomtesse." Which association perplexed him even further! Just who the blazes lived here now?

"Phoebe?" he bawled, once past those posturing clowns, and into the cooler air of the courtyard.

Which had turned into a furniture gallery, it seemed. Couches, wine tables, armoires and cabinets, gilded chairs were everywhere, two-a-penny.

"Ah, Alain, *mon amour*!" a familiar voice called down from the upper floor, and Phoebe appeared in the iron-guarded bedchamber window of the guest room above. "I be down wiz you, immediate, *mon chou*!"

She was wearing a new sack gown, something suitable for presentation at Court, though her hair was down, informal and unpowdered, as she tripped across the flagstones to embrace him.

"What the bloody hell *is* all this, I ask you?" he tried to say sternly, just before she threw her arms around his neck and lifted her feet off the ground. "Phoebe, I'm serious, girl. Don't . . . answer me."

"Oh, Alain, eez merchandise," she replied, waving one hand, to "pooh-pooh" its presence. "I tell you, remembre? Ze *émigrés royaliste*? Zey are sell zer s'ings, *bon marché*. I buy from z'em, an' when people come to San Fiorenzo, zen zey buy from *moi*! *Non* ze *bon marché*! 'Ow do you say, ze uhm . . . profeet, *oui*?"

"You've gone into *trade*?" he huffed, scandalized.

"Non, Alain." She smiled, proud of being so clever. "Non *trade*. I deman' ze cash, on'y, now."

"Phoebe, I thought . . ." he babbled; not knowing *what* he thought!

"*D'avant*, uuhm . . ." she explained, threading an arm through his to lead him inside, skipping girlishly, ". . . in beginning, *oui*, I trade. Zose wiz'ou' furniture, zey 'ave jewelry, an' mus' 'ave beds. Or 'ave gold an' silver plate, *si belle*! But, 'ave no *monnaie* for food, so . . . ze *osteria*, zose nice people, an' *Signore* Bucco 'oo rent to us? Some ozzers, we mak' ze arrangement. Food an' lodgings for trade jewelry, or furnishings. Ooh, Alain, close you' eyes, *plais*! I s'prise you!"

"You've already done that, Phoebe," he declared, though obeying her whim and shutting his eyes, allowing himself to be led inside as her "blindman's buff."

"*Voilà*, Alain!" she cried, giggling a-tiptoe. "*Regardez!*"

"Bloody . . ." He could but weakly gasp at the transformation.

The parlor now held cream-painted, gilded couches and chairs, upholstered in shimmery white moire silk, with gold-flecked filigrees. Deep, rich tables and chests—cherry, mahogany, or rosewood, marbled topped or delicately inlaid with precious ivory. Coin-silver candelabras, tea-things, vases, and trays . . . the kaleidoscopic prism speckling of late-afternoon sunlight glinted off fine crystal gewgaws, or from the magnificent gilt-and-crystal chandeliers! The sooty fireplace had been redone with new marble inlays, dressed in carved stone that was very Romanesque. There were cloisonné, silver, gilt, or Chinese vases, cherubs, candlesticks on the mantel, below a gigantic gold-vein mirror hung above it. Paintings in baroque gilt frames, portraits, landscapes . . . Painted, scoured, papered in some places, elegantly draperied . . . ! The parlor was now a showplace, and not anywhere *near* the gaudy he'd expected from someone of Phoebe's provincial, and untrained, background. Their plebeian lodgings had become a miniature *palazzo*, as genteelly elegant as any fine mansion in the whole of England!

"Sit, *mon chou*. 'Ere. A cool glass, *n'est-ce pas*?"

He *had* to sit; he was too dumbfounded to stand. He fell into a deep, wide, massy armchair done in burgundy chintz over priceless rosewood, so elegantly carved, his senses reeling as she dashed off to fetch him a glass of something.

Joliette appeared, prancing into the parlor with her tail erect. She hopped up on the matching hassock and hunkered down warily, barely out of reach but looking as if she *might* like a petting. Around her slim little ruffed neck, there was a brown velvet riband, from which hung a tiny amber cameo, set in real gold! A cameo of a cat, of course.

There came the promising *thwock*! of a cork being pulled, somewhere off to his right in the kitchen. And a moment later, Phoebe reappeared bearing two exquisitely cut crystal flutes of champagne, followed by a slim, dark-haired maid he'd never clapped eyes on before, who carried a most impressive silver wine tray, and a chilling bucket that held the bottle, a wine bucket as big as a coehorn mortar barrel, heavily ornamented with cherubs, pans, and grapes. Solid silver? he goggled. It had to weigh three or four bloody *pounds*!

"Cool, too," he muttered, after the maid had poured them both a glass, and departed without a word.

"I kep' ze bes', you see?" she informed him, waving a slim hand over her new fineries. "You like ze champagne, Alain? *Bon*. Ve 'ave ze dozen-dozen bottles, now. A *ver'* good year."

"Just how did you ever . . ." he began to marvel.

"I tol' you, Alain," she chided with a pleased little laugh, as she came to sit on the wideish arm of his chair and play her fingers in his hair. "Signore Bucco, 'e is 'ave *beaucoup* 'ouses for to rent, *mais*, ze *émigrés*, zey cannot afford, *n'est-ce pas*? I am shopping, for pretty new s'ings, 'e come to tak' ze old shabbies, as we agree. An', 'e ees afraid-ed zat what we tell 'eem ees *vrai* . . . true . . . zat you' Army will tak' 'ouses non rented. Zen, when I am market, I fin' so many *émigrés* impoverish . . . 'ave s'ings of grande value, but no *monnaies*, for to eat? So I mak' ze arrangement wiz ze Monteverdes at ze *osteria*, 'oo know ze farmers, ze shopkeepers, *aussi, e voilà* . . . ze entreprise we begin. 'E 'ave *monnaies*, I 'ave *une peu*. Pardon, but I see you' agent, 'e advance me *all* ze fif'y pound you leave for me at firs'. Be non to worry, *mon amour*, I pay eet all back, wi'sin ze mont', from my profeet," she said with another pleased chuckle, and a toying with his hair.

"You parleyed fifty pounds into all *this*?"

"*Oui*," she admitted, with a proud cock of her head.

"Bloody hell, you should be in London, at the 'Change!" He gaped. "You'd make a fortune, overnight. And show them how."

"*Merci*, Alain, you are please-ed? *Bon*." Phoebe smiled, rewarding him with a fond kiss. "Now, non more trade. You' Navy, you' Army, so many at San Fiorenzo, 'oo deman' 'ouses, rooms, food an' wine. An' ze refreshment, from ze siege? Ze grande *émigrés*, zey mus' 'ave servants, pay rent, buy food an' wine. An', where are soldiers an' sailors and ze rich, zere come *domestiques*, chefs, ze restaurants an' cafés . . . ooh la, San Fiorenzo ees awaken! Tailors an' dressmakers, zey are mak' money so quick! So, even more people come, from Bastia, Ajaccio . . . all need what we 'ave, *comprende*? Ze people 'oo are jus' depart, zey open ze *maison public* . . . ze 'ore-'ouse, wiz so many beautiful *jeune filles. Maison public mus'* be elegant, 'ave furnishings grande, an' I on'y am 'ave, no one else, so zey buy from *moi*."

"You're in the brothel business?" he yelped in alarm. "That's as good as saying we *both* are! Now, hold on just . . ."

'Course, everyone I knew in the early days said I'd make a hellish grand pimp, he recalled, somewhat ruefully.

"Non, non," she countered heartily. "Sell, on'y ze furnishings. For *monnaie*, an' some wine. Wine, I sell to ozzers, at profeet. You' *officiers Brittanique*, mos'ly. Forgive *plais*, Alain, *mon coeur*, but . . ." She sobered, almost biting her lip shyly. "Mos' of zem, zey are 'aving *très monnaies*, but are . . . *les folletes*—ze leetle fools? Pay any sum I as' for zere port an' claret. An', zey mus' 'ave clubs, *hein*? Where officers go, when zey wish to be *amusant*? Zey need furnishing grande for zose, *aussi*! An', so many gowns, an' jewelry I 'ave tak' in trade. Officers mus' 'ave zere courtesans . . . and courtesans mus' 'ave pretty gowns, or jewelry. Or ze les follettes, zey buy *for* zem, from *moi*."

"So, we're . . . *you're* running a secondhand shop for whores and such," he stated flatly.

"Non!" she declared, aghast, and suddenly losing her gay confidence and pride. "To shop, on'y, Alain, never to . . . I s'ought you be 'appy, zat I do so well. Zat I mak' ze 'ome beautiful, an' eet cos' you nossing!" She began to blubber up, her pouty little lower lip beginning to tremble. "I . . . I s'ought you be *proud* of me!"

"Phoebe . . ." he crooned, abandoning his champagne to take hold of her before she fled in tears, to slide her down onto his lap where he rocked her and stroked her like a heartbroken child. "There there, don't take on so, my girl. Of *course*, I'm proud of you. 'Bout pleased as punch, don't ye know! You're a marvel, so clever, so enterprising . . ."

Hold on there, he thought, though: let's not trowel it on *too* bloody thick! I still don't know what people think of this place. Or my association with it!

"It's just such a surprise, that's all, Phoebe. *Ma cherie*," he told her softly, cradling her head on his chest. "Aye, you *have* done a miracle with this house! I'd not recognize it. And so tasteful! Grand as the Walpoles, grand as the richest house ever I've seen back home in England! But I thought I'd be coming back to our . . . to you, my girl . . . and our little hideaway, where we could be private and intimate. Cozy and pleasant, hey, like you said? And I find people crawling about underfoot, jampacked to the deck heads with stuff like a chandlery, too damn' busy a bustle, bad as the 'Change back home. And some of 'em not the elegant sort you should—a *lady* should—be knowing. Now, where is our privacy in all that, hmm?"

"Ees jus' . . ." Phoebe hiccuped, snuggling closer even as she dashed away her tears with the back of her hand. "You' Prize Court . . . zey tak' so *long*, an' eef *I* mak' *monnaies* zen you non worry 'bout eef you can afford me, Alain! *Merde alors*, eef I lose you, what is zere for me to do? Become ze *putain*, again? Non. Never again, *mon amour!*"

"Phoebe . . ." he gentled, stroking her back. Touched, though, to his heart by her concern for him. He plucked a dainty, gauzy silk handkerchief from the bosom of her elegant gown and began to dry her tears.

"Someday, *oui* . . ." she whispered, turning her face up to his to be gentled. "You go 'way to sea, return to Englan'. Or, we grow tired of each ozzer? I *pray* zat do non 'appen for *très beaucoup ané, mon amour!* All zese I do, so you 'ave nossing to s'ink about but 'ow much you love me, 'ow much I love you! An' 'ow 'appy we are. Zose zat come 'ere . . ." She sniffed, taking the handkerchief for a vigorous swipe at her nose. "Zey non shame you, Alain . . . or *moi*. Zey do non come to trade wiz ze leetle 'hore 'oo 'ave e'spensive s'ings," she swore, all but making the sign of the cross over her heart.

"Non, zey s'ink zey deal wiz *émigré royaliste* from Toulon. Our 'ouse ees non ze salon, or ze *maison public*. Ze courtyard, on'y, ees market. Non 'ere, in 'ouse. Oh, la, I store gowns an' jewelry, in ze ozzer bedchamber, for *sécurité, mais* . . . I do non entertain! An' I am non for sale, ever again, Alain! Eef I mak' *monnaies, honestly* . . . zen I am 'ave *sécurité* so I *never* 'ave to sell myself to men, ever. Give to a man I love, wiz all my 'eart, *oui* . . . but, never sell."

"Dear God," he whispered, in awe of her. "Forgive me for rowing you, Phoebe. Forgive everything I said, or thought. You really are a wonder. A bloody knock-down wonder!"

"Oh, Alain!" she relented, flinging herself upon him once more, this time shuddering with relief, her tears turning to ones of restored joy.

And a poser, *and* a puzzle, and God knows what else, Alan thought, damned well relieved, himself; but above all, girl . . . a sweet, cunning little . . . entrancing dear'un!

CHAPTER

4

"Contessa!" the street vendor greeted her from his flower cart. Followed by some liquid Italian, and the offer of a nosegay of local blooms.

"Contessa?" Lewrie frowned anew. It had been the sixth time in their short evening stroll that he'd heard the word, but the first that he'd associated it directly with her.

"Zey call me zat, Alain." Phoebe shrugged, a bit too artlessly, and with too much nonchalance, though she could not hide her blushing.

"Why is that, exactly?" he inquired, striving for an equally offhand air.

"I do ze bus'nees wiz zem, loan ze *une peu monnaies*, so . . ." She blushed again. "A lady cannot be *padrone, hein*? Zat ees for men. I 'elp 'eem buy donkey for 'ees cart, an' now 'e pay me back, wiz 'ees profits, *oui? Like* ze *padrone* does, *mais* . . ."

Several gentlemen and their ladies, out for a stroll of their own, bowed or curtsied to them—to her, specifically—in the next half block, doffing their hats. Fawning over her, chatting away mostly in Italian, making raving sounds over the miniature portrait of Pascal Paoli that hung on a gold chain about her neck.

"Zey are *patriotes*, Alain," Phoebe said, blushing even more prettily. "I tell zem where I fin' eet, an' zey wish to purchase, *aussi*."

"Don't tell me you paint 'em in your spare time," he teased with a droll expression. "Assumin' you have any, that is."

"Non, non *moi*, Alain." She grinned impishly. "Une of my cousin, 'e ees *artiste*, in Bastia. 'E do ze portraits, 'ave ees own shop. 'E 'ave now three ozzers work for eem. 'E sen' zem to me, I sell for 'eem, place

138

orders for more. For on'y ze *une peu, petite* commission, *n'est-ce pas?*
Mon Dieu merde alors . . . 'e ees kin!"

She'd already explained to him, long before, on the intricacies of Corsican kinships. Which were pretty much on a par with a Scottish clan,
with commerce of the most cutthroat kind thrown in. Immediate family,
down to distant cousins, came first; second was clan loyalty; then God
and Church, with Self coming in a poor fourth, usually. One obeyed the
family *padrone*, then the feudal lords of one's extended clan, who, it
seemed, were forever feuding with each other as bad as Capulets and
Montagues in Shakespeare's *Romeo and Juliet*. Blood was always answerable in blood, and they had longer memories, and grudges, than an entire
pack of abused hounds. The *vendetta*, they called it.

Paoli, everywhere he looked, it seemed, too. Portraits, names of children, names of shops and favorite horses. Troop a large painting or effigy
of Pascal Paoli through the streets, and one might imagine the Second
Coming—or a Saturnalia, with one and all kneeling in tears or hosannahs
like Roosian serfs did to their icons, or their masters. Hero, Saint, Libera-
tor, Caesar—all of them, was Paoli, in the Corsican mind.

"Hmmf!" Phoebe sniffed suddenly, turning her head, and turning up
her nose in remarkable imitation of a grand dowager who'd just delivered
the "Cut Sublime" to some mountebank on The Strand back home.

"What?"

" 'Eem!" She sneered, inclining her head toward a party farther down
the street. "Zat Messieur Jheel-ber' Elliot of you's."

"He's viceroy of the island, Phoebe, representing our good King
George," Lewrie told her patiently. "What's he done to you?"

"Alain," she rejoined, scandalized and reproving, " 'e ees tyrant! *Mon
Dieu merde alors*, Corsica fight ze Genoese hun'erd year, to be independent. Genoa give Corsica to France, an' zen Signore Paoli lead us in fight
zem for year an' year."

"And back in King George the Second's reign, Corsica offered to
become English, as I remember. Sign the whole island over to us," he
countered.

"*Oui*, to rid us of Genoese, so we non become part of France, be free!"
she argued.

"Wait a moment." He scowled, perplexed again. "*You're* French!"

"Papa was Français, Maman was Italian, *mais* . . . Alain, I am *Corsican*, you see? An' now, you' Messieur Elliot, 'e will mak' us British, wiz
monarch. Like you' Scotland . . . poor relation? When what we wish
ees to be Corsica independent. Papa come from France, so long ago, 'e

was Corsican. Maman be born 'ere, in Italian clan, but she was Corsican firs', *hein*? Say Corsican, non Français or Italiana. You' Elliot, 'e say we mus' 'ave king an' parliament, but mus' be *Corsican* king an' parliament, we say. An' zat ees *quel dangereux* . . . 'oo ees king, what clan. Ooh la, you s'ink you see vendetta *now* . . . ! So," she summed up with another snooty heave of her bosom, "ze man 'oo open zat box belong to Pandora, zat man ees ze fool *grande!*"

"But not Republicans," Alan hoped. "Mean t'say, if you don't have a king, you might as well be like those anarchist Americans. Or the French, these days."

"*Mon Dieu*, Alain, non!" Phoebe chuckled. "Oo ees say ev'ryone ees egal, zat ees stupeed! People are non born e . . . equal, ever. 'Ow you 'ave *padrones* an' clan lords, eef paissans conardes be jus' as good as ze noblesse? Zat ees *seelly* idea!"

Add perplexing to the list, Alan thought of his earlier appraisal of Phoebe Aretino; paradoxical . . .

"I 'ope you 'ave ze appetite *grande,* Alain, ze cuisine 'ere ees so ver' good!" she urged, changing subjects, and moods, as quick as the mercurial little minx she was. "Non Français, but Corsican!"

THE RISTORANTE LIBERATORE, with a portrait of Pascal Paoli for its centerpiece, of course, was packed with diners and doing a stock-jobbers' business. But a table was always *reserved*, it seemed for "la contessa bella" Aretino. And, with much smacking of lips, kissing of fingers, crooning "oohs and ahhs!" of welcome joy—along with an occasional smacking of a forehead—they were led to that table that had a commanding view of the harbor and docks, as well as the rest of that crowded dining room, on a slightly elevated upper terrace. And, as they made their way to it, several of the more fashionable diners paid Phoebe "passing honors" with even more glad cries, some almost groveling at her feet in gratitude for some earlier favor. Her hand was kissed and wrung so often Alan thought she seemed more like a Member of Parliament on the hustings, right after he'd trotted out the free gin and roast beef for purchased votes!

Hell of a welcome, he thought; for a little slip of a girl. *And* a retired courtesan, he could not help himself from adding; there must be somethin' Latin in that, surely. God, what a country!

With an almost regal air of true nobility, Phoebe smiled and inclined her head, responding to their greetings, before allowing a squad of unctuous waiters to seat her. And grinning, her eyes alight, gleeful as the cat that ate the canary, over her newfound adulation.

"Oh, there's some poor fellows can't get a table," Alan pointed out. "Damme, it's Nelson and Fremantle." Lewrie allowed himself a tiny smirk, to think he was being treated like a prince consort to a queen as Phoebe's companion, while those two distinguished senior officers were forced to idle in the entryway, pretending with the patience of Job that they weren't famished. Or humiliated. Or almost reduced to groveling or bribery to gain a table, and a meal.

Captain Nelson raised a hand to his right brow, of a sudden, and winced as if in mortal agony, pressing his palm to his eye like he was trapping a persistent Corsican fly. Capt. Thomas Fremantle left off scowling at one and all to turn to him, solicitously. And Alan could almost read their lips, as they debated whether to stay or to go.

"Zose officiers, Alain," Phoebe said as their first wine arrived, a fruity, sparkling blush-pink strawberry something. "Zay are you' *compatriotes*, *oui*? Ze poor man, 'e ees suffer ze *mal de tête*, per'aps? We should let zem join us. Eef you are willing."

"Of course," Alan responded quickly. "This heat, and all. Why, he must be wilting. And, they'll starve to death, else."

Phoebe summoned a waiter who bowed to hear her whispered command, then quickly dashed off to invite the two officers to join them.

"Grateful," Fremantle explained as they shuffled their seats so Nelson didn't have to face the sunset glare off the bay. "Awf'lly. An hellish crowd, hey? Settle for a bread stick . . ."

"Captain Horatio Nelson, Captain Thomas Fremantle, allow me to name to you . . ." Alan began, grinning impishly as he continued in the spirit of the evening, and the sentiments of the town, ". . . la Contessa . . . Mademoiselle Phoebe Aretino? Contessa . . ." He gave her a quick conspiratorial wink, "Captain Horatio Nelson of the *Agamemnon*, and Captain Thomas Fremantle, of the *Inconstant* frigate."

"*Messieurs, enchanté*," Phoebe replied, with another slight incline of her head, as if speaking from a throne to acknowledge lesser barons. Where'd she learn all *this*, so damn' fast? Lewrie wondered to himself. "You appear-ed so, uhm . . . 'ow you say, indispose, *Capitaine* Nelson? Ooh la, I trus' you are well, m'sieur."

"My infinite gratitude for your most gracious invitation, mademoiselle," Nelson rejoined, trying to be sociable even as he seemed to suffer another tiny spasm. "A trifling wound I received the other day."

"Trifling," Fremantle countered with a snort. "Ha."

"Weeks ago," Nelson discounted with a dismissive wave as their waiters returned with more wine, and actual written menus. "Middle of July, actually. I must say . . . this, uhm, *ristorante* is so certain of their supplies they can print their fare, 'stead of chalking it up by the day? Incredible."

"Ah, *oui, m'sieur Capitaine* Nelson," Phoebe answered gaily, and, Lewrie suspected, one of those on the island who had a hand in assuring those regular supplies; what *didn't* she have her hand in by now! he wondered. "You will fin' ze fare ees limit . . . limit-ed? Local *ordinaire*, on'y, *n'est-ce pas, mais* . . . you will fin' eet consistent. An' all ver' tasty. Corsican cuisine."

Odd, Lewrie thought; I'd have thought Nelson was the sort to play up a tale of honorable wounds. Seen him posture and prose before, now, ain't I? To Alan's lights, though, Nelson didn't look particularly cut up. No limp, no bandages . . . a bruise or two, some scabbed-over cuts on his face. Must *have* been too trifling, he concluded; else we'd be sitting deathwatch by his bed, to watch the hero pass over.

"Pardon me for discussing 'shop in the mess,' as it were, sir," Lewrie said, "but I must own that my curiosity has the best of me . . . you both have been up at the siege-work. 'Tis rumored the French are almost ready to give in. I was wondering if there was any truth to it."

"Pray God that will be so, Commander Lewrie," Nelson said, with some heat. And with what almost sounded like a croak of uncharacteristic gloom. "Aye, soon. They simply must, do you see! They're short of almost everything, by now. Save powder and shot. As I learned to my cost," he added, with a faint, deprecatory grin. "Our parallels have been advanced nigh to musket shot of their walls, and our batteries are dominant over their artillery, at last. General Stuart is confident of their surrender within the week. Failing that, an attempt against them might, well . . . a final assault might have to wait, for a time."

"Horrid sickness," Fremantle supplied as Nelson faltered, like a watch spring run down. "We've, what . . . barely two thousand men now? And half of them down, half the time. Bouillabaisse, hmm? Some sort o' fish chowder?" Fremantle wondered, after pondering the menu. "Oysters . . . they might be in it, d'ye think? Like an English meal, back home?"

"Aye, sir. More a brothy fish stew, but *some* oysters," Lewrie informed his superior, hiding his smirk at how provincial most English gentlemen were away from home, how wary they were of unfamiliar dishes. And how un-English he sometimes felt, to delight in the exotic and new.

"Might I offer a toast, sirs." Lewrie grinned, raising his wine. "To our foes, the French, sirs. May they be similarly afflicted. And confused."

"Confusion to our foes," Nelson and Fremantle rejoined, tossing back their sweet, sparkling wine, and echoing the ancient words of the mess or wardroom response to such a toast.

"Frightful campaign weather," Nelson admitted as the waiters topped them up. "Worse than any ever I did see, even in Nicaragua in the last war, for heat, and disease. Bad as the Indies, I must allow!"

"Een Corsica," Phoebe informed him, "we name zis season ze Lion Sun, *Capitaine* Nelson. 'Ow you say, uhm . . ."

"Dog days?" Fremantle offered.

"*Oui, merci, Capitaine* Fremantle. Dog Days . . . Lion Sun, *aussi*," Phoebe went on. "July to October. Ze 'eat, an ze damp! Zis time of year, mos' people stay indoor, an nap s'rough ze wors' of ze day. An' many sick. Many leave us, even so, *quel dommage*. I marvel, zat you' Eenglish soldier, you fight in zis weather. Non wait for cool time."

"As you pointed out, Mademoiselle Aretino," Nelson said, with unconscious pride. "We're English. English *seamen*!"

"Fight in any weather, hey?" Fremantle commented.

"Though 'tis true, mademoiselle," Nelson sobered. "Many leave us. Dear Lord, so many leave us. Why . . . !"

A spasm of grief perhaps, another tic of pain in his brows that quieted him for a moment, but Nelson's voice broke, and he was forced to massage his right temple and brow, as if to knead away whatever agony ailed him with those long, slim, delicate fingers that seemed so out of place on such a wee little fellow, so fond of hard-handed war.

"Oh, do forgive me for . . . for being a killjoy." Nelson frowned after he'd mastered himself. "For even broaching the subject, but . . . Fremantle and I just came from the local churchyard. A fellow officer, Commander Lewrie. You understand, I'm certain?"

"My condolences for your loss, sir," Lewrie gravely offered.

"A most gallant young man, sir," Nelson all but croaked. "One who'd have made a name for himself that would have been on everyone's lips, had he not . . . hmm. Lt. James Moutray, 'board *Victory*. A fine young fellow. Was to have been promoted, soon. His father, Captain Moutray and his mother . . . we were great friends, when I had *Boreas* at Antigua, 'tween the wars. He was Navy Commissioner at English Harbour, d'ye see. And I knew James, from a child. Just a wee lad, back then. It's as if I'd lost my own son, had I . . . as sorrowful a thing as if Fanny and I had lost our dear Josiah."

Fremantle made a tiny face, rolled his eyes in dubious humor, which expression of contempt Lewrie caught.

"Knew you were married, sir," Lewrie prompted, to pique his further curiosity. "But I didn't know you were a parent, as well. Might I offer you congratulations. Some cheer, that he's safe abed in England at this moment."

"Uhm . . ." Nelson was forced to confess, pulling at his long, thin nose. "Stepson, actually. My dearest Fanny and I met on Nevis, while I was in *Boreas*, as well. She'd been widowed, and . . . no, Josiah is with me, Lewrie. In *Agamemnon*. Brought him aboard as a midshipman. To keep a weather eye on his progress, hmm? To assure myself that there will be a successor in the Navy. Why, as I recall, Lewrie, you've sons of your own." Nelson brightened, of a sudden, as mercurial in his grief as he was in his enthusiasms. "Perhaps 'twas Lady Emma Hamilton, in Naples, who spoke of you, when I represented Admiral Lord Hood with King Ferdinand. I'm sure she was the one told me."

"Mmm, well, sir . . ." Lewrie almost winced. Phoebe turned a cool and amused gaze upon him. Though she already knew his marital status, and that he was a father, and didn't *seem* to mind . . . "My eldest, Sewallis, I rather doubt. Now, Hugh, the second son, o' course . . . had to fetch him down from the mizzen stays, just before we left Portsmouth."

"Ees devotion to ees family amaze me, *Capitaine* Nelson." Phoebe chuckled. The other shoe dropped, at last, and Nelson almost flushed as he realized their relationship. Phoebe also took pains to tap the side of her shoe against Lewrie's, under the table, and reward him in public with a cocked eyebrow and tiny smile, hiding her impish teasing for later, in private.

"Mmm, well . . ." Nelson summed up.

"At least the Moutrays may have some comfort, sir," Alan went on, trying to change the subject, and wiggle his way free. "That their son Lieutenant Moutray passed over in an honorable cause, fighting his King's foes."

"Ah, you see, though, Lewrie," Nelson said with a bitter sigh. "God knows why they allowed it, but . . . he was their *only* son and heir. And it wasn't honorable battle, no. 'Twas a fever, so please you! A bloody fever took him, just as . . . a horrid waste of talent, of promise."

Can I dig the grave any deeper, hey? Lewrie asked himself, feeling an urge to look heavenward, where, he was mortal-certain, God was having Himself a knee-slapping good time at Lewrie's expense.

" 'Absent Friends,' " Fremantle harrumphed, raising his glass in toast to bridge the embarrassment of the moment. Embarrassments, rather.

"Wrong day for it, but . . ." Fremantle shrugged. *Absent Friends* was the Sunday toast in the wardroom aboard a King's ship. Lewrie was of a mind, though, to believe that the morrow's—Thursday's—might be more apt; the one Lieutenant Moutray's fellows were probably most callously making at that very moment, now a rival for promotion or command had passed from their midst—*A Bloody War, or a Sickly Season.*

Thankfully, Alan was spared any further chances to embarrass himself by the arrival of their food. Bouillabaisse, aswim with clams and crabmeat, with mussels and a few puny oysters that might please Fremantle, and a host of tiny pink bits of cut-up shrimp peeking coyly from the rosy broth, "decks awash." A fresh wine course, the hard Mediterranean bread sticks, then an appetizer of golden-fried crab cakes, with a remoulade of horseradish, garlic, and a dash of olive oil. Lewrie tucked in, savoring every morsel, though Fremantle and Nelson seemed a bit put off. Nelson ate as if being merely polite. Fremantle muttered, scowled, and inspected every bite, as chary as a customer in some twopenny ordinary who knew a fellow who'd died after eating there. He almost sniffed each new arrival, casting his eyes about as if looking for a hound to try each dish out on first.

He'd have a rough go of it, Alan thought. The *carte de menu* had no roast beef, no smoking joint of mutton to offer. The choices were mostly fish, wild fowl, pigeon, or chicken, eked out from paltriness of portion with rice, pastas, and tomato gravies. Like the goat ragout he had ordered, at Phoebe's insistence, the arrival of which he was awaiting with a great deal of almost lustful anticipation. And some manner of glee. Just to see the look on Fremantle's phyz when he declared what it was he was eating!

Small pheasants or grouse appeared, and with them, a new course of wine. Squab, most like, Alan thought; how many Corsicans had powder or shot with which to hunt, these days. Squab, on a thin bed of rice, colorful with steamed vegetables and a brown sauce.

One of the waiters came to Nelson's right side to fetch off his near-empty glass of rhenish, and replace it with a fresh stem of some red wine. Just as Nelson reached for it, to drain the last of it down to "heeltaps." Their hands collided, the glass turned over, and went smash on the tiled floor.

"Frightfully sorry, tell him," Nelson snapped, now it was his turn to burn with embarrassment. Once more, he massaged his right brow as if to knead a devil out. And wince with more than mortification.

"Just have 'em come under your lee from larboard, from now on," Fremantle attempted to jape. "There's your answer, Nelson."

"Perhaps that *would* be best, Fremantle," Nelson responded, essaying a matching light tone of voice. "My sight, do you see . . . still a bit impaired, sir . . . mademoiselle. Frogs smashed three guns complete to flinders while I was in the battery. Rock, sand . . . splinter of something. I had the misfortune to be within feet of a shell that burst. A temporary affliction, I do trust, yet . . . 'tis hard for me to discern much more than light from dark with this poor eye. Could not spot the fellow to my starboard side."

"Pray God that *will* be temporary, sir," Lewrie said. Should he lose his sight, Alan thought, surely he'd stand a good chance of being "beached," and lose his ship. No wonder he'd not made much heroic ado 'pon it! "Least said, soonest mended," went the old adage. The least-mentioned a commission-ending, career-ending wound, perhaps the soonest forgotten by their superiors!

"Surely, you saw someone . . . ?" Lewrie wondered aloud.

"Oh, of course," Nelson assured him warmly, turning nigh jovial to disguise those very fears, "Doctor Harness, a physician . . . a surgeon Mister Jefferson. Certified me today, as a matter of fact. 'Sawbones' and 'potion pushers,' I tell you. 'Eye of newt and toe of frog,' that's about all they're good for . . . all their kind prescribe. I'm down to see Chambers, surgeon to forces in the entire Mediterranean, in a few days. I am most confident my veil will be lifted, as it were, and full vision restored, by then, or shortly after. A few days' rest . . ."

Lewrie kept an enigmatic expression on his face, though he peered closely at that offending eye. No reason he could see to follow the biblical injunction, to "pluck it out." Yet, it did not seem to wax or wane as a normal eye should. Did not follow in conjunction with the dartings of the left orb. And the faint scar that might have been the result of rock or sand, or a tiny splinter . . . Lewrie kept himself from wincing with nutmeg-shrinking horror when he finally noticed that the scar was not on the brow, only . . . but far down onto the right eyelid itself!

Poor little bastard, Lewrie silently cringed! Raised a glass in mute sympathy. To restore his own courage, too, and damp the fear that he'd ever suffer such a mutilation himself.

There was a commotion at the entryway. Some shouting in the road, and the scruffing of urgent feet. Calvi, blah blah blah . . . ! Louder in

Italian, inside the door. *I Francesi*! Calvi! Waiters translating for a party
of British infantry officers on the main floor, and a host of loud hosannas
of triumph from them, once the news had been digested.

I Francesi, esse arrendere Calvi, di mattina!

Applause and cheers arose from everyone in the ristorante, Corsican
or émigré French, Italian, or British. The French would surrender Calvi
in the morning. And British forces had, at last, won an important victory
in the Mediterranean, to expunge last year's shame of Toulon and its
abandonment. And something worthwhile, too; the total ownership of
the strategically valuable island of Corsica!

Nelson appeared weary, yet relieved, and wore a faint, bemused smile.
He applauded briefly, but remained seated. Fremantle, though, rose to
cheer cock-a-whoop, abandoning even those half-mute essays of his at
complete sentences to howl and cheer, not even trying to form recogniz-
able words for a minute. Until recalling that English gentlemen weren't
supposed to be seen enthusing, and sat back down, abashed.

Thank Bloody Christ, Alan thought, getting to his own feet, and dancing Phoebe about, using the joy of the moment to embrace her in a most
un-English expression of joy. The fleet'll be fully manned again, he speculated; all those seamen and Marines back aboard from the siege. We'll
put to sea again, and fight the Frogs proper, at sea! Sail into Golfe Jouan
or Gorjean Bay, whatever they call it, and shoot the Frog fleet to kindling, if they won't come out to fight! And get the damn' war over in
another three months or so! Austrians, Piedmont, Genoese all ready to
march west, into France, and them without ships to serve their troops,
protect their seaward flank . . . why, we'll chop them to Hindu chutney
sauce!

And prizes, he further speculated! With few warships left, the French
coasting trade would lay wide open and unprotected to his guns. In
another three months, *Jester* could reap a bountiful harvest. Then he
could go home the hero, wearing the laurel wreath corona. A *gilded*
laurel-wreath hero's crown, he crowed to himself! With enough money to
buy his rented land from damnable old uncle Phineas Chiswick, buy even
more acres, have that London town house, at last, into the bargain . . . !

And see Caroline and the children. Enchanting mistress or no, he'd
been on the beach too long before, those four years between commissions, and where his heart lay, and where his lust romped, were two
different places entirely. Only one letter had come from Anglesgreen, so
far, in reply to the half dozen he'd sent off.

Aye, get this over with quickly, he mused, as he resat Phoebe at their table; she's a fetchin' little mort, but she'll land on her feet, when I'm gone.

"You gentlemen will permit me?" Alan asked them. "In the spirit of the news, I think a brace of champagne might be in order."

Spumante was the best the house could boast; overly sweet, for most tastes, a bit on the cloudy side. But sparkling and spritely on the tongue, frothy with pearly bubbles as they charged their glasses.

"Sirs . . . mademoiselle contessa . . ." Lewrie posed to them. "A toast. To a complete and convincing victory over our enemies. And an even greater one, *at sea*, soon to follow."

"Here, here!" they all agreed.

Book IV

Haec deus in melius crudelia somnia vertat
et iubeat tepidos inrita ferra Notos.

May a god turn this cruel dream to good, or bid the
hot South Wind carry it away without fulfillment.

> Book III, "Lygdamus's Dream"
> 95–96
> Albius Tibullus

CHAPTER

1

"It's working," Lieutenant Knolles exclaimed, with the sound of true wonder in his voice. "It is actually working."

"Well, o' course, it is, sir," Mister Buchanon chided his earlier skepticism. "Th' cap'um knows a thing'r two."

Lee guns run out in-battery, though aimed at nothing; weather artillery run into loading position, and *Jester* forced to sail over on her shoulder, canting her deck as if she were beating close-hauled instead of sailing with the scant wind large on her larboard quarters.

It was a thing old Lieutenant Lilycrop of the *Shrike* brig had taught his first lieutenant during the tail end of the American War, and it might not avail aboard a larger ship of the line—to heel a shallow draughted brig-sloop or ship-sloop in very light airs, reducing drag created by her hull, by reducing the total area of her quick-work, which was immersed.

And it was working, for *Jester* was slowly forging ahead of the main line of battle, on the lee side where frigates and lighter ships belonged of course, to catch up with *Agamemnon* and *Cumberland*, which were almost up to gun range of the fleeing French. Four-and-a-half knots, at best; but that was at least a knot-and-a-half quicker than anyone else at the moment, as the fickle weather of the Ligurian Sea in midsummer played its usual coy games.

"Deck, there!" came Rushing's call from the foremast. "Cape Sepet, two points off th' weather bows!"

"Never catch 'em up," Lewrie glumly predicted. "God, what an opportunity wasted. Again!"

"Cape Garonne, two points off th' lee bows!" Rushing further informed them. "Signals Cross is a'workin' on Sepet!"

"Four bloody days, all the way to Toulon, and . . . damn 'em!"

The van squadron of the French Mediterranean fleet, now a much reinforced assemblage after ships from the Biscay ports had slipped in past the weak guard at Gibraltar as soon as milder spring weather had freed them, would be almost abeam of the Croix de Signeaux atop Cape Sepet. The wind—what wind there was—was coming more southerly, directly into the Bay of Toulon. Before noon, the main body, perhaps the lead ships of the rear squadron, would be inside the two horns of the bay's wide entrance, able to shelter under the heavy artillery of Toulon's many formidable fortresses.

"Signal from *Brittania*, sir!" Midshipman Hyde shouted. "And, from the repeating frigates. 'Discontinue the Action,' sir!"

Lewrie turned aft to watch every ship of the line hoist replies, to watch every frigate on the disengaged lee side hoist the blue-and-yellow checker. "Mister Hyde, hoist the repeat," Lewrie ordered with a sour grimace. "So *everyone* knows we're useless. *Damn* him!"

On *Agamemnon*, of course, there flew the "Query." Trust Nelson to dare to challenge Vice Admiral Hotham's decision. No "Respectfully Submit . . . ," this time, as there had been after the last fiasco. Then, Nelson had gone aboard *Brittania* to plead that the two French 74's he had taken—*Ça Ira* and *Censeur*—be left astern under guard of some frigates, and the pursuit continued. Admiral Comte Martin didn't have the stomach for a real fight; he'd continue to run in rough disorder, and his trailing ships could be overhauled and battered into surrender in penny packets. But no, Hotham had demurred. And even days after, Nelson had been pinch-mouthed and pale with anger when he'd repeated Hotham's words to Lewrie. "No, we've taken two. We've really done very well, Nelson. We must be content."

Those two taken, but *Illustrious* had been mauled after she had come up to aid *Agamemnon* and the lead frigates. She'd been taken in tow by the *Meleager* frigate, but blown onto a rocky shoal off Avenca on the Genoese coast, and lost. HMS *Berwick* captured alone, too. Tit for tat.

And today . . . one French ship of the line shot to rags, set on fire, and her colors struck to *Agamemnon* and her tiny squadron. But she'd blown up before she could be taken as prize. And Admiral Hotham was most like content . . . again! . . with the results! One for nought. Tit for tat. What a bargain, Alan thought; why, by the turn of the century, we'll surely've whittled 'em down to a manageable number!

"He's a glass on me, sir," Hyde carped, referring to the signals mid-shipman aboard *Agamemnon*, not half a nautical mile ahead, and to their right. "Surely, he sees our repeat signal."

"I'd imagine his captain is trying to digest it first, Mister Hyde," Lewrie snarled. "Farts! A brace of farts, the pair of them! Their Martin . . . *and* our Hotham. Goddamned rabbit-hearted . . . dismal, cowering farts stagg'rin' about in a bloody . . . fucking . . . *trance!*"

There, at last; *Agamemnon* hauled down her "Query," and hoisted the proper repeater reply. *Cumberland* answered a moment later, along with Fremantle's *Inconstant*, Captain Cockburn's *Meleager*, and the rest of Captain Nelson's small detached squadron, which had ended up far in the lead of the battle line, as usual.

"Mister Knolles, secure the hands from quarters," Lewrie said. "Run out the larboard battery and bowse up to the bulwarks. Same with the starboard battery. Get her flat on her keel again, and ready to comply with any alteration of course *Agamemnon* directs."

"Aye, sir," Knolles grunted in disappointment. "Uhm, I s'pose sir . . ."

"Aye, Mister Knolles?" Lewrie snapped.

"Well, sir. At least we chased 'em back to their kennel. That must be worth something. Kept 'em from escorting a grain convoy from North Africa." Knolles posed with a wistful hopefulness.

To which his captain replied with a dismissive, "Shit!"

"Well, sir . . ." Knolles shrugged.

"Martin came straight for us, chased us a day and a night from nigh to Genoa back to San Fiorenzo, Mister Knolles," Lewrie commented. "As close to looking for an engagement as *that* mouse will ever get . . . while the grain convoy most like went sou'west, near the Balearics so we'd be feinted away from any hope of intercepting it. Four damn' days we've been playing tail chase, far off to the north and east. I'll lay you any odds you like they're loaded by now, and heading home. And I'll lay you even *better* odds our Admiral Hotham will trundle back to Corsica, as pleased as a pig in shit, and never think to detach scouting frigates to look for 'em, till they're back in Marseilles. We've been buggered, in short. Again. Now, attend to my orders, sir. I've no time . . . nor any reason . . . to discuss tactics or strategy. Not when our commanding admiral is so bereft of understanding either."

"Aye aye, sir," Knolles almost wilted under the unaccustomed heat of Lewrie's bile. He was not usually the target for his captain's wrath.

Philosophically, he realized though, that anyone would suffice for the moment, and that it wasn't in any way personal. Or permanent.

"He's having one of his days," Knolles said to Bosun's Mate Cony a few minutes later, once the guns had been secured; powder bags and shot drawn, flint-lock strikers removed, touch-holes and vents covered, and tampions inserted in the barrels. "Poor bugger."

"Ya might say that, Mister Knolles, sir," Cony allowed, looking aft at the moody, impatiently pacing captain, all hunched over like some plow-ox brooding on remembered goads. "But, he's had a power o' worry t'fret on, 'side's how we look t'be losin' this 'ere war, so far, sir. But th' latest news from home'z better. An', he's the sunny sort. I 'spect he's weathered th' worst. Sing small fr a few more days, Mister Knolles. Till we're t'Genoa proper, an' he'll be himself, again. But right now, he don't need no more frustin'."

"Point taken, Mister Cony," Knolles grinned shyly. "No more of our petty, uuhm . . . frustrations?" he suggested diplomatically.

"Now 'at's th' very word I wuz lookin' for, sir. Th' very word."

Got to stop taking things out on the people, Lewrie chided himself, massaging his temples, and the bridge of his nose, as if trying to scrub himself into a better humor.

But it had been a horrible winter, a miserable spring, and looked to be a dismal and frustrating summer, this fine new year of 1795. Both professionally—saddled with an inept, sluggard of a shit-brain fool as commander of the fleet—and lately, personally, as well. In fact, for a time it had been a terrifying time; though that was somewhat eased by his brother-in-law's last letters.

For perhaps the hundredth time, he wished he'd never made that bold, smug toast to Nelson and Fremantle. How hollow that wish for victory seemed now, how rashly he'd tempted fickle Fate.

With Corsica theirs, and Lord Hood worn down to a nubbin by the pressures of command, he'd struck his flag the previous September, just after Calvi surrendered, and had sailed for home in his flagship, HMS *Victory*. And had taken victory, or any hopes of one, with her. Hood had promised intentions of returning, refreshed, sometime in the new year, but "Black Dick" Howe had kept his promise to retire, and Hood had been retained as senior admiral in London, ashore. Vice Admiral Hotham had taken over the Mediterranean fleet, after Sir Hyde Parker had stood in for the interim.

Parker was cautious and conservative, to be sure, but competent.

Hotham, now, well . . . cautious was about as much as anyone might allow. Dull, dithering, slow as molasses, unable to commit, or make a decision. His favorite color was rumored to be "plaid." But he was so senior he couldn't be passed over, too healthy to ship home as unfit. And had far too much patronage to be trifled with even by Lord Hood, the Board of Admiralty, or the Prime Minister, Pitt.

Perhaps Hood was too exhausted to care, Lewrie brooded in foul humor; though the signs had been evident long before. While *Jester* was fitting out at Gibraltar to go home in the early spring of '94, Hotham had been at sea near Toulon. He'd loped back to Corsica just as soon as the French put out, to join up with Hood, though he'd been an equal match for Admiral Comte Martin's fleet, and could have won himself an epic victory, if he'd even lifted one finger to try. French seamanship was abysmal back then, the jumped-up *matelots* from the lower decks who'd commanded hadn't the first clue, and it could have been a proper massacre! But for Hotham's caution. By the time Hood sailed from San Fiorenzo, Martin had staggered into Golfe Jouan, and got himself blockaded for seven months . . . as out of the game as a legless pensioner at Greenwich Naval Hospital.

With Hood's departure, though . . . it was like taking tea water off the boil, and setting it out on a windowsill without pouring into the pot. Their "brew" had gone tepid, unleaved; then positively cold.

The winter gales had set in around November, and Hotham had so reduced poor Rear Admiral Goodall's blockading squadron that once he'd been blown off-station, Martin had been free to nip along the coast to Toulon and refit toward the end of the month.

Then, like locking the stable door after the horses had bolted, Hotham had assigned the *proper* number of frigates and lesser warships to watch Marseilles, Toulon, Hyeres Bay, and Gourjean Bay, when no one but an utter drooling idiot in Bedlam would have *thought* of sailing.

And *Jester* had been one of those lesser ships, one of the very unlucky, and had spent up to twelve days at a stretch, at times, heaving and bobbing like a wine cork under storm trys'ls, or heaved-to and bare-poled, trusting to sea-anchor drogues to keep her bows-on to wind and sea so she wouldn't broach or capsize. And a very merry Christmas season that had been!

Then in the spring of '95, once the weather had cleared, Martin had come out, much better armed, refitted, and trained, as well as reinforced.

Probably threatened from Paris with the guillotine, he had at least *pretended* to try to retake Corsica. He'd left his 18,000 men and transports at Toulon, thinking he had to clear the seas of the Royal Navy, first. And where was Hotham and the fleet? At San Fiorenzo Bay, where they could guard Corsica? Good Christ, no, he'd taken them over to Leghorn on the Tuscan coast, no matter that the Mediterranean was so full of spies and informers you could purchase two with dinner. Surely Hotham had been told, hadn't he? Had an inkling? And if the line-of-battle ships had needed refits, then why hadn't he fetched the supplies to Corsica, rather than sailing over to them?

"So everyone could come down with the pox," Lewrie muttered in acidic jest. Leghorn was a hotbed, a paradise, of vice and venery—and hip-deep in diseased whores of every persuasion, something for just about anyone's purse, or taste. San Fiorenzo by comparison was almost stuffy and Calvinist, and dull as Scotland on a Sunday.

And what better way to erode the efficiency of his ships, than to expose officers and men to the debilitating effects of the pox and the Mercury Cure.

God, even Nelson and Fremantle had succumbed! Fremantle had met some Greek doxy through old John Udney, the British Consul. Another of the Prize Agent, Prize Court set, and Lewrie strongly suspected he also lined his purse as a pimp to the visiting squirearchy. Nelson took up with one Adelaide Correglia. No raving beauty, that; no sylphlike armful! The night Lewrie had dined aboard *Agamemnon* at anchor, that doxy—who'd moved into the great-cabins with Nelson, for God's sake!—had trotted out to table in little more than a sheer nightgown and dressing robe. So tight bodices or corsets wouldn't aggravate the abscess in her side she temporarily suffered, so please you! Prating, silly, and inane, twittering and tittering—and that went for the pair of them.

Why, the man'd made a perfect *ass* of himself over the mort, all but cutting her meat for her, and feeding her forkfuls, all but wiping her chin, and toasting her so lovey-dovey every five minutes it'd damn' near made him spew. And, as Fremantle had put it on their way back to their gigs, "makes himself ridiculous with that woman. Damned bad supper, to boot!"

No, Hotham had been just as bedazzled, and as buggered, as any of his officers, and when word finally came, he'd scrambled to sortie, with only thirteen of the line. Well, fourteen, if one could count a Neapolitan 3rd Rate-74 as seaworthy, or battle-ready.

* * *

THAT FIRST SET-TO in March had been in weather as scant, and a wind as light, as today's. Three days pussy-footing about—*farting* about!—and unable to close each other. And, even with twenty-two sail of the line, Martin had proved to be just as timorous as Hotham. And just about as benighted, with no eagerness to do much of anything.

While the rest of the fleet had almost posed for paintings atop a mirror-smooth sea, Nelson in *Agamemnon*, thankfully without Adelaide Correglia, had forged ahead, dragging Fremantle's *Inconstant*, Cockburn's *Meleager* frigate, and a few more with him to harry the tail end of the French, who had been content to run for home and Mother, with their tails tucked between their legs. *Jester* had been right up with them, and for a time, it had seemed as if that epic sea battle would occur.

Two French 74's shot to lace, *Ça Ira* and *Censeur*, after Nelson fought them for two-and-a-half hours of close cannonading. Over 100 men killed or wounded aboard *Ça Ira* alone, as opposed to only seven wounded aboard *Agamemnon*!

Which shows what a proper-drilled ship can do, Lewrie thought; and what a barking shambles a bad'un can be.

But what could have been accomplished if Hotham hadn't broken off that action, too? Hadn't said ". . . we must be content, we've done pretty well."

THEN, AFTER "SAVING" Corsica, Hotham had scattered his frigates and such to the four winds on patrol duties and ineffective blockades, trundling his "liners" back to Leghorn. Perhaps Mister Udney had a doxy lined up for *him*?

Jester had at least scooped up two more prizes from that spell of duty, though they'd not seen a penny of the prize money for them yet, either. One of them, a supposedly neutral Danish merchant brig, was still anchored at San Fiorenzo, while the Prize Court nattered as to whether her papers were colorable or not, even though she'd been crammed to her deck heads with warlike material.

Another bad comparison between Hood and Hotham; at least under Hood, the Prize Court had been a *tad* less venal and corrupt. Less so than what anyone familiar with a court's doings could expect. Hotham in charge, though . . .

No, not in *charge*, Lewrie sneered; just bloody *here*, but never in charge, even of his own bowel movements!

Now, TODAY'S MUDDLED fiasco. Again, there'd been rumors that Martin was to come out, this time to escort merchant ships to North Africa to pick up corn so the south of France wouldn't starve, or riot, when their own crops failed for two summers in a row. The piratical Barbary States had grain aplenty, and were more friendly with France than anyone else they pirated.

Yet what had Hotham done with that information? Go look for a convoy? Cover Marseilles and Toulon so tightly that no merchantmen might come out?

No, again! He'd sat as "sulled up" as a bullfrog at San Fiorenzo, conserving what little energy he was still thought to possess, and had detached Nelson with a squadron of the *very* sort of ships that should have been prowling the seas in search of the French convoy, or their fleet; not west to interdict—but east, to Genoa! To buck up the Austrians, who didn't have a navy to play with, and were loath to advance one foot west of Genoa without a guard on their seaward flank.

Nelson in *Agamemnon*, clinging to his half-worn-out 64-gunner like she was a lucky talisman, even though he'd been offered command of newer, larger ships time and again. Fremantle's *Inconstant* and a fine 32-gun frigate the *Southampton*, Cockburn's *Meleager*, two brigs of war, *Tarleton* and *Tartar*, the frigate *Ariadne, Jester*, and a small 14-gun brig-sloop, HMS *Speedy*, and the humble cutter *Resolution*.

How satisfying it had been, six days earlier, to set sail for Genoa and Vado Bay, under a commander who could at least be trusted to charge into battle. And to get away from Admiral Hotham.

Naturally, it'd turned into a farce. Not a day out, they'd run into Admiral Martin's entire fleet, twenty-three sail of the line, and supporting frigates, stooging about northeast of Corsica! They'd spent a day and a night being chased themselves this time, turning to combine against any French frigates that got too near, then spinning away when the odds became too daunting. Chased all the way back to San Fiorenzo, and Hotham's "aid."

Seven hours it had taken him to rescue them, to recall his shore parties and libertymen, to weigh anchor and lumber out on a poor wind to their rescue. Seven hours of damned fine seamanship to stand off-and-on San

Fiorenzo Bay and not be crushed like bugs by the weight of the approaching French line-of-battle ships before Hotham could save them!

AND THEN HAD come these last four days of slack-weather pursuit, to end
up off Toulon, letting Martin get away again. Toothless hounds too feeble
to bark; chasing each other back and forth without even a nip on the
hindquarters to show for it, as if making a show for the young dogs in the
neighborhood; that they still knew how to beat the hounds. Even if
neither one couldn't have cared less if they'd actually caught the other.
Or remembered what it was a dog really did with a rival dog.

"Piss on the gatepost," Alan snickered with dismal amusement, "and
toddle off with yer tail high."

"Sir?" Midshipman Spendlove inquired, close at hand.

"Just maundering, Mister Spendlove. Pay me no mind," Alan said,
blushing to have been overheard, and glowering hellish-black.

"Aye aye, sir," Spendlove replied meekly, scuttling away from his captain's possible wrath.

AS IF SERVING under Hotham were not plague enough, as if a pagan god
had decided to muck about with his life of a sudden, everything he held
dear seemed to be tumbling down like a house of cards.

Prize Court, Phoebe . . . *Caroline!*

He shook himself and shrugged deeper into his coat, turned his face to
the dubious freshness of the wind to blank his thoughts of how near he'd
come to being a widower.

After Calvi had surrendered, as if a floodgate had been opened, letters
from home had begun to arrive on an almost monthly schedule to keep
him informed of hearth and family. Caroline was a highly intelligent
woman, witty and expressive, and her many letters well-crafted and filled
with newsy, chatty gossip, local lore, the farm's doings, what his children
had got up to. And how much she loved him.

All of which had made him squirm, but only a little, with shame of his
betrayal. Yet it was a socially acceptable betrayal, was it not? Most English gentlemen of his stripe married more for connections or land than
love, in the beginning. One had to be careful; it took a rich man's purse
to attain a Bill of Divorcement from some unsuitable mort, so they
weighed their options, and the girl, and the material benefits she could
bring to the marriage, with care. Beauty was valued, as was a pleasant

and agreeable demeanor. Mean t'say, if one were stuck forever-
more . . . !

But once at least one male heir was assured of living to adulthood—
two or three was much better—it was expected by both parties in the
better sort of Society that the man would keep a mistress for his pleasure,
sparing his wife the perils of further childbirth. They might be civil,
sociable, and agreeable to each other, still. But it was understood, and
tacitly accepted; as long as one had discretion. Many wives even wel-
comed such an arrangement, and felt a sense of relief. Some few men
with the purse, and the *ton*, for it, kept more than one mistress. A man
had his needs, after all! Especially one facing such a lengthy separation,
in time and distance.

But Caroline's letters had stopped arriving toward the end of January.
Gales and storms in the Channel, the Bay of Biscay? A packet ship lost
on-passage, and her latest missive with it? The risk of correspondence
over such a long distance that every Navy man faced, Lewrie could have
thought. Yet there were letters from London that still arrived, letters
from Burgess Chiswick, and his father, in India.

Finally, in April, just after the first indecisive set-to against the French
fleet, a letter had come from his brother-in-law Governor in Anglesgreen. And worry, and longing, coupled with his lingering sense of guilt,
in *spite* of being such a smug hound with purse, needs, and *ton*, had
chilled him to the bone as soon as it was in his hands.

Alan, I most sadly take pen in hand to discover unto you, and most strictly
against my dear Sister Caroline's Wishes, and most rigorous Instructions,
that both she, and your Children, have been on the very verge of Death.

There'd been wave after wave of illness in the parish, beginning sometime after the harvests were in, and continuing into the new year. Flux,
grippe, the influenza and fevers. Many of the elderly and weak, the very
old and very young about Anglesgreen had been taken to their beds, and
a fair number never rose from them, but had joined what the vicar at St.
George's termed The Great Majority.

First to succumb had been little Charlotte, then Hugh, lastly Sewallis,
all within two days and nights. First sniffles, headaches and fevers, followed by incontinent bowels, vomiting, chills and the most heartrend-
ingly wet, racking coughs.

No cordials, no herbal teas or purchased nostrums or folklore reme-
dies had helped, not even warming pans, hot and dry flannels, or hot and

steamy flanneling. The local surgeon-apothecary was an idiot. They'd
sent at last to Guildford for a gentleman-physician educated at Edin-
burgh, whose Jesuit's bark, opium, and antimonies had broken their
fevers, whose bleeding had restored the balance of their humors, and
whose pills and drops had quieted their coughs, and allowed them to
draw breath once more.

Passing quiet, restful nights seemed to restore them wondrous well, though
they were for days afterward listless and languorous, quite febrile and
weak, with but the most delicate digestions or appetites, as you may well
imagine.

Caroline had been too busy to write, Governor further imagined he
might understand; later, worn down and too exhausted by her valiant
struggle to preserve her dear children's very lives. So, at the very instant
that the family could feel relief, and give thanks to a merciful God,
Caroline had also come down with chills and fever, headaches and sniffles, then collapsed over supper, pale as Death itself!

Before she took to her bed, she enjoined us all, dear brother-in-law, that
we were, under the sternest threats, not to communicate to you any of their
travails, so that you, so nobly and honorably in Arduous Service for King
and Country, should have no distracting Worries, no additional Burden
that might affect that Service. I thought it quite daft but demurred, for the
nonce. However, now that . . .

They'd despaired so much of her life, as Caroline suffered very much
more than the children had, that they'd sent to Guildford for the physician once more, and he had all but thrown up his hands, and told them to
expect the worst.

Governor Chiswick was also a skilled writer, much *too* damned skilled!
Like some droning bore who relished describing every agony of his own
surgery for a stone, Governor had gone to wretched, terrifying and overly
excessive details, painting a picture so vivid and ghastly of Caroline's, and
the children's, every moan, of how haggard and bedraggled, how skeletal
her visage had appeared as she'd sunk to the last extremes. How scant
her breath, how thready her pulse . . . !

Christ, if he was here now, I'd strangle him, Lewrie thought in once-
more impotently distanced rage; and quite damn' gladly, too! By God,
he's done me no favors!

Yet, miracle of miracles, and with the unstinting, damned near ferociously tender care of Sophie de Maubeuge, Caroline had rallied . . . she'd lived! The crisis was over, sometime in late February, and since Caroline was well on her way to a full restoration of her health, but still too weak to pen much more than spidery hen-scratches, Governor thought it was time he was told. In morbidly excruciating detail.

AND WHAT THE hell was I doin' in late February, Lewrie sneered to himself, scathing himself again with self-loathing? Why, I was on top of a Corsican whore, dickerin' with criminal prize agents . . . too full o' lust for Mammon . . . an' just plain old lust! . . . t'give family more'n the idle, passin' thought!

When did I get his damned letter? Late April. Just after a night ashore with Phoebe, damn my blood! Feelin' like the Devil's Own Buck-of-the-First-Head, with nothin' on my mind but more quim, and breakfast! Noble, honorable . . . Arduous Service, mine arse!

He felt guilt, a shipload of raging, bellowing Guilt. Not just for his dalliances, for his venal concerns placed ahead of family, but for his smugness, his conceit, his blithe disregard for life's lessons.

How fortunate he'd been so far, and how cocksure he'd breezed through. Battle, wounds . . . that he'd not lost an eye like Nelson, or a limb like Lilycrop; that he'd been exposed to the most hellish fevers in *both* the Indies, China, that he hadn't come down with sepsis or lockjaw fever from a cut in battle, or those two unspeakably daft duels he'd fought in his callow, feckless youth. That it was such a wonder he'd lived *this* long was some assurance that he always would!

Or that those close to him would be just as fortunate, and that he could pay them no mind, dismiss them from his thoughts once he had sailed them under the horizon—and gaily assume that they'd be there at home, unchanged, pristine and untouched, like porcelain gewgaws he might collect, like marionettes stashed in a glass-front cabinet until the next performance. Which would occur whenever it suited *his* lights!

Sobering, to think he could have lost them all. Wife, children, heir, love, and joy . . . shameful and sobering, to consider what he'd been up to while all this near-horror had happened.

Hadn't he *seen* it? How many couples birthed ten, twelve babes, and ended burying all but two? A man with means, and the best physicians on retainer, might lose two, three wives to child-bed fever before they interred him, as well, at the "ripe old age" of fifty!

✻ ✻ ✻

THAT LETTER, AND the ones that had followed from Governor and his mother-in-law Charlotte, finally a shaky one from his dearest Caroline herself, had brought him relief, but little joy. Perhaps this was what the reverends called an epiphany. Perhaps it had occurred in some ironic conjunction with seeing a stern, tarry-handed fire-eater such as Horatio Nelson spoon and coo over his mort, Adelaide Correglia, making an utter fool of himself, even though he still spoke of his dear Fanny back in Norfolk as some sort of household goddess. Or of seeing the dour, taciturn, and inarticulate Capt. Thomas Fremantle chortle and blush as he tried to play the *gallant* with his Greek doxy at the opera in Leghorn.

How much of a purblind fool do *I* look? he'd wondered. How huge the quim-struck cully have *I* been? Hmm . . .

Whatever. As drenched as a dog doused with a bucket of water to get him off a bitch in season, he'd cooled to Phoebe. Turned surly and short. Made excuses, invented duties that kept him aboard *Jester* until he could hide from her no more.

AND WHAT A muck I made o' *that*, he squirmed, working his mouth on his weakness as the squadron stood on nor'west toward Cape Sepet.

He'd gone to break it off, cut swift and clean. To make amends to Caroline, even if she never learned of it. Pray *God* she never learned of it! But, in explaining himself, and his reasons . . . And it hadn't helped that Phoebe that day had looked so fetching, so damned handsome! Neither had it helped that her huge brown eyes had filled with tears so readily at his sudden, and inexplicable, dismissal and betrayal.

Frankly, their *rencontre* had not been one of his shining moments.

"*PAUVRE HOMME*," SHE'D muttered brokenly, her face crammed into a lace handkerchief, and she'd rushed to throw herself into his arms—to comfort *him*! Crying and clucking, stroking and soothing, as if *he* was the one to worry about!

"Phoebe, I *do* love them all, more than my own life, d'ye see . . ." he'd muttered. "And nearly lost them, so . . . mean t'say . . . this. We . . ."

"But, zey are recover', Alain *mon amour, merci a Dieu!*" Phoebe had shusshed. " 'Ow 'orrid eet mus' 'ave been fo' you. 'Ow thankful you mus' be, *mon coeur*! An' no one, you may tell. But, you tell *me*."

There had been that; what captain could unbend, let his tears flow, show weakness before his inferiors. Oh, he'd had Cony and Cox'n Andrews in, given them the bald facts, with hopes that Maggy Cony, and their infant son might be weathering it. But, how long he'd pondered, fretted, wished to weep, to scream, to beg God to spare 'em . . .

"Surely, you must see, dear Phoebe . . ." he'd stammered. "Mademoiselle Aretino, rather, hahumm!—that this, that our . . ."

"You mus' tell me ev'rysing, dear Alain!" she'd insisted.

So he had. Sitting together on a sofa. Embraced. And his own tears had, at last, come, no matter that he'd held them in control this long, and what was another hour of a sad duty?

Wept on her damn' tits, Lewrie railed at himself! Went to end it, and I ended up toppin' her! Again! Yorktown . . . Toulon . . . there'd been a power of rogerin', the days before the end o' both, 'twixt soldiers an' camp followers. Like tellin' Death t'go bugger himself. Long as we're playin' at life-makin', you can just piss off!

He'd taken his comfort with Phoebe, the comfort and sympathy she had been so eager to offer. And he'd been so grateful to receive. But it had felt so perverse a thing to do, even more worthy of guilt than before, when he'd been unaware, that he'd ended despising her to her face. Which was to say, that he'd despised himself, and had simply found a suitable target.

They'd had a high old row; shouting, cursing, flinging expensive gewgaws at each other. And damn his blood, if they hadn't gone right back to ranti-polin' in the heat of the moment! He'd spent the night. And had awakened even more confused, even more dithering than when he'd climbed the hill-street to her . . . no, "their" house.

The sudden transfer to Nelson's squadron had come as a godsend. If he couldn't make up his own bloody-weak mind, he thought, then the Navy would make it up for him. If he hadn't the "nutmegs" to tell Phoebe off proper, then perhaps time and distance from San Fiorenzo'd do it for him.

GOD, Y'ER SUCH a bloody coward, me lad, Alan told himself; such a weak, venal, spineless . . . but, damme, why's she have to be so sweet about it, so . . . ?

"Still no signal for a change of course, sir," Lieutenant Knolles said at his side. "We're standing in rather close to Cape Sepet, and those batteries."

"Hmm?" Lewrie grunted in alarm, certain his quavery musings had been spoken aloud, in even a tiny mutter or whisper. That just bloody *everyone* knew his business; or soon would.

"Standing on, sir," Knolles repeated, with a quizzical expression. He took off his hat, ran his fingers through his blond hair, and clapped it on again, in a gesture Lewrie had come to know as concern.

"Why, for spite, I s'pose, Mister Knolles," Lewrie allowed, now he was back in the real world. "To trail our coats right to their doorstep. Rub their cowardly noses in it."

"I see, sir." Knolles nodded, with a slight, wolfish grin.

"Though, just what it is we're rubbing their noses *in* is beyond me, at the moment." Lewrie shrugged, damned by his irresolute dithering beyond all glee of his own witticism. Knolles, though, and those on the quarterdeck nearest them, rewarded him with a tiny, appreciative chuckle, even so. As if to mollify the mourner.

The word had surely spread through the ship, as the word always will, in an eye-blink, Lewrie was certain. Since then, the people had been walking on eggshells around him. Though they certainly sympathized with his plight, they couldn't commiserate until he allowed it, till he even mentioned his family. He was approached like a new widower who was barely launched into his period of mourning; cosseted gently, without actually broaching the subject of what he needed cosseting for!

Hellish challenge, Lewrie thought; to be captain of a ship, and thought lucky. Sure, they're wond'rin' . . . if I'm not blessed, if I can have a near-fatal sickness back home, am I suddenly just a run-of-the-mill captain? *Jester* still a lucky ship, or . . .

To their north, the French fleet was entering harbor, just as he had predicted, without even trying to turn and show their fangs. Their van was already inside the bay, only their topmasts showing above the rugged heights of Cape Sepet, and the main body around their flagship brailing up square sails to slow as they entered the Bay of Toulon.

" 'Ere's a sloop o' war, fetched to, sir," Mister Buchanon pointed out to their left. "Just below th' batt'ries at Cape Sepet. One o' 'eir corvettes, like us. 'Bout our size, sir. Twenty—twenty-two guns, I make her."

A most sleek and jaunty corvette she was, too, presenting her larboard profile to them, about two miles off and about an equal distance from the sheltering guns. New, Lewrie thought, noting her yellow pale upperworks, still pristine and virginal under a fresh-from-the-yards first

coat of linseed oils. A black lower chain wale that set off her saucily
curved sheer line, and a broad white gunwale. Though her sails belied
that newness; they were of a more-worn dun than most French ships
sported, from spending more time at sea since her launching.

"Signal, from *Agamemnon*, sir!" Hyde interrupted at last. "The squadron . . ." he read off slowly, "Wear . . . to starboard tack. Course easterly. And, make all sail conformable with the weather, sir."

"For Genoa." Lewrie nodded, suddenly feeling a weight depart his
weary shoulders. Dither enough, and someone else'll make your decision
for you; and have sense enough to be damn' grateful when they do, Alan
almost snickered in relief. "With the Frogs run back to their pond, I trust
we'll have a *much* quieter passage, this time, hey, Mister Knolles?"

"Indeed, sir," Knolles replied, chuckling.

"Very well, Mister Hyde. Hoist the Affirmative. Mister Knolles, pipe
Hands to Stations to Wear Ship."

A glance astern to *Agamemnon*, then past her to Hotham's line of
battle, which had already begun to turn east in rigid line-ahead order; the
lead ship hardening up across what little wind there was, and the one
next astern of her sheeting home and bracing in to turn in her wake, once
the lead ship's stern galleries were midships abeam. Going back to San
Fiorenzo Bay, he supposed, their dubiously performed duties done, for
the time being. And another fine chance for a victory lost.

"Signal's down, sir!" Hyde shouted.

"Wear-ho, Mister Knolles," Lewrie directed moodily. "Put the ship
about to the starboard tack."

There was a thin warlike sound down to leeward that turned his attention north once more, a flat, slamming thud of a gun. That French
corvette had just shot off a lee gun, the traditional challenge to combat!
The misty single bloom of gun smoke rose over her decks, obscured by
her hull and sails.

Would they . . . ? But *Agamemnon* showed no sign that Nelson had
even taken notice; no directions to *Jester*, or another of the powerful
frigates in the squadron to go teach that Frenchman some manners.

"What a lot of gall, I must say, sir!" Knolles all but yelped in spite of
himself, once the ship had her head around.

"That's the French for you, Mister Knolles." Lewrie felt like japing.
"Just like women. Always have to have the last bloody word, d'ye see
. . . in everything. And . . . full to their hairlines with 'Gaul,' don't ye
know." He simpered.

"Oh, merciful God, sir," Midshipman Spendlove groaned at just how bad a jape it was. "Ow!"

"You wouldn't be just the slightest bit French, yourself, would you, Mister Spendlove?" Lewrie snickered, feeling his mood brightening at last, now that *Jester*'s bowsprit pointed to someplace more promising. "Do I detect a touch of 'Gaul' in you, as well, sir?"

"God, no, sir!" Spendlove countered. "That was good old English cheek. The sort allowed midshipmen. A different matter entirely, sir!"

"I stand corrected about your antecedence, young sir," he said with a mock bow. As Lewrie turned away, he missed the wink exchanged between Hyde and Spendlove, the smiles of relief among the crew. The captain had cracked a jest, and a smile, after weeks without. Perhaps the bad times were over. For him, and for them all.

So long, Corsica, Lewrie thought, peering sou'west, though that isle was far under the horizon, a hundred mile or more. So long, my shore house. *And* my damn' rent money! And Phoebe, and my . . . well.

Free of Hotham, free of the fleet, under an energetic commander such as Horatio Nelson, Lewrie was sure there'd be action galore, and the reek of fired guns. Bags of other things to deal with, to think about; so much that he would no longer have a chance to remain venal or weak. A chance for redemption, perhaps?

Daft as a March hare . . . reedy as a willow wand, was Nelson, but Lewrie was coming to like his direct, and enthusiastic aggressiveness. And who'd o' thought it, the first time he'd met him. *Or* the second.

And this time, please God . . . he prayed silently. I promise to keep me member buttoned snug in me breeches; swear on a stack o' Bibles, if you like. Just steer us to action, so I can stay out o' trouble.

Mostly, he amended quickly.

And, he could not help smiling ruefully; there was a phrase he had heard, mostly on the lower deck, the wry wisdom of a frazzled sailor who had bitten off more than he could chew. And, it even rhymed!

> *When in trouble, when in doubt . . .*
> *hoist th' main,*
> *and fuck-off out!*

"Ahum." He coughed into his fist. "Steady as she goes, Mister Brauer. East-sou'east. Thus."

CHAPTER

2

PIPES SQUEALING, MARINE muskets and deck-officers' swords presented in salute, as Commander Lewrie attained the entry port of *Agamemnon*, just after Captain Cockburn. The dance of gigs roundabout to line up in order of seniority had almost seemed laughable; had it not been deadly serious to some of the participants.

"Welcome aboard, sir," an *Agamemnon* Lieutenant greeted Lewrie's safe arrival on the starboard gangways. "Might you join the rest, on the quarterdeck yonder, for just a moment, sir, till . . ."

"Certainly, sir." Alan smiled, looking forward to an opportunity to speak to Fremantle again, that tall, laconic stalwart; and, to become acquainted with the rest of the captains of their squadron, who had so far been faceless names aboard distant ships.

"Captain Fremantle, good morning to you, sir."

"Lewrie . . . hey," Thomas Fremantle replied, never known for the use of five words, when one or two would do. "Keep well?"

"Indeed, sir. And free of our admiral, sure to keep better."

An audible sniff to his right, which turned Lewrie's attention to a very young post-captain, a prim, upright, almost delicately handsome sprog with an eager and earnest expression on his "phyz." Though at first glance, a moment before, that "phyz" had borne the not-quite-with-us-yet blandness and perpetual weak-mouthed pout of someone from the peerage, the sort who felt nigh-overwhelmed but was determined not to show it to lesser mortals. Now, a long vane of a nose, with a pug-tilted tip was lifted high in what appeared to be sudden revulsion.

"Allow me to name myself, sir. Alan Lewrie, the *Jester* sloop." Lewrie beamed with malicious glee to so discomfit such a paragon. "And I believe you are Captain Cockburn, of the *Meleager* frigate?"

Of course, he'd known; all he'd had to do was see from where a captain's gig had come, and observe the rigid order of boarding.

"It's announced *Coe*-burn, sir," the young sprog announced in a testy snap, looking Lewrie up and down like a disbelieving tailor.

"Your servant, Captain Coe-burn," Lewrie offered. "And I stand corrected." Beaming on, as if nothing could deter a sunny smile.

"Really, Commander Lewrie, our admiral . . ." Cockburn's petulant thin-lipped mouth grimaced in disapproval.

"Savior of Corsica, sir," Lewrie asserted quite cheerfully.

"Uhm, yess . . . though you sounded less than supportive of . . ." Cockburn frowned, as if disarmed; or at least confused.

"Spot o' bother at home, we heard, Lewrie?" Fremantle interjected quickly, to defuse the situation. "Better now?"

"Quite, Captain Fremantle," Alan said, allowing his intercessor to lead him away, quite thankfully. "Winter agues. 'Twas a near thing but my wife and children have recovered, sir, and thankee for askin'."

He caught a testy sniff from Cockburn, to his rear. Was he one of those hidebound in the Navy who had no use for a married officer, suspecting them of a lack of zeal and attention to duties?

Damn him, then, Lewrie thought quickly; senior to me or no, he's barely a jot over twenty-one. Already made "post" when most his age are lucky to be commissioned, at all? As much the "boy-captain" as Nelson looked at Turk's Island, I swear. Touch of the brogue or burr to him, no matter how "plumby" he speaks, too. Irish or Scottish? Lewrie wondered to himself. No, definitely a burr—maybe Lowland variety. Fair complected like a Scot. Your daddy a trewed Lowland Scot laird, young Captain *Coe*-burn? No knees for the proper kilt?

As he and Fremantle conversed, he turned a corner of his eye to measure Cockburn; just an inch or so taller than his own five-feet-nine, perhaps no heavier than his own twelve stone. Courtier-slim, elegant in his carriage . . . aware of himself, too.

Lt. George Andrews, *Agamemnon's* first officer, joined them, and Fremantle drifted away. "Bit of a rigid stick, hmm? Cockburn?" Alan inquired softly. "Know much about him, do you, sir?"

"Oh, him sir?" Lieutenant Andrews shrugged. "The usual story, Commander Lewrie. A long schooling, like most of us, carried on ship's books without actually serving, till he was fourteen or so." Andrews smiled. "Went into his first ship in eighty-six . . . passed his board, first try, in ninety-two, I believe. Was aboard *Brittania*, with Hotham, when the war began . . ."

"No wonder he didn't like my scurrilous comments." Lewrie almost winced, beginning to wonder if he'd tromped through the manure again, in his best boots.

"A scurrilous comment 'bout our admiral, sir?" Andrews recoiled in mock horror. "Probably not a jot on what I've already heard, but . . . then into *Victory* under Hood as tenth lieutenant. Then into *Speedy* after a few months. You know the benefits of the flagship's wardroom, and may we all thank God for it, I say. Had *Speedy* for just a little over four months, and did incredibly good service in her, too. Then was jumped to "post" into *Inconstant* when Captain Montgomerie had to ask for relief."

"Mercurial." Lewrie sighed.

"A month in her, then into *Meleager*, Commander Lewrie." Andrews chuckled. "No, I should think mercurial can't *quite* convey how quickly he's rising! A good enough sort, I've gathered. Captain Nelson thinks the world of him. Sober, high-minded, a taut hand . . . though a bit of a stickler. Stiff and stuffy, but . . ." Andrews shrugged again. "Why?"

"Just want to know with whom I'm dealing, Lieutenant Andrews," Lewrie discounted. "After all, we'll be depending on each other . . ."

"Oh, I get your meaning, sir." Andrews brightened. "Haven't a worry in the world with him at your back, sir. When it comes to combat, Captain Cockburn's a perfect Tartar. Doesn't *look* the sort, does he? But then, neither does Captain Nelson, were one to judge solely 'pon a fellow's appearance, Commander Lewrie. Though I must say, *you* appear as . . . dare I say, sir? . . . as dashing as your past exploits repute you to be?" Andrews drew a finger down his own cheek, as if to scribe the cutlass scar on Lewrie's. "God help the French, Commander Lewrie, our captain remarked when he learned *Jester*, and 'Ram-Cat' Lewrie were to be part of our squadron."

It was quite refreshing for Lewrie, now that he was somewhat a "senior" officer, to be toadied to, gushed at, to have a subordinate "piss down his back" as he had over the years to senior officers. All he could do was blush in surprise, scuff his shoes, and make a stab at "shy" noises.

"Ah?" Lieutenant Andrews chirped, when a midshipman came to his side. "Very well, Mister Nisbet. Gentlemen, sirs? Captain Nelson is now able to receive you, and allow me to express his apologies for keeping you waiting. If you will follow me, sirs . . . ?"

Nelson's stepson, Josiah Nisbet, Lewrie gathered, looking that somewhat portly, smug young man over; God help Nelson, he thought; as bad as old Forrester, back in *Desperate*. And thinking about old times in the American Revolution, he could not help wondering . . . one of his old captains, aboard *Desperate*—Tobias Treghues—one of God's Own Cuckoos, he. Offend him once, and you were in his bad books forever. And I think I just offended another of his tribe, Cockburn. Well then, God help *me* . . . again!

STEWARDS CIRCULATED, TROTTING out glasses and wine as senior men took seats near Nelson's desk, and the rest stood as close as they were able. It was a Tuscan red, a tad dry and puckery, but it was as close as Nelson might come to a proper "Welcome Aboard" claret, after a year or more in the Mediterranean.

"Gentlemen, good day to you all," Nelson began once they were supplied. "I should like to start by proposing a toast. To our squadron. To us."

"To us!" they chorused, tipping back their glasses.

"It is a fragile, and may soon seem like an arduous and frustrating, task upon which we have been embarked," Nelson continued. "One, I trust . . . given your zeal for its performance . . . which shall *not* prove to be unrewarding, or absolutely vital to our cause. But one that may seem to pose you on tenterhooks, should this duty be pursued properly. Top-up for you? And then I will reveal it to you."

The stewards came around again, and Lewrie found a place to slouch against a carline post with his second glass in his hand.

"We are, as you may know, under orders to liaise with the Austrian Army, and their allies the Piedmontese, commanded by General de Vins. To be his left flank, as it were, and act as a wing of his cavalry might, at sea, to scout out and discover, then harass and destroy, any attempt by the French to advance eastward along the coast. General de Vins aims to advance west, clearing the French from those ports and fortified towns of the Genoese Riviera, containing French expansion, then driving them back behind their own borders. Eventually, it is hoped," Nelson said forcefully, "he will bring them to battle and destroy them, clearing the way for a second invasion of the French portion of the Riviera and Provence. That task is made daunting by the nature of the country. Inland, there are steep mountain roads, little better than Corsican goat paths, these narrow passes that are easily defended. Suppling his army inland will be most difficult. And equally difficult for the French, do you see," he said, sweeping a hand over a large map on his desk, at which they all craned their necks to peruse.

"The French aim is to spread eastward, seizing the Genoese Republic, Piedmont . . . then all of the Italian peninsula. We've checked them at sea, so far, so the army France assembled to retake Corsica has been diverted . . . to here, east of Toulon. They come forward slowly, depending on coastal merchant ships for supply. Hence the necessity for our squadron in these waters, to harass their trade . . . and to protect ours. We are, gentlemen, much like a cavalry vedette or piquet-post, a force flung forward-most, at the very lance-tip of contact with our foe. We may help delay, therefore assuring the defeat of, their plans. Or, we may most surely lose this campaign entire. For the time," Nelson told them proudly, "we are the most vital naval squadron in the Mediterranean. Perhaps in all of European waters. Things . . ." Nelson was forced to admit, sobering, "have not gone entirely in our favor . . ."

He outlined the reverses the Coalition had suffered. The Austrian army under General Coburg had been defeated, and run out of Belgium. An Austro-Prussian force across the Rhine had been run back to the east side, which forced the Prussians to split off from the Austrians, and sign the Treaty of Basle with France. Holland had been overrun, its ice-bound navy captured—by French cavalry charging over the ice!—and was now a mostly enthusiastic French Republican possession called the Batavian Republic. And the unfortunate Duke of York's army, mostly Hessian and Hanoverian mercenaries, had been run from Dunkirk into Flanders, then into Holland as it was being conquered, and finally into Germany, where the Royal Navy had fetched off the officers, their baggage, and a large part of the supply train . . . but the men had mostly been abandoned, and lost. Spain, never much of an ally, anyway, had just signed a treaty with France, and had quit the Coalition!

Closer to home, Austria and Sardinia were still officially in . . . but Genoa and Tuscany were wavering, and what the Kingdom of the Two Sicilies in Naples might do from one moment to the next was . . . iffy. With Tuscany now neutral, Leghorn and Porto Especia could no longer be considered allied, Royal Navy, bases, though they could refit and victual individually during a limited stay . . . as could *every* belligerent's warships! Genoa, directly in the path of both armies, maintained her shaky, but still friendly, neutrality; quite unable, or unwilling to defend her own territories. Or too frightened of the consequences!

"The trade with the French is bolstered by many Danish, Dutch, Tuscan of a certainty, vessels. Perhaps we shall see Spanish vessels seek-

ing to profit, presenting the most plausible, but colorable, papers. Even
Genoese ships are suspect. And must be stopped."

Hullo, Alan gawped, slouching a bit less; *hell* of a way to deal with a
neutral . . . almost an ally!

"This coast now occupied by the French, properly of the Genoese
Republic, along here west of Vado Bay . . ." Nelson said with a sweep of
his hand over the map, which encompassed Porto Mauritio in the far
west, the harbors of Oneglia, Diano and Alassio, Luano and Finale, as
well as a host of lesser ports, fishing villages tucked into almost every
sheltered inlet on that steep-to, rocky coast, all the way to the wide sweep
of Porto Vado and Vado Bay. Even further west, along the coast of
formerly Sardinian Savoia—from Cape Antibes, Nice, and San Remo—
the Riviera presented a hundred places where shoal-draught coastal trading ships could shelter, almost take to the shingly, stony beaches overnight, like ancient Greek or Roman galleys. It had more hidey-holes than
a well-wormed cheese!

"To be perfectly charitable and humane, sirs," Nelson glowered
sternly, "one might expect us to turn a blind eye to the Genoese trying to
relieve the sufferings of their own subjects, who have been invaded and
trampled under the conqueror's heel, through no fault of their own.
Genoa cannot rescue them, free them of the tyrant's yoke. And, we may
be certain, with their coastal trade cut off, and the French Army foraging
from their larders, they shall certainly go hungry, until such time as
General de Vins may liberate them. Short-commons may be the least of
the suffering the French bring to them. You understand the callous and
rapacious nature of triumphant soldiery . . . Yet, every morsel of pasta,
every swig of wine or cup of flour that might charitably nourish a Genoese, may just as easily end in the gullet of a French Republican soldier.
So, hard though it may be for me, and I am certain for you gentlemen, to
contemplate . . . yet must we interdict that trade, completely. Mister
Drake, our minister to the Tuscans and the Genoese Republic, and his
agents . . . assure me that such a trade already flourishes."

"Excuse me, sir," Lewrie simply had to say, which drew another reproving sniff from Captain Cockburn, seated close to Nelson's desk and
alternately frowning in humane concern, or beaming in rapture at his
words. "We're to base here, just off the Genoa Mole, and in Vado Bay.
Might we not make the Genoese so angry with us that they order us out?
And ally themselves with the Frogs?"

"A point well taken, Commander Lewrie," Nelson allowed without a
trace of rancor. "Indeed, there is that risk. Mister Drake and I have

wrestled with that *contretemps* many an anxious hour. But I believe it a sea officer's duty to not only have the moral, physical courage that our calling demands, but political courage as well. If it is political courage that the Genoese lack, then there is also the possibility that they will accede, temporarily, in the face of the greater good; that is to say, the preservation of their well-professed love of independence.''

"But are you not, sir . . . that is to say, *we* would be, uhmm . . ." Captain Cockburn fretted softly. "Acting against orders? I mind . . ."

"Aye, Captain Cockburn," Nelson confessed. "There are extant instructions from home, which state that 'our warships are to avoid giving just cause of offense to any foreign power in amity with His Majesty's Government.' I am, in fact, acting without not only direct and specific orders and instructions from Admiral Hotham, but I am in some measure acting directly contrary to them."

And good on *you*, Lewrie thought with rising expectations, feeling his face crease in a wolfish, rebellious grin. Anything that goes contrary to Hotham's edicts is probably the best course of all. Damn' fool!

"Genoa may qualify . . . loosely . . . as a foreign power in amity," Nelson all but smirked, "but they have proven too irresolute in defense of their neutrality, and their amity with us is but grudging. We *will* stop up the trade along the coast entirely. No matter which flag is presented. Horrible as it may be to make innocent civilians pay for a war, as against the honorable and Christian usage of a military campaign this may be, I am sure that I have the support of His Majesty's ministers both at Turin and Genoa . . . and a consciousness that I am doing the right and proper service of our King and Country."

"Well, sir . . . !" Captain Cockburn grinned bashfully, sounding as if he had been turned around to a new way of thinking, and was enthusiastic.

"Aye, we are acting contrary to whatever orders *might* have come from our senior admiral," Nelson further confessed.

Means he didn't think to issue any, that *might've*, Alan thought.

"Aye, we face the risk of litigation over illegal seizures, of political, diplomatic wrangles." Nelson went on. "No one knows more than I . . . and Commander Lewrie, I recall? . . . of how fraught with possible cost to career and purse such lawsuits that might be brought in Admiralty Court against us. Lewrie and I had a rough old time of it in the West Indies, 'tween the wars, did we not, sir? But we persevered, and succeeded in suppressing illegal foreign trade, in upholding lawful Naviga-

tion Acts. And in hanging a few pirates, in the end. Of bringing the
biggest rogues to book. So, this is what we shall do, sirs . . .

"The harbor at Vado Bay will become our main anchorage, and where
we will fetch all seizures, no matter how small. Mister Drake, here in the
capitol, is arranging agents to inspect and condemn our prizes, to pay the
freight, release the vessels, sell their cargoes, and hold the monies for us
until a real Admiralty Court may adjudicate them. Neutrals may be
released, once emptied, should their papers prove legitimate and proper.
But, *without* cargoes, or profit, thus hopefully deterring them from a
second attempt. Vessels of belligerent nations to be kept as Droits of the
Admiralty, subject to prize money. As will any ship, neutral or belligerent, found to be carrying warlike stores. Now, here are my specific
orders, which you will also receive written . . .

"You will stop and inspect *all* ships bound for France, or any port now
occupied by France, no matter how inconsequential such ships may be,"
Nelson ticked off on his fingers. "You will be careful not to give too great
an offense, but stop them you will. You will prevent any embezzlement of
their cargoes, taking inventory as best you are able against the manifests,
should they still be aboard after seizure. The masters will be kept aboard,
so they have no certifiable complaints to level against us at some future
Court. You may take out of them such people as may be deemed by you
improper to remain aboard, either of the crew or the passengers. Most
especially those you deem suspect, or who cannot provide proper *bona
fides*. Should they offer any resistance to you, then on their heads be it.
As long as your responding force is commensurate and requisite to the
situation, I assure you I will uphold you to the utmost of my power, as
long as you feel you did your duty honorably, and as best you saw it."

That cheered them up considerably. What Horatio Nelson proposed
was fraught with risks; professional ruin, a court-martial, financial disaster and years of litigation so expensive, with possible judgment against
error so steep, they'd die in debtor's prison, without even a penny for
beer on Sundays!

"I know it is not the usual thing," Nelson said with a smile on his face,
a bit shy, "that a senior officer explain himself so elaborately. But I have
found, gentlemen, that hastily issued, unexplained or mystifyingly pur-
poseless orders are never half so diligently pursued as those that are
made clear, concise, and the sense, the reason for them, fully shared. I
promise you all that I will endeavor to share with you all pertinent
information, as soon as I come to know it, which pertains to our situation.
So that you may feel free to act with more certainty, knowing that you are

in full obedience, and full agreement with me, as well. So that we may
diligently, enthusiastically, and cooperatively, function more as a like-
minded band of supportive men toward the greater good, instead of at
half-guessed loggerheads."

That, too, drew a "good on *you*!" from Lewrie's thoughts. He'd been
clueless too often in the Navy, too compartmented and menial, to suspect why most admirals issued orders, while holding the reasons as close
to their waistcoats as whist players with a good hand.

"Well then, gentlemen, a final glass to success in our new endeavor,
and we'll be about it," Nelson suggested, summoning his stewards once
more. "Written orders that illuminate the points I raised will be given
you. The port of Genoa is—at present, mind—cooperative toward port
visits and victualing rights. Which ships require supply before putting to
sea?"

Half the captains' hands went up, Lewrie's included; victims of capricious, mystifying, and conflicting orders to join the squadron at San
Fiorenzo before victualing, before they'd tangled with the French this
last time, and San Fiorenzo already short of supplies.

Nelson gave them a wry expression, perhaps verging upon shammed
horror; no captain would usually put to sea without every water butt or
bread-bag bungful, his stored rations, especially livestock and fresh meat
or flour, crammed into any odd nook or cranny available. And well Nelson knew that fear of running short, or of being deprived. He might have
urged them to sail with what they had, but seemed to shrug off the
"greed" for oversufficiency philosophically.

"In that case, then, uhm . . . Captain Cockburn?"

The young man perked up, his phyz turned all noble and enterprising,
and conscious of being singled out.

"Since your *Meleager* is better stored than others, you are most ready
to put to sea," Nelson told him. "You will cruise off Vado Bay, in company with, uhm . . . the *Tarleton* brig, and the *Resolution* cutter. And
in temporary charge. Mister Drake informs me that there is rumor of a
Genoese convoy. Keep your eyes peeled for it. Some talk of monies, plate
and jewels, to be transported east from Marseilles in Genoese bottoms,
the interception and seizure· of which, I am certain, would be most
discomfiting to the French cause. Along with the grain."

"I would be honored, sir," Cockburn preened.

Could a man swagger, still seated . . . !, Lewrie thought sourly; regretting his own selfish desire to cram *Jester* with last-minute supplies.
Lucky bastard! Still . . . even though *Jester* barely drew more than two

fathoms, this duty would involve inshore work, cutting out a merchant-man in shoal water, from under the very noses of forts, almost in musket range of the cliffs or beaches. *Jester* had but two boats on her tiers to use for this, and they were both too small to hold a crew of raiders *and* oarsmen. He reckoned he might use the delay in harbor to chivvy up something larger, something Mediterranean-looking, shabby but stout, to serve as *Jester*'s tender.

Something so commonplace that her arrival in an occupied port would go unnoticed, until . . . Damme if I'll cheat myself out of a shot at plate, gold, and jewels! Something just big enough to bear the weight and recoil of swivels, or one of the "Smashers"? he mused.

The other captains seemed regretful of their avidity, too, bereft that they'd ceded a chance for untold riches in prize money for the lack of a ha'porth of tar, or a stoupful of water.

"I *could* . . . !" *Ariadne*'s captain grudgingly offered, now he saw the fortune he had missed.

"No no, sir," Nelson countered amicably. "Do fulfill your every need first, so your *Ariadne* may keep the seas without stinting your men and thus reducing your effectiveness once there."

You damn' clever hound, Lewrie realized, gaining a sudden appreciation for Nelson's nacky wits; you want us like-minded and all that—but you want us hungry for loot, too! No better way to light a fire in 'em, than dangle baubles in their faces. Were it just orders, or grain, we'd be keen enough, but now . . . ! He's more than the dashing, heedless bugger I thought him. Hmm . . .

"Lucky dog, sir," Fremantle crowed at Cockburn's luck, once they were on deck once more, queuing up to depart in reverse order of seniority, and their gigs aligning themselves in a like circle.

"But for firewood and water, sir . . ." Cockburn simpered, seeming modest; but more than a little certain of how high in Nelson's regard he really was, compared to the others. Stiff, stuffy, aye, like Lieutenant Andrews said, Lewrie thought; but more prissy than prim. Like a woman with a new ball gown. I don't think I'm going to like him very much. All *my* good fortune and patronage aside, being in the right place at the right time—bein' *damn'* successful, too!—and he made "post" in a little more'n a Dog Watch, got a *frigate* . . . doin' less than *half* of what I . . . !

Right, add Jealous, to Weak and Venal! he scowled. And had to snicker at his own pretensions. Oh, well.

"Good fortune, sir," Lewrie offered Cockburn, "and good huntin'." Extending a hand to be Christian about it, jealous or no.

"Thankee, Commander," Cockburn replied stiffly. "One may hope, hey? I'll try and leave something for you."

"That'd be *damn'* good of you, sir," Alan forced himself to say with a smile. You vauntin' turd! Damn' limp hand and wrist, cold an' weak as some . . . !

"Well, urhm . . ." Cockburn said, retrieving his hand, seeming as if he felt a sudden urge to wash it. "Before we sail, sir. Allow me to give you the name of a rather decent Genoese tailor." He cocked a brow and gave Lewrie another of those searching, top-to-bottom looks. "Perhaps your delay in port will give you time to obtain the requisite epaulet and lace, Commander Lewrie? One must be properly attired, d'ye see . . . else our so-called 'neutral' traffickers might not take you as seriously as they ought."

"Kind of you, sir," Lewrie rejoined, stifling the fiery retort he really wished to say back. It was possible that Cockburn was genuine with his offer, that he really *was* such a stickler for details. Or was such a toplofty sod he didn't understand when he gave offense.

Lewrie, though, had never been more than ready to be chary of other men's motives, and was pretty sure he was being deliberately galled.

"For the nonce, sir," he continued, still with a thankful smile on his face, "I'll have to let my guns be my guinea stamp."

"Ah!" Fremantle coughed with sudden relief. "M'boat. Good day t'you all, sirs. Captain Cockburn . . . Commander Lewrie. Confusion to the French."

Alan had to admit he was a bit behind the latest Regulations for Sea Officers' dress. But then, they almost all were. The latest directives ordained the addition of a vertical scallop "slash-cuff" over the sleeve rings of rank, with the gilt buttons moved inside, and vertical instead of horizontal. And finally, after years of grumbling that the senior naval uniforms were too plain compared to the Army's, they were allowed to wear epaulets. Commanders got a plain, fringed gold-bullion epaulet on their left shoulder. Captains of less than three years' seniority got one on the right, while full post-captains were to sport the full pair. Cockburn had already obtained his, though few of the others had so far bothered, so much at sea where it didn't make one damned bit of difference, on a foreign station out of sight of Admiralty or fussy port admirals.

"My thanks for your excellent suggestion, Captain *Coe*-burn, sir," Lewrie said, continuing to doff his hat, turning to include Cockburn in the salute he'd just given Fremantle. "I'll toddle on down the queue, if you will excuse me? B'lieve your boat is next anyway, sir?"

"Quite," Cockburn replied, giving him a brief, jerky head-bow.

As LEWRIE WEDGED in astern of *Ariadne*'s captain but before the juniors who commanded the lesser ships, he took time to look over the harbor, searching for a useful boat he could purchase as a tender to *Jester*. Even with a replacement cutter on her boat-tier beams, he had three *small* boats to work with. A local-built tartane, lateen-rigged fishing boat or small coaster would best suit his purpose, he decided, something around fifty-feet long, or so, about half *Jester*'s length. A two-master, perhaps, which would be fast enough to chase, shoal-draught enough to go very close inshore . . . and could pay for herself at least fifty times over, were they lucky.

Another thought struck him, as he was at last being rowed back to *Jester* in his gig. Were they to wage full-fledged commerce warfare, then why were they limited to the *Genoese* coast? While Nelson had said little about Savoian ports—nothing, really—hadn't his hands encompassed them when he'd shown them the chart?

Wait a bit, Lewrie enthused, squirming on his padded thwart; he had! ". . . any ships bound for France, or any port *now occupied* by the French," he'd directed.

Better pickings, he speculated; easier pickings? Troops all off far to the east, with only small garrisons left in the backwaters, and shipmasters thinking themselves safe as houses that far west. Around Cape Antibes and San Remo, he thought, defenses might be lighter, yet the effect of a raid could hurt the long French supply trains just as badly. Maybe worse; they'd have to divert troops and guns from their march on Genoa to protect those neglected ports, spread their ships too thin, which escorted or patrolled . . . ! And, most profitably, yield the value of contraband cargoes as prize money, with no other British warships "In Sight"!

Confusion to the French, indeed, he thought with a feral grin of anticipation. Eager to be at it. And to get ashore quickly to grab a tender before the others thought of it. And get those changes to his uniforms done, after all; as long as he was at it.

CHAPTER

3

LEWRIE'S PROBLEM WAS being a bit "skint" himself, short of the where-withal to pay the outrageous prices Genoese masters or captains asked for their fishing boats. So *Jester* had departed Genoa in mid-July without a tender. Once at sea, though, he'd simply taken a suitable vessel.

Bombolo, her owner had named her, a *tartane* of only forty feet in length, tubby and broad-beamed. She'd been running along the Riviera coast, fat, dumb, and happy—Thomas Mountjoy, whose command of Italian idiom was growing by leaps and bounds, told him her name meant "A Fat Person," and was therefore particularly apt—off San Remo. There'd been no beach to ground on, no convenient inlet into which she could slip, and *Jester* had cut inshore of her. She was Savoian, and empty of anything of value, save for a few casks of fresh-caught fish. But she had attempted to flee, which Lewrie wrote up in his report as the sort of "suspicious activity" Nelson's orders had warned him to be on the lookout for.

A quick palaver, at gunpoint, with her terrified captain, and the deal had been struck. With three casks of their catch in her longboat, the captain and his small crew allowed their freedom to row away—and Lewrie's offer of £30, in silver shillings—he'd "bought" her.

"QUOINS FULL OUT. When you're quite ready, Mister Bittfield," Lewrie ordered.

"Number one larboard gun . . . fire!" Bittfield shouted. A ranging shot howled away for the tiny, extemporized "fort" sited on a low bluff overlooking the entrance to the harbor of Bordighera. A sleepy town awoke to the clap of thunder, and the crunching rattle of rocky soil and shale blasted loose from the bluff, just below the redoubt.

There was an answering bang from the shore, as one of the guns in the three-gun battery returned fire, adding a bloom of smoke to the cloud of dust that hazed the morning air below the thin flagpole and French Tricolor.

"Cold iron," Lewrie spat to Mister Buchanon, as he saw the shot fall far short, and wide to the left by at least a hundred yards. And if the battery corrected their lateral aim, they'd still fire astern of *Jester*, for at least their first or second full salvos.

"Number two gun . . . fire!" Bittfield shouted, pacing aft as if he were firing a timed salute, with the Prussian quarter-gunner Rahl almost frantic as he scampered in advance of him, tugging and trimming the aim and elevation, casting urgent glances over his shoulder to Mister Bittfield, to see if he was still scowling at him.

A touch higher, a touch to the right, that second shot; fountaining gravel and dirt just short of the low stone rampart. An officer on horseback appeared, with one or two aides, to the right of the battery, and unslung a telescope. So close was *Jester* to the steep-diving shore that they could hear the faint, whistle-through-your-teeth tootle of the garrison being called to battle by fifes and drums.

"Number three gun . . . fire!" Bittfield barked.

"Oh, bloody lovely!" Lewrie beamed.

That shot scored a direct hit on the rampart; nine pounds of iron ball striking between the two right-hand embrasures. Poor mortar, or no mortar—perhaps the wall had been quickly erected with its stones laid as loose as a Welsh pasture fence—but when the dust cleared, down it had come, creating a fourth embrasure on the seaward side, a ragged gap, with a skree-slope of tumbled rock below it.

"Number four gun . . . fire!"

Down the deck the tolling went, gun after gun lurching backward on its truck carriage, to chip away at the top of the rampart, smash in low on the wall, skim just over it, or pummel the soil beneath, making a pall of dust and smoke to obscure the French gunners' aim.

"Larboard batt'ry . . . make ready for broadside!" Bittfield cried, raising a fist in the air. "Wait for *it*! On the uproll . . . *Fire!*"

Nine carriage guns went off as one, this time, shaking *Jester* to her very bones, reeling her sideways to windward a foot or two. A shot amputated the flagpole, bringing down the tricolor; the rest battered down a stretch

of wall, flinging rocks as big as men's heads into space. The officer on
horseback fought to control his terrified, rearing mount, and the
mounted aides vanished. As the dust and smoke cleared, Lewrie could
see at least one French field-artillery piece laying canted on a smashed
wheel and carriage through the vast gap his guns had blown.

"Mister Hyde!" Lewrie shouted, fanning in front of his face for fresh
air. "Hoist the signal to Mister Knolles. Mister Buchanon, we'll put the
ship about on the larboard tack. Porter? Pipe 'Stations for Stays' and
ready to come about!"

Little *Bombolo* wheeled about from her position astern and to seaward
of *Jester*, easing the set of her conventional jib, winging out her large
lateen mains'l, and bore off north for the harbor entrance. At the same
time, *Jester* swung south into the wind, tacked, and sailed to her support,
to re-engage what was left of the battery with her right-hand guns.

"Steady . . . thus," Lewrie told the helmsmen. "All yours, Mister
Bittfield!"

"Starboard batt'ry . . . ready broadside . . . on the uproll . . .
Fire!"

Closer, this time, within a quarter-mile of the shore, and even the
carronades blazing away from foc's'le and quarterdeck bulwarks. A hailstorm of round-shot savaged the entrance face of the battery, and more
stone flew in the air, more gravel and dirt slipped down the hillside to
patter into the sea. One shot from the French, who had gamely wheeled
one of their light field guns to a spare embrasure, from that unequal
combat on the sea face. A shot that went warbling low astern to raise a
tiny splash seaward of *Jester*'s wake. The tricolor showed itself again,
risen on the stump of the flagpole by some brave soul . . . now only a
little higher than an infantry regiment's banner.

" 'Ey got spirit, Cap'um," Buchanon commented, when he took his
attention off the sea to starboard for a moment.

"We'll shoot that out of 'em, sir." Lewrie grinned.

"Ah, 'ere's 'at rock ledge . . . well t'starb'd. Missed it by at *least* a
quarter-cable, sir." Buchanon grunted with professional pride. "No worries. Deep water, clear t'th' entrance."

With the fort so busy with *Jester*, and being pounded into road gravel,
little *Bombolo* was free to breeze into the small harbor without a shot
being fired at her. Around the point, behind the bluff fort, there sounded
the panicky patter of musketry, fired at impossible range.

"Broadside . . . ready . . . on the uproll . . . *Fire!*"

And another exchange of shots. Two French guns, this time, but still badly laid and aimed. One ball struck short, skipped twice, and struck *Jester's* starboard side, just below the mainmast chains with a dull *thud*. It hung for a second in the dent it had created in the oak planking just below the stout chain wale, then dribbled off to splash into the sea. The second whined overhead, not even clipping rope.

Once more the tricolor went down, as the fort shivered to the monstrous weight of iron, and the wall between the embrasures slumped. Flinty sparks, smoke, and dust flew. Then the *Whoomph!* of gunpowder cartridges as a reserve went off like a miniature Vesuvius, flinging rock and gravel a hundred yards offshore, creating a rising gout of smoke, and the hint of flames at its base.

"Near midchannel. Ease her, Quartermaster. We'll enter harbor in midchannel. Mister Buchanon, hands to the braces," Lewrie called. "Wind's from the sou'east. Wear us for a run, with the wind large on the starboard quarter."

Around the point and under the bluff, the land fell away toward the town on the right-hand side, the shoreline of the harbor almost a full circle, as if cut from the rocky coast with the rim of a cup, with high hills all about behind the bluff's short peninsula. He could see that Bordighera held slim pickings. There were three shabby locally built *tartanes* tied up to a stone quay near the center of town, a narrow and rocky beach to the right, and a much wider, softer beach to the left of the inlet, where at least two-dozen small fishing boats no bigger than the ship's jolly boat rested with their bows on the shingle and gravel.

Bombolo was coasting toward the quay, prompting the crews of the *tartanes* to flee ashore, into the streets leading uphill. But down from the battery, at least a hundred French infantry—two companies? Alan thought—that had formed a line midway between the fort and the town, were jogging townward to intercede. The mounted officer appeared again, this time at the infantrymen's backs, his sword drawn, to spur them on.

"Mister Bittfield, that lot!" Lewrie shouted. "Load with grape and canister. Quartermaster, put your helm alee two points, to lay us closer inshore o' those buggers."

Pistols were popping on the quay. With his telescope, Alan saw a few men in French naval uniforms, falling back from their vessels to the buildings as Knolles's raiding party came alongside the largest of the *tartanes*. No more than half-a-dozen, against Knolles's fifteen, he thought, abandoned by the rest but still game. A swivel gun banged and a uniformed Frenchman went down. A two-pounder boat gun went off aboard *Bombolo,* spraying canister into the front of an impressive shorefront commercial building, and dropped another. The rest at last fled, far outnumbered and outgunned.

"Loaded an' run out, sir," Bittfield reported. "Range 'bout two cables. Too far forrud o' th' carriage-gun ports, but we're sailin' faster'n they can trot, sir!"

"Steady, Quartermaster. We'll stand on a little closer. Do you be ready, Mister Bittfield."

"Ready!" Bittfield yelled to his gun captains. Tacklemen and loaders, rammermen and powder monkeys stepped clear of recoil, of the rope tackle that could ensnare a foot and have it off. Lanyards were pulled taut to the flint-lock strikers. Quarter-gunner Rahl, more used to the employment of artillery against troops in the field, scampered onto the forecastle, after directing the train of the forward-most gun.

The French soldiers were intent on getting to the quay, to stop Knolles from taking those small coasters, of getting into the town and the main square just above the quay, to volley or snipe from cover. A moment more, Lewrie thought, wondering if those local charts were right, and he had depth enough along that shore. But for the creak and groan of the hull, the swash of water, and the rustle of the wind and sails, it was, for a moment, peacefully silent. He could distinctly hear the rattle and thud of boots on the roadway, of musket butts clapping upon bayonet scabbards and sheathed short swords, canteens and metal plates and cups hung from knapsacks tinkering one another, as they jogged at the double-quick.

"Helm up to windward, Quartermaster. Lay us parallel to them," Lewrie said at last.

"*Wait* for it!" Bittfield soothed as *Jester* swung her bows about, and the shoreline road and its panting target appeared in the gun ports. "Wait for *ittt!*" He squatted to point over the number one nine-pounder.

"Nein, Herr Bittfield!" Rahl countered from the foc's'le. "*Der mitte kanon!* Middle, zir!" He fanned his hands to mime the spread of shot of a full-dozen barrels; carronades and long guns. "*Verbreitung* . . . der spread!"

Bittfield swore under his breath, but trotted aft to the waist.

Wiser than the small French garrison, the Savoians of Bordighera had gone to earth, or run for the hills above their hard-scrabble little town. The dusty harbor street down which the infantry pounded, among the first shantylike outlying homes and tiny shops, was shuttered and closed, not even a dog or curious cat in sight.

"Proceed, Mister Bittfield."

"On the uproll . . . !" Bittfield screeched, drawing breath for his final shout.

The mounted officer reined in his horse savagely, making it rear once more, as if suddenly realizing he'd bitten off more than he or his men could chew. The rear-rank men at the tail of the column, the file closest to the low stone boundary markers of the shoreline road, suddenly shrank in on themselves, looking over their shoulders, hunched as pensioners.

"*Fire!*"

It was not over 300 yards from ship to shore when that broadside erupted. Canister, so Army artillery texts stated, was most effective out to nearly 500 yards. And, in Army usage, *Jester* carried the equivalent of three four-gun batteries a battalion of guns!

The ship shuddered and complained with wooden groans as gun smoke blotted out the view. Ashore, it was an avalanche that swept everything away in a twinkling. Dust flew, low shrubbery wavered and frothed, and the stucco fronts of low houses and shops were dimpled and crazed to the brick beneath, and roof tiles were flung into the air, some in shards, or whole. Precious glass windows shattered, wood shutters and awnings disappeared, all those screechings and crashings lost in the terror-stricken wails—the death screams—of the infantrymen, who were scythed away. Plebeian dun stucco was splattered or sheeted with gore. The officer's horse was flung over a waist-high fence of a pigsty, its rider—minus an arm and a leg—flung the opposite direction, and his gleaming sword did a silvery pirouette, twirling over and over.

When the smoke cleared, there weren't a dozen Frenchmen who still stood, to stagger blindly away. For another long moment, all was quiet. Then the moaning began, the panicky yelps and whimpers of the dying, as they felt themselves over to discover their mortal hurts.

"Reload," Lewrie barked, though his knees juddered as he beheld the enormity, and the suddenness, of that slaughter. "Round-shot this time, Mister Bittfield."

"Aye aye, sir," the master gunner muttered, in awe himself.

"Mister Buchanon, hands to the braces. Ready to wear about, to the larboard tack. We'll circle the harbor, until Mister Knolles has way on the prizes. Mister Porter? Clew up courses and tops'ls. Keep way on her with t'gallants, jibs, and spanker."

"Fire on the town, sir?" Bittfield inquired from the gun deck. "Those fishin' boats?"

"No, Mister Bittfield." Lewrie grimaced. "No call to ruin the civilians' lives. Unless we're fired upon, that is. Andrews?"

"Heah, sah," his cox'n replied, leaving his quarterdeck carronade.

"Three prizes, and *Bombolo* to manage. Take my gig, with a full boat crew, and row over to join Mister Knolles's party. My compliments to him on his quick seizure, and he is to get them underway as soon as possible. He is to . . ." Lewrie ordered, then paused, looking astern. "He is to lay off the entrance, until I join him. I'll be tending to that damn' battery."

"Aye aye, sah." Andrews nodded, dashing off to gather the men who usually made up the captain's boat crew.

"Sergeant Bootheby?" Lewrie called. "Mister Porter? Join me on the quarterdeck, if you please."

"Sah!" *Jester*'s most-senior Marine barked, in his best parade-ground fashion. The Admiralty put little faith in the abilities of a lowly second lieutenant to lead a shipboard detachment. Post-ships got a Marine captain, with at least one lieutenant as his assistant, while vessels below the rate such as *Jester* rated only a senior, but experienced, noncommissioned officer.

"Mister Porter, lead the cutter and jolly boat around from the stern," Lewrie instructed. "Full crews for both boats. Sergeant, I would like you to take your men ashore, and spike those guns. Better yet, tumble them down the bluff, into the sea. Take powder and oil . . . so you may set their carriages alight, too. I'll send Mister Meggs the armorer, and Mister Crewe the gunner's mate, to assist you. We've shot most of the garrison to rags, I expect, so there should be little opposition."

"Aye aye, sah!" Sergeant Bootheby bellowed fiercely, pleased to get a chance to shine at something more useful than polishing brass.

"We'll debark your party as we sail back out toward the bluff. Five minutes, I make it, before we let you slip. Hurry."

Lewrie looked back toward the quay as Bootheby assembled troops, calling some of them from the guns to dash below and fetch their coats and hats, spatter-dash gaiters, belts, and gear. Knolles had the lines cast off, and the first rags of sail were being hoisted. Andrews with the gig was almost to them, and he could see shouted exchanges as his cox'n relayed his orders.

Above Bordighera, some civilians at last showed themselves, on the rocky, low-shrubbed heights. No threat there . . . yet, Alan thought grimly, as he eyed them with his glass. No sign of reinforcements, or that Bordighera had had a larger garrison. The crowd grew larger, and thinking themselves safely distanced, began to wave their fists, shout silent imprecations and curses. A few mounted men, waving swords about in the air, though they were dressed as civilians. No, there were some few men in uniform climbing up to them. Stragglers from the *tartanes*, he surmised; in French Navy uniforms, what appeared to be a lieutenant leading them. No sign of firearms, though. Or not too many, he told himself. At that distance, it would be hard to discern a musket from a manure fork!

What could they be so angry about? he wondered. They were Savoians, conquered by Frogs, ripped away from their longtime allegiance to Sardinia!

Rather a lot of fit young men up there, he frowned; and them the angriest. Don't tell me they *prefer* the Frogs, he gawped to himself! Worse than Yankee Doodles, I swear . . . !

Throw off your kings, your princes, the French cooed. Stand up and be free men, with liberty, equality, fraternity for all. Had their blandishments taken root here, in tiny, sleepy Bordighera? In spite of how butcherous the French Revolution really was, how two-faced the real motives were . . . they weren't out to liberate Europe, they were out for conquest and domination! . . . as callous and canting . . .

Well, there *was* Holland. Sensible damned people, peaceful, and prosperous. In point of fact, rather a damned *dull* people, the ones he had met. Yet thousands had been elated to see their nation conquered, a Batavian Republic proclaimed, and thousands more had enlisted in the army, to fight alongside the Frogs. What on *earth*, Lewrie puzzled; it don't make sense, the allure the Frogs had on people!

He lowered his glass as the quartermasters steered *Jester* along the western beach, crabbing up into the wind and preparing to tack, to make a short board across the harbor toward the peninsula, and those bluffs, where the shattered battery still smoldered. The winds were scant, as usual, and she barely ghosted. Across her bows, Lieutenant Knolles aboard *Bombolo* was leading out their prizes toward the entrance channel. Waving and shouting in glee. Lewrie counted heads. Not a single man down, no casualties! That'd make good reading in his report.

"We could wear off th' wind, sir," Buchanon suggested. "Or we could fetch-to. Light as 'is wind be, do we bare a jib or th' driver, it'd be as good as heavin' in on a spring line, 'thout anchorin'.'"

"Fetch-to, Mister Buchanon," Lewrie decided. "So we may keep the larboard battery directed at the shoreline road. Should that mob work up its courage, the sight of our guns should daunt 'em."

"Aye, sir."

"Landing party's ready, sir!" Porter reported.

"Away, the landing party, Mister Porter."

Now he could do nothing but wait. Oh, a dashing captain might go
ashore himself. That made hellish-good reading in reports, too, at the
Admiralty. Made for good fiction, Lewrie snorted in derision; the plucky,
aspiring young captain at the head of his troops, doing what a junior
officer was hired on for. Lieutenants were expendable; and he'd been
"expended," or nigh to it, often enough in his past to know that, now
hadn't he? Under the right circumstances, he still might have to exert
himself beyond his captain's role. But if one wished officers in one's
wardroom to aspire, one gave them first shot at the sharp end of the dirty
stick, and didn't go about trying to hog *all* the glory at their expense. How
else were *they* to rise, without getting their name mentioned in dispatches? They usually resented that type of captain.

A QUARTER-HOUR OF fidgeting and fretting that his plan misfired, that he
hadn't thought of everything. A captain's *proper* duties, Alan glowered,
worrying without showing it; about French cavalry, a battalion appearing
over the heights, a battery of siege guns that might just be in-transit on
the coast road toward San Remo and pop up to take *Jester* under fire,
forcing him to sail off or lose her, abandoning the Marines. Survivors
lurking in the kinky shrubs behind the battery, sniping and skirmishing.
A French warship happening by out to sea, espying smoke from the bluff,
and . . . That damned mob gathering its courage?

At last!

Smoke curling and wavering over the battery. Thicker smoke and the
red flicker of flames as field carriages, wheels, limbers and shot and
powder caissons were set ablaze. A gun barrel, man-hauled by rope about
its cascabel, went rumbling down the steep slope of the entrance face, to
tumble and roll, turning muzzle-up as the heavier weight of the breech
dragged it. And trailing a plume of dust, gravel, and rock behind it as it
fell, so that it looked as if it reeked powder smoke after being fired. A
second followed it, and with his telescope, he could determine that
Meggs and Crewe had done a very thorough job of it; trunnions blown or
hammered off, making it impossible to mount it on a carriage again, even
should the French recover it from the shoal beneath the bluffs.

As overburdened as the supply roads already were, useless but valuable guns sent back to a foundry to be recast or repaired might be an
even greater delay to the French, taking precious draught animals from
moving things *forward*! Lewrie strongly suspected they'd rust out where

they lay, alongside the detritus of Roman triremes, till the Last Trumpet, too hard to dredge for, or raise.

Bootheby and his Marines appeared, a slim scarlet snake curving down the bluff road. A fife and drum playing, a short column of twos tramping in good order, with skirmishers thrown out ahead and to both sides. And sailors in slop clothing a shambling blot in the rear. A five-minute march, and they'd be at the boats again. Lewrie heaved a *huge* sigh of relief. It was almost done. He turned to look at *Bombolo*, which drifted bare-poled about one cable seaward of the channel. There was no signal from her that an enemy ship had come into sight, either!

That mob . . .

Finally, they were moving downhill, the mounted men leading them. Nothing like an army, it was still a righteous but disordered mob, with women and children alongside. No fight in them, Lewrie thought with even more relief; they just want a good excuse to shout. Probably hasn't been this much excitement in Bordighera since the Crusades, he allowed himself to chuckle.

And along the eastern shore road, where the two French companies had been slaughtered. Hullo, there were Bordigherans there, he started. No, no threat in them, either. Old women in black, a few younger women in gayer gowns, some gaffers and kids.

Keening and wailing over the broken dead, some of them.

The wind brought thin screams, wails, and prayers to *Jester*, as civilians raised their hands in supplication, beat their breasts, and wrenched at their undone hair, throwing their heads back to howl like hounds in mourning.

" 'Ey've profesh'nal mourners back home beat all hollow, sir," Buchanon grunted, as the civilians began to drag off the badly wounded, or prop up those lesser hurt and get them to their feet to stagger off, crying and weeping with agony.

"Might give these local lads a bellyful of war, Mister Buchanon," Lewrie spat. "*Were* they of a mind to volunteer before, well . . ."

"Mourners, my eyes, sir!" Buchanon said with an outraged snort. "Looters, more like. Look yonder, sir."

Sure enough, once Lewrie raised his telescope again, he could see pockets being turned out, boots and stockings stripped off, the bloody knapsacks being rifled. Taking his first close-up look at his handiwork, Lewrie could view horribly wounded men being rolled over, so the loot-ers could get at their valuables, flailing their hands weakly, or screaming in protest, shaking their heads to be left alone to die, in peace. Those hands being stripped of rings, bloody purses, or tobacco pouches torn away from punctured waistcoat pockets. Urchin children quarreling over corpses, and their pitiful wealth, like buzzards. A few of the younger women honestly grieved, and took no part in looting.

Simple little fishing-town girls, Lewrie thought, bedazzled by romantic young soldiers, so exotic, from so far away, bragging about booty and plunder and glory. When conquered, there were always those who'd snuggle up to the victors who could offer power, money, or food when everyone else went hungry. Or could offer novel adventure, love . . . yet even a few of those weeping young girls had the common sense to pick their dying lovers' pockets. For mementos. Or a token of security for their own precarious futures.

"Mister Bittfield!" Lewrie howled. "A round-shot over their heads! *Well* over, mind. But scare those harpies off!"

"Aye *aye*, sir!"

Boom! went a larboard nine-pounder, its ball a rising black dash-mark aimed with the quoin below the breech fully out. A redoubling of the wailing ashore, but for their own safety now as they scattered, running in all directions, skirts hiked up to their knees. The shot struck earth a full mile away, but they weren't to know that. Again, the road was as empty of life as it had been just after the broadside.

Another, larger *boom!* atop the bluff, as the assembled powder charges and spare kegs exploded. Another Vesuvius-like eruption that flung charred gun tools and carriage timbers into the midmorning sky, and a patter of rock and gravel that rained down as far as the Marines re-embarking on the narrow beach.

The mob, which had been so intent upon re-entering their town, perhaps advancing toward the battery, had also scattered to the four winds. Bordighera was as devoid of people, of a sudden, as Stonehenge.

Five minutes more, Lewrie swore, pulling out his watch in spite of his best intentions to appear calm and unruffled. The boats would be back alongside, the people aboard, and he could quit this horrible place. And he didn't much care if those three *tartanes* were full of gold bullion. He didn't much care for the taste in his mouth.

"ALL WELL, SERGEANT Bootheby?" he asked, as the last Marines and sailors gained the gangway, and the boats were led astern for towing once more.

"Not a scratch, sir!" Bootheby boasted, his grizzled bear-face glowing with pleasure in a soldier's proper job well done. "And *thank* you, Captain sir! From me and all the lads. That were a rare treat, sir. Anytime, sir. We're ready, anytime."

"Damn' well done, Sergeant, and aye, I'll keep that in mind," Lewrie promised, smiling now that they could depart. "Mister Buchanon? Hands to sheets and halliards. Hands to the braces. Get sail on her, and get us underway. Once around the point, and well offshore, set a course for Vado Bay."

"With pleasure, sir," Buchanon agreed, working his mouth as if he'd been chewing on something disagreeable, too.

CHAPTER
4

ONCE WELL OUT to sea and headed east, shepherding their prizes, Lewrie had hoisted "Captain Repair on Board" to summon Knolles, so he could write his report on the action. To their surprise, Knolles had fetched along a French prisoner of war, a surly, coldly sneering lout in a midshipman's uniform that was a very tight fit, so bad that he appeared as if he'd stripped a much shorter and slenderer lad for his clothes; all out at the elbows and wrists, breeches that buckled up *above* his knees—had they buckled at all. A tall and lanky thatch-hair, who wore it long and unclubbed to either side of his face, like a parted curtain. Midshipman Jules Hainaut altogether resembled a very dim-witted peasant, just off the turnip wagon, who'd been clad in some cast-off theatrical costume as a jape.

"Speaks damn-all English, of course, sir," Lieutenant Knolles said with an apologetic shrug. "And only a word or two of Italian . . . those mostly food, drink, or something to do with whores . . . so Mister Mountjoy's skills as a linguist might not avail, either. He's French, I've determined . . . but from where, God only knows, sir. He's no French I ever learned. A Parisian would send him to the guillotine for bad pronunciation."

"However did you catch him, Mister Knolles?" Lewrie asked.

"He was aboard the largest *tartane*, sir . . . the armed one. Popped off with a brace of horse pistols, missed by a mile, and dropped to the deck when Cony shot back at him." Knolles laughed easily, savoring his small triumph at the quayside. "Rather clumsily, at that."

"So the Frog Committee for Public Safety, or Directory," Lewrie said, chuckling, "appears to have their own 'Bad Bargains,' as does our King?"

"Aye, sir," Knolles agreed.

"Now, the prizes, Mister Knolles!" Lewrie urged, turning to more rewarding thoughts, and dismissing the French midshipman immediately.

"Lord, sir!" Knolles exclaimed. "Arms, uniforms, boots, packs . . . everything to equip and feed, and field two regiments. The smaller *tartanes* are Savoian, I've determined. The larger one is French. She carries some four-pounders, swivels, and a pair of twelve-pounder French-cast carronades, sir. Rather clever mounting, fore-and-aft, in the middle of the forecastle and at the taffrail. The slide-carriages are built atop a round wood platform, which can point in about three-quarters of a full circle. Quite ingenious, really. Pinned through the deck just like a sea-mortar platform. On a small vessel, without a lot of standing rigging to impede one's aim, sir, well . . . ! She could employ them even closing or fleeing, on a bow-and-quarter line."

"And her cargo?" Lewrie pressed.

"Powder, made cartouches, cartridge paper, tents and blankets, mostly, sir. She escorted the others to Bordighera. I got *that* much from our French mute. But her main load was a company of French infantry, to do the training, sir. Half of that lot you erased on the shore road. They were raising at least one Savoian regiment of volunteers, Captain. With hopes of another, do you see." Knolles crowed himself. "And we put paid to *that* scheme, sir!"

"But her crew?" Lewrie wondered aloud. "Where'd they gone when we closed them? They could have given you one hell of a scrap."

"Oh, them, sir." Knolles sneered. "Savoians, too, for the most part. Fisherman and such, 'pressed' into French service. They offered a joining bounty, some fraternity cant . . . and gaol as the other option, if they didn't, uhm . . . willingly volunteer, sir. Even our lout yonder thinks them scum. Scampered off, soon as we sailed in, leaving their Frog masters to do the honorable thing."

"Well, we've had ourselves quite a productive morning, Mister Knolles." Lewrie grinned. "And hurt the French cause, no end. Your part in it was gallantly carried, and I'll stress that in my report."

"Thankee kindly, sir." Knolles all but blushed, thinking it was necessary to appear modest and unassuming.

"Lord, don't scuff your shoes like a schoolboy, Mister Knolles," Lewrie genially chided him. "Save that for Captain Nelson, and your patrons. Just 'twixt you and me, it's quite all right to admit you're 'all the go.' "

"Aye, sir." Knolles grinned, lifting his eyes. "If you say so."

"Yon Frog *tartane*, Mister Knolles . . ." Lewrie pondered. "She's a bit stouter than our little *Bombolo*? And a tad longer?"

"About sixty feet, altogether, sir," Knolles supplied. "Cleaner, certainly. And doesn't reek of fish."

"Condemned as a lawful prize, she'll swing idle for months, and then get disarmed and sold out," Lewrie griped. "How many four-pounders did you say?"

"Six, sir," Knolles informed him.

"Damme, let's keep her. And those novel swiveling carronades," Lewrie decided quickly. "Shift your crew over to her, and leave just a barebones crew aboard *Bombolo*. You'd best shift our two-pounders aboard her, too. And the swivels. That'd be easier than stripping her, then rearming *Bombolo*. What's her name, by the way?"

"*La Follette*, sir," Knolles said, snickering. "The Little Fool."

"Really!" Lewrie gaped with amazement, then began to laugh in hearty appreciation. "Most apt. The little fool, tender to a jester. Well, damme . . . it can't be coincidental, d'ye think?"

"God knows, sir." Knolles shrugged. "But it sounds . . . lucky."

There it was again, that thing of his, and *Jester*'s luck. But perhaps it wasn't coincidental. Perhaps, with her capture, his luck, and his ship's, were turning for the better.

"Very well, Mister Knolles, carry on. Send me Andrews, soon as you can. Cony to serve as your acting bosun. Five hands for *Bombolo*, same as the other two prize *tartanes*, and we *may* have enough men to go around, till we drop anchor at Vado Bay. It's only eighty sea miles or so. With this sou'east wind, we could be there by dusk, pray God."

"Aye aye, sir."

A LATE DINNER, bites taken between writing. And fending off his young ram-cat, who was ever fascinated by the waving plume of his quill pen. "No, Toulon. Sweetlin'? Can't you go play with mousey?" Lewrie attempted to cajole. "Aspinall?"

"Sir?" his steward replied from the pantry.

"Dangle something tempting, will you, for God's sake?"

"Monkey-fist, Toulon," Aspinall offered. "See it swing, hey? Wanna fight yer monkey-fist, hey cat?"

Toulon would. With an excited trill, he jumped down to dash for the pantry door, where a newish toy of intricately plaited small-stuff swung and jerked alluringly. It was Aspinall's first successful stab at decorative knot-work, a skill he was picking up from Andrews. There were rather good place mats woven from sennet in the great-cabins now, a set of restraining ropes in the pantry where he labored, prettily served with turk's-heads, so he wouldn't go arse-over-tit in the next spell of nasty weather. But Andrews had done half of those himself as examples.

Crash! came the sound of a Marine guard's musket beyond the door. "Cap'um's clark, Mister Mountjoy . . . sah!"

"Enter." Lewrie sighed around a chunk of salami and goat cheese.

"Excuse me, sir," Mountjoy said as he entered. "But I expect you're almost ready for me to make a fair copy of the report from your rough, sir?"

"Just about, Mister Mountjoy. Glass o' chianti?"

"Aye, sir, that'd be welcome."

"A tad puckerish, is chianti," Lewrie admitted. "But it grows on one. Aspinall, a glass for Mister Mountjoy. And a top-up for me."

"Aye, sir."

"A bit of news, too, sir," Mountjoy offered. "That French prisoner Mister Knolles brought aboard is Flemish. Did as you bid, sir, tried to speak with him, but I do declare, sir, I've never heard worse French in all my born days. But, most happily, Mister Rahl the quarter-gunner happened by."

"Mister Rahl," Lewrie posed, a trifle dubious. Rahl couldn't put four words of the King's English together with a pistol pointed at his head.

"The Austrian Netherlands, sir. Or rather, should I say, what was *once* the Austrian Netherlands," Mountjoy explained. "A polyglot, sir. Flemish, Waloon, bastard Dutch, a version of French as far from good French as Birmingham 'mumbletonian' is to English. But they do still know the tongue of their conquerors, sir. German. Mister Rahl was *'Wie Gehts?'* and *'Was Machts Du?'* with the clod, quick as a wink, sir. Our M'sieur Hainaut is the usual story these days. A 'prentice seaman, from Antwerp, or thereabouts, of French blood, sir. Joined up eager as anything, soon as the Frogs drove the Austrians out. Bad as the Frogs need skilled men, they took him on as a petty officer, much like Mister Cony . . ."

"Bosun's mate," Aspinall said, almost under his breath, back to entertaining the cat after fetching the wine.

"Uhm, quite . . ." Mountjoy frowned. "Anyway, sir, Hainaut rose to become a midshipman, double-quick. Acting, one might suppose. And poorly paid, if that's the best uniform he could afford, what? Earned the notice of a senior officer, came under his wing . . ."

"Patronage," Lewrie supplied to enlighten Mountjoy's continuing ignorance.

"Oddly, he won't tell me who he is, sir. Just refers to him as *'Die Narbe.'* Rahl tells me that means 'The Scar,' Captain. *Capitaine de Vaisseau* Scar, sir. Might be another German who threw in his lot on the French side, but Mister Rahl believes it's more a nickname, sir. But then, German names, I've found, are much like Red Indian names . . . holdovers from tribal times, when 'Strong Arm' and 'Bear-Killer' were popular. So it could be a proper name, no matter what Mister Rahl believes. I gather this Captain 'Scar' is in charge of coastal convoys and their escorts." Mountjoy blithely shrugged off, taking a sip of his wine.

"*Sail ho!*" came the interruption, making Lewrie almost tip his glass over.

"Later, Mister Mountjoy," Lewrie said, getting to his feet and into his coat and hat; and finishing his wine. First things first, he told himself. "Do you go ahead with the fair copy of the report, while I see to this." A final pat on Toulon's head, and he was out the door and pounding up the ladder to the quarterdeck.

"Where away, Mister Buchanon?"

"Three points off th' starboard bows, sir," the sailing master told him, pointing an arm in the general direction. "T'gallants 'bove th' horizon, so far, Cap'um. I make us 'bout ten miles off th' coast, an' 'bout ten miles east o' San Remo. She's almost bows-on, sir, an' that could mean she's on a course t' a French-held port."

"From somewhere to the sou'east, then . . ." Lewrie mused. "From Leghorn? To San Remo?"

"Very possible, sir. Might be one o' 'em so-called neutrals 'ey told us t'watch for," Buchanon agreed.

"Check with the signalman-striker, Mister Buchanon. Have him fetch out that French Tricolor we used off Ushant. And order Lieutenant Knolles in *La Follette* to come under my lee. I'm sure *he* has a tricolor aboard . . . but he'll be needing one of our smaller ensigns, to declare his proper identity when the time comes. A boat ensign'll do."

"One aboard *Bombolo* now, sir," Buchanon reminded him.

"Very well, have him send a boat for that one," Lewrie schemed. "Damme, Mister Buchanon, were you an Italian captain, running goods to the Frogs, what would you make of our motley group?"

"Be relieved, sir," Buchanon guffawed. "Couple o' French warships, escortin' a three-ship convoy 'long th' coast? Just th' thing. Better'n runnin' afoul o' one o' 'em nasty Englishmen!"

"Would you be tempted to come close enough to speak them, sir?"

"Were I worried 'bout any Royal Navy ships in th' area, I would, sir. Aye, I surely would sail right up an' ask, 'fore I put in to San Remo. Might have too much wagered to lose, else."

"Let us devoutly hope, Mister Buchanon," Lewrie enthused along with him. "Once we've our flag situation settled, we'll harden up to windward a point, as if we're standing out to 'smoak' him. Like what a properly wary escort'd do."

"Very well, sir."

"I'll send Knolles a quick note. Tell him to guard the prizes while we're gone. And what we're about. And conform to my flag when I show them false colors. Damme!" Alan swore in wonder again. "I do believe this could turn out to be a Dev'lish profitable day!"

"It could, at that, sir!"

"Oh! Mister Rydell," Lewrie said, snapping his fingers at the small lad. "Nip below and order Mister Mountjoy to come to the quarterdeck. And for him to fetch my new gold-laced coat, with the epaulet. And my full dress hat. Has the gentleman a sword, he's to fetch that from his cabin, as well."

"Aye aye, sir," Little Rydell replied with a puzzled look.

Thankee, Captain *Coe*-burn, Lewrie thought with a wry grin; one of us, at least, is going to look very convincing to that ship.

CHAPTER

5

"Ooh Law', Sah," Andrews drawled, doffing his hat and making a formal leg, "but don' ya look pretty. Why, ah expects dey ain' nevah been *such* a dashin' lookin' cap'um in de whole Royal Navy, sah."

"I really . . ." Mountjoy protested bashfully, aware that he was the object of the entire ship's amusement. "Sir, how can I pose . . . ?"

"Put your hands in the small of your back, sir," Lewrie said, beaming. "Frown a lot. Right, Mister Spenser?"

" 'At's a cap'um's way, sir," Spenser said from the wheel.

"And when you speak, do it from deep down in your chest," Alan further instructed Mountjoy. "And shout. Shout very loud," he said, handing him a brass speaking trumpet. "Imagine you've not had a spot of joy your last ten years, entire, sir. *Or* the gout. Whichever you think makes you the gloomiest. Begin in French. Should they wish to, switch over to Italian. I'll be right by your elbow, prompting you to the proper commands in English, so you can shout orders to the crew in Frog. I'll pass them, in English, through Mister Rydell to Mister Porter and the master gunner, soft enough so they won't hear me. I must say, though, Mister Mountjoy," Lewrie was forced to snicker, "but you do cut a most dashing, and nautical picture."

"Uhm, sir." Mountjoy sighed, feeling put upon, in spite of the necessity for him to be tricked out in Lewrie's best coat and hat, and wearing a spare sword borrowed from the gunroom. "But wouldn't it be best, sir, to pose as *your* first officer, while . . . ?"

"No, sir," Lewrie countered. "That might have been the way in the *Royal* French Navy, beneath the dignity of a titled captain. But a captain

come up through the hawsehole'll shout his own questions. Be ready,
she's within half a league of us. Practice bein' a Tartar. A *loud* Tartar,
mind. Scoggins? Hoist the French colors."

"Aye aye, sir!" the signalman-striker shouted back, hauling at a flag
halliard on the mizzenmast.

With the most powerful glass aboard, Lewrie could almost recognize
the shivers of relief that went through the people on the strange brig's
quarterdeck. Instead of edging astern, as she had been to shy away, she
now resumed her old course, straight for them.

"Mister Knolles's hoisted his own false colors, sir," Buchanon said,
almost in a conspiratorial whisper at Lewrie's side.

"Very well, Mister Buchanon, thankee." Lewrie nodded emphatically,
edgy and fidgety with worry of all that might still go awry. It was many a
slip, 'twixt the crouch and the leap, as Caroline ever said.

"Her own colors," Mountjoy drawled out in a regular voice, an arm
extended to point. "Mean t'say . . . *there's* her own damn' flag, at last!"
he amended, suddenly gruff, and rather loud, too, in what Alan feared
was a fairly accurate impersonation of his own style.

Damme, do I sound *that* fearsome? he asked himself.

"Tuscan, sir," Buchanon identified first. "And a house flag I don't
know."

"Let's pray it's a house flag," Lewrie said, "and not a secret recognition
signal." They'd tried, in the hour that HMS *Jester* and the strange brig
had taken to close each other, to interrogate the French midshipman, but
he'd gone even surlier, and more mute, once the subject had been
broached. *Surely* there were signals, Lewrie thought; must be, if they're
to approach French forts that could blow 'em to flinders! A godsend for
the entire squadron would be the discovery aboard the brig of her
codebook, which would let them raid any harbor they wished for a time,
before the French changed the signals.

"Wearin', sir," Buchanon grunted. "Two cable up t'windward."

"Helm alee, Mister Spenser. Two points to weather. Close her. On
tippy toes," Lewrie told the helmsmen. "Nothing too sudden."

"Two points t'weather, sir. 'Andsomely," Spenser replied, chuckling.

"Can they hear us yet, do you think, sir?" Mountjoy asked.

"Not upwind of us," Lewrie scoffed. "Nor in the middle of a jibe.
Mister Porter? Brail up, and reduce sail," he shouted.

The rather pretty brig wore her stern across the wind, and took in sail
herself, slowing and sloughing atop her bow wave, and falling leeward at

a slight angle. Warily keeping the wind gauge of *Jester* but approaching to as close as half a cable, possibly less.

"She'll be fine catch, sir," Buchanon murmured, rubbing fingers as if shining a guinea between them. "A damn' handsome thing."

Dark green gunwale over well-oiled oak, with only a miser's pale yellow gloss paint in lieu of a braggart's gilt, was the brig. Rigging was well set up, the wood of her yards and lower masts freshly painted in white, and her running rigging was almost golden-hemp new. Lewrie eyed her with his glass, estimating her length at around eighty-five or ninety feet, just a little larger than their brig-sloop *Speedy*. And there *was* gilt on her, he noted; a figurehead lady was gilded, as were the upper beak-head rails, and the trim around her quarter galleries.

A pretty thing, he thought; *and* a richly done'un!

A shout from her quarterdeck, as she fell down alee, within two hundred yards. In French! *"Qui va la?"*

"Answer them, Mister Mountjoy," Lewrie prompted.

"Uhm . . ." Mountjoy quivered nervously, coughing and practicing a false *basso*, sounding like a mastiff with a chest cold.

"La corvette Emeraude, *Marine de guerre Français!"* Mountjoy said through the speaking trumpet, sounding a bit shriller than Lewrie might have liked, a touch too quavery. *"Ici capitaine de frégate* . . . Hainaut! *Et vous? Qui vive?"*

"Il Briosco!" came the wail of a shouted reply. *"En partance pour San Remo! Parlez-vous Italien, m'sieur, s'il vous plais?"*

"Got you, you bastard!" Lewrie hissed with fierce glee.

"Should I repeat *that* to him, sir?" Mountjoy whispered from a corner of his mouth, with an expression on his phyz that questioned his captain's sanity.

"Mine arse on a bandbox, sir, o' course not! Just palaver with 'em in Dago, till she drifts a little closer!" Lewrie spluttered. And wondered about Mountjoy's sanity. "Be ready, Mister Bittfield."

"He asks about any British ships in the area," Mountjoy went on.

"Tell him no, not this far west," Lewrie prompted.

Damme, how'd he know of our ships even beginning patrols so quick, Lewrie frowned in puzzlement. "Home port," he demanded, jogging Mountjoy in the small of his back.

"Leghorn, sir," Mountjoy muttered, turning his head a trifle to speak from the side of his mouth again, after posing the question.

"That's at least a two-day passage, and we only arrived *four* days ago, so . . ." Lewrie frowned again. "Damme. Close enough, sir."

The brig had made a little leeway, sailing alongside *Jester*, while Spenser and Brauer had been edging the helm over, spoke at a time, to go up to her. There weren't a hundred yards between the two hulls, wakes creaming slowly, their outer wave fronts beginning to mingle astern.

"Gun ports open, and run out!" Lewrie screeched suddenly. "True colors aloft! Marines, up!"

Up, the port lids flew, and truck carriages squealed and roared as wood wheels rumbled over oak decks. Down came the French Tricolor, to be replaced with the White Ensign with the Union Jack in the canton. Up, the Marines bounded, from kneeling behind the bulwarks of the starboard gangway, half turned, muskets at half cock and ready to aim.

"Heave-to or I will open upon you!" Lewrie snarled to Mountjoy. "Resist, and I will blow you to hell, tell him! Mister Porter, cutter to the starboard main chains! Muster the boarding party!"

Andrews, a boat crew, four spare sailors, and six Marines under Corporal Summerall trotted to the entry port, as the cutter was led out from being towed astern.

"Mister Buchanon, you have the deck, until my return, sir," Alan instructed. "Mister Mountjoy . . . *you* have my coat and hat! I'll thank you for 'em back."

"Yes, sir, uhm . . . could I go with you, sir?" Mountjoy pleaded as he stripped to shirt and waistcoat. "They speak either French or Italian, sir. And their papers will be in Italian, most likely. I'd do best at translating for you, or searching. Speed us along, sir?"

"Right, then. Come on." Lewrie nodded, retrieving his uniform. "Keep that sword on you. But try not to cut yourself."

"Thank you, sir!" Mountjoy gushed, breathless with excitement.

Down they went into the cutter, without ceremony, clambering on the boarding battens to the chain platform low on the chain wale, then timing leaps into the gently bobbing cutter.

"Ship starboahd oars!" Andrews snapped. "Toss larboahd. Shove off, bow man, and fend off forrud. Back-watuh, starboahd! Fend off, larboahd aft . . . easy all! Now, ship oars, larboahd. And give us way, togethah!"

The brig had let fly all, clewing up her courses and tops'ls, her jibs and spanker flogging. It was a short row to her, and within a minute they were hooked on and boarding; Lewrie first with a pistol in his waistband and his sword dangling from his right wrist from a leather lanyard. Four cutlass and pistol-armed sailors next preceded the Marines.

A damn' well-kept little brig, Lewrie thought happily as he saw how

clean, how "Navy Fashion" her decks had been holystoned or swept. He
waited for his sailors to join him, glaring at the crew that gathered near
the main cargo hatch and the entry port in her waist. They didn't appear
much concerned of their capture. Nor cowed, either, he thought. Defiant, smug; and only a trifle hangdog. As if they knew Nelson's orders that
they'd soon be released?

Aft was a bit of the same story, as he paced along the gangway to the
brig's quarterdeck. Helmsman, after-guard, a couple of men in plain blue
coats and cocked hats who were probably the mates, and one dapper
little fellow with gray hair and a close-trimmed gray beard in a fancier
coat and hat he took for the captain. Two further civilians in the latest
fashion, one drab in snuff-brown and boots, and the last a silken peacock,
clad in an almost metallic-gleaming electric blue and silver-trimmed coat
with dark-blue velvet cuffs. Clerk and owner, Alan speculated?

"Signores," Lewrie stated. "Commander Lewrie, the *Jester* sloop. *Reg-
gia Marina Britannico.*" He knew *that* much Italian, anyway. "With me
yet, Mister Mountjoy?"

"Here, sir," Mountjoy replied from his right rear.

"Tell these gentlemen that . . ."

There was a hefty splash from starboard and astern.

"Papers, sir!" Mountjoy wailed.

"Corp'rl Summerall, the great-cabins!" Lewrie barked. "Move!"

A sneer on the peacock's face, crude grins on the mates'. And from her
captain, an attempt to remain bland, but a daunting smug look of satisfaction in spite of his best efforts. Only his lively wee eyes laughed.

"Damn them!" Lewrie spat. "They think this is some bloody game?"

"Perhaps, sir," Mountjoy confessed softly.

"Introduce me, tell 'em they're prisoners, and that we're taking this
brig into Vado Bay." Lewrie sighed bitterly, working up the enthusiasm
for an air of false bravado, and success, in spite of them. And in spite of
his dashed hopes that he'd discover just how they knew to fear a British
squadron along the Genoese Riviera so quickly.

"Then, sir?" Mountjoy asked, once he'd delivered that news.

"Tell 'em no harm will come to them, but they're to be searched for
weapons, then confined until we drop anchor. Officers, passengers, and
crew. We'll search their personal belongings and cabins . . ."

A muffled bang from below! Followed by several louder reports!

"What the Devil . . . ?" Lewrie shouted, wheeling toward a ladder to
the waist. "Watch 'em, Andrews."

"Aye, sah," Andrews drawled, drawing his pistol and pulling it back to full cock. He might not have been tall enough, or beef to the heel enough to seem menacing; but his feral grin, and the unspoken and exotic danger of a dark-skinned man with a gun did the trick for him.

"What happened, Corporal Summerall?" Lewrie demanded once he'd gained the great-cabins.

"Civilian, sir," Summerall reported from rigid attention, eyes fixed over Lewrie's shoulder on a cabin door. "Caught 'im pilin' up a mess o' papers an' such, sir! Drew a pistol, sir! Fired at us. Returned fire, sir. No 'elpin' it, Cap'um, sir!"

He might have been a servant, a valet to one of the gentlemen on deck. A wiry-haired fellow approaching middle years, his hair gray and neatly dressed. An aging clerk's soft hands and cherubic face. But he now lay sprawled between two open chests or traveling trunks, amid the blizzard of loose and bound correspondence he'd tried to jettison. His clothes were quite good. Much better than a servant usually received as part of his wages. Castoffs, Lewrie thought, kneeling down? No, they were too new, of good fabric, and elegant cut. Drab gray trousers, not breeches, but of excellent wool. A black waistcoat, now torn and gory. A fine cambric linen shirt with lots of lace, slowly turning rusty red.

"You're a damn' fool, sir," Lewrie told him, as his eyes opened and his breath, which had seemed stopped, heaved his chest.

"Aaahh . . ." He whimpered. A trickle of blood appeared along his mouth. Lung shot, or gut shot, and goin' fast, Lewrie grimaced.

"Who are you, sir? Anyone we should write?" Lewrie offered as he knelt down beside him. "Tell your family? *Familia*? *Famille*?"

"In . . ." The little fellow almost chuckled, though he was choking on his filling lungs. "*Inconnu* . . ." And with a rictus of a grin, he closed his eyes. A racking cough, the gout of blood that drowned him, flooded his mouth.

"Dammit!" Lewrie groused, sliding back on his knees to escape the last coughed blood. "*Inconnu*?"

"In French, sir, that is to say . . ."

"I *know* what it means, Mountjoy! 'Unknown,' was what the damn' fool said," Lewrie fumed, getting to his feet. "Having his last wee jest. See his eyes twinkle for a second there? Means whatever there was worth finding went overboard. And he died 'fore we could interrogate him. Might've planned it that way. Couldn't find the 'nutmegs' to put a pistol to his own skull, but he could make us do it for him."

"French agent, without a doubt, sir," Mountjoy flatly stated. "No one sane would kill himself for loss of profit." Mountjoy looked a little

queasy, as if he were suffering seasickness again. So far, there hadn't
been much dying aboard *Jester* for him to witness, for the young gentleman to wade through. "Hellish business, sir. Still . . . I say, Corporal
Summerall? Was he still trying to gather bundles of his papers, as if there
was something left to toss into the sea?"

"Aye, Mister Mountjoy, sir. Saw us, dropped 'em, then snatched up 'at
pistol, sir," Summerall reported, turned to face them but still speaking to
windowsills and the like.

"There is a remote possibility, sir," Mountjoy posed.

"Have at it, then, sir," Lewrie agreed with a weary air.

"And, sir?"

"Aye?"

"That fellow in the snuff-brown, sir, did you notice?"

"Notice what, Mister Mountjoy?"

"Well, sir, he was the only one of the principals aboard this ship who
didn't look pleased when they heard that splash, sir," Thomas Mountjoy
pointed out. "Didn't look . . . anything. Stone-faced as a good gambler,
sir. Pinched his eyes at the shots. For an instant, I recall a trace of
sadness. Then, back to his pose, sir. As if he *knew* this'n was going to die
beforehand. Didn't flinch or jump, like the others, that's what made me
remark him, sir."

"Well, damme, Mister Mountjoy, that's . . ." Lewrie gawped, as if
Toulon had begun forming words and speaking in English. "That's sharp
of you, I must say. However did you come by this . . . talent of yours?"

"A barrister I clerked for, sir, when I was reading the law, he discovered to me certain quirks people have when they give testimony in the
dock. Had he feigned surprise, I might have dismissed my first impression of this fellow, but . . ." Mountjoy shyly confessed. "Lead them on
with innocuous prattle, sir. Then rock 'em back on their heels hard, with
a question they don't expect. Then read their reactions."

"And, since you speak Italian and French so well, in addition to this
most welcome skill of yours, Mister Mountjoy," Lewrie decided, "I will
put you in charge of not only perusing what remains, but of quizzing our
prisoners, as well. Especially our snuff-brown friend."

"Er . . . thankee, sir. I think," Mountjoy all but preened. Just before
he realized how much, and how arduous a labor that would be.

"Him, last, I should think," Lewrie speculated. "Let him stew over
what the other missed."

"An admirable idea, sir. I'll see to it."

"Lock them all up, separate cabins. No personal belongings, I think

would be best. These trunks and chests, ready for debarking at San Remo
. . . could you go through them all?"

"These two, particularly, sir. This dead fellow seemed anxious to purge
just these two open ones." Mountjoy dared to grin. Excited, again, to be
useful. "Why just these two? His . . . and the snuff-brown man's, I'd
wager? Rather plain, good leather, but unremarkable, hmm. Nothing as
gaudy as those. I'd strongly suspect the fancy ones belong to the elegant
gentleman. Might be the ship's owner, do you not think, sir? Might have
bags of incriminating stuff crammed in his, but *these* got the attention, as
if this ship's problems, and theirs, were . . . !"

"I leave it to you, sir," Lewrie interrupted. "I have to get way on her,
sort out her crew, disarm and inspect 'em. Shuffle hands about—again!—
to man all our prizes, and such. We'll speak later, once we're safe and
snug in Vado Bay." And knowing, too, that once his clerk got enthused
about something, he'd talk six ways 'round whatever had heated his
blood, and waste the rest of the Day Watch doing it, too!

"Manifests," Lewrie said, snapping his fingers, delaying his departure
for the upper decks. "Bills of lading, ship's papers, crew and passenger
lists. I'll send you Mister Giles and his jack-in-the-bread-room to take
inventory of the cargo, so you may see if it conforms."

"Very good, sir. I mean, aye aye, sir."

Lawyers, Lewrie thought, pounding up the companionway ladders:
Minds like snake's nests, God save us!

CHAPTER

6

"A MOST GALLANT action, Commander Lewrie," Horatio Nelson told him, waving a hand toward a cut-glass decanter of newly arrived claret. "Perhaps a *bit* beyond our brief, to raid a Savoian port rather than a Genoese. But one which has no doubt discomfited the French, no end."

"Thankee, sir," Lewrie replied, making free with that welcome claret, and feeling like God's Own Damme-Boy to win praise from a man so aggressive himself.

"And most circumspect of you, as well, sir," Nelson went on, "to confine your findings concerning the merchant brig, and your suspicions, to a separate report."

"Mine and my clerk's, sir, Mister Thomas Mountjoy's," Alan added. He'd won almost gushing praise—there was enough and more to go around. And Mountjoy, surprisingly, had done almost as much as Knolles, Bootheby, Cony, or any of the others he'd cited for significant contributions to their overall success.

Too far from the entry door to be able to respond to the musket butt rapped on the deck, Nelson's next comment was cut off by the knock at the louvred partition door to the day-cabin.

"Excuse me, sir, but Captain Cockburn is come aboard, as you bid him," Lieutenant Andrews informed him, "and is just without."

"Ah, show him in, sir!" Nelson brightened. "Devil of a fellow, Cockburn. Took a Genoese just off Finale, 'bout the same time as your *Jester* was at Bordighera, Lewrie. And, in much the same mysterious . . . ah, here he is! Come in, Captain Cockburn! Come in, sir! Do you join us. And join us in a glass," Nelson offered. "New-come claret!"

"Captain Nelson, sir, good morning to you. Lewrie." Cockburn nodded, almost affably. Especially since Lewrie was sporting his newer full-dress coat, with the suggested epaulet and slash cuffs.

Small talk was made for a few minutes, a review of Cockburn's doings off Finale, which Lewrie felt politic to beam over; Lewrie's doings far to the west, over which Cockburn raised a brow and simpered, almost politely.

"And both of you have taken merchantmen violating our unofficial embargo," Nelson summed up. "Ships that present to us a most striking and mystifying similarity of circumstances. One might initially think that their coinciding similarities were simply that; coincidence. But I now am coming to suspect that any similarity between them is a first inkling of something planned, do you see. First off, Captain Cockburn brings in *Il Furioso*, a ship of Genoese registry. All her papers *seem* to be in order, though she was observed departing Finale, a port that is now French-held. Her Captain Bavastro and her crew abandon her just as soon as they are able. She attempted to prevent *Meleager*'s gallant First Officer, Lt. Thomas Hardy, from boarding. Her guns were loaded with canister and langridge, and her matches lit. Hardly the acts of a declared neutral, and therefore liable to legitimate seizure. Laden with valuables, too. Coin, gold bullion, silver plate, and such in her master's great-cabins. Which are now here aboard *Agamemnon*."

Damme, but Cockburn's a lucky bugger, Lewrie groaned to himself!

"Odd, though, that so far, Mister Francis Drake, ashore, cannot seem to find anyone who knows her as *Il Furioso*, or has ever heard of a ship by that name clearing from Genoa. More perplexing is the presence of a different name on her transom. *Nostra Signora di Belvedere*," Horatio Nelson posed.

"And mine, sirs . . ." Lewrie exclaimed, sitting up straighter.

"*Il Briosco*," Nelson agreed. "That is to say, *Lively*, as in a 'lively tune.' But bearing the name *Nostra Signora di Capraia* across her stern. Of Tuscan registry. Or at least, flying a Tuscan flag when taken. Lured in by *Jester* flying false French colors, and playacting as escort to a convoy, which were really his prizes and tender, Captain Cockburn. I strongly hold that only the nearness of *Il Briosco* to her captor, and her run-out battery . . . *and* the suddenness of Lewrie's revelation as a British ship, which took them all aback, prevented them from resisting. Her guns, too, were loaded but not run-out. With langridge and canister," Nelson stressed, lifting a finger, "one person, at least, did resist below, whom Lewrie suspects was a French spy, intent upon jettisoning a bag of incriminating documents. The man succeeded. Just as someone aboard *Il Furioso* did, Commander Lewrie."

"As if it were the drill, sir?" Lewrie puzzled. "No, it hardly sounds like coincidence at all!"

"Take him, sir?" Cockburn asked.

"Shot dead, in an exchange of fire with my Marines, sir," Alan had to admit. "There's a second, though, whom my clerk thinks might be another Frenchman, traveling under a false identity. Gave us a name . . . Enzio Brughera . . . but his companion, who called himself 'Inconnu' in his dying breath, didn't *quite* empty this Brughera's chest. There was a purse of Italian coinage, and a hefty purse of French gold, too. We found some odds and ends that show at least two more Italian names."

"I have him below, in irons," Nelson said. "I intend to hold him here, until Mister Francis Drake may contact some, uhm . . . associates, more used to this sort of chicanery."

"And out of the hands of the civil authorities, sir," Lewrie added. "Who might feel pressed, politically or militarily, to set him free. Or look the wrong way for a minute or two."

"Quite." Nelson nodded grimly. "While your French midshipman may go ashore, once he's given his parole, and may be exchanged, along with the civilian sailors and those passengers we *think* are legitimate."

"Another mystifying thing, sirs," Lewrie commented, "is Captain Menzi of *Il Briosco*, or *Our Thing-gummy*—whichever—departed Leghorn two days after we arrived off Genoa Mole and set off on our blockade . . . yet, he *knew* to inquire about the presence of our ships along the Genoese Riviera, and off San Remo. Why was that?"

"That, too, is intriguing, I'll grant you," Nelson agreed with him, waving a hand toward the decanter, so Lewrie could play "Mother," and top them all up.

"Well, sir." Cockburn sniffed. "It is not as if British ships have been completely absent from these waters. They were engaged in a smuggling endeavor, after all."

"Genoese ships might know it is now considered smuggling, sir," Lewrie countered. "But how did a vessel ostensibly Tuscan come to know of it, and so quickly? That, too, smacks of chicanery, of an organized and well-informed combination."

"Latins," Nelson chuckled with a world-weary sigh and a raising of his good brow. "Gossip, and informing, is in their temperaments, I do declare—bred into their very bones and blood."

"Something larger than turning a quick profit, or any charitable mo-

tive, if you will allow me to color it so, sirs," Lewrie continued. "Both of
these ships feared the presence of the Royal Navy . . . not since we just
did intend to stop up all coastal trade . . . but because they were engaged in trade with the *French*, sirs. Someone, perhaps a great many
someones, are eager to aid their cause, beyond turning a profit. Those
two agents aboard *Il Briosco*, the similarity of the subterfuge . . . then,
too, there is the possibility that influential or simply corrupt people
actually believe in the exportation of French Republicanism and revolution. And would do anything possible, 'long as they may make a fortune
from it, to aid the Frogs. Undermine their own governments."

"A very *large* supposition, Commander Lewrie," Cockburn drawled,
pulling a face. "Nor one spun from whole cloth, but only a few raveled
strands, as of yet."

"Well, perhaps the French may pay more than we can offer, sir,"
Lewrie rejoined. "All the wealth seized from Royalists, from guillotined
aristocrats, the Catholic Church in France. And what they looted from
their recent conquests."

"We'll leave it to the proper authorities," Nelson decided for them,
raising a brow slightly as he detected the slightest hints of animus between them. "We don't have all the facts, and cannot discover more from
Leghorn or Tuscany. Commander Lewrie, you did recover commercial
documents from *Il Briosco*, which lead you to suspect, at least, a financial
combination?" he urged.

"*Il Briosco* is owned by a Leghorn joint-stock company, much like the
East India Company," Lewrie said, sitting back in his chair. "Men invest
as ship's husbands, or as risk-coverers such as Lloyd's, sharing the risk,
and the possible profits. It's called the *Compagnia di Commercia Mare di
Liguria*. Rather confusing, though. Neither my clerk nor I can make
heads or tails of it, so far, sirs. Captain Menzi is shown as a shareholder in
some papers, just a hired captain in others. The super-cargo aboard, a
Signore Gallacio, admitted he's a shipowner, not a shareholder. Yet,
there's an inscrutable little ledger book Mister Mountjoy turned up that
shows several people, or organizations, and their share of the profits of
the ship's voyage. There's a 'G-G,' which I take to stand for Guilio
Gallacio. The rest are just initials, and no telling what they really mean,
sir. I find it odd, though, for a Tuscan company to call itself a *Ligurian*
sea-trading firm."

"We *are* in the Ligurian Sea, sir!" Cockburn snorted.

"Liguria is also the ancient Roman name for the entire coastal region,
sir. *North* of Leghorn or Porto Especia. Were they really a Tuscan con-

cern, sir, why did they not use their own sea, the Tyrrhennian, or the entire Mediterranean, to describe their intended trading area?"

"Another matter for Mister Drake's associates, Commander Lewrie," Nelson suggested. "After inquiries may be made in Tuscany. Should it be registered proper, the names of the major stockholders will be revealed to us. And if some of those majority owners turn out to be Genoese, or agents representing Genoese investors, *then* we may be able to say that it is, without a doubt, an illegal combination."

"And, most likely, such an inquiry may also reveal the names of ships to be on the lookout for," Cockburn said with a sly chuckle, a tap of his finger against his temple. "With such information, we may concentrate on the largest, best-organized, smugglers. Their capture or elimination from the trade would daunt the smaller players. Were their ships to be seized often enough, they'd throw in their hands as a poor wager."

"If it is merely financial, and not political, sir," Alan said, unwilling to concede the point, on principal certainly, because he still suspected the presence of French agents hinted at something dangerous. And hating to give the smug bastard the last word, in anything!

"I daresay, Lewrie," Cockburn allowed with a bemused expression, "that there is the possibility of the French being involved, taking full advantage of the greed, or the humane efforts of the Genoese to aid their occupied compatriots. Anything to undermine resistance in Italy. But, as I also said before . . . we simply do not know enough to take a leap of logic, into the speculative."

"I see, sir," Lewrie relented. A bit truculently, it must be said; resenting being lectured to by a man ten years his junior. "But I will lay a wager with you, this very moment, sir," he added with a sly grin. "That when we do come to discover all, there *will* be French collusion, and French gold, at the root of it. Name your sum, sir."

"Five hundred pounds." Cockburn grinned back, just as slyly.

Sufferin' Jesus, Alan thought, his mind awhirl; now I'm for it! Even if the Prize Court came through with what I'm due, I'd still be bankrupt, if I'm wrong! Borrow it from Phoebe . . . No!

"Gentlemen, really . . ." Nelson chided them, with the affable, and amazed, tone of a father interceding between two headstrong brothers. "Make it a shore supper, or a case of wine. And the terms are vague. Of course, the French are involved. Whether they are the instigators, or the recipients of a fortuitous accident, which they hope to exploit. Hardly a proper wager at all, really. It lacks the 'either, or.' "

"A shore supper, then, sir," Lewrie amended. "That it is the full cabal, set up by the Frogs."

"And I say they are exploiting the greed of misguided, short-sighted . . . tradesmen," Cockburn countered. "Aye, a shore supper."

"Done!" Lewrie cried, offering his hand to seal the bargain.

"Done, and done, then." Nelson laughed. "Well, I think that's about it. We must *suspect* a formal, organized attempt to trade with, and succor, the French. The valuables suggest that. *Il Briosco* had a full cargo of flour, salt, boots, and shoes, what else . . . ?"

"About a ton of tanned leather, sir, suitable for harnesses or belts and pouches," Lewrie was happy to supply. "Cast-off military accoutrements, sail cloth suitable for tents, blankets . . . and quite a lot of naval stores. Salt meats, sausages and salami, cheese, and all the rough wine in the world."

"Which will fetch a pretty penny at Mister Drake's sales." Nelson beamed, rising to dismiss them. "And deny the French any joy of it. I think that will be all, until we know more. Gentlemen, thank you both for coming aboard, and sharing your information with me. And with each other, hmm? So you may cooperate in future, more attuned?"

That wasn't a hope; that was an order, Lewrie almost winced.

"Stay a moment, Commander Lewrie, there is one other matter," Nelson directed before they said their good-byes.

"Aye, sir?" he prompted, once Cockburn had gone.

"The matter of your tender, sir," Nelson said, squinting over his report, impatiently turning for the best light in the great-cabins for his one good eye. "This little *Bombolo*. Quite a good idea. Most ingenious of you. Though you were *damned* fortunate, against such odds."

"Thank you, sir." Lewrie smiled, glad it wasn't to be a tongue-lashing for being at odds with Cockburn.

"I fear you'll have to keep her," Nelson said soberly. "This *La Follette*. Better-armed, I grant you, and a valuable seizure. But she is a French ship of war, little or no, and must be properly condemned, then bought into the Royal Navy before I could possibly condone her addition to our squadron."

"I see, sir." Lewrie sighed.

"There are certain customs and usages of the fleet that even I cannot ignore, no matter the situation, do you see, Lewrie." Captain Nelson laughed softly. "Only *so* many orders I may flaunt, or act contrary to. No, I am sorry, but she must go to San Fiorenzo. Our admiral may wish to inspect her unique carronade armament. That she is armed with carronades, at all, in the first instance. And the novel training platform beneath them, in the second. And, after all . . . I doubt if you would wish to give up your First Officer, Mister Knolles."

"Sir?"

"You would, you know, were she taken in or sent off. She's a lieutenant's command, not merely a tender to another ship," Nelson told him. "*Could* I condemn her myself, and buy her in, well . . . I fear there are other lieutenants senior to Mister Knolles more deserving of command. And, were she a part of this squadron this instant, I would assign her to work inshore with *Meleager, Inconstant,* or *Southampton,* allowing one of the deep-draught frigates a shallow-draught companion. I fear you must recover your swivels and two-pounders from *La Follette,* and rearm *Bombolo.* You can tow her astern, ready for another bold raid on the French. But you can't come nigh to hoisting your own broad pendant as an *ex-officio* squadron commander with her your consort."

"Oh well, sir . . ." Lewrie shrugged sheepishly, putting a good face on it.

"I trust, though, that the prize money from her capture mollifies you, Lewrie," Nelson offered by way of condolence.

"Should the Court ever see their way clear to paying it, sir," Lewrie reminded him, "then, aye, I s'pose it must."

"Aye, those . . . !" Nelson seethed for a moment. "I tell you, sir, I am *determined* to become an admiral! To have say in matters, redress so many shortcomings. Prize-Court doings, not the least of them, but . . ." he said coming around his desk to steer Lewrie to the door of his day-cabin. "Until then, there is the satisfaction that you did your duty, as best you saw it, with aggressiveness, pluck and daring. And, more than your own portion of good fortune. Confounded French recruiting, perhaps; certainly destroyed a battery, a garrison, and took those coasting bottoms they'll sorely miss. And captured a French national ship into the bargain. This fellow who runs their convoys must, this very instant, be tearing out his hair in frustration."

"Confusion to the French, sir," Lewrie boasted.

"Amen to that, sir," Nelson exclaimed, as a send-off. "Amen to that. Now, off with you, Lewrie. Recover your tender and we'll be off about the King's Business. Perhaps not quite so far as Cape Antibes . . . hmm? A little closer to home. A daily cruise west, returning to read my signals. Mister Drake suggests a large convoy, soon, a rich one . . ."

"Aye aye, sir!" Lewrie heartily agreed.

"Scour the coast for me, Lewrie. And good hunting."

CHAPTER

7

"You . . . !" THE SCARRED man sneered, his permanently scrub-pink complexion mottling with an anger so fatal it could have killed, just by itself, straight across the desk in the great-cabins of the French National corvette *La Vengeance*.

Vengeance was at anchor in the port of Nice, but a southerly, a sirocco, blew into the harbor, making the agile 350-ton corvette do an edgy dance. Which didn't do Lt. Henri Becquet's attempts at composure any good, either, as he suffered the well-deserved tirade. As Lt. Henri Becquet attempted to find a way to wriggle free of responsibility—and the threat of court-martial and the guillotine. France did not suffer its fools gladly, had no use for failure, or excuses for it.

"You . . . !" the scarred Capitaine de Vaisseau hissed again. He partially hid his brutally scarred face with a black silk mask, an eye patch that extended upward to cover a broken-lined brow, downward to hide a cheek that had been slashed to the bone. There was no disguising, though, the tyrannical mouth, the upper lip and part of a nostril that had been savaged and crudely sewn, making him an offset harelip. "You stupid . . . goddamned . . . *fool!*" he thundered. "Idiot!"

"M'sieur . . ." Lieutenant Becquet shivered so violently that his teeth chattered. His very life depended on the next few moments, suspended in midair at the end of a figurative single skein of light thread . . . and Le Hideux the one with the razor blade! Perversely, Becquet cast a glance to the civilian aft near the transom windows, who was a dark, brooding shadow against the midday glare. Le Hideux was showing off, performing for the civilian, Becquet suspected. Covering his own failures with a spectacular rant, if the civilian was down from Paris, to inquire why the convoys failed so often, so much was lost . . . ?

"What can you do?" the senior captain asked the ether, with a soft toss of his hands, and a look toward the deck head. He rose and paced slowly, his weakened left calf supported by a stiff knee boot reinforced with an iron brace. Clump, shuffle . . . clump, shuffle, and Lieutenant Becquet began to sweat an icy flood as Le Hideux approached him. "Here is the very sort of laziness I continually fight against, Citizen," he said to the civilian. For his benefit . . . and his own. "Idiots, fools, shit for brains. Oh, they spout all the right slogans, cheer when you tell them, Citizen Pouzin. As if halfhearted *enthusiasm* for the Revolution was enough, *n'est-ce pas*? But, deep in their souls, they stay shop clerks! Open on time, *pretend* to work, then run for the cafés or the brothels, as soon as the door is shut for the evening. Without a thought of working! Without a care for anything but their comforts!"

Clump, shuffle . . . clump, shuffle, behind Becquet, who kept his gaze straight ahead at the silhouetted Citizen Pouzin, pleading with his eyes. And expecting a dagger in his kidneys.

"A gun captain, did you know that, Citizen Pouzin?" Le Hideux sneered. "From the Garonne, where they do not understand the sea. A *river* man. A gun captain who turned against his 'aristo' masters when he saw which way the wind was blowing. When we broke up that elitist naval artillery corps, that pack of bootlickers! . . . Becquet turned on them. To save his hide, hein? So he could have his soup and bread, a ready supply of coin, only. For his wine, and his *whores*! Got promoted because he shouted the loudest. So he could make even more money to waste on wine and *whores*?" Le Hideux accused, shouting into the lieutenant's ear so close that spittle from his ravaged lips bedewed Becquet, as cold as Antarctic ice crystals.

"*Capitaine*, I did my duty, I . . ."

"Too hard a task, was it, Becquet?" Le Hideux scoffed. "Too much to ask, to *unload* the cargo, as soon as you got to Bordighera? Even if you had to work past closing time, *hein*? But you *had* time. You docked at dusk? Answer!"

"*Oui, Capitaine*, just at dusk, but the Savoians . . ."

"Let the infantry company go ashore, instead of ordering them to help unload," Le Hideux growled, stumping back into his sight. "I ordered you to unload quickly, did I not? Dash in, dash out, before a 'Bloody' patrol saw you. So that the convoy would be safe. So those Savoian volunteers would get their arms and equipment. A direct order, and an important task. Which you nodded and parroted back to me, did you not, here in this cabin, Becquet? Swore on your honor you'd fulfill, to the letter, *hein? Oui?*"

"*Oui, Capitaine* . . . but . . . !*"

"Thought one puny three-gun battery of light fieldpieces would be protection enough, did you? For ships in your charge? To protect your lazy hide? Were you aboard *La Follette* when the 'Bloodies' opened fire on the battery?"

"*Certainment, Capitaine!*" Becquet declared.

"Liar," Citizen Pouzin asserted calmly, snapping Becquet's head around. "A letter from your midshipman, Hainaut."

"*Oui*, Hainaut!" Le Hideux chimed in. "Not four days since his capture, and we already have a letter he sent, asking for his exchange. *He*, at least, did his duty. You were *not* aboard. Where were you, in bed with a whore, up in the town? A whole half hour they took, before the battery was silenced. Were you so taken with wine that you needed a whole half hour to wake up? A half hour, Becquet. A real man would have mustered his crew, sailed out, and supported the battery. With the guns you had aboard *La Follette*, you could have deterred them entering. But what did you do with that precious time? *Nothing!*"

"The crew, they ran off, *Capitaine*, I *tried* to muster them . . ."

"Not run off," Citizen Pouzin countered, coming closer. "You gave them shore leave for the night. How convenient."

"They didn't come back, I . . ." Becquet almost swooned in fear. "Some did. I brought them . . ."

"From the same brothel where you wallowed?" Le Hideux scoffed.

"The 'Bloody' corvette entered, and the few who'd stayed, or the few who'd come back with me, they . . ."

"*Hainaut* had mustered them for you," Le Hideux accused. "Hainaut had sense enough to load the artillery. To *load* the *artillery*, do you hear, Citizen Pouzin? The gun-captain's guns were unloaded! Were they even loaded for the voyage, you idle fool?"

"We drew the charges, once we tied up. Accidents, new allies . . ."

"Convenient," Pouzin whispered, coming close enough from those harsh shadows at last, so Becquet could see him. A square-cut, hefty man, quite handsome in a rough-and-ready way, with a blunt chin and a square head. All business. "Perhaps, *Capitaine*, too much so."

"All you had thought for was a bottle or two, a good supper, and a plump whore, wasn't it, Becquet?" Le Hideux snapped. "Crew let go for the night, so they could have a good, easy time of it with you, so they would *like* you? Perhaps a bit too *much liberté, egalité, fraternité, hein?*"

Citizen Pouzin lifted a bushy brow at that statement. A French officer was supposed to be no better than the commonest man beneath him, due no more dignity. There was *supposed* to be brotherhood among them, a true comradeship in the service of The Cause.

"Time enough for that when the voyage is over, when you had completed your mission," Le Hideux added in a softer voice. Pouzin was in charge of intelligence, and had as many connections in Paris as did Le Hideux; as many ears into which he could pour poison against him. "Then, and only then," he continued, glaring at Pouzin to show how heartfelt were his sentiments. And how innocent. "May you let your guard down. Had you lost your ship in battle, I'd be kissing you on both cheeks, Becquet. Had you hurt the 'Bloodies,' gotten the cargo ashore, it would have been bad luck, bad timing, their arrival, but . . ."

"But it seems such a total lack of diligence, and caution, we might be able to think of it as treachery," Pouzin challenged in his gruff, maddeningly calm voice. "How else may we explain the suddenly foolish actions of a man so well regarded, just weeks ago. With such a diligent, able, and unblemished record in the Republican Navy?"

"M'sieur, oh God, I . . . !"

"Citizen," Pouzin corrected, with a warning hiss.

"Now your Savoian hands have run away, and will never come back, *hein?*" Le Hideux summed up, goading Becquet with a cruel leer. "The Savoians delayed training and arms. When they seemed *so* eager to join us. A brave French garrison turned to blood soup, a valuable company of experienced, battle-hardened officers and men who would have trained them, lost. How much enthusiasm for military service do you think the Savoians have now, hein? There is no doubt word has spread deep into the mountains. Of how inept French warships, of how ludicrous the French Army, look. And, it's all . . . *your* . . . *fault!*"

"Dear God, sir . . . !" Becquet whimpered, almost pissing himself.

"But you will atone for this, *mon pauvre petit* Gun Captain," Le Hideux promised in a caressing whisper, that whisper more threatening than his loudest rants. "Oh, indeed you will. On your *head* be it."

"Sir . . . !"

"By the authority given me by the Committee of Public Safety," Le Hideux intoned, stumping away to lean on his desk to rest his leg. "I order you be held in irons until the time of your trial by court-martial, where you will answer charges of grave dereliction of duty . . . cowardice in the face of the enemy . . . the loss of your command without a shot being fired . . . the loss of your convoy and their cargo . . ."

"And treason against the Republic," Pouzin tacked on, heaving a huge shrug. "Trafficking with the enemy and conspiring to . . ."

There was a thud as Becquet's wits left him, and he swooned to the deck, a spreading wet stain on his trousers.

"At five, this afternoon," Le Hideux grunted. "Guards! Take this cowardly scum away!"

"A FOREGONE CONCLUSION." Pouzin sighed, heading for the cabinet to pour them both glasses of wine. "A court packed with officers, and men . . . of sound Republican, Revolutionary spirit . . ."

"Of a certainty," Le Hideux agreed, wincing as he sat down, to rest that continual dull ache that had been his burden the past nine years. The bastard who'd cut him with his sword, laying his face open, had also slashed his left calf, after he was down and disarmed, writhing and howling with agony . . . ! *"Pour encourager les autres*, Citizen. The grand revolutionary, Thomas Jefferson . . . he said that the Tree of Liberty must be watered with the blood of patriots. I water it with the blood of fools and cowards. Of shop clerks! So the others might become *true* patriots. Even if they come to their patriotism from fear. You see what I contend with, hein, Citizen Pouzin? The idleness, the thoughtlessness I endure? I am surrounded by incompetence, and lackluster pinheads. What I would give for just a *few* more Bretons here, a few more with the hardy, seafaring courage of the ancient Celts . . ."

Pouzin rolled his eyes, bored that Le Hideux was harping upon his favorite theory. He'd heard quite enough of it in the full year they'd cooperated together. Most warily cooperated, that is. Neither was superior to the other, running their separate operations in parallel; sometimes at cross-purposes, sometimes hand in glove. And writing to Paris, to their own superiors, and patrons, of a certainty, reporting on each other. They were both in the same business, really, this horrid little deformed ogre Le Hideux, and Pouzin the spy (if Pouzin was indeed his right name), that of seeking out defectors, traitors, failures, and fools, such as Becquet. Of inspiring the others to keep the ardent flame of passion for the Revolution alive in every breast. To weed the unworthy, the lazy, the smugly satisfied, so that France, so threatened from without (and quite possibly within, such as in the Vendee where resistance still sputtered) might survive, then march to the ends of the earth to spread her glorious

doctrines. If that took a thousand bad bargains and traitors to the guillotine . . . *et alors?* . . . Pouzin thought philosophically.

"And the brutal logic, the innate *sense* of the Breton peasant." Le
Hideux sighed in longing. "Not these shortsighted, city-bred . . ." He
took a sip of wine to cool his melancholia. "I envy you, Pouzin. The zeal
and dedication of the people who work for you. Do you ever
face . . . ?"

"A different sort of worry, *Capitaine.*" Pouzin chuckled. "I worry
about who is loyal, who is lying to me. Of which reports can I trust, and
which are made up to please me, to earn my gold. Who works for the
other side, or both. But, thankfully no, no lack of zeal. It is far too
profitable to them. And, for the good ones, too much fun. A good spy
thoroughly enjoys his work. Now then . . . the rest of the bad news.
This ship that raided Bordighera . . . your Hainaut tells us, quite inno-
cently in his letter to the parole commission, that she was named *Jester.*
Even worse, she took one of the ships we . . . arranged . . . off San
Remo. Aboard were two of my best agents, returning from Leghorn. One
is dead, the other a captive."

"That's bad," Le Hideux commiserated. "But, far west of where we
expected this embargo to reach, in a backwater. Had your people in
Genoa told us this, I would definitely have provided escort within fifty
sea miles of the coast. Though my few poor ships are stretched so thin,"
he added, to excuse himself. Pouzin could smell a brave but exculpatory
report to Paris; his *and* Le Hideux's.

"I grant you," Pouzin allowed. "And I sympathize with your lack of
suitable warships. Yet . . ." he posed, with another Gallic shrug.

"Two ships lost," Le Hideux rasped, running a hand over a rough and
patchy beard and short mustache he'd grown to help disguise his injuries.
"Another taken off Finale? Again, where my vessels dare not go, except
in squadron strength."

"Our principals in Genoa, and Leghorn, are upset, that our mutual
arrangement unravels so quickly," Pouzin gloomed. "There are so many
other ships naturally. But the captains and crews must take even more
risk now. And one of our Tuscan principals was temporarily detained. He
is not a man of stout courage. It will take more gold, he writes."

"He is robbing us, and he knows it," Le Hideux spat. "A chance
encounter off San Remo. An idiot who should have put back into Finale,
under the protection of the castle's guns, as soon as he saw a 'Bloody'
frigate. Two out of dozens? The vagaries of war. Which they agreed to
happily. The bulk of the goods, messages, and money get through."

"*Certainment, Capitaine,*" Pouzin quickly agreed. Certainly, Le Hideux was ruthless, a monster in human guise . . . but he'd been successful enough to keep his command—and his head—this long. Grain from North Africa, coastal convoys that lost ships, also of a certainty, but mostly delivered the goods to support the advance of the Army. And allow Pouzin to maintain his far-flung spiderweb. "But with the British squadron in Vado Bay, and our army threatened by de Vins . . . a greater effort is called for. No matter the cost."

"Get me Hainaut back," Le Hideux said, of a sudden. "He's not a Breton, but he's of the ancient blood, of the Belgae. In his head he has information we need, Pouzin. He's been in Vado Bay, aboard this . . . *Jester*. He may be only a midshipman . . . now. But, he's *paissan connard*, a wily one. A cunning one. He has a great future. He's counted their guns, can tell us of their ships, their schedules . . ."

"But we know them," Pouzin countered. He could not relate what his latest secret letter from Genoa hinted, from one of their principals aboard *Il Briosco;* that Hainaut had been taken so easily, so clumsily, that the "Bloody" sailors laughed at him. A cunning peasant, yes, he was, Pouzin was sure; cunning enough to have a very strong streak for self-preservation. "A sixty-four-gun ship of the line, three frigates, a pair of what we would call *corvettes*, a pair of brigs of war, a brig-sloop of fourteen guns, and a cutter."

"We know the ships, yes, Pouzin, but not the men who command," Le Hideux demanded. "Hainaut will know to listen and learn, to probe and discover their faults. You will get him back quickly."

"I will get him paroled," Pouzin promised; it was easier than saying no, though how long it might take . . . "There are midshipmen of equal value from the *Berwick* Admiral Comte Martin took in his initial try against them. But . . ."

"Now *there's* a head that should tumble into the basket, Pouzin," Le Hideux sneered, tossing back his wine and reaching for another. "A coward and a fool, who abandoned *Ça Ira* and *Censeur*. Another Becquet. Another time-server. Another shop clerk! Hainaut is ten times that Martin's worth. At least he is dedicated, and zealous. You don't see, do you? Have I not told you of the ancient Chinois general, Sun T'zu? The man who knows his enemy, as well as he knows himself, will never be defeated. Especially if he knows himself, best of all. What are their faults, their strengths? Their vices, their weaknesses . . . what have we learned about them, so far, I ask you?"

That was an indictment of Pouzin's intelligence-gathering, and could not go unanswered.

"A fair amount, *Capitaine*," Pouzin retorted, baring his teeth. "We know that this Nelson took both *Ça Ira* and *Censeur*. Traded fire with *Alcide* before she blew up. He was a favorite of Hood. Led the battle line both times Martin fought Hotham. A very aggressive man. Our principal met him, when he represented Hood in Genoa, last year, and was highly impressed. A little fellow, a bit frail . . ."

"Watch out for the little ones, Pouzin, the minnikins have more ambition than most," Le Hideux cackled. "He will be vaunting, brave. Perhaps too ambitious and eager for glory. Ah ha!"

"The frigate *Inconstant*," Pouzin went on, proving his worth to Le Hideux, and hating every minute of justifying himself to such a hideous fellow. "Her Captain Fremantle . . . dull, dogged, quiet. Capable, but inarticulate."

"A follower," Le Hideux dismissed. "A gundog. The others?"

"The one off Finale, *Meleager*. Her Captain Cockburn is a young man, a minor 'aristo' from lower Scotland. Very prim and proper, but . . ."

"His family rich?"

"I don't know," Pouzin intoned, the phrase he hated most of all!

"A rich 'aristo' will be smug, easily satisfied. A poor one will be all ambition and nose-high airs, too proud to listen to anyone. He's lucky once, but again? Go on. Tell me of this *Jester*'s captain."

"A commander, in his early thirties. She has eighteen cannon on her main deck . . . nine-pounders. Carronades, of course. They all seem to have them, almost doubling their armament. She was a French corvette, once . . . *Sans Culottes* . . . taken off Toulon after the 'Bloodies' . . ."

"But you don't know his identity," Le Hideux purred.

"Not yet. He has not set foot in Genoa, so no one . . . but your Midshipman Hainaut, has seen him, so far." Pouzin sighed in surrender. It appeared that he would *have* to get Hainaut exchanged, and as quickly as possible, after all. "We know little more about her. An agent from Calvi—when we still had communications with him—reported *Jester*'s arrival at San Fiorenzo. Last June, or July, as I recall. I don't have my records with me. I doubt that agent is willing to make inquiries now, since Corsica is occupied. Getting a letter to him is almost imp . . ."

"Try Genoa, first. I know the 'Bloodies.' There's nothing they like more than a stroll ashore, an invitation to a supper, or a ball. A coupling with a whore? You can arrange that, Pouzin?"

"Of course, *Capitaine*," Pouzin agreed with a tiny smile. "Poxed, or otherwise?"

"Oh, the 'Bloodies,' so many of them are already poxed. Look at how little effect it had, after their long stay at Leghorn." Le Hideux chuckled. "I want to know who he is, what he's like . . . so I can lay the trap that kills him, Pouzin. He's dangerous, this one, whoever he may be. He's hurt our Cause, made us look like fools, *le salaud intrigant!*"

Made *you* look the fool, Pouzin thought, his face a stony mask.

"I will move the squadron east, Pouzin," Le Hideux announced suddenly. "I must. Our presence at sea must be seen, by the Savoians, and our unwitting . . . traders, *hein*?"

"Escorted convoys?" Pouzin hoped aloud.

"We must," Le Hideux growled. "Else we risk losing more ships, more supplies, which the Army needs so badly. And soon, before de Vins masses his Austrians. Or the Genoese at last find a scrap of courage. We must both use our influence . . . or our threats . . . against Toulon, to force Martin to give me the strength I need. He *hoards* corvettes and frigates, refuses me any of the trained men or experienced officers I need. Yet expects me to work miracles with my castoffs and converted merchantmen. Here, *here*, is where the Navy should be, Pouzin! Facing the 'Bloodies' with a large squadron, under my command. Four of our little armed *tartane* expedients could never outgun or outfight *one* British frigate. Yet, how *dare* they sneer when we fail! If we wish to defeat the Austrians, and guard our borders, they must release to me the proper ships, at last. I cannot face this embargo, otherwise."

"Well, there is a way, perhaps, to weaken it," Pouzin hinted coyly. "While you prevail upon Toulon to send more warships. *Jester* fired a shot over the heads of those looters who were desecrating our brave soldiers. But, can we not allege that the damage to their buildings came from an indiscriminate broadside . . . against Bordigheran civilians? That this British ship fired on innocent, helpless villagers, *hein*? We both know the 'Bloodies' have no real love for Savoians, or the Genoese. They mean to exploit them, use them in the most cynical manner, to uphold rich 'aristos' and landowners, at the poor people's expense. A broadside of our own . . . a *paper* broadside, *hein*? . . . might make infuriating reading in Genoa. A slaughter on the docks, too, when the poor people came down to save their town from being burned to the ground?"

"I see." Le Hideux nodded, his eyes widening with the possibilities. "But," he countered with a petulant air, "they might send this *Jester* away from the coast, put her at patrol duties far out to sea . . . where I cannot reach her with the force I now have. A Jester took my Little Fool at Bordighera. But I will not be this man's fool, Pouzin. *I* will not laugh at his jests. He must pay. *Oui*, we must weaken the embargo, and embarrass the 'Bloodies.' If it takes your lies to do it, *et alors*. But it is bloodless. The Italian states must see British blood for French blood. We must have victories to boast of, so they come to fear us. Or admire us. We *must* be seen able to punish this *Jester*, don't you *see*?" Le Hideux insisted, his eyes bulging, and a livid purple-red cast coming to his scars, in a flushed ginger face. "And you *will* aid me in arranging it," Le Hideux concluded, with the sureness of the delusional demented.

"A hid . . ." Pouzin began to say, but checked himself. "A titanic task," he amended. Too late. Le Hideux's good eye had slitted in black fury. No one but Hainaut had ever been able to mention his maiming, without suffering for it. Die Narbe, he named him in admiration and a *respectful* jest. Something Pouzin was not allowed, would never be allowed. Too many slips of the tongue like that, and Pouzin would pay, with his head on the block beneath the blade, one day!

Pouzin flinched a trifle, though he meant to stare calmly, turn bland and innocuous. Since his first sight of Le Hideux, Brutto Faccia, Die Narbe . . . however men called him . . . he'd felt ice water trickle down his spine in dread of him, had felt his "coulles" shrivel up inside his groin. And had felt his stomach turn in utter loathing of the outward appearance, as well as the soul within.

"I will compose the rumor at once, *Capitaine*," Pouzin swore. "And get it off east. And arrange for *Jester*'s captain to be studied. Hainaut to be paroled and exchanged for someone off *Berwick*. And you still plan the convoy to Alassio? I must make arrangements for them to meet it," Pouzin ticked off, trying not to sound rushed, though he felt a tremendous urge to be away from the poisonous little monster. "You will extend your escorts east, to protect this convoy, and offer battle to the 'Bloodies,' *hein*?"

"*Oui*," Le Hideux confirmed, his remaining eye hooded with venom.

"*Au revoir*, then, *Capitaine*."

"*Au revoir*, Citizen," Le Hideux snapped coldly.

IT WAS QUITE a clever plan, the hideously scarred captain mused, and Hainaut's "testimony" to an alleged massacre, once he'd been coached on what he was to "remember," would be even more official, and convincing. Citizen Pouzin indeed was very good at what he did. And being master of an intelligence ring was most likely as great a delight to him as "the deadly game" was to his minions. A tireless, and clever, worker, one totally dedicated to furthering the Revolution. Look what Samuel Adams's lies about the "Boston Massacre" had started!

Even if he *had* been a commercial importer-exporter from L'Orient before the Terror, and a minor representative in the fledgling Assembly. An *elevated* shop clerk—*and* a nattering lawyer—Le Hideux glowered; a *rich* man, as exalted as any "aristo"!

Pouzin was not to know it, but Le Hideux had already discovered his true identity through his own intelligence network of informers and collaborators, minor functionaries of local or naval committees, and a host of officials in the Ministry of Marine. There were skeletons in Pouzin's closet; some Royalist sentiments in the family, a cousin conveniently sent to Boston, and Pouzin's attempt to purchase a title back in 1786 of the old calendar. Someday, Le Hideux was sure he would use that information to damn Pouzin, if he persisted in ogling him like a carnival monster, or sneering behind his back at his mutilation. Not anytime soon, though, Le Hideux sighed. A new guard was taking over, the original patriots being supplanted, deposed, or guillotined after show trials, and the unctuous lawyers and *bien élevé* schemers were now in the saddle, no better than the haughty "aristos" they'd helped kill. The professional politicians, Le Hideux sneered; it is ever thus! Men who thought him an ogre, too, a frightening, crippled *toad* who rose in the patronage of the giants of the Revolution that they'd replaced. A time to lie low, he decided, to escape their notice. And to give them such a military and naval success that his witch-finding activities for the original rebels could be conveniently forgotten. When Genoa became theirs . . . he could become *their* scourge, a shabby but useful tool for the sneering *arrivistes*. And take his chances.

There'd never been a time when he hadn't felt like a tool, an implement to be discarded. Safer, perhaps, to have remained a Breton peasant, in the fisheries with his father. He might have come to own three or four luggers, by now. But still go home each evening to a drab, and limited, village cottage, stinking of fish and shiny with their scales. The ambitions his father had, that he had had . . . He *could* have become a priest, a pampered sycophant of the "aristos." Even without a cassock, the Jesuits had taught him much, had declared him to be a wondrous pupil. Had they not introduced him to Machiavelli's writings? How apt a preparation the Jesuits and their coldly calculating logic had been to him . . . to ready him for the time when he *was* better to be feared, than loved! His acceptance into the old Royal French Navy, the best he had been allowed, since getting into the glorious old aristocratic *Armée* was impossible for a fisherman's son. The sneers and jibes there, too, as the smelly fishmonger's boy, the dirty-arsed coastal peasant . . . !

He'd risen, though, by doing their dirty work, by being better than anyone else. By taking on the tasks the idle "aristos" wouldn't, or couldn't. But, successful though he'd been, until his downfall in the Far East, he'd been their despicable tool, a brute instrument best kept on the orlop until needed. Then cast him aside, with a pittance for a disability pension, as soon as . . .

He'd made them pay, all those who had sneered at him, derided him, passed him over so some simpering frailty with a weak chin, but a perfect lineage, could advance. Revenge had been so sweet, and their terror so savory, when they'd beheld his new appearance. He'd hunted them down, with the diligence of a starving ferret clawing his way into a henhouse. Found them, denounced them no matter how secure they were in the new order, along with the "aristos" who truly deserved the guillotine, the weak, the foolish, the idle . . .

No, despite the appalling risk he ran to remain in power, even at the gall of his soul to *remain* the tool of more powerful men, the power was heady. Tried in the fire, he'd been—by his failure, and all the years he'd suffered the jeers and curses in the streets, the urchins who taunted him and imitated his limp, or ran screaming at the sight of him—for the fun of it!

Now, he knew how to use his hideousness to terrorize, in making handsome men jump when he gave an order. Or shiver like an aspic with a single glare! And the women . . . the ones who'd turned away, crossed the street, and crossed themselves for luck against him. Even whores who'd laughed him to scorn, or refused his trade, well . . . he'd hunted down a few of those, too, and their families. And made them pay their comeuppance in his cells, before their trials and beheadings.

Fear was a wonderful aphrodisiac, fear of his physical person, and fear of his power; greater and more coercive than mere political power. More brutal and direct, to get what he wanted. No woman anywhere in France could dare refuse him now.

And those officers' wives and daughters, oh *yes!*, the daughters best! What a thrill it was to have them without the mask, candles lit so they *must see him*, so he could savor their revulsion, the stomach-churning shame and horror on their faces. All so he might spare their husband, their father, from the guillotine, indictment or denunciation. The perverse duties they'd performed, weeping, to keep them alive. Only the prettiest now, only the slimmest, most graceful . . . and, youngest! As long as he held on to his power, he could enslave an adolescent for months, keep her father in chains all that time, until he'd tired of her, and his preordained but delayed sentence was . . . !

Hardly Jesuitical, he thought with a leer, dragging pen and ink to him. There must be a letter to Toulon, no longer begging for ships but demanding—threatening. If he failed for lack of support, they would go down with him, those time-serving, timorous shop clerks! A set of orders to ships of his squadron, to escort the Alassio convoy. A letter to the captain of *La Resolve*, a corvette only victualing at Nice, to consider himself permanently attached. Bayard, a devilishly handsome rogue, who knew better than to sneer, or gape, but . . .

Bayard, Le Hideux pondered. What tale had he told him . . .

"Etienne," he shouted for his clerk.

"*Oui, Capitaine?*" The careworn little nonentity quavered at the door, leaning in as if scared to be alone with his employer.

"Something nags at me, Etienne," Le Hideux replied, distracted. "Two things. You have a retentive mind, perhaps you may recall. Early last summer. Reports from Citizen Pouzin regarding the arrival at San Fiorenzo of a British ship named *Jester*. All engagements or sightings mentioning *identified* 'Bloody' ships since the fall of Bastia. Or at least before Calvi surrendered. Search my files and find it. Secondly, *Capitaine* Bayard told us a tale at dinner from his time with the Brest fleet. Something concerning a British vessel that he witnessed. Do you remember his story?"

"No, sir, sorry," Etienne stammered, ever in fear of failing his master, of *paying* for it . . . ! "Y . . . you might do best to ask of Bayard, sir. The other, though . . . *Jester?* Something akin to *Le Buffon*, or *Le Plaisantin?* I do recall that, I think. Around the time the convoy to Calvi was . . . lost?" he dared remind Le Hideux of that debacle.

"*Oui*, find it, *vite!*" Le Hideux glared so fiercely that clerk Etienne went quite pale, and fell on his knees before a large chest of documents and reports, hands shaking and palms wet. It took several *long* minutes for him to produce, all the while aware of the scratching of the senior captain's quill. Then the drumming of his fingers on the desktop after he'd finished his letters and was . . . waiting!

"*Voilà, Capitaine!*" Etienne sighed with relief. "In Lieutenant de Malleret's report. From *La Flèche?* The British ship she fought . . . when Lieutenant Michaud was slain, was *Jester*. He saw it on her transom."

"*Salaud intrigant!*" Le Hideux exclaimed with an inward hiss of air. "The meddlesome bastard!"

The ship that had taken his convoy at Bordighera, the British ship that had savaged *La Flèche* and taken another convoy . . . killed a promising fellow Malouin, a Breton champion, Lieutenant Michaud . . . they were the *same*?

"*Oui*, Capitaine, quel dommage . . ."

"Send for Bayard. I must know what his story was about. There was a name *he* mentioned, but . . . !" Le Hideux ordered, seething. "This one, this *Jester*. We must destroy her, Etienne. And her captain, too! This I vow. Whoever he is. I will eat his brains and shit in his skull!"

"*Oui, Capitaine.*" Etienne nodded, mouth agape. He'd never seen this ginger-haired ogre this angry, not even when presiding at a trial of an "aristo"! Trial? he thought. A good excuse to become scarce.

"Ah . . . I have the charges drawn up for your signature, *Capitaine*. Becquet's?"

"*Oui*, give them here, Etienne. Once you've sent to *La Resolve* for Bayard, finish searching all the files for any further mention of this *Jester*. I must *know* her. Him. Pouzin promises, but I cannot wait on him . . ."

Le Hideux—Brutto Faccia—Die Narbe—he went by an entire host of sobriquets; none of them flattering or reassuring. He dipped his quill and signed Becquet's fate; charges *and* expected sentence:

Citoyen Guillaume Choundas—Capitaine de Vaisseau.

CHAPTER
8

A BEST-SILK-STOCKINGS EVENING, Lewrie elated, all tricked out in low-cut shoes and breeches, and his best full dress. Feeling the winds, though, after getting used to slop trousers or his London-made Hessian boots with the gold braid and tassels. His shoes, it must be admitted, as well as his conscience, were pinching him sore.

Letters come from Caroline, and from Phoebe, in the same post, and held aboard *Agamemnon* for *Jester*'s return to Vado Bay. Fond, and loving devotion from Caroline, now quite recovered, as gay as larks at being able to ride their acres, again, of how glorious was an English country summer, how desperately she missed him, and would never withhold vital information from him again! A note from Sewallis, replete with paw prints from his dogs, a scrawl from Hugh, and . . .

And from Phoebe, such desperate longing, tearful phrases, words of love and . . . devotion, too, dammit! Chatty, newsy, delightful, as if a light touch might cajole him into believing their relationship had never suffered a grounding. Time and distance from her had caused him to forget just how delightfully cheery she really was. Her use of English had grown so skillful that he might have imagined (minus news of children, of course!) that the signatures of wife and mistress were interchangeable, that either missive could have come from the other!

"A WELCOME AND diverting amusement," Nelson had promised them, so he had scrubbed up, shaved, and donned his best for a night ashore in

Genoa, as welcome guests of a very influential and powerful member of
their Senate, one extremely close to the Doge, himself.

Genoa was indeed more distracting, and impressive, than Naples. And
Lewrie had been most impressed by Naples. Every other house was a
magnificent palace, he could have sworn, each one richer and grander
than the last, in a merchant city that had been rich as far back as Julius
Caesar's times, and had hoarded and multiplied its vast seaborne wealth
ever since. Surely, he thought—a sailor would find warm welcome in
Genoa!

THEIR HOST'S PALACE was truly magnificent, if a bit overdone. Gilt, coin-
silver, solid gold gewgaws, silk wallpaper, silk hangings, crystal chandeliers ablaze with two hundred or more beeswax candles at a time.
Precious . . . everything in *sight* was precious, rare, priceless, including
the clothes of the guests, their jewels and fripperies. Bare-shouldered
ladies, bodices half exposed, the heat of candles and too many bodies
gusted the confined night air, fanned overly sweet or musky scents of
Hungary Water, gentlemen's cologne, or ladies' perfume over him like a
Levanter, along with the dry talc aroma of face powder or hair powder,
the tang of rouges and pastes. And admittedly a sour reek of past and
present perspiration from those expensive suitings or gowns, and the
poor toilette or bathing habits of the rich and noble.

A bit off-putting, certainly; but a flower bed compared to the odors of
a warship full of men.

Nelson and his Lt. George Andrews, Cockburn and his Thomas
Hardy, Lewrie, and Knolles, along with a gaggle of midshipmen from
their respective ships, were led down the receiving line by Mister Francis
Drake, their Sovereign's representative to Genoa, a grossly untidy man
who appeared most unlike what a king's agent should be. Nelson had
wondered if he was even an English gentleman!

"Lovely place," Cockburn commented.

"His town palace," Drake muttered, swiveling about like an ill-tem-
pered bear, as if looking for a place to spit. It was rumored that he
chewed. "You should see his real one, up in the hills. Tremendous estates, owns half of the Republic, damn' near. Quite handy place for him
to leave the wife and kiddies."

"Really," Cockburn drawled with a dubious note in his voice.

"Quite small in comparison, this pile," Drake tittered, with a rogueish nudge in Cockburn's ribs. " 'Tis said he's a mistress cached in either wing. Rough life, hey, Captain? Ah, here we go, then."

"Ahum!" Cockburn sniffed in displeasure as he was left astern; as they queued up to be introduced. Drake did the honors in passable Italian with their host, the Genoese Senator, Marcello di Silvano.

". . . further allow me to name to your excellency Commander Alan Lewrie, captain of HMS *Jester* . . . Commander Lewrie, our distinguished host . . ." Drake simpered like a mastiff after a bone.

"Your servant, sir," Alan offered in his best social purr.

"*Signore Comandante, benvenuto*," Marcello di Silvano replied in a deep, cultured *basso*. He was, for a senator of a Republic that gave at least lip service to electing its leaders (though only from the rich or noble) dressed more like a prince. Di Silvano wore a glaring white suit of figured satin with silk cuffs, pocket flaps, and lapel turn-backs of a very regal reddish-purple. Cloth-of-gold satin waistcoat, white silk hose, and solid gold knee buckles on his breeches, solid gold shoe buckles, set with rubies and diamonds! A sash of office crossed from one shoulder to a rosette on his hip in Genoese colors. A gold chain and medallion of office rested on the snowy white breast of his heavily laced shirt. There were some civil or military decorations on coat and sash, as well. Signore di Silvano was a devilishly handsome man in his mid-to-late forties, with a lean, hard, firm-chinned patrician face as genteelly weathered as Lewrie might expect to see on old Roman coins in celebration of a successful general, or a new emperor; as if di Silvano spent time at sea or out hunting, and didn't care a fig for a courtier's more-fashionable, powder-aided pallor. The signore offered his hand, a rough-textured hand, taut and muscular, and as strong as a sailor's. Alan imagined a gilt-wreath corona would suit the man better than the high white periwig he wore. The hand was withdrawn, and sensing that his time was done, Lewrie began to turn to his right . . .

Merciful God in heaven, he gasped to himself, quite nonplussed; *nobody* has poonts *that* big! The ethereal, bewitching beauty next to . . . !

"*Cara mia* . . . *Comandante* Lewrie, *capitano di 'Asch-Emma-Essa'* . . . *Jester* . . . *simile il motteggiare*, hmm?" Senator di Silvano informed her, inclining slightly to her and leering with amusement. "*Comandante* Lewrie . . . *Signorina* Claudia Mastandrea."

"Your servant, *signorina* . . ." Lewrie said with a deeper incline of his head and bow than his usual wont. So he could peer at those impressive tits directly, instead of ogling her under his lashes.

I've died and gone to heaven, he exulted as she dropped him her curtsy, leaning *forward* a bit to incline her own head, and . . . ! And to rise from that curtsy to look him directly in the eyes and smile, curl the corner of her mouth up with a veiled, mischievous amusement, as if she knew exactly where his eyes had been. She kept her head inclined to the side, in wry acknowledgment, her entrancing amber-brown eyes twinkling as she looked him over as if taking his measure.

"Uhm, aye . . ." he stammered, turning to lumber down the line.

"A pleasure to meet you, Commander Lewrie," she murmured in a more than passable English, in a surprisingly husky, seductive voice.

"Pleasure was all mine, ma'am," Alan assured her, fighting for an air of gracious, gentlemanly gravity. And to keep his hands to himself! He broke off, at last, wondering if he'd been slobbering on his shoes, feeling the urge to wipe his chin free of drool, to be introduced to the lesser lights. But could not help glancing back, furtively now and again, just to see . . . *idly* curious, no more'n that . . .

Damme, he gasped again, feeling his innards lurch! She leaned forward a bit, past some shoulders and wigs, looking back at him. A miss-ish sort of minx might have ducked her head, hidden behind lashes or a fan. Nothing brazen about her, but . . . ! He met a hooded smile, a long, approving blink, which was as good as the nod, anytime!

"Dear Lord," he muttered, free of the line at last, desperately in need of drink, and male company, to buck up those tattering vows of his. "Mister Knolles!" he cried in relief, snagging a passing waiter with a tray of fine cut-crystal stems of *spumante*. "For you, sir?"

"Thankee, Captain, I'm fair parched a'ready." Knolles beamed, as he handed his first officer a glass. "Can't they open some doors, some windows? So bloody hot in here . . ."

"Must be his mistress, that, uhm . . . ?" Lewrie speculated. "D'ye think? That Claudia Mastandrea? Wonder if she's his East wing or his West wing ride?"

"Rich as he is, the Friday'un, I'd say, sir," Knolles said with an appreciative leer of his own. "Were I that 'John Company' nabob-wealthy, I'd have one for every day of the week, save Sundays. Wonder what his wife's like, if . . . ?"

"I'll lay you odds, Mister Knolles, we'll not discover that!" he snickered back. "Doubt there's even a miniature of her, hereabouts."

Gorgeous bloody creature, though, Lewrie thought; brown-eyed blonde, I'll wager. Those eyebrows were . . . pale down on her arms . . . those *catheads*! He was forced to gulp again, and slosh back most of his champagne. And took another surreptitious look across the room.

Most fashionable ladies he knew used tight corset laces to push themselves anywhere near such bounty, attain such a deep cleavage. Or crammed cotton stockings up underneath. He'd been rooked before, hey? Those few who had been so . . . *blessed*! he groaned . . . fought it, laced or banded themselves flat under a higher bodice so they'd not be taken for strumpets. Or fondled by the bully-bucks in the streets! This'un, though . . .

He watched Signorina Mastandrea gaily swirl beside her keeper on the way to a wine table. Four or five inches shorter than his five-and-three-quarter feet, he recalled, almost petite, which was why her husky voice had surprised him, coming from such a slip of a girl. Woman, he corrected himself as he snagged another glass of wine. Styles changed, though, and he didn't think a corset could explain her slim back, her narrow waist. Acres of underpinnings and petticoats were passé, as were hip pads and concealing whalebone frames. The way her matching white satin gown clung to her, swished against her limbs . . . why, she'd be slim as an eel, he speculated! Very slim legs, narrow hips, almost childish bottom . . . ! He'd seen a few like that, those who seemed overblessed by nature in one area, but deprived in the rest of their person. And that was a *damned* intriguing . . .

Stop it, damn you, he told himself; take a deep breath, a round turn and two half hitches! Can't keep a vow, with a pistol to my *own* head! Tup a senator's doxy? Mine host's doxy? Jesus!

"Excuse me, sir, but . . . do you think there will be dancing later?" Midshipman Hyde asked at his elbow. He turned to give the wiry, ginger-haired lad a peek, but Hyde was casting a shy but ardent look off toward the walls; where stood a slim, light-haired beauty, perhaps no more than fifteen or so, in the tow of a female chaperone, who was gazing back at Hyde with wide-eyed admiration, the coy, covert art of a fan quite forgotten.

"Close your mouth, Mister Hyde . . ." Lewrie chuckled. "Before a fly pops in. Aye, let's hope there is dancing . . . for your sake. Just be careful. She more'n like don't speak the King's English. And they take the ravishin' o' their daughters more serious. Or promises, hmm? As in betrothals?"

"God *yes*, sir!" Hyde replied, blushing furiously. Yes to *what*, Lewrie hadn't a clue, and expected he'd prefer not to know.

"Well, hold the British end up, Mister Hyde," Lewrie warned.

Lewrie expected there would be dancing, later. Large as Signore di Silvano's town *palazzo* was, he could see no sign of a hall set for dining tables. Almost like a basilica, it was—a round central hall or rotunda, beneath a soaring dome with marble stairs and balconies up at least three stories, with three projecting wings. The longer two, to east and west, lay open to the rotunda, salons each as big as two 1st Rates lying hull to hull. One was lined with chairs around its entire girth, the handsome and intricate inlaid tile floor bare, with all the carpets removed. A chamber orchestra played from the balcony above its entrance. All they had do was turn their chairs to face the salon, to supply music for dancing.

"Sparse damn' place," Lewrie muttered. In spite of all those rich silk hangings, the drapes, the wallpapers and such, it sported more dressed stone than people would be comfortable with back home . . . niches filled with rare old vases, amphorae and statuary that ran to the Classic, Heroic vein. Like a Roman basilica when they were homes or palaces, or imposing public buildings—before they'd been turned to churches. The matching salon on the other wing did seem to be the public offices, the parlors and libraries, the music room . . . lined up one after the other with all the massive, impressively tall doorways opened to flaunt and overawe. Marble columns, painted wood columns, arches, and insets . . . Some few civilians dared tread the carpets down that wing, oohing and ahhing—and careful with their drinks.

The rotunda, though, held the food and drink. Table after table groaning under their host's largesse; there a long table for twenty-four minus chairs, topped by a tapering pile of pastries, surmounted by a statuary group of winged cherubs and doves. Another bore taxidermied wild fowl, suspended on the wing or roosting in the branches of tree boles and short limbs—that was where the goose, duck, partridge, or pheasant meat could be found.

Wine tables, too, each with a fountain plashing colored water—or real wine?—down a series of miniature waterfalls; each in the color of the wine offered. The white wines and *spumante* tables bore statuary carved from ice, resting against what looked to be snowfields in which spare unopened bottles chilled!

"A bit . . . gaudy, d'ye think?" Cockburn commented to Nelson as they wandered by, nodding pleasantly to one and all. They'd sampled the victuals already, having visited the pork table, with its gigantic papier-mâché porker and nursing piglets, the fruit table with its titanic cornucopia, the fish table, the pasta, and made-dish table. Alan goggled in wonder, noticing that Cockburn and Nelson were eating from real gold plates, held gold-and-silver damascened utensils!

"Knows how to impress, I must admit," Nelson whispered back to

Cockburn, using his free hand to pull at his nose, and play up a nasal Norfolk twang in ironic commentary.

"Makes King Midas look like a publican at a two-penny ordinary," Lewrie japed. "What fine greasy wooden trenchers you gentlemen hold. Anything particularly good, sir? Or merely showy."

"All quite good," Nelson allowed, still too much in awe. "But do allow me to recommend the vinegared pressed beef. Levant-style, I was told. Particularly spicy and tangy." Cockburn agreed, though he and Nelson both bore a dubious look, as if to say that an Englishman'd never act the fool so, as to lay on such a raree-show. It was heathen . . . Hindu Grand Moghul . . . and not quite the hearty country thing.

The aromas, stronger and more alluring than those of the guests around him, drew Lewrie to the tables, where he began to graze, taking a small taste of everything before finding something exceptional that pleased him most. Nod, smile . . . shrug and chew. Nod, smile, shrug in perplexity . . . and take a sip of wine. Knowing Latin didn't do him the slightest bit of good when it came to conversing in Italian; one word in twenty, perhaps . . . just enough to get him in trouble. All he could be was mutely agreeable.

Making the rounds, he crossed Drake's hawse, winced to watch him load his plate to overflowing, then tuck it in quickly, all the while gab-bling and gesticulating with both hands in hearty conversation with the Genoese. Lewrie encountered Cockburn and Nelson again, hands free of plates, at last.

"God, what a scruffy fellow," Cockburn muttered. "I find it hard to believe that he isn't some excellent imposter. A bosun's mate who's run, and gulled the Genoese, like Doctor Gulliver in Lilliput."

"Much my opinion, too, at first, sir," Nelson confided to them. "Last year, his repute with these people was odious. Hasn't a shred of respect from even the lowliest Genoese. Yet, sirs . . . one comes to discover he's a man of more parts than a first impression might allow. I find him . . . like Sir William Hamilton at Naples . . . to be a fellow with whom I may do direct business. Some, less direct, do you follow?" he added with a cryptic smirk.

"Oh, God!" Lewrie cried suddenly. "Shrimp, sirs. A whole fresh bowl of 'em. My soul is lost. You will excuse me, sirs?" A cauldron would have been more like it, which took two strong servitors to carry, abrim with peeled and boiled shrimp as big as his thumbs! He made his way to the fish table quickly, trying not to trample civilians to beat them to them.

"Bloody marvelous!" He sighed, once he had a gold plate laden, with a fiery hot sauce in which to dip them. "What *is* it? How did . . ."

"A sauce from the Far East, *Comandante* Lewrie," his host said from across the wide table. Lewrie had been oblivious of everything, and everyone, his whole attention greedily focused on the shrimp.

"The Far East, really, sir?"

"They name it *kai-t'sap, Comandante*," Senator di Silvano told him with another smug expression, as if once more secretly amused with Englishmen in general, and Lewrie's ignorance in particular. "Spices, peppers, vinegar. To which, Italia contributes its humble marinating to-mato sauce. I see that you relish it, hmm?"

Damme, the wretch speaks some English, Lewrie thought; huzzah! And his wench is with him, too. Huzzah, again!

"Allow me to compliment you, *signore*, on the . . . *kai-t'sap*, and Italia's improvements on it . . . *and* your remarkably skilled fluency." He toadied. "And aye, I do relish it, most wondrously well. Almost as much as good old hot English mustard or Worcester sauce."

"But the Worcester sauce of which you speak, *Signore Comandante*, is not English," Signore di Silvano chided him. "*Scusa*, but when Roman legions conquered your island, they brought with them their *garum*, the salty fish spice. You English sweetened it by adding fruit, but it is still made the Roman way, first, *Comandante*. You still begin with the boiling and fermenting of the sardines."

We *do*? Lewrie wondered to himself. Feeling a touch of acid of a sudden. Well, wasn't it said, one didn't ever wish to see sausage, or legislation, made? It didn't signify. He *liked* Worcester sauce.

"My compliments, as well as my thanks, *signore*," Lewrie went on, fighting the urge to dart a glance at di Silvano's bewitching mistress, "for your kind invitation, and the bounty . . . the excellence of the bounty, you put before us."

"Ah, bounty." Senator di Silvano sighed, turning sad. "Thank you for your compliment, *Signore Comandante*. But I wonder . . . much as we enjoy ourselves tonight, as well as we fare . . . what do you call it . . . the short commons? *Si*, short commons? *Grazie*. The poor people of the Riviera. Do you believe they enjoy short commons tonight, *signore*? What hope do they have of ever eating half as well as they did before, as when you began your embargo?"

Uh oh, Lewrie thought, casting his eyes about for Drake, Nelson, or a senior officer. But they were too far away from where he had been waylaid to aid him, sandwiched in between lash-fluttering ladies three tables or more off. Damn this bastard, Lewrie snarled to himself; he did this o' purpose! Raised his voice, by design, to gather a crowd.

And Claudia Mastandrea was gazing at him, quite coolly, waiting his reply, and how he'd handle himself. Bitch, he accused; in with the smarmy shit, aren't you? Enjoying yerself, hmm?

"*Signore* di Silvano," he began carefully, "civilians are always the sufferers, in wars. Especially those occupied and enslaved by the plague of locusts we call the French. Do they ever hope to enjoy the fruits of their own harvests . . . they'd best do something to help beat the bastards. And pray God General de Vins and his Austrians crushes the French soon. So they're no longer saddled by a pack of robbers."

"Yet, what may they do, *Signore* Lewrie," di Silvano posited in a hand-wringing gesture of seeming concern. "The little people, those *paisans* . . ." Aye, he'd gathered a crowd of sycophants, Lewrie noted; there certainly by design. "Is their suffering, their starvation the only thing you wish of them? To be supine, and waste away?"

"Perhaps arise, like Cincinnatus called from his plough, sir," Lewrie suggested. "Resist, like . . . like Robin Hood did against Prince John, in Sherwood Forest."

"I cannot pretend to know *English* folklore, *signore*," his host said with a dismissive air, as if it was an Irish tale of fairy circles. "But I do know the fate of the Huguenots of La Rochelle . . . the fate of the Royalists of Toulon . . . the armed resistance offered by the Vendee, against French Revolutionary forces. Slaughter. Extermination!" he declared, switching to Italian to share the pith of his argument among the onlookers, who were properly outraged, and horrified.

"Then pray for an Austrian victory to liberate them from 'neath the tyrants' heels, *signore*," Lewrie rejoined. "Though, 'tis said . . . God helps those who help themselves. Were Genoa . . ."

He bit the rest of that off; Genoa would never take up arms, too terrified of failing.

"Ah, the *Austrians*." Di Silvano sneered. "You are a student of history, *Comandante*, to reach back to your own past?"

"Somewhat, sir," Lewrie answered. Though his school days *had* been a trifle spotty.

"Are you versed in Italia's past?" di Silvano queried. "With us, it has *always* been the Germans. Teutons against Marius . . . Goths, then Huns, Lombards and Vandals who conquered the Old Empire, made us broken pottery, so many little feuding kingdoms, unable to resist . . ."

"Oh, much like the Holy Roman Empire in the Germanies, sir?" Lewrie pointed out quickly. "So fragmented and weak?"

Score one for me, he thought happily, seeing di Silvano almost wince and grit his teeth in a too-wide smile.

"*Si,*" the senator allowed grudgingly. "And like our Empire's last decadent days, we must call once more upon our Goths to rescue us. Summon the barely civilized barbarian legions, accede to whatever they demand of us, to save us. But, *signore,* do not even *you* deem what it is they do so far a very *slow* sort of rescue? How long, I ask you . . ."

"First of all, Your Excellency," Lewrie interrupted, quite full of himself by then, feeling able to hold the British end up. "Our Mister Gibbon writes that Rome was Christian, hardly decadent, when she fell. Your Gothic legions and generals prevailed because no one Roman cared to soil his hands with combat any longer. The Austrians, I am certain, are *quite* civilized enough these days. Does their campaign against the French go slowly, it is only because a successful campaign takes time to marshal and amass, *Signore* di Silvano."

There, that was safe enough, without implying criticism of an ally. General de Vins barely made half-a-mile a day, and that, mostly shuffling without actually advancing. Mostly sitting on his hands and decrying how badly he was outnumbered by the Frogs, he'd heard. Alan was quite grateful, though, to espy Mister Drake conferring with Nelson, pointing in the direction of the senator's diatribe and loud questions. Aid was in the offing, he sighed!

"Besides, Your Excellency," Lewrie went on, basking in the intense regard of Signorina Claudia Mastandrea, who was following their word-play closely. "One must recall that, do you fear a barbarian invasion into Italy again, the most-recent invaders who are sworn to conquer you and annex you to *their* new Empire of the Common Man, if I may so style it . . . were originally Franks. A Germanic tribe who came late to the party. And, like scavengers, took what they could. The leavings of those who preceded them. Franks, and Gauls. Julius Caesar's bane, sir . . . Gauls. I should think any Italian, be he Genoese, Savoian, or Tuscan, Piedmontese, or Neapolitan, would prefer the whole of Italy be left alone, free of tyrannical Franks . . . and Gauls, *signore.*"

Oh, well *shot,* look at him squirm, Lewrie exulted!

Senator di Silvano had gone as stern and choleric as a hanged spaniel, his tanned complexion suffused. Yet, of a sudden, he got a sly look. Hurry up, damn you, Lewrie urged Drake and Nelson.

"We do, *signore Comandante,*" di Silvano assured him, turning suave once more. "Almost as much as we wish the north of Italia free of Austrians, hmm? Yet, how may we do this? How may the many states in Italy resist? Or cooperate? As you said, so fragmented and weak."

"Well, perhaps what you need do, *signore*, is to find yourselves another Marius, another Julius Caesar, to beat back your invaders," he breezed off. "Better to stand up and fight, like Horatio at the Bridge . . . than cringe and wring your hands. Throw your lot in . . . temporarily? . . . with the Coalition."

"They were despots. Dictators, *signore Comandante*," his host reminded him. "Once in power, they became oppressive tyrants."

"Better the temporary dictator, *signore*, from the old neighborhood," Lewrie said with a grin, "than the eternal conqueror from France."

"Ah ha!" di Silvano barked of a sudden, hands on his hips, and seeming terribly pleased with himself.

Have I stepped in the horse turds, Lewrie thought; again? He's too damn' pleased for my liking. I must have fallen into a trap he's laid, some subtle debater's ruse, or . . . When he'd sailed to Naples, he'd been presented to King Ferdinand in his fried-fish shop, told him a tale of British derring-do that had bucked him up, gotten Naples and the Kingdom of the Two Sicilies into the Coalition. Well, that'd been arranged *sub rosa* long before, but he *had* added the last straw to the camel's load, hadn't he? Perhaps tonight, he could cajole Genoa . . . ?

"I mean . . . what could a united Italian army not do, were their kings and princes of the same mind, sir?" Lewrie added quickly, with a view to backing off.

"Perhaps, *Signore* Lewrie . . . rid ourselves of Germans, at last?" the senator hinted.

"Rid yourselves of a plague of Frogs, *first*, sir," Lewrie said. "Then, were you of a mind . . ."

"Even though our days of glory are long gone, *signore*? You say Cincinnatus at his plough. Yet, our modern-day Cincinnatuses will not leave their fields to defend the soil. They wish to rest." His host almost sneered. "A man of his hands, *and* of his head. *Si*, a modern Marius or Caesar is what we need. But where are we to find him?"

"Well, that's pretty much up to you, sir," Lewrie allowed.

"Up to me?" di Silvano replied, turning almost teasing. "Up to me personally, *signore*?"

"Well, you and your fellow senators, *Signore* di Silvano." Alan shrugged, reaching for another shrimp on his plate, at long last. With a generous dredge through the *kai-t'sap*. "I'd expect you'd know your fellow Italians best."

"You surprise me, *Signore* Lewrie." The senator beamed elatedly. "You really do. I would not think an Englishman . . ."

"Ah, Your Excellency!" Drake bellowed, finally coming to Alan's rescue through a purposely maddening maze of strollers and wine-bibbers. "Have you and the commander been having a good chat?"

"A most excellent one, *Signore* Drake," di Silvano assured him with a pleased purr. "Though he gives me no reassurances for the poor people of the Riviera, my fellow Genoese. But that . . ."

"But that, Marcello," Claudia Mastandrea interjected with a *moue* of boredom, and a sulky tone, "is best taken up with the good *Signore* Drake, or his *ammiraglio piccolo*. Politics, Marcello!" She pouted. "They bore me. And you must argue with *Comandante* Lewrie . . . a guest!"

"Our squadron commander, you mean, *signorina*?" Drake amended.

"*Signore* Nelson," she said, turning to him with a sly expression. "*Si*, he is *piccolo*. A *very* little *ammiraglio*."

Lewrie coughed some *kai-t'sap* up his nose as he snorted in appreciation of her wordplay. Piccolo, he thought; have to remember it! Horatio Piccolo, haw haw!

"Scusa, *Signore* Lewrie," di Silvano offered, reaching across to shake his hand right manly and gentlemanly. "My enthusiasm, my concern . . . we must speak again. Of Rome and its past glories. Of a new Rome, and its possibilities. Most intriguing."

"I should be delighted, Your Excellency." Lewrie beamed, glad to be free.

"You will allow the *Comandante* Lewrie to escort me, Marcello?" Signorina Mastandrea cajoled. "He is in need of more wine. As am I."

"But of course, *cara mia*, of course," di Silvano said magnanimously. "You will be in the care of a fine English gentleman."

Thankee, Jesus, Alan exulted! No, *wait*! Maybe not, there's . . . well . . . oh, to hell with it!

He put down his plate, offered the crook of his arm to her once around the table, upon which she could rest her forearm and hand.

"I apologize for Marcello, *Signore Comandante*," she said, with a delicious tilt of her head in his direction, an intimate, conspiratorial tilt, revealing strands of strawberry-gold blond hair peeking from beneath her high-piled white wig. Huzzah, she *is* a blonde, he smirked! "He must be seen concerned, you know. He has many estates, now taken by the French, many *paisans* depending on him as their protector he cannot help, until the French are driven away. But he must show concern for the welfare of all of the people of the Riviera, since none of this was Genoa's doing. Your embargo, or the French occupation."

"I quite understand, *signorina*. Though it was a bit touch-and-go there, for a bit." Lewrie decided to shrug off. "I still don't understand why, though, your senator, and his fellows, won't take steps."

"To complain against you is all they *can* do, *Signore* Lewrie." She shrugged. "All Marcello can do, for the moment. He is of a mind to resist, he alone of them, but . . . what may one out of many do?"

"You are from the Riviera yourself, *signorina*?" Lewrie asked as they got to a *spumante* fountain.

"Oh pooh, *signore*!" She pouted again. "Claudia. I allow you."

"*Signorina* Claudia, thankee," he said with a short bow.

"No, I am not from the Riviera. I am from the north. Bergamo."

"Pardon me, but . . ." Lewrie snickered. "Wouldn't that make you one of his detestable Germans?"

"Marcello has forgiven me my blood, long ago, *Signore* Lewrie," Claudia whispered close to him, leaning toward him as a waiter handed them their glasses of sparkling wine. Husky, breathy . . . A rare, and costly aroma exuded from her shoulders and bountifully filled bodice, a seductive citron and sandalwood. "He assures me that many clans of the Republic and early Empire were *rufios* . . . mixed with the original Celts. Alexander the Great of Macedonia was of the *celtoi*. So you see, he is *so* forgiving. Of almost anything I do," she promised him with another husky chuckle, her eyes hooded.

"Er . . ." Alan croaked, wishing he could bite a knuckle to fight his urges; bite *something*. "Even when you tell him he's boresome?" he japed, striving for flippancy.

She tossed back her head and laughed a deep-toned guffaw, not a simpering twit's titter or giggle. "You struck a chord, *signore*. Alan Lewrie? I call you Alan, as you call me Claudia, *si*? *Grazie*. A very *Roman* chord. Come. Walk with me, while we sip our wine."

He offered his arm again and they began a languid stroll toward the far salon wing, against the tide of guests drifting into the salon readied for dancing, circling the rotunda counterclockwise.

"Marcello is of *very* ancient family, you see?" Claudia imparted, walking so close their hips brushed, sending a shock through him. "Of a patrician, senatorial family since the days of Rome's first wall. So what is more apt, that he is a senator now? The di Silvanos come from the Silvanii, a prominent Roman clan. Many senators, tribunes, and generals.

Pagans, even after the reign of Constantine. Or so he tells me. You will see how fond Marcello is of Rome's ancient glories. Statuary, the picture gallery, the armory that holds so many things he has had unearthed, or purchased from others. Perhaps the library, at the far end . . . ?" she cooed, as promisingly as a new bride after the last of the wedding guests had been shooed away.

Dear Christ, I'm *trying*, he groaned! Some credit in that, hey?

"So he surely must be upset that Italy is fragmented, controlled by Austrians, not what it once was. Or could be," Lewrie temporized. "And he wishes there would come a new Caesar? Himself, perhaps?"

"Ah no, he is not a professional soldier," Claudia pouted quite prettily as they neared the first massy double doors leading from the rotunda to that dimly lit far wing. "But he believes he might be the new Cato. The one who might arouse the passion for a unified Italy . . . a New Republic . . . in people's hearts. A liberated Italy, a power to be reckoned with. There is a map, in the library . . . you must see it. Do you wish to see it, Alan? A map of what might be. Should be."

She had come around a little before him, looking up in his eyes, no longer veiled in her meaning or her carriage.

"Uhm . . . the dance, *signorina*," Alan flummoxed. "Isn't it just about to . . . ?"

"Oh, pooh." She breathed in a sultry, silken mutter. "You are more interested in a silly dance or two, than in allowing me to display Marcello's most-prized treasures to you?"

He looked down at *two* of 'em, in a hellish quandary. Firm, and big as bloody pineapples, or coconuts, shifting up and down along with her every deep breath, larboard or starboard as she swayed sideways as if keeping time with her own dance.

Christ on a Cross, he begged; just a *little* help here! Didn't bring my cundums ashore o' purpose, just in case some mort was just *too* temptin' . . . oh my God, look at her . . . !

The intricately pleated and ruched folds of her already strained bodice *un*pleated, as two proud nipples hardened and puckered behind a single layer of cloth—all that stood between him and bliss. Lewrie tore his gaze upward to her face, to a smile that seemed to promise everything, those amber eyes going so wide . . .

"Perhaps, uhm . . ." He coughed, unable to look away, mesmerized. " 'Tis been so long since I've danced, d'ye see . . . enjoy it, rather, and . . . two years or more in active commission, and a short refit back

home. The wife and I . . . ah . . ." Hmm . . . didn't hurt so much to
say . . .

By God I *do* have self-control, he exulted! Lookit! I'm turnin' down
the bounciest quim ever I did see! See, God . . . morals?

"We had no chance to dance at Portsmouth. And, with our kiddies
along . . ." he felt emboldened to add. "I would request you save me at
least the one turn around the floor, *signorina*. For a wondrous memory of
Genoa, but . . . perhaps we should enter the salon. And dance?"

"So honorable," she whispered, so softly he had to lean to her to hear.
"So decent an English gentleman," Claudia crooned, eyes wet in wonder.
She glided a half step to him, her breasts brushing at his shirtfront and
waistcoat buttons, her lips open in a half smile, her eyes going even wider
and more besotting. Within inches of a first kiss, her lips opening. And
Lewrie knew he was a lying hound, after all.

God, just a dab o' backbone, he pleaded, ready to succumb, in spite of
his best efforts; I'm a cunt-struck cully, always was, always will be, I'm
tryin' t'help meself, so where's yer . . . ?

"Ahem, Commander Lewrie?" A very welcome voice intruded behind
him, a very plumby, cultured English voice!

Thankee Jesus, Alan thought, whirling in alarm, and an immense relief. Which turned to wide-eyed amazement, seasoned with just the
slightest dash of terror, when he beheld his rescuer.

How the Devil'd *he* get here? He gawped. And should I be glad or not.

"Allow me to name myself to you, sir." The impossibly tall and skele-
tally lean old beak blathered on quickly, stalking up to offer a hand to be
shook. Thin hair brushed back severely, above a weathered face that was
all angles and hollows in the cheeks, temples, and eyes. Agate-y buzzard's
eyes that glinted hard and merciless as gunflints over a long hawk's nose.
"Simon Silberberg, sir. Your servant, sir. From Coutts's Bank, in London?" he purred as he shook Alan's quite-nerveless hand.

"Mister . . . Silberberg, sir," Lewrie continued to gawp, clapping his
astonished mouth shut.

"Agent of the bank, sir," Silberberg rattled on. "In Genoa on business,
don't ye know . . . commercial interests . . . well, when I heard we
were both invited to the same ball, Commander Lewrie, I took it 'pon
myself to make my acquaintance of you. Hoping we might meet . . .
your solicitor Mister Matthew Mountjoy mentioned you to me, just before I sailed? Wished me to convey his greetings. Do you have a moment,
sir? Just the one triflin' moment. Took it 'pon myself, sir, to list ev'ry bank
customer in the Mediterranean, make them familiar with me, impart

details of new services for serving officers on foreign stations." The lean old fellow in his "ditto" suit of somber black almost whinnied in shy urgency, playing the perfect overeducated, underemployed fool of a tradesman. "Can't hope to rise in Coutts's, sir, 'less . . ."

"Of course, Mister . . . Silberberg," Lewrie allowed. "This won't take much time, though, will it? The dancing, d'ye see."

"Of course not, sir. Won't interrupt yer pleasures," Silberberg promised, casting a sidelong, significant glance at Claudia Mastandrea.

"You will excuse me, *signorina*," Lewrie said to the mort. "Do save me at least the one dance, I pray you. Until later, hmm?"

"The night is young, *Signore* Lewrie," Claudia huffed, a bit beyond "cooled" from her ardor; downright snippy, in fact. "Perhaps you will accompany me later. *Ciao, signore.*"

"Should I escort you . . . ?" Lewrie offered, but she swept away.

"Up to your old tricks, are we, Lewrie?" Silberberg sniffed in aspersion, his lips suddenly hairline thin and cramped together. And suddenly not half the hand-wringing senior clerk he'd seemed.

"Up to yours, are we . . . Twigg?" Lewrie scowled back.

"Yes," the spy from the Foreign Office, the cold-blooded manipulator Lewrie had known in the Far East as Zachariah Twigg drawled in a toplofty sneer. "In point of fact . . . I am."

CHAPTER
9

"SILBERBERG?" LEWRIE SNEERED softly. "However did you come by that? And, ain't you slightly out of your usual bounds, sir?"

"A half-addled banking clerk of the Hebrew persuasion may be an object of amusement, Lewrie . . . of some derision," Twigg replied with a conspirator's mutter, though sounding pleased with his alias. "Hardly one to suspect as a spy, though. *We*, after all, finance *their* wars for them. Apolitically, mind . . . with suspected loyalties only to the bank, the guinea, and one's tribe. As for my presence, the Far East became more a military, or a naval problem, of the overt sort. And, too, our last escapade made me too well-known there. With French influence limited to Pondichery or their Indian Ocean islands, their trade dried up, and with trade their hopes to service informers, agents provocateurs, pirates, well . . ."

Twigg shrugged expressively, then with the dropping of his arms he seemed to fall back into his assumed character. They paced toward a wine table, Twigg all but fawning and bobbing, anxious to please.

"You will remember it *is* Silberberg, not Twigg, from now on, I trust, sir?" He wheedled in a whisper, laying a finger to his fleshy-tipped nose, the end-pad of which would have made a walrus jealous. A louder voice for his next statement. "So *very* sorry to take you from your amusements, Commander Lewrie, but since you're so much at sea, I have so few opportunities. If not tonight, sir, perhaps you may do me the honor of allowing me to call upon you, aboard ship, before *Jester* departs? Oh my, sir . . . your account prospers, indeed it *does*. Prize money, the Four Percents. Though you *are* aware there is talk of a tax on income, sir?

Hideous notion, truly hideous, but there it is. Now, had we a moment, Commander Lewrie, I believe I may make to you such a proposition of investments to safeguard your farm income, making less of it subject to any future levy, as would warm the very cockles of yer heart. A glass of wine with you, sir? A true nautical hero? One such as I have so few opportunities . . . dine out on it for years, I could."

"Oh for God's sake," Lewrie whispered, frowning crossly. "Bit less of it, hey?"

The waiter turned away after pouring them each some claret, run in from France, of a certainty.

"Your ship, instanter," Silberberg hissed softly, as Twigg, a finger to his thin lips. "We have *so* much to discuss, sir. Oh my, yes!" He gushed for the waiter's benefit, as Silberberg.

"But . . ." Lewrie protested, as the opening strains of a gay air soared from the far salon to the rotunda. He knew there was nothing he could say or do, but go along with Twigg's dictate. Again!

"YOUR FATHER'S WELL, sir," Twigg told him as they tossed their hats and gloves in his great-cabins. "Made a brigadier, imagine that. He'll know of it, soon enough. This come from Leadenhall Street with me. Your brother-in-law Burgess Chiswick will become a major."

"That's gratifyin'." Lewrie sighed, opening his wine cabinet.

"So sorry to spoil your fun," Twigg posed, one brow lifted in amusement as Alan grudgingly gave him a snifter of brandy. "And, such bountiful fun it would have been, too."

"Didn't think a cypher such as you'd notice, Twigg," Alan spat.

"*Au contraire*, Lewrie, I have always had an eye for the ladies." Twigg chuckled. "Though I may hardly say that my face, or my choice of career, has ever stood me in such good stead as yours, in that regard. Such a splendid run of luck *you've* had, though. A lovely wife, truly lovely, is your Caroline. As is your Corsican doxy, the, uhm . . . shall I say the *contessa* Aretino?"

"Now why would you wish to know so much about me, Twigg?"

"I know a lot about everybody, Lewrie. That's my job."

"So you can use 'em, I s'pose. And that, most cynically," Alan accused. "Leave my wife and . . . mistress . . . out of this, Twigg."

"Only if you will, sir," Twigg shot back, even more amused with Lewrie's sullen truculence, his past grievances. "*I* will not use them, cynically or otherwise. I leave that to you, Lewrie. No matter. Now, sir.

Might you summon your clerk, Mister Thomas Mountjoy? I confess I was quite struck by your clandestine report to Nelson, in which Mountjoy played so prominent a part. I've gotten little from our Frenchman you captured, and I wish to go over that report, fleshing out the sparsity of the written account with both your recollections."

"Sentry?" Lewrie called to the Marine at the door. "Pass the word for my clerk. Come at once, tell him."

"Aye aye, Cap'um . . . SAH!" the muffled voice shouted back.

"*Inconnu*, my God," Twigg mused, slouching in the sofa cushions. "How dramatic. How French! Fellow could have put on a fool's face and gotten clean away, since he'd purged his own chest so thoroughly. That partner of his, he's the same stubborn sort. All fired with adoration for his Revolution. Might as well make a Hindu kill a cow, as get him to talk. Bloody amateur, in his own theatric."

"What did you learn of him?" Lewrie asked, wincing as he remembered Twigg on a captured Lanun Rover *prao*, with a wavy-bladed *krees* at a pirate prisoner's throat. Which Twigg had most dispassionately cut, after slicing and torturing what little he could from him. "And how? Up to *all* your old tricks, Mister Twigg?"

"And why not, now and again, sir?" Twigg allowed coolly. "I find they more than suffice. No, Lewrie, he lives. Shaken, one may hope, but no permanent harm done. An amateur, as I said. Marks on a pile of dirty linen, with several aliases, from several cities. Some of them most embarrassingly French. And caught red-handed, laden with gold, in a ship laden with military goods. Should have taken another vessel, traveled separately from his dead compatriot, that unlamented romantic, *Inconnu*. Secret writings . . . the lemon-juice variety 'tween the lines of innocent correspondence. Smell it, by God! A dead giveaway, everytime. No, a more elaborate cypher would have served them better, but I doubt the poor fellow in charge of French spies in the region has much to work with yet. And, he's no Richelieu, himself, exactly. Learnin' . . . give him that much." Twigg shrugged again, and took a sip to toast his worthy opponent. "Fellow'll be turned off in a fortnight, though. Hung for spying, soon as a military court at Corsica has him in."

"And the French midshipman?"

"That clumsy lout, God no, Lewrie! He's to be exchanged. Too many of our squirearchy's slack-jawed sons aboard *Berwick*, those with *such* a lot of 'interest,' are festerin' in France. Midshipman Hainaut will be reporting back to his masters, and the less said about *me* the better. Best he suffer an accident on the way, he knows too much already, seen too much, but . . ." Twigg sighed, as if to say "what can you do?" "Knows who you are, Lewrie, he does. Not as thickheaded a peasant as he looks. Scrub him up, dress his hair . . . a proper uniform, and the sky's the limit for him. His Die Narbe will take care of that, I assure you."

"Yer clerk, Mister Mountjoy . . . SAH!" the Marine shouted.

"Of Die Narbe, more later," Twigg promised smugly, rising for his introduction. Mountjoy, as usual, disappointed. He'd risen from a deep slumber, dressed haphazardly, and presented himself in a pair of bear-hide carpet slippers, bare ankles, and dark-blue slop trousers, into which he'd crammed the tail of his knee-length nightshirt, with a ratty old drab-brown wool dressing gown atop. Mountjoy still wore a tasseled sleeping cap over his unruly hair, too.

"You sent for me, sir?" he said, yawning and blinking from the sudden change to lanthorn light in the great-cabins. Scratching a bit, too, it must be admitted.

"Good God, what's that?" Twigg growled, stiffening.

"Mountjoy, my clerk," Lewrie puzzled.

"No, I mean *that*, Lewrie!" Twigg grumbled, pointing.

"That, sir . . . is a cat," Lewrie enlightened him. "You know . . . *felis domesticus*? Name's Toulon. He's the *same* sort o' disaster."

"I despise cats!" Twigg glowered, hellish-black.

"We wake you up from a good nap . . . sweetlin'?" Lewrie asked of Toulon, bending down to scratch the top of Toulon's head, concealing a small smirk of sudden pleasure.

"Mister Mountjoy, the name that you are to remember, on pain of your life, sir . . . is Silberberg. Simon Silberberg," Twigg began, and riveting Mountjoy's attention, turning the beginnings of a yawn into a gape of awe. "From Coutts's, do you follow? A representative of your captain's bank, do you understand, sir? But . . . and this you will forget immediately I'm gone . . . damme!"

Toulon, following the perverse wont of his tribe, had gone for Twigg immediately, purring with secret, malicious delight to discover a cat-hater—to twine around his ankles, sniff at his shoes and silk stockings, which were new, fascinating . . . and perhaps might require a sprayed marking . . . or a few clawed snags to make 'em simply *perfect*!

"Get that . . . *that* . . . beast away from me, Lewrie!" Mister Twigg demanded, skittering as if he were going to do a dance to Saint Vitus—or hop atop the sofa like a lady who'd seen a mouse.

"Here, Toulon. Mousey," Lewrie tempted, fetching out the wool scrap toy on a length of small-stuff. "Leave the bad old man alone." He singsonged to his ram-cat, which was a perfect excuse to expose a childlike smile of fiendish glee.

Think I *really* love you, puss, he thought quite warmly.

TWIGG, IN HIS guise of Simon Silberberg from Coutts's, had been in Leghorn and Porto Especia, with an occasional jog inland to Florence, as a commercial representative ought, when Mister Drake had sent a messenger to him, regarding the seizures of *Il Furioso* and *Il Briosco*. He'd not found ships registered as Tuscan under those names, indeed, had not discovered any public record of a trading company calling itself the *Compagnia di Commercia Mare di Liguria*.

"No public stock offer on what passes for their exchange, sirs," Twigg/Silberberg told them over an eye-opening glass of brandy. "Nor any articles of corporation filed with their government. Pretty much the same murky situation as obtains here in Genoa that so puzzled Mister Drake. It was helpful in the extreme, though, Mister Mountjoy, to receive a fair-hand copy of the entries in that small ledger book you found. Cryptic as the headings were, still I was able to form an educated guess as to the identities of the principals."

"Guilio Gallacio, sir?" Mountjoy inquired eagerly, quite awake by then, though they'd been at it for at least an hour.

"To the tee, young sir," Twigg replied quickly, with an admiring smile, though a damn' thin'un, as was his wont. "Unfortunately, I cannot 'front' him in any fashion, and he's much too prominent for me to . . . uhm, spirit away, for a probing interrogation. Though, I'm told he was quite upset, and shaken, by his capture so early on in the life of their venture. I have arranged for his correspondence to be intercepted, and read. More of the vinegar or lemon-juice secret writing, as I mentioned earlier, you recall, Lewrie?"

"Uhm," Alan commented, feet up on his desk and slouched down in a padded chair, with Toulon now quietly napping in his lap.

"Unfortunately, too," Twigg went on, as if he, and *ergo* them, had all the time in the world, though it was growing quite late. "I cannot substitute correspondence, either overt or covert, to cause confusion. Indeed, until we are certain of all the principals, we cannot strike at any of them."

"There is the niggling problem that they're neutrals, citizens of a sovereign Tuscany," Lewrie pointed out. "But that never stopped you much before."

"My Lord, this is fascinating, sir!" Mountjoy cried, wriggling in his chair with excitement.

"You do me too much injustice, Lewrie, 'deed you do, sir," the old spy carped. "Why, were I a passionate man, I'd take a grave exception to it. Though, fencing words with you *is* amusing, at times . . ." He tossed Lewrie a beatific smile; another damn' brief un. "No, I fear I can do little, for the nonce. It will be up to you, and your Nelson, to . . . how *did* Captain Ayscough put it, Lewrie? That I should hold his coat, and let another batsman have his innings? No, to lop off conspiracy at the root may be beyond us, but I shall be quite content should your squadron take as many of their ships as possible, cutting profits to nil . . . and disabusing the conspirators of the notion that they may aid France and prosper. Or that France will aid them in their plans."

"So it goes beyond profit, sir?" Mountjoy gushed.

"Indeed it does, Mister Mountjoy. Lewrie, I'm told you have a wager with Captain Cockburn? He'll buy you that shore dinner. May I suggest roast crow for him? No, sirs. This exceeds humanity, or care for their fellows, from the Genoese. Or for the neutrality, the very sovereignty of Tuscany. *Signore* Gallacio, I have learned, is part of a salon group of like-minded progressives, quite taken with the American Revolution, and with its ideals. Overeducated, overwealthy dilletantes and intellectual wastrels. Idealists, some of them."

"Perhaps they see in French occupation a new order, sir?" Alan asked, reminded of his talk with Senator di Silvano earlier. Or, with his besotting mistress, at the least. "Mean to say, surely there are some benighted fools who believe all this Democratic, Mob-ocracy cant. Liberty, Equality, Fraternity . . . the franchise given to just anybody."

"Granted, Lewrie," Twigg allowed. "Rather perceptive of *you*, I must say. Yes, sirs . . . even at home, well. Priestley and those of his ilk, the gimlet-eyed . . . Reformers. Fortunately, they're not rich enough to afford private armies and mobs of thugs, nor do they possess constitutions of an active nature that might allow them to conspire . . . beyond printing a few odd penny tracts. And we've shut all that down, quite successfully. In Ireland, there are more worrisome combinations . . . but then in Ireland, there bloody always are! Gallacio is, for his rather advanced age, very active in certain societies . . ."

"So, do you know his associations, Mister . . . Silberberg," Thomas Mountjoy interrupted, "you may discover the principal conspirators in Tuscany. And I suppose you have already done that, or are in the way of doing it?"

"Quite so, young sir," Twigg said with relish. "Though it is rather like playing a good hand of whist, with no cooperation from a partner you've never met, right after the first distribution of the cards. Knowing the deck has been arranged beforehand . . . but in whose favor, hmm? One discovers information as to who holds what, one bid or lay-down at a time. An intellectual passion. Rather, a most cold and logical *dis*passion. But, hugely enjoyable, even so."

"I should quite imagine it is, sir!" Mountjoy enthused. "So . . . you know who the others are, some of them?"

"I fear I must play my cards close to my chest, Mister Mountjoy," Twigg said, disappointing him. "Though I have found the identity of another large financial risk-taker. The others, I suspect, are talkers, rather than doers. In Tuscany, there was . . . 'B-R' . . . do you recall?"

"Aye, sir . . . 'B-R' was owed twenty percent, do we believe what was in the small ledger, and not the captain's."

"Bruno Randazzo . . . a very prominent young fellow. Educated in Paris, not so long ago. Travels widely," Twigg ticked off. "Was in the south of France, overland, about the time of Toulon. From what I believe to be correct, three other sets of initials belong to men from Tuscany, five-percenters. They fit, they match the names . . . they are in Randazzo's, and Gallacio's, social circles. A few, however, conform to no one."

"Those, you believe are Genoan, I take it," Lewrie said, as his cat shifted about, settling back to sleep with a little grunt. "Which is why you're here?"

"That, sir," Twigg said, turning in his chair to face him, "and the fact that, as you suspected, this combination of ships' owners, and ardent conspirators, have good intelligence of our squadron's arrival . . . in the first instance . . . and of its movements in the second . . . three of the sets of initials, I have come to believe, reside in Genoa. Two of them are five-percenters . . . while the last commands . . ."

"Thirty percent, sir," Mountjoy announced. "The lion's share. He must be a player even bigger than Gallacio. A richer man, perhaps. Or, one more devoted to Genoa's conquest, and the coming of a French-enforced new order."

"Or a cabal of three, or six, or thirty . . ." Lewrie shrugged. "And I suppose our captive Frog spy told you nothing in that regard."

"Absolutely nothing, I'm afraid." Twigg sighed, massaging the bridge of his nose. "There's a very good possibility that the wretch never dealt

face-to-face with any of the larger principals, at all. I strongly suspect it
was done through anonymous representatives, agents, or ships' captains.
Solicitors or mistresses, that sort of thing. A good conspirator never tips
his own hand . . . when he may use some poor cully more expendable
as a go-between. I had hopes my noble opponent, being so new and
unused to the 'trade,' might not have developed the sophistication as of
yet, but it appears he has. The French have always been good at spy-
craft. In their damn' blood, worse than Italian schemers."

"It may be, sir, that one of the five-percenters from Tuscany may be
more important to their plot than *Signore* Gallacio," Mountjoy posed
with a puzzled look. "Gallacio may be in full sympathy, and in complete
accord with one more political. And is throwing his wealth, his ships and
money into it. The same may obtain in Genoa."

"Oh, very good, sir. Yes, I'd thought of that," Twigg complimented.
"But . . . one must consider that for a wealthy man to expend a considerable part of his fortune 'pon a conspiracy against his native people, he'd
wish more say than the rest in the outcome. More so than a coffeehouse
schemer, or a street-corner ranter. There are revolutionaries, with
scythes in their hands . . . *and*, there are the political animals, who pull
the strings of the puppet show. The ones who end up top dog when the
others have faded back to their ineffectual ditherings, once the revolution's accomplished."

"So, who do you suspect, Mister Twigg?" Lewrie asked, yawning.

"The initials in the ledger, as your Mountjoy could have told you,
Lewrie, are . . . 'U-R,' " Twigg announced, though barely above his
most ominous whisper. "Our French spy knew no one by any name,
which might coincide. He's not a practiced liar, but intractably mute
upon almost every subject. Nor does our Mister Drake, who is familiar
with all the merchant class, or ruling class, who might have a deep-
enough purse to be our 'U-R.' Nor do any of the romantically idealist
young men of Genoa match. He has suspicions among those, as to the
identity of our 'sardines' . . . but nothing of the biggest of fish, whom
we seek. Nor do I. But I shall, in time," Twigg prophesied with a cunning
leer of eventual, almost foreordained triumph. With the great pleasure it
would be to see this mysterious "U-R" ruined, once he was revealed.

"Now, as to the matter of the French knowing our ship movements so
quickly, Lewrie . . ." Twigg snapped, turning brusque once more.

"Easily solved, sir." Lewrie yawned again, recrossing his legs so one
foot didn't fall asleep, too. "Every bloody Genoese would sell his mother

for a groat. Might as well try to eradicate cockroaches, as dam up the flood of information."

"I expected no less, sir." Twigg glared. " 'Tis not the first time I've been in this part of the world, d'ye know. What I was about to say . . . before your blithe dismissal, *sir* . . . was that while we cannot hope, indeed, to limit, much less totally eliminate, the many informers along the Riviera, who do it out of spite for our embargo, love of Frog radical Republicanism, money, or a love of intrigue . . . we may turn it to our advantage. This Midshipman Hainaut, for example, who's to be exchanged. Mister Mountjoy might be quite useful, in planting with that young man some false scents, some superficially convincing truth, along with a hard kernel of falsehood, to confuse them. Feel up to playing a part, Mister Mountjoy?"

"Aye, sir. Sounds intriguing," Mountjoy replied, barely able to contain himself at the prospect of being "useful."

"Mister Drake and I have some . . . uhm, associates," Twigg said, his death skull of a face creasing in malicious good humor. "We are privy to certain information about the French, as well. For instance, there is to be a convoy, soon. The presence of this squadron has cost the French the ability to supply their army with coasters sailing independently. You'll know it when you hear it, not before, Lewrie. We are told that several small warships of a counterpart French coastal squadron will guard them to their destination. But were the Frogs to believe that our squadron would be off at sea, under the horizon, out to stage another raid such as yours on Bordighera, to descend upon a *larger* Savoian port, well . . . there you are, then. A weakening of the convoy escort, a dispersion of force to the wrong place, at the wrong time . . . yet an important convoy full of supplies taken."

"And the French unable to trust in the complete accuracy of all they hear, in future, I take it, Mister Tw . . . Silberberg?" Mountjoy exclaimed with a giggle.

"He's smart, Lewrie. Smart as paint, as you sea dogs say." Mister Twigg beamed again. "I will give you the particulars, Mister Mountjoy. Hainaut will carry it to his master. I will arrange for his immediate exchange, to speed things along, since they do need speeding, given . . ."

"The timing of the convoy's arrival, wherever," Lewrie gathered.

"That, and a few more important items," Twigg agreed.

"I am at your complete disposal, sir," Mountjoy volunteered.

"Then let us repair to yon dining area, for a moment or two," Twigg decided. "So I may coach you on what it is you need to say for Hainaut to repeat. And how it might be best discovered to him. May I prevail upon you, Lewrie . . . to borrow your dining room, and your clerk for a further time?"

"Have at it, sir," Lewrie said, unable to say much opposed. He was certain Twigg had risen considerably in the Foreign Office's secret bureaus since the Far East, and had the ear and patronage of people who could crush a pipsqueak naval commander if Twigg wished it. There was spite enough, of the lingering kind, between them already.

"And I will thank you, on your honor, sir," Twigg cautioned him with a sternly risen finger. "To go aft. There are matters you are not to know yet. Or at the least, be able truthfully to deny knowing."

"You . . . !" Lewrie spluttered, getting to his feet in anger. "I swear, you're too full of yourself, sir, to row me, in my own cabins . . . !"

"Our sovereign's writ allows me, sir," Twigg cautioned. Though he showed all signs of relishing Lewrie's embarrassment.

"THERE, DONE NOW?" Lewrie snapped, once Mountjoy had been told what to do, and had departed for his cot. "How dare you, Twigg. There is the matter of respect from my officers and crew that a captain can't allow to be trampled! By a goddamned *civilian*! An outsider, a . . . !"

"Oh, do sit down and cease your pious rant, Commander Lewrie." Twigg sighed wearily, making free with Alan's brandy bottle. "I know you of old, sir . . . perhaps a great deal better than you shall ever, of yourself . . . one more word, and I might decide, in the King's Name . . ."

Twigg left his full threat unspoken. But he had invoked enough.

Lewrie shut up. And sat down.

"First of all, sir, you know how impatient I am with the custom and usage of naval or military blockheads."

"You made that perfectly clear in the Pacific. Sir."

"Secondly, sir," Twigg went on, ignoring Lewrie's bile. "Your use of my true name, after I cautioned you to not . . . and in that rather loud voice, too. Tsk tsk. Were it to result in my death, sir, should one of your crewmen blab inadvertently, well. That is one thing. But the utter confusion of a great many schemes, should the enemy come to know of me, or my involvement, were they to begin to suspect that I'm a spy, would unravel more enterprises than this. And result in death, or torture, for a great many others. So I will instruct you this one last time to keep your wits about you, in spite of your resenting me, and kindly refer to me, even in your dreams, as Simon Silberberg, the harmless bank clerk, too 'gooseberry' ineffectual to be any harm. Can you do that, Lewrie?"

"Aye. Sir." Alan glowered.

"Good. Sir," Twigg mocked. "You may not believe this, Lewrie, but . . . I rather like you. I have a great admiration for your qualities as a sailor, and a doer. As a commission sea officer."

"Oh, bloody . . ." Alan groaned. "Pull the other one."

"No, I do!" Twigg smiled cadaverously. "Whatever made you the greedy, grasping opportunist you've become, so much more dangerous and useful than the usual sea dog, I know not. But when you're *of* a mind to put your mind to a problem, 'stead of loafing, or muddling, through like the rest, you're bloody inspired. Desperation, perhaps? It's no matter. I value you men like you, Lewrie, they're damn' rare. Damme! Bordighera! Caught 'em with their breeches down, and buggered 'em, as deep as a mop stick would reach, my word! And *Il Briosco*? How many of your contemporaries would be that clever, sir? That devious?"

"You're pissing down my back . . . Mister Silberberg." Lewrie smiled back, a wickedly mirthless smile of ill-humor. "Sounds like I'm set up for something. Know *you* of old, I do. You use people."

"Aye, I do," Twigg most amiably admitted.

"Now you think you're going to use *me*, again?"

"Of a certainty." Twigg chuckled. "There's even a possibility you'll enjoy it. This fellow Hainaut will be rejoining soon, his mentor and patron. This French senior officer. Know who he is?"

"Die Narbe . . . Capt'n Scar," Lewrie shot back, happy to have a bit of knowledge that Twigg perhaps didn't, for once. "Early on, last summer, we heard he also went by 'Ugly Face' or 'Hideous.' Ran convoys to Corsica, too, before it fell."

"And do you know many French naval officers, Lewrie? Personally, I mean. Know any of past acquaintance who might fit those frightening sobriquets?" Twigg posed happily. "Think back, sir, do."

"We don't run to the same clubs, so . . ." Lewrie began to sneer, then got an icy chill of dread, felt his stomach contract. "Oh bloody . . . !" Alan gasped, as the shoe finally dropped. He leaned back in utter astonishment, his face paling for a second. "No! *Couldn't* be! Didn't we do for him? They cashiered him, surely . . ."

"Guillaume Choundas, his horrible little self," Twigg cackled softly. "Twice as mean . . . and thanks to your efforts, twice as ugly. Cashiered, yes. Pensioned off as a cripple. Not the sort of face one wishes to see in one's wardroom, hmm? Not handsome enough to wear the uniform of an officer. Always did hate aristocrats, though. Recall . . . a peasant, father a Breton fisherman, out of Saint Malo? Forever going on about the Veneti, those godlike Celtic sailormen of his? Educated, in a fashion. Jesuits, I learned."

"*That'd* make him twisted as an Irish walking stick."

"Who best to volunteer, to espouse the Revolution?" Twigg asked. "One of the first to the barricades and all that, and deeply, truly in love and league with everything the Revolution in France means. Active service again, as an officer. A chance to shine again. A chance for Choundas to take revenge on every petty Frog who ever even looked sidewise at him. To lop off a hundred aristocratic heads, a thousand . . ."

"And he's here, in charge against us," Lewrie spat, with weary and bitter amusement. "Well, I'm damned. We should have killed him, long ago, when we had the chance. He was *damned* good. Might have gotten even better."

"You'll soon find out, Lewrie," Twigg informed him with a knowing leer. "Once Hainaut tells him who it was stopped his business at Bordighera . . . as I intend for Hainaut to do . . . he'll come looking for you. Personally. I'm counting on it."

Knew I should have become a bloody farmer, Alan thought! Pimp in London . . . my early aspiration? Safe as houses, that . . . consid'rin'.

"Sir," Lewrie glowered. "Are you trying to get me killed, on purpose, you scheming old . . ."

"Not at *all*, Lewrie!" Twigg was quick to assure him; simpering though, which didn't sound like much assurance at all. "As I say, I do like you. Professionally speaking. Your sort aren't worth a tinker's damn for much beyond war, and well you know it. Neither am I, I must confess . . . but then, my sort of war is eternal. Back home in peacetime I expect I'd find you boringly conceited and unscrupulously smarmy, an idle wastrel and lecher. As I expect you did, too, 'tween commissions, hmm? But that's what makes you so valuable at war. Laze your way into idle foolishness, then shovel your way from 'neath a wagon-load of manure, and come up smelling like a rose. With guineas in your fists. Do it quite ruthlessly, 'cause you're too impatient, or desperate, to play by the rules the *proper* sorts believe in. I'm counting on that remarkable ability of yours. Should you two actually meet again."

"So you'd sport a small wager on the home side?" Alan snorted.

"Stake my last shilling on you, sir . . . my entire fortune, had I the chance," Twigg snickered for a moment before turning forebodingly dark and somber. "Choundas is clever, but he's much like you, Lewrie. He's ultimately ruled by his heart, not his head, no matter how clever he is. *I* play my game dispassionately. But oh, Lewrie, what a *marvelous* diversion it is! A personal involvement that misdirects could be fatal for me. So rarely do I allow personal motives to intrude, or allow a motive, or those who would fulfill it, to become personal."

"Believe me, sir," Lewrie sneered heavily, "I've noticed."

"In this instance, though," Twigg said with a frown, "I do not think that I err, in allowing myself to *feel*, just once. Had I been on that beach with you when you chopped Choundas to flinders, I'd have ordered you to complete the work. Had you not, I'd have broken you, then scragged him myself. *Knew* the work wasn't done, even though it looked that Spanish officials would hang him as a pirate. Even then, I felt a gnawing suspicion that, ruined as he was, he'd cause us mischief, in future."

"So you want *me* to kill him, personally?" Lewrie blanched.

"I most passionately, most eagerly, wish his death, Lewrie," Mister Twigg said with unwonted heat. "Even as a legless cripple, holed up in some noisome Paris cellar, with others to do his bidding, I fear he would still be dangerous. You, personally? More than likely not, sir. I wish to unbalance him, distract him with rage, as I did in Canton, after he had my old partner Thom Wythy murdered. You're my chink into his armor, Lewrie. Knowing you're near, the man who maimed him, he'll be more eager to hunt you than do his duty, his cold and evil logic all confounded and diverted. You'll be the bait . . . my bait, which . . ."

"Oh, just thankee, so *much*!" Lewrie whispered.

". . . draws him to fatal folly." Twigg pounded on. "And, should he creep to my trap, he will die, at last, no matter who does it. But should he find *you* . . . should the chance arise . . . I count on you being the one who kills him dead. In fact, *should* you two meet again, then I insist 'pon it. You are to kill him dead!"

CHAPTER
10

"SIGNAL IS DOWN, sir!" Spendlove shouted.

"Maintain course, Quartermaster," Lewrie ordered. "And God help the French. It's going to be a lovely day. What little joy of it they'll have. Buggered 'em, by God!"

"If only we were in on the buggering, sir." Knolles laughed.

It was, indeed, a lovely morning, for late August in the Ligurian Sea. There was a noticeable swell, now and then the hint of some foamy chop to the folding wave tops, and a decently brisk breeze for a change. All under a brilliant blue sky, wisped with benign clouds.

Fremantle's *Inconstant* led, breaking away westward, accompanied by the *Tartar* brig to cover the westernmost small town of Languelia, in the Bay of Alassio. *Meleager* and *Speedy* went more easterly, to tackle one of the warships at anchor, what looked to be a French corvette. While Nelson in *Agamemnon*, being handled like a frigate instead of a tired sixty-four-gunner, *Southampton* and *Ariadne* charged directly for the clutch of merchant ships.

Jester stood on, tail end of the informal battle line that had approached the coast, to remain offshore as the seaward guard for the rest, as they achieved their victory. She stayed on course, alone.

" 'Least we'll be in-sight, sir," Buchanon grumbled. "Share in the take."

"There is that, Mister Buchanon," Lewrie smirked. "Though, we could wait till hell freezes over before the Prize Courts approve those shares. Easy money, today. Ah, well."

No sign of Guillaume Choundas, either, Lewrie was more than happy to note, which partly explained his sense of content. Rumor had it that "Le Hideux" had a corvette as his flagship, and there were two of them anchored in Alassio Bay this moment, caught napping and facing the heavier twelve-pounder guns of *Southampton, Inconstant,* and *Meleager,* those crushing heavy guns aboard *Agamemnon's* lower deck. If he *was* there in Alassio Bay, and someone else stopped his business, then . . . Facing the wily Frenchman, who'd had the Devil's own luck, was someone else's joy, and Lewrie wished them well of it. Ever since Twigg had come aboard with his disturbing news, Lewrie had felt a distinct twanging of nerves.

Only sheer, dumb luck had saved Lewrie's bacon in the Far East, when he'd gone up against Choundas before; only desperate derring-do, and neck-or-nothing chance had kept him alive. Why, the bastard would have slain me, if I hadn't kicked him in the "wedding tackle," Lewrie thought with a queasy feeling. Could one divide a single second . . . that was how close he had been to being spitted on the man's sword! A normal foe, now . . . but Choundas? Again? he shivered. Sorry, but the Navy don't pay anyone *near* enough to tackle that clever fiend!

He raised his telescope to watch, glad to be an observer, as the squadron stood into the bay, creating as much confusion and fear aboard the French convoy as a fox might among the chickens. His lips curled in silent delight. They'd made it to Alassio, the destination Twigg and Drake had discovered; dropped their "hooks" and prepared to carry their cargoes ashore, certain that the British squadron was far away to the west. On that shore, he could see tiny antlike figures in the dark blue-and-white uniforms of the French Army, the colors adopted from their old second-line National Guard. Thousands of Frogs, foot, horse, and perhaps some light artillery. Rather a lot of cavalry, he surmised; or draught animals assembled to tow the heavy wagons that the convoy's goods would have filled?

Cannon fire, now; blooms of smoke staining the oaken sides of *Agamemnon* and the rest. Even upwind, the slamming and drumming boom of artillery was lung-rattling. Some scattered return fire from shore, or from the armed ships that had escorted them in. For show, Lewrie thought smugly; a broadside or two so their captains could claim that resistance had been offered, but then . . .

Neither of the French corvettes appeared to be trying to hoist sail, or save their anchors. The dull glint of iron upon their forecastles. Cutting cable? Yet, so slowly, so raggedly.

"He's not here," Lewrie muttered, lowering his glass, and gnawing on the lining of his mouth in disappointment that Choundas had not been caught with his trousers down. And worry. That he was still out there, somewhere. And that Twigg would arrange for him to fight him.

"Damme, I could have thought . . ."

"LET THIS BE a lesson to you, Hainaut," Le Hideux grumbled, as he awkwardly paced his quarterdeck in bleak fury. "Never believe what is offered to you too easily."

"Citizen Pouzin thought it was authentic, so . . ." the lanky midshipman shrugged. He looked a little better. The British had been so good as to present him with a pair of slop trousers, which fit better than his old castoff breeches. A gift, that civilian clerk had told him.

"Ah, Citizen Pouzin, *oui*." Choundas scowled, lifting the good corner of his mouth in a brief grin. "So easily gulled, that one. I will make sure Paris knows of his gullibility. Should he have gotten the timing wrong, we sail for nothing. But, if this is a ploy to expose the convoy, then he will pay for it."

So many places to cover; Nice, Sam Remo, Cagnes, Antibes, and Cannes. Martin had yet to send him his needed ships, so he could not hope to cover them all. Nor hope to stand out to sea, but not so *far* out that he could not espy signal fires to alert him where the British might strike. Nor hope to confront them in equal combat, ship against ship, either.

He glanced at Hainaut, wondering . . .

Never believe what is offered *me* too easily, either, Guillaume Choundas frowned. So quickly exchanged, bearing his cunningly gathered information about the British squadron. And the greatest news of all! That *Jester*, and that bastard Lewrie who'd maimed him, were one and the same!

When the British did not appear on the horizon, where he'd been assured they would, he'd begun to fret. First in anger, that a chance for revenge was delayed, that he'd have to wait to capture *Jester*, and carve her smirking bastard Englishman into stew meat, as he had lusted to do these past nine years! So close at hand, yet . . . !

Anger had cooled, replaced by trepidation; that he'd been told a lie, a cunning English lie, that someone was in league with them and had passed the lie on. Who would wish him humiliated? Pouzin? Yes, that could be it. He'd seemed so anxious to know the date of sailing, so he could make his arrangement, he'd said, but that could have been his way of getting what he needed to know, which he'd told the enemy! There might *never* have been a smuggled letter from Genoa, at all! It could have been Pouzin's fabrication.

Alan Lewrie, though, Choundas fumed in silence, clump-shuffling about the deck, oblivious for once to his crippled state. Lieutenant Alan Lewrie . . . Commander Alan Lewrie . . . Lewrie, Lewrie, Lewrie. *Hate him*! In the days since Hainaut had returned with that startling revelation of who his foe was, how close he was to vengeance, that name and what he wished to do to the person bearing that name had become almost a litany, like what he had once mumbled in rote duty over rosary beads.

But now, at sea, where a cooler head could prevail, he had begun to wonder about the timing of that revelation. Why now? Just before a convoy, a vitally important convoy . . .

It was late August, almost September. Soon, the weather would turn, the gales arise, cutting seaborne supplies by half, even without a British squadron on the Riviera. The first snows would fall in those mountain passes, and soldiers of both sides would go into winter quarters, unable to wage war until spring, bogged or snowbound.

To *use* me, he sneered, at last, when a blinding epiphany struck! To delude me, disarm me . . . to blind me with the brightness of revenge! Someone on the opposing side, someone incalculably clever, had revealed this to me, through Hainaut and perhaps even through Pouzin. Waiting, watching . . . being fed information by traitors and greedy *shop clerks* . . . biding his time until this could be used against me.

La Vengeance now stood on East, racing with every scrap of canvas spread aloft, bounding and soaring, cleaving foam with a sibilant, spiteful hiss, like an adder aroused and dangerous, warning everything in sight to get out of striking distance. She stood on alone, though. The rest of his patchwork squadron was too weak, too slow, too thin-scantlinged for what she might discover. The winds had not been that good, the last few days; the convoy and escort force could still be caught up, if they'd found scant winds or foul. There was a chance that Capitaine de Fregate Bayard, the too-handsome beast, would use his innate cleverness, and put in each night in a snug harbor, not daring an evening passage on the open sea. Would he be that clever? Choundas devoutly wished. One of the rare ones, clever *and* pretty, was Bayard.

Yet, how many tiny seaports had they passed, getting closer to Alassio, and no sign of them. It didn't mean that they were really a target,

Choundas could tell himself. Perhaps the British didn't know of their presence. That everything would turn out fine.

Diano, to larboard and now astern. Only a few miles more, once around the headland that formed the spine of the western heights of the Bay of Alassio. No sign of any enemy warships further out to sea. A thought did cross his mind, that it was a trap; that whoever that very clever fellow was in the British camp, they'd passed the tale, knowing he would do this—rush to the scene, to assure himself. It made the right sort of sense, to Choundas. Who was more important to the war effort than he? With all modesty, he could not think of anyone else whose loss would do more harm to the cause of the Revolution. It was not *hubris*, that awareness; it was merely his studied opinion, after coolly weighing the facts, and the rest of the participants. Lewrie. Would Lewrie be there? Would anyone? As bait, or . . .

"Artillery!" sang out a watch officer. "I hear gunfire!"

"*Hé, merde!*" Choundas groaned, biting his lip in anguish.

"Sail Ho!" Sang out the foremast lookout. "Dead on the bow!"

He could hear it himself, now. Stuttering. Dull brumbles. A single flat bark. An irregular cannonading, around the headlands. His convoy! The "L'Anglais"—the "Bloodies"—were in Alassio Bay!

"Sail is ship-rigged!" the lookout cried again. "Standing out to sea . . . larboard tack!"

"Her flag!" Choundas howled aloft, cupping his hands.

"Corvette!" the lookout shouted. "Warship!"

"Her flag! Her damned flag!" Choundas screeched again.

"*C'est l'Anglais!*"

"*Timonier*, helm down a point, alee," Choundas snapped, turning clumsily. "Close-haul to windward. Brail up courses, and chain-sling the yards. We will fight her. Drum us to Action!"

"Sail Ho!"

"Where, away?"

"*One* point off th' *star*-b'd bows!"

Lewrie scaled the mizzen shrouds on the starboard side, telescope in hand, so he could see for himself. A ship, a proper ship, he thought; not one of those lateen-rigged locals. She was bows-on to *Jester*, aiming directly at her under a press of sail, flinging a great mustache of sea foam about her forefoot and cutwater, her arrogantly thrust bowsprit and jib boom cocking up and down as she rocked. No more than a league to leeward, standing on nor'east close-hauled, and about four miles off-shore. The strange ship's courses, tops'ls, t'gallants, and royals were cusped to the wind, their leaches almost edge-on to him.

Something diff'rent, though . . . ? Even as he watched, the greater drum-taut billow astern of her fore-course went slack, winging out alee.

"Brailing up her main course!" Lewrie shouted down to his deck officers. "To fight! She's a French warship! Mister Bittfield, run out the starboard battery, now! Hoist signal, 'Enemy in Sight'!"

He clambered down, to hop the last three feet to the quarterdeck and stride to the nettings overlooking the waist. He lifted his glass again. Should *Jester* stand on, she'd keep the wind gauge above the foe, but allow her to slip astern. That French ship . . . a *frigate*, perhaps? . . . was as close to the wind as she could lie, already, and would slide aft as she stood on. Unless she tacked and bore away south to offer battle.

Has to be a frigate, Alan frowned; a lesser ship'd haul her wind and not be confident of the outcome. But she's so close inshore . . . I think I like her there. I allow her to tack out to deeper water, she's all the maneuvering room in the world, then. Aye, stand on as we are, for a bit more, but then haul our wind and wear down to *her*. Then, if her captain feels he's trapped himself, he'll *have* to come about, tack 'cross the wind. But I'll *still* have the wind gauge of her. *And* rake her, bows-on to me and helpless. She'd *have* to haul away west . . . ?

"Brail up the main course, Mister Porter. Rig out the boarding nets. Loose, sloppy bights, mind." Lewrie smiled. "Quartermaster . . . half a point to weather."

Without the force of the main course, *Jester* slowed, sailing off the wind toward the sou'west, the beginnings of a Levanter, an easterly, on her larboard quarters. Altering course, making it more of a run down-wind, which took away the apparent wind, making her seem slower still as she moved no faster than the breeze itself.

"Full-rigged ship, right enough, Captain," Mister Knolles stated. "Small frigate, or large corvette . . . about our equal?"

"Unless she's a thirty-two-gun frigate, with twelve-pounders, Mister Knolles," Alan speculated with a cautious growl. "Two points off our bow, and a mile nearer. She'll shave the western headland by at least two miles, should she stand on as she is."

He cast a glance to *Jester*'s rear, back toward the bay that lay off her starboard quarter. Surely, there was enough noise coming from there, enough high-piled rags of gun smoke, to tell this Frenchman that there were other British ships about. He rather doubted that she'd be foolish enough to go much further east than the headland's tip, or risk being trapped between *Jester* and the rest of the squadron's guns.

"Let her slide aft to about . . . four points, *almost* but not quite abeam before we wear, Mister Knolles," Lewrie decided aloud. "Perhaps half a point less than four. Then she'll be between . . ." He felt the urge to snicker, "between *Jester* and the Deep-Blue Sea! Let's prepare. Hands to Stations for Wearing Ship."

"Aye aye, sir. Mister Porter?" Lieutenant Knolles bellowed, causing a stir, a chorus of piping, a stampede of bare horny feet.

"*Three* point off th' *star*-b'd bows!" a lookout cried over that preparatory din, as hands hauled taut on braces and sheets.

"Tacking!" another lookout shouted, followed by the others in a reedy chorus of alarm.

"Avast, Mister Knolles!" Lewrie snapped, countering the order. "Quartermaster, up your helm. Course, due west. Ease her onto a run, wind fine on the larboard quarter!"

It was just possible that the Frenchman had the slant, around the headland's tip, to see all he wished to see, and had spotted the powder palls, perhaps one or two more British warships. The French ship came about across the eye of the wind, slowing and luffing, beginning to present her larboard side to *Jester*.

"Well-handled, sir," Buchanon noted with professional interest. "None o' 'at lubberly cock-billin' an' floggin' you'd expect."

"Aye, she is, Mister Buchanon." Lewrie frowned, feeling a sudden foreboding. A taut ship's company, a rarity among the Frogs, from what they'd seen so far. A captain who acted with alacrity, and pugnacious aggressiveness; an eagerness, it seemed, for a stand-up fight. Another rarity, that. The Frenchman had come about due south, close-hauled hard on the wind once more, as if to claw himself up and take the wind gauge from *Jester*. Less than two miles away now, but they were approaching each other quickly.

"Mister Knolles, we'll harden up a mite. Quartermaster, put yer helm alee. Lay her head west-sou'west. Leadin' wind, sir."

"Seed 'er *afore*, sir!" Seaman Rushing, high aloft on the foremast cried. "Corvette! Toulon, there!"

Aye, it was the pretty corvette that had fired the insolent challenge off Cape Sepet. Lewrie eyed her in his glass. What had they determined . . . twenty, or twenty-two guns? French eight-pounders, more'n like. Which were the equal of his, rated as nine-pounders. Her pale golden-yellow upperworks had gone to seed since, she'd faded and dulled, turned darker as more linseed, tar, or paint had been slapped on to control the ravages of exposure. Her white gunwale was still bright, though, and the black chain wale . . .

"Damme!" Lewrie shivered, lowering his telescope. Feeling real fear at the prospect of a fight for the first time, instead of the taut nervousness he usually experienced; the nervousness that had almost come to be a high-strung, but manageable, alertness. *"Poisson D'or!"*

"Sir?" Knolles queried. "You know her, Captain?"

"Just like his old ship . . ." Alan muttered, feeling as shuddery and weak as he usually did after a fight was ended. He slammed the telescoping tubes of his glass together, striving to disguise the trembles in his fingers. Painted, tarted-up just like his old . . . It was *him*!

"No, Mister Knolles," Lewrie told him, trying for a grim amusement. "But I think I know her captain. We're in for a real scrap."

He looked astern again, back into the Bay of Alassio. Had any ship read his hoist yet, come about to sail out to aid him? It didn't look like it. *Jester* was on her own against the Devil, Choundas!

Think, he warned himself; what'll he do! Once we close to gun range, I can go close-hauled, upwind of him, headed south. Else he's a chance to bow-rake us. He's French, he'll fire high. Chain-shot . . . multiple bar-shot to take our rigging down and cripple us. He wears, he exposes his stern to my guns. He tacks again, though, after first broadsides . . . it'd be *our* stern wide open to raking! What to expect? He was always so clever, so beastly *good* at it, unpredictable . . .

"It's her, *Capitaine*!" Hainaut exclaimed. *"Jester!"*

"Then God is good to us." Guillaume Choundas nodded, his caricature of a human face made even fiercer by a smile of feral pleasure. "Sextant, Hainaut," Capitaine Choundas demanded. Lewrie's *Jester* had once been French; he could measure the height of her mastheads above the sea and determine when his guns might reach.

"Not quite yet." He sighed with impatience, willing himself to wait. But soon, my brutal English beast. Soon!

So swaggering, that Lewrie, so conceited and cocksure of just how gently life should treat the handsome and well-formed, the landed aristocracy—the son of a British knight. Money, servants, the best schools . . . best of everything. Dissolute, a randy rabbit, and a wag, he'd learned of him; thought himself infinitely clever, those informers' reports told him once he'd regained access to Ministry of Marine files after '89, so he could begin seeking his tormentor. But never quite as clever as he believed. Again, just like the English, who depended upon Luck, Fate, and breeding to "muddle through," instead of applying themselves diligently. They threw money at problems, as if that would keep them safe, hired others to do their dirty work, like dismissing pregnant household servant girls. Never really tried in the fire, never . . .

A bit more, and his guns would reach at extreme elevation, with mast-damaging shot, he concluded. A precious minute more in which to enjoy the taste of success at meeting him face to face.

Stand on, my dim-witted beast, stand on, pretty one! Be so very English, and expect me to be conveniently clumsy, like the other shop clerks. Do you know who you face, yet? This time, I will beat you!

"READY, ABOUT!" LEWRIE cried, of a sudden, after long thought.

"*Give* her the wind gauge, sir?" Knolles wondered.

"Damn the wind gauge, sir!" Lewrie roared. "Stations to Wear! Mister Bittfield, double-shot the larboard battery now, for later."

He was too fearful, covering it with bluster, too impatient and edgy with frightful expectations of the unexpected. He had to do *something*, even if it was wrong. Besides, wearing *Jester* north would sail her back to the headland, able to flee into the bay should Guillaume Choundas cripple her aloft. And it would force Choundas to maneuver, might upset the careful aim of his gunners with their first broadside of disabling shot.

"Hands at stations, sir . . . hauled taut," Knolles reported.

"Mile and a bit, I make it," Lewrie muttered, twining fingers nervously, rocking on his feet, unable to stand stolid. "A long shot, but . . . his and ours. Mister Bittfield, we'll engage with the starboard battery, at extreme elevation!"

"Ready, sir!" the master gunner replied, sounding as dubious as his first officer.

"Mile, just about . . ." Lewrie sighed, rising on his toes with anticipation. "Wait . . . wait . . . Mister Bittfield . . . fire!"

"On the uproll . . . *Fire!*"

A broadside from the long Nines, the great-guns, crashed out in angry roars and a sudden fog-bank of smoke and sparks erupted from her starboard side. With the wind gauge, *Jester* was heeled too far over for her solid round-shot to score crippling damage aloft, the disadvantage of firing from upwind. Fall short, perhaps, skip into the enemy . . .

"Secure the starboard battery at run-in. Ready about? Helm a'weather! New course, nor'west, Quartermaster. Wear ship!"

He could feel his vessel wheel, her decks coming level, the wind coming stronger on the nape of his neck, as she pivoted within the pall of her broadside, which was hazing and misting as it expanded, thinning to show him the French corvette, which was . . .

Firing!

Moans, warbles . . . eldritch screeches, wailing higher and higher in tone, even as Choundas's ship was suddenly surrounded by feathers of spray as his own shot arrived. Fired high, elevating quoins fully out and breeches resting on the carriages . . . and her decks angled upward to the force of the wind on her full-and-by course to windward.

Crashes aloft, crashes and bangs. The royal mast and yard upon the main was shattered at the doublings, bringing down the commissioning pendant, sails and ropes, in a blizzard. The fore t'gallant twitched as it was punctured by bar-shot and star-shot, punctures ripping open from luff to leach in an eye-blink. Fore-stays snapped, and the outer flying jib lashed out to leeward, shivering like a spook!

"Nor'west, sir!" Spenser called, easing his helm, watching the main tops'l for a clue to his luff and winds, with the pendant gone.

"Ready, larboard batt'ry, sir!" Bittfield reported.

Mile, or *less*, Lewrie judged, glad to have drawn first blood; or first honors, at the least. Better shootin' range.

"Fire, Mister Bittfield!" he urged, gripping the railing with one hand, chopping at the air with the other as if it held his sword.

Cripple him, Bittfield, he thought grimly; save my poor arse!

"Sure o' yer aim, now, wait for *itt*!" Bittfield cautioned his gun captains, still not trusting Rahl to scamper about and train those barrels inward, so their shot would converge amidships of their target. Following along behind quickly, sensing how *Jester* rode the sea, when she'd rise up, decks almost level, pent on the uproll. Waiting for a good one, perhaps, a convergence of wave and counterwave.

Come on, you perverse bloody perfectionist, Alan wished to yell!

"Ready . . . on the uproll . . . *Fire!*"

A stunning blast of sound, explosions, and the scream of truck carriages running inward, axles and wheels howling, breeching ropes and restraining bolts juddering bar-taut making thick cable squeal, forged iron moan.

"Eat it, you *bastarrddd!*" Lewrie howled, too jittery to remain stoic and captainly. He never had been—never would be—*any* good at stoic.

At least, fear had turned to something useful, now that he was getting into a battle fever, the insatiable kind that would leave him wringing wet, spent, and gasping.

The French corvette returned the favor, again slightly later, just as *Jester*'s double-shotted barrage reached her. There were more crashes aloft. The foremast fighting-top seemed to explode into dust, as a solid shot smashed into the upper mast, bringing down the tops'l and t'gallant together, cleaving away stays for both the inner jib and fore-topmast stays'l. Topmen aloft, swivel gunners and Marines in the top, came spilling out and down, riding the wreckage or flung bodily by the force of the strike! Two massive flashes of sparks and oaken splinters erupted along-side, amidships, as the main chains and stays writhed like disturbed asps, and the entire upper mainmast groaned and creaked, and supporting lower shrouds let go under the suddenly unequaled tension, popping as loud as musket fire!

"Hullin' her, sir!" Knolles cried. "Hullin' her, 'twixt wind and water!" he hooted as he pointed to larboard at their foe. Plumes of spray skipped in lines toward the French ship, some almost on her waterline, bursts of dust and wood splinters as she was hit above the water, around her midships gun ports.

"Half a mile, sir," Buchanon adjudged, more calmly.

"Run-out!" Bittfield was screaming, his voice breaking on all the reeking smoke, and his emotions. "Point yer guns! Carronades as well . . . stand clear? Ready . . . *fire*! Whoohoo!" He was gun-drunk.

"That's the way, that's the way!" Lewrie snarled, pounding his fist on the railing, just as caught up in the stink and roar of those monsters, his beautiful, reeking, but beloved guns, as the "Smashers" on the quarter-deck came reeling backward on their slide-carriages in a bitter cloud of spent powder. "Quartermaster, steer half a point to loo'rd. Close her."

He can't come up higher to the wind on me, all he can do is haul off, he thought with scintillating but frenetic crystal clarity. We'll rake his stern, unless he wears away. Or tacks! Twigg made sure he'd know I was here, available—he can't scamper off 'thout *trying* to do me in!

Moanings and warbles, dire humming, and this time round-shot hit lower. *Jester* reeled like a punch-drunk boxer as she was hulled, shuddering with each savage blow taken. A portion of the larboard gangway bulwark caved in, scattering waisters and brace-tenders. Splinters and shards from shattered iron shot keened amid the sudden screams of pain and fright. Men were down, lucky *Jester*'s lucky people were bleeding, dying!

"He's tacking! Sir, he's tacking!" Spendlove wailed from the larboard side. "Swinging sou'east, into wind!"

"Broadside, Mister Bittfield, now! Aim high!" Lewrie ordered. "Take her rigging down while she's busy comin' about! Knolles, ready to wear about to east-nor'east!"

"*Er ist* vounded, zir!" Rahl cried up from the waist, "I send to Herr Crewe . . . ?" Even as Crewe boiled up from the midships hatchway ladders, still in his white apron and list slippers from the magazine.

"The stays, sir," Knolles panted beside him, smudged with soot and smoke, his hat askew. "Might bring *all* the main topmasts down if we come about."

"The windward stays are sound, sir. Might ease the lee'uns, if we wear. Hands to the braces, ready to wear, sir," Lewrie retorted.

"Run *out* yer guns . . ." Mister Crewe intoned more calmly. "*Prime* yer guns . . . cock yer *locks!*"

"Porter, hands to the braces, ready to wear nor'east!" Knolles bellowed into his brass speaking trumpet.

"*Point* yer guns . . . ! Quoins half out . . . ready . . . fire!"

No, dammit . . . Lewrie groaned to himself; you rushed 'em, they'll shoot too low, and . . . !

In, they lurched, all but number five larboard nine-pounder, which had been struck dead on the muzzle, and blown backward off its truck carriage, trunnions ripped from the cap-squares, and its crew savaged.

Brutal noise and a hellish reek of the roasting damned, *Jester* shaking and rattling under Lewrie's feet and hands, the enemy blotted out by the massive gush of burned niters.

"Ready, sir," Knolles gasped.

"Wear ship! Helm alee!" he snapped, soon as he heard, scampering to the larboard side so he could *see*, pressing up against the bulwarks to peer out through all that smoke to see if he'd hurt Choundas.

Being flung backward, thrown off his feet as a ball blasted in just above the gunwale, splinters and shards flying upward, an erose chunk carving the face of the bulwark down to the thickness of a single plank! Feeling his ship being pummeled and punctured beneath him, her stout scantlings wailing in agony!

"Sah, you kilt?" Andrews demanded, looming over him, filling his entire vision. Lewrie blinked, and kept on blinking, to clear the red haze that kept blinding him.

Blind, he gibbered wildly; blind as Nelson! Oh, the bastard . . . he's done for me! He flailed his arms and legs, found that they still were attached and obeying. Rolled to his side and retched the coppery taste from his mouth, knowing what blind fear tasted like at last . . .

A crumpled calico handkerchief smeared his face, mildewy and redolent of tobacco. Blinking mindlessly, panting and gasping air in terror of what bad news might be coming. But his sight cleared, with Andrews's ministrations. A firm hand clasped the handkerchief to his scalp.

"Carry on, Mister Crewe!" he heard Knolles rasp. People were walking around him, as uncaring as if he were a misplaced hammock roll.

He felt the guns go off, the deck on which he lay shiver as the ship was punched sidewise by her own recoil. There was a regular beat of juddering coming from her hull, even more insistent than his racing heart. God, there'd be another broadside in reply, soon!

"You tell me, Andrews . . . *am* I killed?"

"Got yah scalp shaved, sah. Blood in ya eyes, but . . ."

"Help me up."

"Best hold dat right dar, sah . . . firmlike. Staunch de blood."

He held the cloth with his left hand, clung to the railing over the waist with his right, and almost swooned and saw double. The pain was coming, and he sucked air between his teeth as the first wave hit, going cross-eyed with it. He swabbed his face, his eye sockets, with his right sleeve, forever staining that fancy gold lace slash-cuff . . . but he could see, with both eyes.

"Ooh, Law'," Andrews flinched for both of them, as a broadside came inboard.

More smashing timbers, more screaming side planking, as French carronade shot joined their long guns. That juddering got noticeable, became a deep, plucking hum instead of an unnatural motion. Through it all, the gun crews slaved away, swabbing and overhauling tackle, rushing up cartridge and shot, ramming it home and pricking the vents.

"Run *out* yer guns . . . !" Crewe roared, not so calm anymore, and caught up in the madness.

Alan took another suck of breath! There lay Choundas's vessel, not one cable to leeward of *Jester*'s left side, just a little ahead, and sailing parallel to them, her own side looking gnawed at, stove-in here and there, her pristine white gunwale turning gray with spent powder stains.

"On the uproll . . . fire!" Mister Crewe bugled. A ragged broadside crashed out, stuttering up and down *Jester*'s ports. The enemy corvette lurched and seemed to wince as she was struck again by a hailstorm of shot, delaying the run-out of her own guns a precious moment.

"Payin' off, sir!" Spenser called from the wheel. "No jibs . . ."

Jester could not lay close to the wind without them, and slowly swung leeward, in spite of a large portion of lee-helm. She and that corvette would angle together slowly, closing the range, if Choundas held his course. Lewrie groaned as he saw that the wind would let her pinch up to weather, at least one point or more. Choundas could throw his ship up so close to luffing that he could bow-rake *Jester*, at nigh musket shot, in another minute.

"Mister Knolles, ready to haul our wind, course nor-nor'east," Lewrie snapped, the effort of shouting making his head seem to explode with fresh pain. "Mister Crewe, one more broadside, then switch over to the starboard battery! We'll rake his stern!"

"Oh, Lord," someone whispered in awe as Choundas's corvette lit up in flames, flinging long thrusts of smoke at them. She fired another broadside!

Jester was pummeled, sent reeling, as iron smashed home, aimed at her midships. There was a tremendous pillar of spray alongside, then a second, the shuddery twist of the hull as it was struck, down low by a graze, then a direct hit, and a mighty *thonk* of rupture. A groan aloft, that juddery humming ended suddenly. Replaced by a wail of pine and fir as her mainmast began to topple—everything beyond the fighting-top swayed over the larboard side, coming down like some sawn tree! The main chains had taken another hit, and everything was shot away that held it upright! All they could do was duck and pray as it collapsed, crashing down into the ocean in a rat's nest of torn sails, tangled rigging, and broken yards, to dangle on the gangway or bulwarks, further tangled with the collapsed boarding nettings, blinding the guns. A discharge from one of the nine-pounders might set alight the ruins. *Jester* was disarmed and powerless!

"Mister Crewe, starboard battery! Waisters and idlers," Alan cried in despair. "Chop all that away, now, Mister Porter! Spenser, steer due north, best you're able with all that dragging. Hurry!"

There was nothing left aloft for drive but the mizzen sails—spanker, top's'l, and t'gallant, and they'd be lucky indeed to be able to steer effectively, if at all, with all that force so far astern.

"Spare stays'l, jury-rigged from foc's'le to the foretop!" Knolles was shouting forward to the hands digging free of the ruins.

Jester had slowed, drastically, dragging herself almost to a stop, bereft of wind power. Beyond crippled. Almost conquered.

He's going to win, damn him, Alan felt like weeping! His ship turned to scrap lumber, defenseless against whatever might come. He suspected

Choundas would close and board, to take her as prize. Take *his ship*, in a sea of bloodshed. Take him prisoner, and what he felt like inflicting on him, once they were anchored in a French port, he . . . no, By God! You want me, you'll have to kill me! You want *Jester* . . . then you'll have her over my dead body!

Lewrie drew his sword and let it glisten in the sun.

"Starboard batt'ry ready, sir!" Crewe rasped. He looked down on his gun deck. On his people. The ports were open, the artillery run-out. Grimy, bleeding from cuts and splinters, mouths agape with terror, and some of them shivering, amid the carnage, the dead.

"They'll not have us!" Lewrie roared. "They'll not have *her*! If they try, we'll kill every last mother-son of 'em! Close shooting, and make 'em *pay*, Mister Crewe!"

And he was amazed, that they could raise a cheer! A weak one, aye. But an angry, defiant cheer for their ship.

Choundas had slipped ahead, of course, his rigging mostly free of damage and his sails still drawing power. Headed east-nor'east on the wind, but even then easing her braces and sheets to fall off, and employ her larboard guns. And her stern, her vulnerably thin stern . . . !

"Fire as you bear, Mister Crewe! Hold her, Spenser! Nothing to loo'rd, for just a minute!" he pleaded.

"Aye aye, sir!" Spenser grunted, as he and Brauer and two more hands threw all their weight on the spokes to hold full lee-helm, the rudder jammed hard-over.

"Point . . . !" Crewe ordered. "As you bear . . . *Fire!*"

From the foc's'le carronade, then aft to the quarterdeck, some swivels firing, too; a controlled, steady tolling, the guns so hot by now they leaped off the deck with recoil, titanic crashes and bellows of rage, deafening thunders and harsh ejaculations of gunpowder, all dun gray and brown, shot through with embers and flaming bits of wad. The range was little over a cable, and the results were immediate.

The corvette's stern was caved in! Glass sash-windows blown in, both quarter-galleries shattered, her taffrail and flag lockers blown skyward. The name board and dead lights to the officers' wardroom all were smashed beyond recognition. Her transom post was whittled by shot, and her rudder twitched like a hound's ear. And there would be carnage further forward, as hard nine-pound shot caromed down the length of her open gun deck, breaking into hundreds of jagged shards on gun barrels and carriages, creating a maelstrom of wood splinters to quill her crew, to rip and rend! They could hear her, and them, wail, they imagined!

"Can't 'old 'er, sir," Spenser gasped. "Sorry, but they's too much drag t'larboard. Payin' off, again. Make due north, just."

"Reload, Mister Crewe!" Alan demanded. "One more time!"

"Tackin'!" Knolles countered. "She's going over to larboard, sir!"

"Now she'll rake *our* stern," Lewrie groaned. Once she gets settled down on larboard tack, she'll make sou'west, easy, he thought. "Get that raffle chopped away, Porter! Hurry with that stays'l. And rig the main topmast stays'l from the maintop to a foc's'le ladder, if that's all you have. I need jibs. *Any* sort o' jibs! Now!"

Close as Choundas was, he'd get a quartering slant across HMS *Jester*'s stern. At about the same range as the shot she'd delivered! Lewrie paced to the larboard side, to see the last of the mess going over the side, the last raveled stays and braces cut. With a great splash, the last of the upper masts hit the water to float away aft.

"Better, sir!" Spenser encouraged, spinning the spokes.

"Due east?" Lewrie asked him.

"*Mebbe*, sir!" Spenser allowed, chomping on his tobacco quid in a frenzy. "Nor'east, at best, I think, Cap'm. We're so slow."

"Good enough, then. Ready, Mister Crewe? We're coming about to weather some more for you!"

"We'll be ready, sir!" Crewe stolidly assured him.

"Give him a broadside, while he's tacking, then. Then load and run out, quick as you can. Soon as he's in arcs."

Choundas was standing away southerly, already on the eyes of the wind, sails rustling and luffing, and jibs just beginning to fill, and draw. His ship would heel over as she felt the force of the wind upon her braced-around square sails, delaying that raking broadside a little. Until she was more in control, her decks more level. And then . . .

"*Meleager*, sir!" Hyde crowed. "Signal, sir! 'Do You Require Assistance!' "

"Hoist 'Affirmative,' Mister Hyde!" Lewrie yelped in relief. "You're goddamned right we do!"

And there she was, about a mile off and coming hard, beating to windward with a bone in her teeth, guns run out and ready! She'd clear that western headland by miles, pass ahead of *Jester*'s bows even if she managed to attain nor'east. And chase this foe away!

Lewrie went to the starboard side of his quarterdeck, wincing in agony with each step, left hand still clamped atop his skull. Choundas was there, he was certain. Even at 200 yards, he thought there was a man on that opposing quarterdeck, a slight man with pale skin and dull reddish hair. A man who wore a large black patch. A man who was shaking his fists at him, his mouth open to howl curses at him.

"Got jibs, sir, at last!" Buchanon told him. "Come a'weather?"

"Close as she'll lay, aye, Mister Buchanon," Alan replied, with the shuddery sort of giggle a condemned felon might essay right after a hanging rope snapped and dumped him alive in the mud under the gallows.

Jester came up toward the wind, struggling to lay nor'east. As Choundas heeled over and stood out to sea, bearing sou'west. Men were aloft, letting the corvette's royals fall. Stern-to-stern, they were separating, no guns able to bear. Choundas had been driven away, not able to deal with a frigate's fire. *Jester* had been saved, would go on living. It was over.

For the moment, Lewrie thought wearily. There'd be a next time. Twigg would see to that, damn his blood! Pray God Cockburn catches him up and shoots him to toothpicks! Spares me the . . . *spares* me!

"We continue on this course, sir, we'll block *Meleager*'s course," Buchanon cautioned, close by his side. Buchanon put a steadying arm to Lewrie, as he swayed and sagged, utterly spent.

"Aye, come about, again, Mister Buchanon. Due north, steer for the western headland, so Cockburn gets a clear passage to seaward close-hauled. Unless he wishes to come inshore of us, cut the corner . . . ?"

Too tired to think, as if he'd gone fifteen rounds with a bully-buck at a village fair; it always was this way after a hard fight with him. He leaned on the bulwarks, tried to sheath his sword.

"Mister Hyde, hoist 'Submit,' followed by 'Pursue the Enemy More Closely.' 'Vast coming about,' Mister Buchanon. We'll stand on. Cockburn can gain on the bastard, if he cuts inshore of us. Stand on," Lewrie decided. He'd wait until *Meleager* was abeam, then come about, into the shelter of Alassio Bay. *Jester* would need quick repairs, perhaps even a tow, to get back to safety at Vado. She'd never crawl there on her own.

"Porter?" he shouted, wincing again. "Pipe 'Secure from Quarters,' then let's see what needs doing we can do for ourselves."

"Er . . . aye aye, sir!" Will Cony shouted back. He shrugged and pointed to a broken figure being borne below by the surgeon's loblolly boys on a carrying board. Bosun Porter was groaning and writhing over several large, jagged splinters, his right arm ravaged and soaked with gore. "I'll tend t' h'it, sir," Cony assured him, beginning to rouse stunned hands back to their posts.

"Fancy a sip o' somet'in', Cap'um?" Andrews tempted, offering a small pewter flask, on the sly. "Neat rum, sah. Put de fire back in yah belly."

"Thankee, Andrews." Lewrie sighed, taking a small sip.

And wondering what thanks he'd have to give Cockburn, for saving his bacon. He grimaced at the sharp bite of the rum; and how even more insufferable Captain Cockburn might be, in future. Or how low he'd be groveling in gratitude, pretending to like the taste of boot polish.

Grateful, aye . . . Alan realized with a small, mournful groan of relief. He takes him or kills him, 'stead of me, I'll buss his blind cheeks! I don't ever wish to cross that bastard's hawse again. Ever!

CHAPTER
11

"A DESPERATE ACTION, sir," Nelson told him in the privacy of *Agamemnon*'s great-cabins. "Gallantly carried," he added. A bit more praise, very similar to their last meeting; though thrown out rather offhandedly, not quite so congratulatory, and bitten off, delivered in a moody, frownful snappishness. "Five dead, a dozen wounded? I am sorry for your losses. The only losses the squadron suffered in our cutting-out expedition. Not a single man even hurt aboard the rest. My condolences."

"The rest of the squadron didn't have to contend with Choundas, sir," Alan told him, a bit put off by Nelson's less than charitable air, wondering if the killed and wounded had ruined what might have been a fine report for Nelson to submit to Admiral Hotham.

"You're quite sure it was him, I take it?" Nelson demanded of him. "My opposite number, this will-o'-the-wisp, Choundas?"

"No error, sir. Saw him with my glass as he hauled his wind to break off the action, stern-to to us. A mite uglier than last I saw of him in the Far . . ."

"So this Mister . . . Silberberg wrote to me, Lewrie," Captain Nelson grumbled, his long dainty fingers fretting papers on his desk, still standing and looking down distractedly. "I do not very much care for spy-craft, nor for those who engage in it. Valuable though their information may be at times . . . they . . . some of them, put far too little emphasis or value on the fighting man, take too much upon themselves, and too much of the credit . . ."

"It sounds as if Mister Silberberg is now attempting to dictate to you as well, sir?" Alan scoffed, offering a commiserating grin. And thinking Twigg had a challenge on his hands, for once.

"That is of no matter, sir," Nelson grunted, vexing his mouth in annoyance, or a bad memory. He looked up at last, as if resolved to the solution of a matter that plagued him. "There are before me, Commander Lewrie, at least three grave items anent you and your ship. Items most vexing. I thought it best to discuss them with you here, in total privacy, before they become formal complaints, answerable to higher authorities. Perhaps a court."

"What . . . a court?" Lewrie gawped. He creased his brow in utter puzzlement, which caused pain in his shaved and restitched scalp wound, and wriggled in his chair, recrossing his legs in defense.

"The first, sir," Nelson bleakly intoned, perhaps even with some anger (which was something new about him for Alan to discover) "concerns your raid on Bordighera. There's a letter of complaint just given Mister Drake, from the Savoian government, that your ship, cited by name, fired upon the town center, their fishing fleet, and homes and shops along the eastern shore, resulting in damage and destruction, and in some civilian injuries and deaths. I am told that Mister Drake is on warning that their former masters, our Sardinian allies, also contemplate a formal diplomatic grievance. The Genoese have also formally demanded an explanation. As to whether the charges are true, and if so, is this the way we mean to enforce our embargo—by the indiscriminate slaughter of innocents, and the destruction of civilian property. Now, sir . . . for the record, did you engage in any indiscriminate firing?" he coldly demanded.

"What the . . . no, sir! By God I did *not*, sir!" Lewrie countered quickly, outraged. "You have my report. We fired shoreward just twice, once we'd silenced the battery and entered harbor. First, to eliminate the French troops, so my Lieutenant Knolles had a free hand. Our aim was those soldiers, with canister and grape, not solid-shot to level buildings. A bit of damage might have been done, I grant you, sir . . . windows smashed and such, but . . . ! We never fired on the town proper, never fired upon the beached fishing boats, since they were Bordighera's livelihood. Our second was a single round-shot over the heads of the looters to dissuade them pillaging the French dead and wounded, sir. Far over, sir. Fall-of-shot was beyond the town, in the eastern hills. We were about two cables off the beach, sir, and fired at maximum elevation, quoin out, so there's no *way* any civilians could have been harmed, sir!"

"A bit unfortunate, though. Perhaps unnecessary," Nelson said gloomily. "The specific charges are replete with eyewitness testimony that you loosed a full broadside, not a single round, killing or wounding many of those who'd come out to *succor* the wounded."

"Succor, mine arse, sir!" Alan spat. "That, sir, is a lying packet, concocted by the Frogs. They were looting, pure and simple. I put a stop to it. French soldiers or no, sir, they didn't deserve that pawing and stripping as they were dying. Besides, sir, the Savoian government's a pack of toadies and bootlickers to their new Frog masters."

"One witness purports to be a French midshipman, Jules Hainaut," Nelson informed him. "The prisoner you took, just exchanged?"

"How convenient, sir," Alan griped. "A toady to Choundas, he is. Consider the source, sir. Do you ask Mister Silberberg . . ."

"I have, Lewrie. I know of your past association with this man, and the reasons Choundas might have to wish to see you ruined," Nelson agreed, albeit reluctantly. "And the good use he made of returning this Hainaut to him. The problem, though . . ."

"Well, there you are, then, sir," Alan grinned, relaxing.

"You will not interrupt, sir!" Nelson burst forth, mottling with sudden rage. "Clap your goddamned mouth shut and listen, sir!"

"Aye, sir!" Lewrie mumbled in astonishment to hear the minnikin, *ammiraglio piccolo* Nelson shouting—cursing!

"Of course it's a lie, Lewrie!" Nelson fumed, lowering his voice from a quarterdeck bellow. "A damnable lie, but one the Genoese, and everyone else, will believe! The city mob takes it as bloody gospel . . . and it doesn't help that their own government's letter in question has given it an official stamp! Whatever your reasons for firing that shot, you did it, and I can't deny it. Can't refute the whole damned thing, just quibble 'bout the particulars, and do you know how *lame* that makes us sound? God Almighty, Lewrie! This might undermine the embargo, tie my hands . . . result in correspondence back and forth with Admiral Hotham . . . perhaps even London! It might result in our sudden withdrawal, under a cloud! And make this squadron, the Royal Navy, and His Majesty's Government a foul and clumsy jape . . . a laughingstock!"

Alan opened his mouth to make a contradiction, just what he didn't know right off . . . but Nelson's steely glare shushed him anew.

"Making matters worse, sir," Nelson hammered onward relentlessly, "there are flyers making the rounds in several Italian cities adverting this incident, as well as Captain Cockburn's seizure of *Il Furioso*, as a continuing compendium of British . . . atrocities!"

"But those were successfully answered, and settled, sir."

"All a packet of lies, start to finish, I grant you. But what recognition Genoa made of their own breach of neutrality, and their acquiescence 'pon the matter, is *not* recorded. So it becomes another nail in our coffin. Another victory in a war of words and opinions, which we are losing!" Nelson almost snarled; half at Lewrie, half at a form of war conducted by cowardly, faceless innuendo and lying. "Also cited in these flyers, Lewrie . . . though of yet not mentioned anywhere official, is a further, even more serious charge 'gainst you and your ship, sir."

Dear Christ, what else? Lewrie quavered.

"You told me last year 'bout being off Ushant, at the Glorious First of June battle, Lewrie." Nelson posed, solemn again. "As another example of England's supposed perfidy . . . the flyers allege you and your ship . . . mentioned both by name . . . entered combat flying false colors, that you engaged a French frigate under their flag. May we, at least, be able to successfully refute *that*, sir? And in so doing, cast doubt 'pon the whole?"

"Uhm . . ." Lewrie squirmed, innards icing up in fear. "Well . . . not *exactly*, sir."

"What?" Nelson bellowed. "Goddamn you for a cod's-head, sir!"

Oh, Christ, I'm in the quag for certain, now, Alan thought!

"To my best recollection, sir," he began to explain, again most carefully, "we hoisted French colors as we neared the lee side of the French line of battle, so their seventy-four's at the hind-end, which we had to tack around, wouldn't riddle us, sir. I hoped it might fool the frigate that had been pursuing us since daybreak, but he wasn't taken in. He opened 'pon *us*, sir, first. We put the ship about to shave the end of their line, and had to return fire if we wished to escape. We *opened* fire under their tricolor, sir, which fact my first pointed out to me, at which time their flag was lowered, and the Red Ensign hoisted. We began under French colors, but concluded several broadsides properly declared. Just after tacking, sir, but not yet flaked down or belayed. And that quickly done, sir."

And that's the truth . . . isn't it? he asked himself. Where had that come from, of a sudden? And, does he believe me?

Nelson glared at him, silent, his fine sense of honor outraged beyond all temperance, breathing high and shallow off the tops of his lungs, his lip beginning to curl in disdain.

"I wrote a report of it, sir." Lewrie explained further. "Gave it to Admiral Howe's captain of the fleet to be sent to the Admiralty. I've received no reference to the event, since."

That, he was certain was a true statement. But then, after such a glorious victory, who'd mar its odor with even a hint of a sanction, or sully the Navy's worldwide good opinion by even mentioning it?

Christ, one tiny slip, a quarter-minute's inattention, out of a fifteen-year career, and I'm to be ruined? he gasped to himself. Court-martialed and cashiered as dishonorable, in *shame*? A lucky ship, hey, a lucky captain, mine arse! And where's bloody Lir when you *need* that bastard? Mine arse on a bandbox!

"I promised all my captains I'd uphold them, Lewrie," Captain Nelson muttered more softly, though aflame with righteous anger. "As long as they did their duty, as best they saw it. You, however, make that vow rather *more* than difficult to fulfill. Damn you, sir! Whether you were half sunk, on your beam-ends, in the middle of a hurricane or pissed as a newt, *honor* was *breached*, sir! No matter how briefly, no matter how momentary your hair-splitting explanation may excuse it. Of all the blockheaded, slipshod things you ever thought of doing! Accident or design, it doesn't signify. It casts the foulest asperions on Navy, King, and Country. And, at a time when I, indeed England and what is left of the Coalition can least afford it. Made our task here even harder. And at the worst possible time. Do you see that, Lewrie?"

"Aye, sir," Alan groaned, sure he was a goner.

"Perhaps it's of no matter." Nelson sighed heavily. "I cannot print flyers of mine own to counter any of these charges, without giving them greater circulation. To deign to notice them is to show fear, which gives them even further veracity. And, sir . . . I cannot stoop to rebut this compounded slur in good conscience. That would be creating lies, to counter lies. To then be *caught* lying, later . . ."

"That's what Mister Silberberg is paid to do, sir," Alan said with a miserable shrug, but a touch of gallows humor in spite of all.

"The Admiralty took no notice of it?" Nelson inquired, with a very small sound of hopefulness.

"No, sir. Not a word."

"Nor have the French complained," Nelson glowered, sitting at his desk, at last. "Now it's public knowledge here, though, there is a chance Paris might find it useful against us, throughout Europe. As soon as this Choundas person, or his superiors, gloat over what they've gained by local exposure. Good God Almighty," he brooded, lowering his head and massaging his injured brow. "Admiral Hotham must be told, do you see, Lewrie. Loath as I am to communicate it to him, this is a matter we cannot sweep under the rug. He may assemble a court at San Fiorenzo."

"I see that, sir." Lewrie sighed, just as morosely.

"Thought better of you, I did, sir," Nelson declared softly. "Turk's Island, the way you spoke so movingly in your captain's behalf when he was wounded . . . way he spoke so well of you. Toulon. Taking *Jester* just after, saving all those refugees. *Knew* you were reputed to be a trifle rakehellish, one who'd tiptoe right to the edge. The Hamiltons in Naples spoke well of you, too. Lady Emma, especially. I have found her to be a shrewd judge of character, in the main."

Lewrie bit on a knuckle, diplomatically, wondering what Nelson'd think, if he knew he'd got the leg over Lady Emma back in '93?

"Trouble is, though, Lewrie, you're slipshod, slapdash. More so than a proper captain ought be," Nelson accused. "Given your previous good repute, though, I *am* given to believe your explanation. Your actions at Bordighera *were* honorable. Give me copies of all officers' journals, log entries, and such, concerning Ushant, so I may satisfy myself, one way or the other, before I communicate it to Admiral Hotham. There is always the possibility that he will deem it unworthy of note. Or, given the circumstances that obtain of late . . . he may consider it *inexpedient* to notice, do you follow, sir?"

"Aye, sir." Lewrie nodded hopefully. Hotham had trouble with recalling what he had for breakfast, his bloody hat size; or dither so long in making up what passed for his mind, he'd soon forget it.

"In the meantime, I may perfectly justify sending you away, then. Though I am already badly in need of reinforcement," Nelson stated.

"Sent away, sir. I see," Lewrie stammered.

"Your ship took damage, sir," Nelson said, brightening a trifle. "I believe you've been eighteen months without a refit, as well. Leghorn is the place for you, Lewrie. With *Jester* away . . . out of sight, out of mind? . . . the rabble-rousers who spread these filthy lies will have to cut new ones from whole cloth to inflame Italian resentments. You will perform such limited repairs as you may here at Vado Bay, then go to Leghorn to complete them, and do a proper refit. Take your time, there. No need to rush back. Once back, I may find you useful again. Perhaps well offshore, still out of sight. And operating under a set of orders and cautions, which I pray will spare us the risk of future embarrassments."

"I see, sir," Lewrie said, even more gloomily. "Well, I'd best be about it, then. Was that all, sir? You said three . . . ?"

"Ah." Nelson frowned sternly again, getting to his feet, with his hands in the small of his back. "Yes. There was."

God what bloody *else*, Alan sagged; adultery?

"It is Captain Cockburn's complaint, sir . . . that you impeded his pursuit of Choundas's vessel . . . an enemy then flying . . . by the placement of your ship, by not obeying his flag signals to give him way seaward. Further, that your replies were preemptory and unsuitable for a junior to send to a senior officer."

"Well, damme . . ." Lewrie muttered, quite nonplussed.

"A close-run thing already, I warn you, sir," Nelson rejoined.

"He asked 'Do You Require Assistance?' sir," Lewrie explained, feeling like he'd been doing so his entire bloody life! "My signals midshipman Mister Hyde's deck log will show that, sir. To which I sent 'Affirmative,' taking it to mean did I need *rescuing* from Choundas . . . and I most heartily *did*, sir!"

He laid out his crippled state, barely under control and unable to steer clear, barely underway and almost dead in the water. How he had sent "Submit," meaning that Cockburn should cut inshore, cutting a corner off the pursuit.

"We did *manage* to claw about northerly, sir, when he ordered us to haul our wind. I had no intent to impede him, far from it. I meant no disrespect, or wished to 'serve him sauce,' either, sir. Were he to catch Choundas up and murder the bastard, I'd be the first one to sport him a royal fireworks, *and* a concert! That man needs killing more than anyone ever I did see, sir, and if Captain Cockburn got the credit for it, then I'd be the last man on earth to complain. Had he cut inshore, well . . . he broke off his pursuit not an hour later, so . . ."

Nelson cut off his blathering with a chop of his hand.

"I've already sensed animosity between you before, sir. And did I not warn you both that I wished my captains to work together? Did I not make that plain enough, sir?" Nelson intoned harshly. "I cannot tolerate officers under me who can't put aside personal grudges so the greater good is achieved. With due deference, and mutual respect."

"But I was trying to communicate to him how best my situation, and his desire for a fight, might coincide, sir."

"He may be young, to your lights, Lewrie," Nelson pointed out. "May have attained a great deal, perhaps an unseemly great deal in so short a time. But I find him to be one of the ablest, most honest and courageous officers it has ever been my pleasure to meet. Intelligent, with steel in his hand, and aggressive, with a burning desire to close with, and destroy the foe."

"Well, of course, sir," Alan wriggled.

"How many battles has England lost, sir?" Nelson sighed, gazing off in the middle distance, half turned away from him. "How many opportunities have we let slip, because of bickering and rancor, when they might have resulted in stupendous, crushing victories? All due to the spite and jealousy of our leaders, I tell you. You were at the Battle of the Chesapeake in eighty-one, I believe, sir?" Nelson snapped, turning to face him again. "Hood and Graves, sir, confusing signals? I doubt it. There was lingering animosity 'tween them, and Hood disgusted that his superior allowed de Grasse to stand out and exit the capes in good order, so he held his division back from engaging, and Graves left unable to prevail, unsupported. Hard as it pains me to say about our mutual patron, and as fine a sailor, a gentleman, and officer as we may ever know, he is not free of human failings. There *must* be trust, respect, and cooperation between us, sir!" Nelson cried, a messianic glint in his eye. "We must allow nothing to get in the way of Duty. Nothing! Mankind will never be free of spite, never become so contented with their lot, or with one another, that they march in lockstep, like some wind-up, clock-work toys. I cannot hope, nor order, that my officers *love* one another, Lewrie. But it is not too much to wish that they are respectful of one another, and the others' individual talents. Like a houseful of good-natured brothers and cousins might deal among themselves. Chaffer at home, with no vindictiveness, but ready to spring to the defense of each individual with as much alacrity as they would for their family's good name. I will not tolerate an officer who cannot work cheerfully with his fellows, Lewrie. Nor one who would play the serpent in the Garden of Eden behind the others' backs."

"Aye, sir," Lewrie replied, cowed by the vehemence with which Nelson spoke, his stubborn enthusiasm.

"You will write Cockburn and make amends to him," Nelson told him; ordered him. "Explain yourself, and your signals, and the spirit in which they were intended. You might also thank him, even though you have already done so, for rescuing you at your weakest moment. Quarter-hour more, and you'd have been forced to strike, no matter how doughty a defense you presented, isn't that what you wrote in your report? It would not hurt to tell Cockburn that."

"Perhaps it may mollify him, were I to offer him my tender, sir? Little *Bombolo*? I'll have no need of her at Leghorn," Lewrie offered, hard as it pained him.

"I should think that would be received as a most welcome, and a most gracious gift, Lewrie," Nelson replied with a tiny smile; a first of a gruesome half-hour's cobbing. He offered his hand.

Now there's a wonder, Lewrie thought, rising to shake it, taking it for dismissal, at last, thank God.

"I will make the strongest representation to Admiral Hotham that we've been hoodwinked by a clever and malicious French plot. A letter from that fellow Silberberg of yours, may be of aid, as well. That is, should your logs and journals satisfy me," Nelson stated levelly.

"Aye, sir," Lewrie flummoxed, seeing escape from Nelson's ire, and his predicament. "Assuming that Mister Silberberg is of a mind to be forgiving, since I didn't kill Choundas for him."

"That was his intent?" Nelson frowned, pulling at his nose.

"For someone to do it, sir, didn't matter whom. I was the bait to get at him. Just didn't expect him to pop up where he did, and so quickly. Crippling his squadron as we did, sir, that was only a part of it. Same with scooping up his convoy to Alassio."

And, barring the fight with Choundas, it *had* been a red-letter day; a corvette *La Resolve* taken, along with a small corvette *La Republique*, and two Barbary Pirate-type *xebecs*, three-masted-armed galleys, plus a total of seven assorted merchant ships crammed with munitions and food.

"Now we've bested him, sir," Lewrie dared to suggest, with *his* first grin of the last half hour as well, "his superiors might turn him out, and give you an honorable foe. Probably a man less dangerous, do you see. Then, it'll be Silberberg's pigeon. Poison in the man's soup, or a knife in the back in a dark alley . . . his stock-in-trade. Find himself an assassin who can . . ."

"This Choundas may be a wily foe, Lewrie," Nelson objected with revulsion, "as large a monster as he is painted, aye . . . but I doubt that anyone is so vital to the French, nor our fortunes grown so bleak, that we would ever sanction cold-blooded murder. To bring him to book, gun-to-gun, or with crossed steel is one thing, but . . . that's repugnant to me, to any honorable gentleman or Christian."

"War to the knife, sir. As Mister Silberberg put it, long ago."

"You associate with the wrong sort of people, sir," Nelson said with a sniff of disdain.

And don't I, just! Alan thought, fighting a rueful smile.

"Not exactly my choice, sir," Alan told him. "He's very good at using people, whether they like it or not."

"By God, sir, he will not use me!" Nelson declared. Which gave Alan as much joy as could be expected, given the circumstances.

BOOK V

Aut tuam mortem aut meam.

Your life or mine.

Hercules Furens, 427
Lucius Annaeus Seneca

CHAPTER

1

LEWRIE HAD ALWAYS been pretty sure that there were some quite positive things to be said for Greed, and Lust for Mammon. Positive things most likely said from the comfort of an expensive club chair. Though Tuscany may have gotten some of those inflammatory flyers, and a few of the merchants, some few of the shipyard workers of Leghorn may have resented, perhaps even despised *Jester*'s presence at the careenage, in the graving dock, or moored stern-to at a stone quay, Dago fashion, they didn't allow personal grudges to mix with business, or a chance to turn a handsome profit on her repairs, and her refit.

One hellacious profit, if Mister Giles's ledgers, old Mister Udney's receipts, and Cony's stores' lists were anything to go by. There were other profits to be made, ashore, too, and Leghorn's brothels and taverns, food stalls and chandlers, pimps and bumboat marketers were as apolitically avaricious as the rest when it came to shillings or gold guineas. And the resulting claims for damages to taverns and brothels, when those of *Jester*'s people reliable enough to be trusted with shore leave occasionally went on "a high ramble," and were sometimes fetched back alongside in the custody of the neighborhood watch.

Certainly, glum and ever unsatisfied Mister Howse their surgeon, was prospering. He, LeGoff, Mister Paschal the sailmaker, and one of the loblolly boys who'd been a glovemaker's assistant were making a killing on manufacturing cundums—or administering the Mercury Cure for the Pox. Howse's purchases of mercury were beginning to rival what a small, but thriving, silver refinery might consume.

"Can't you put saltpeter in their food, or something, Mister Howse?"

Lewrie crossly inquired of him. "I mind a rumor around more than a few schools I attended that it was done regular, to reduce the parish pregnancy rates blamed on students. Or faculty buggery."

"I have no definitive proof that such an admixture is efficacious, Captain," Howse grumbled. "An old wive's tale, more like. And, should medical science admit it as a proper medicament . . . I am operating on a strictly limited Admiralty allotment *per annum* for the purchase of . . ."

"Which seems to be going for sheep gut and mercury." His much put-upon captain sighed in frustration over another damned indenture form from his medical staff.

"Should you order the ship back into Discipline, sir, keep our men aboard and away from the whores, you would find my expenditures . . . and the crew's good health, and their moral state, much improved, I'm certain," Howse said, in that truculent, edge-of-accusatory way he'd perfected. "To allow the people to engage in such licentious manner, to 'spend' on whores their vital and precious bodily essences . . . which weakens their bodies and minds, renders them lackluster and feeble of wits . . . incites continual thoughts of lust, contributing to their perpetual moral decline, well . . . I'll say no more, sir."

"I should *certainly* hope so, Mister Howse," Lewrie snapped, at his breaking point. The reek of fresh paint being slathered on by the barricoe, the din of hammering and sawing, had had him in an ill humor for days. That, and their enforced idleness. "What would you have of me . . . sir! Lash 'em below, seal the hatches on 'em, and let 'em free only when we need 'em? Sir? Would you be happier if they flogged the palms of their hands raw from 'boxing the Jesuit'? Or would you like a bugger's orgy in the cable-tiers . . . sir? By God, sir, you hired on as a naval surgeon, not a hedge-priest. Sew their wounds, cure their *bodily* ills . . . not Society's. Sorry your flock need to gambol like a pack of spring lambs, Mister Howse. Get blind-drunk and put the leg over some poll, now and then. They're *men*, sir, not your social experiment!"

"I can see, sir, that discussion at this point is . . ." Howse sulked.

"You take that tone with me one more time, sir," Lewrie warned him, glad to have someone or something to rant at for release, "do you *dare* look cutty-eyed at me when we suffer casualties doing our duty . . . and I'll bloody break you, Mister Howse! Men get hurt at sea, whether it's peace or war. Men die! I'm not your heartless monster to sneer at 'cause we've lost a few since you came aboard. Men *I* knew, men who served with me *long* before you brought your disdain, you . . ."

Lewrie turned away and took a sip of his coffee, on the verge of being personally insulting, of abusing a gentleman. Howse did deserve that distinction, at least. The coffee was tepid. And it stank from paint, tasted like cool enamel.

"That'll be all, sir. Get out," Lewrie ordered.

"Very well, sir." Howse all but coughed in outrage, but determined to be his captain's moral and intellectual superior to the end.

"GODDAMN HIM!" LEWRIE whispered, tossing his coffee overboard, out the opened sash-windows in the transom. Porter, minus his arm and pensioned off discharged, Bittfield off in hospital at San Fiorenzo . . . sure to die of sepsis; Rushing atop the amputated fore topmast. Five dead, a dozen wounded aye, and four of those maimed so badly they'd be cripples and pensioners once they got back to England. Teenaged topmen, first-voyage Marines too young to shave proper. Not too many of the petty officers, thank God, Lewrie thought, or the able seamen the ship depended on. Mostly the feckless young. The worst slaughter was usually reserved for them. The worst heartbreak . . .

Dolorous as the crew had been when they'd anchored at Leghorn, Lewrie had known . . . as Mister Howse never would . . . that sailors were a resilient lot. Beaten and terrorized as they'd been with Choundas close-aboard, they'd stood game, ready to dare to the last. Stubborn pride, courage . . . fear of letting mates down, revenge for the fallen friends, or that ineffable spirit of English sailors that their ship would win, that their *Jester*, their home, would never strike. That had been what kept them from falling apart, then. And what would save them now. A great deal of physical labor, beginning with stripping her down to the fighting tops and gant lines, hoisting out artillery, shot, powder, and stores to float her onto a careenage shore so they could scorch off the weed on her bottom, chip off barnacles, search for rot and missing copper. Physical labor took their minds off fell musings.

A long-delayed distribution of a portion of the prize money they had earned had helped. That, and the chance for a spell ashore, while *Jester* was uninhabitable, and days Out of Discipline once she was back afloat, so they could caterwaul and carouse their way back to feeling like men who were unbeatable.

Poxed, some might have been, staggering dizzily with their teeth gone gray from the Mercury Cure, which no matter Howse's lofty disdain fetched him fifteen shillings per sufferer, but they were still Jesters.

Floating catamaran work-stages alongside, bosun's chairs or wood tres-
tles slung overboard so they could paint and tar, a perceptive ear could
ascertain that they were working cheerfully. Fiddle and fife played to
divert them. Hands near the great-cabin's quarter galleries chatted and
joshed one another. Cursing the bosun, of course, for putting them to
such a messy chore, for tar stains and paint splotches on even their worst
old slop trousers. Which was about all they wore at the moment, rolled to
their knees. The scuttlebutts were kept full and handy for all, the amount
of thirst-slaking water unrationed for once. Mister Giles, with only mild
objections to the expense, supplied small-beer in liberal amounts. There
was fresh food come from shore almost every day, along with the tons of
chandlers' goods.

Lewrie sat down to read it over, again, mind-boggled that he had
been allowed so much, that Udney and the local Admiralty shore agent
at Leghorn were so prodigal with Navy funds. Well, almost prodigal,
Alan thought with a rare grin; the prices local chandlers charged were
downright sinful, and limited the largesse he might take aboard.

New canvas and thread, new rope cable for standing rigging, and
running rigging, new replacement masts and spars—all Tuscan pine or
Levant cedar—of the highest, best-seasoned quality. Tar, turpentine,
pitch, white-lead, and copper to pay the bottom with barnacle-poison-
ing, weed-killing lead over canvas and felt, thin sheet-copper to seal
that so *Jester* would be as smooth as a baby's arse, and slip across the
sea like a thoroughbred once more. Timber and planking of the best
Adriatic oak to replace smashed or wormed hull members and blown-in
bulwarks.

And paint, Lewrie gagged again, as the breeze shifted, bringing the
heavy odor into his day-cabin. He threw his quill pen on the desk and
leaned back in his chair, recalling what a captain outfitting back home in
an English port had written the Admiralty, once he'd received the usual,
meager, ration of paint from HM Dockyards:

"Which *side* of the ship do you wish me to do, sirs?" Alan asked the
echoing cabins, with a faint chuckle.

Toulon came slinking in from up forrud, low to the deck, imitating a
caterpillar, with a distressed, grumpy trilling yowl, on a beeline for
Lewrie's lap. Where, once ensconced, he could make his strongest complaints over some new cat-galling disaster. Rather loudly!

"Poor puss, what's got you . . . ?" Alan cooed. His hand came off
Toulon's hindquarters wet with dull red inboard-bulwarks paint, which

was used to disguise bloodstains. "Christ, you clumsy litl'un. You've put your tail in the paint pot? Aspinall?"

"Sir?"

"Fetch a cloth, 'fore it dries on him. Might need one dipped in turpentine, too. No, Toulon, don't lick it . . . God . . . !"

There was a pair of kerseymere breeches that had seen their last Day Watch, Lewrie sighed; a good shirt, too, if I'm not . . .

"I'll ask Mister Cony, sir," Aspinall vowed. "Back in a trice."

Mister Cony. With Porter gone, Will Cony had risen to bosun, and Able Seaman Sadler, one of the old Cockerels from the times at Toulon had become bosun's mate. Just as Mister Crewe was now the acting master gunner, Yeoman of the Powder Room Hogge was gunner's mate, and the Prussian Rahl was acting yeoman. Another Cockerel, Preston, had become quarter-gunner, though Lewrie wasn't sure that Rahl's eye for gunnery wasn't wasted below, in the magazines.

"Cap'um clerk, Mister Mountjoy . . . Sah!"

"Enter," Lewrie snapped, trying to hold Toulon still and not get paint-stained until Aspinall returned.

"Letter's come aboard for you, sir," Mountjoy announced. He coughed into his fist, looking cutty-eyed to all corners. More softly he added, "and this, too, sir. From your, uhm . . . banker? He's ashore and wishes permission to come aboard."

"Sergeant Bootheby to muster his Marines, Mister Mountjoy," Lewrie growled, opening Twigg's note first, no matter how he hated doing that; it was official, after all. "Full 'bullock' kit, red tunics and pipe-clay. We'll execute him by musketry, at the taffrail, *à la* Admiral Byng."

"Can . . . can you *do* that, sir?" Mountjoy gaped. "Should, I mean."

"No, but I can wish, sir." Alan sighed futilely. "Very well . . . tell the devious bastard he may come aboard. A *tradesman*'s welcome, do you inform the harbor watch. No honors."

Aspinall returned, to take Toulon from him and carry him off to the pantry for a cleaning with some dishcloths moistened with turpentine.

"Well I'm damned . . ." Lewrie whispered as he opened the second.

It was from Signorina Claudia Mastandrea!

He'd gotten several supportive, kindly letters from her, and her keeper Senator Marcello di Silvano. He'd sent the senator the expected "thankee" for his invitation, with apologies for missing the ball that followed. Twigg's doing, damn his eyes! Maybe just as well, though . . . ?

Claudia's first note had been just before *Jester* sailed, and more than the usual social obligation to a new acquaintance; so pleased she met him, sorry we missed our promised dance, do forgive the forwardness and blah-blah-blah . . . But laden with so much double meaning, that she might have rewarded him with more than one turn around the floor, that he still *must* allow her to show him that map, that collection . . . those *treasures*? That there should be perfect freedom between them? Hmm . . .

After the battle with Choundas, another brace of letters. The one from Signore di Silvano so outraged that he was being smeared with such a scurrillous set of lies; promises to get to the bottom of it and refute them, in concert with Drake and Nelson; how di Silvano had spoken to his fellow senators and the Doge, would use his every good office to maintain Genoese neutrality, *and* independence. That Lewrie should consider him a friend, with many mutual, historical interests to discuss when he returned from Leghorn.

Claudia's though . . . it was almost tearful, that a good and decent man had been falsely accused, and her remorse that Genoa was so ungrateful to him. A stronger hint, concerning her high regard, her inability to get him out of her mind, a wistfulness . . . ? Hmm . . .

Now, this'un:

. . . patron travels to Leghorn and Florence on family and commercial affairs, and I must confess I have conspired to accompany him. Though once in the city we will be too little together most days, and a great many evenings, for he will be much upon the town and *so very busy*, while I languish. Many evenings he must attend the rich and prominent in their homes or at the theaters, accompanied by their wives and children, to which I am not invited though his hosts, being substantial men, covertly maintain their own convenient, pleasing, and similar "fictions"?

"Hmm, hmm, hmm!" Lewrie harrumphed, feeling a stirring, in spite of himself, in his nether regions.

Though our acquaintance has been so brief thus far, I am constantly mindful of you, and struck by how warm is my regard. How often I muse that after knowing you much better, I could not form a more perfect appraisal and appreciation of your fine qualities. Marcello will invite you ashore soon, to renew his budding friendship. Do please accept, so you and I may renew our own. Further, should the needs of your ship allow, you will then be free to call upon me while we are in Leghorn, or inform me of a shore residence you may use, so we may dine . . .

Would it not taste pretty much like lead paint or turpentine, he felt badly in need of a glass of something for "Dutch Courage," at that very moment. "To dine *intime*, well, well . . . just the two of us, alone?

Lewrie brooded, it must be admitted on his behalf, on past error. And they were legion. Whenever he'd been so idle, so out of sorts, and so sunk in the "Blue Devils." So close to shore, and all its allures. Betty Hillwood, Dolly Fenton, Lady Delia Cantner, Soft Rabbit, Phoebe . . . and a host of others whose names he'd forgotten, if not their charms.

More than two months since Alassio Bay, staying aboard most of the time, or in communal shore lodgings while *Jester* had been careened and empty. Male-only suppers, park strolls, the opera that was in Italian and wasn't meant to be understood, anyway, or concerts where the music didn't puzzle overly much, with Knolles, Mountjoy, Buchanon, or the midshipmen as unwitting chaperons. Then back aboard sober, *alone* . . .

But what was good for the geese was good for the gander. He'd let the hands have their ruts, so why not . . . ?

No, damme . . . in enough bloody trouble already, ain't I, he told himself sadly, turning her note over and over in his fingers; should I start again, I'll make a *pig* of meself. He did espy, and quickly take to memory, the carefully written return address, however. Duty, refit . . . so little time? Well, I *have* to write her, o' course, to beg off . . . ? Pig—piglet—teats—bouncers—God, *stop* me 'fore I *tup* again!

"Mister Silberberg is without, sir," Mountjoy interrupted.

"Have the vicious, two-faced fart come in, then, Mister Mountjoy," Lewrie barked in a quarterdeck voice loud enough for Twigg to hear beyond on the gun deck. And slipped the too-tempting note from Signorina Mastandrea into the middle drawer of his desk. "And fetch me poor old Toulon, soon's he's paint-free . . . th' widdle darlin' . . ." Lewrie said with a sudden surge of spite.

"How very clever, Lewrie," Twigg/Silberberg whispered, feigning amusement, though pale with sullen anger.

"So good to see you again, Mister Silberberg. And how's me shares doin', hey?" Alan chortled. "You'll pardon me if I don't rise."

"You press me too far, sir!" Twigg hissed, but softly. "I vow you'll overreach someday, to your regret!"

"Pretty much what I thought of you, sir," Lewrie whispered in return. "After you damn near got my arse knackered. Four dead, four crippled.

Like the score so far, do you . . . Mister Silberberg? Press *me* too far
. . . someday, and . . ." Alan shrugged, flashing a toothy grin.

"We need to talk, sir. Privately," Twigg instructed, tossing his head to
the pantry, where Aspinall hummed and crooned over Toulon to gentle
him. "You and I. No others."

"And what about him?" Lewrie asked, his notice drawn to a side of
beef in a dark suit who had accompanied Twigg aboard. "Feel need of
bodyguarding, sir? A fine ox-carcass you've hired, I must say."

"Here 'e be, sir, good'z new, I reckon," Aspinall announced as he
fetched the cat back. "Got all 'at paint off 'im, I did, sir. He weren't fond
o' th' scrubbin', though."

Toulon was set upon the desktop, fluffed up with insult, tail bottled up
and lashing. He would have finished washing his flank all by himself, but
for the odor, and the presence of strangers. With a mean-spirited growl
and hiss, ears laid back—which made Twigg pale even more and cringe
far back in his chair—Toulon leapt away to go hide under something,
where he could sulk in private, carping to cat-gods of how abused his
pride was, how unfair Life's Portion.

"That'll be all, Aspinall," Lewrie said. "Go on deck, if you please. We'll
fetch our own glasses. You, too, Mister Mountjoy."

"Yes, sir," Mountjoy replied, mournful that he wasn't included this
time.

"Now, sir. What do you and I have to discuss, private or otherwise?"
Lewrie asked, rising to open the wine cabinet for them. Brandy was too
good, he thought; let 'em drink this cheap Dago red!

"You failed, Lewrie. Failed me." Twigg began, swiveling about to keep
his eyes on him.

"Not for want of trying, sir. Or have you not noticed how bad *Jester*
was knocked about? Didn't know you'd whistle him up quite that quickly,
else I would have swallowed my pride and requested *Meleager* to stay
seaward with me."

"Then he'd have never dared, sir," Twigg snapped impatiently as he
accepted a glass, a pour, and tossed his wine back. He made a face,
lurching back as if he'd been poisoned, and eyeing Lewrie hellish-sharp,
as if he wouldn't put poison past him!

"You, sir?" Lewrie asked of the hulking stranger, so tanned and fit, so
martial in his carriage. "Whoever you are?"

"Yes, sir, thankee," the apparition spoke at last, taking wine and sip-
ping at it, showing no trace of disappointment with its taste.

"One of my associates, Lewrie," Twigg grumbled. "A most competent fellow. Ex-Household Cavalry. Allow me . . ."

"Looks *far* too intelligent to be Household Cavalry," Alan said tongue-in-cheek, "nor British Cavalry, at *all*! And, *if* intelligent . . . then how'd he come to be stupid enough to associate with you, sir?"

"One should never kick strange dogs, sir," the dark fellow said with a faint smile, yet an air of menace. "They've been known to bite."

Officer, Lewrie surmised by his squirearchy, perhaps Kentish accent; ex-officer. Abscond with the mess funds, did you? Or your major's daughter?

"Enough of this rancor, Lewrie," Twigg warned. "As you refer to me, 'pon your life, as Silberberg . . . you will take as gospel that my man is ever to be referred to as Mister Peel. Or ex-Captain Peel."

"Not 'John Peel,' surely," Alan snickered, reminded of the old hunting song.

"No, 'tis *James*, sir . . . James Peel," the fellow purred, offering his hand, which Lewrie had to shake.

"Right, then . . . Captain Peel, Mister Silberberg," Lewrie said, sitting down, regretting his choice of wines, which he also was forced to drink. Thin, too fruity, and acidy; and fresh-poured already had a redolence of paint thinner. "So, what is so important that you sailed down from Genoa?"

"Coached," Twigg griped, shifting as if in pain. "As to that gruesome necessity, more later. What is important, Lewrie, is killing Guillaume Choundas. Still."

"Is that really necessary, sir?" Lewrie frowned. "We buggered him and his reputation, took his convoy at Alassio, and bagged four of his warships, such as they were. And, in spite of serving us as good as he got, we damaged his own corvette. I'd think his stock was quite low, by now."

"Can you forget the Far East, sir?" Twigg insisted. "Whenever we thought we'd truly crippled him, he wriggled free, and came back to bedevil us, twice as strong as before? No, sir. It won't be over till I've his head in a sack, for all to see."

"When last we met, Mister . . . Silberberg, you told me you prided yourself on keeping things coolly logical and objective," Lewrie said with a dubious look. "Frankly, I think Choundas is become your bug-a-bear. It sounds entirely personal and revengeful, to me. What can he hope to accomplish, with the few ships he has left? With Nelson commanding the Riviera coast? And with your . . . connections . . . alerting us to every convoy? In the Far East, he was the *only* pirate, privateer . . . whatever, that Paris would sanction, so eliminating him was important. Wartime, though . . . he's just another ship's captain at the moment, a commander of a minor squadron. There must be a hundred men in France just as potentially troubling."

"He's in *my* bailiwick, Lewrie," Twigg objected stubbornly, "in charge of the squadron that runs supplies to support the French Army, which will gobble up all of northern Italy if they're not stopped. It makes him *my* preeminent problem, no matter our past connection. If he is killed, I save another region the grief of facing him. If he dies, Choundas rises no higher. He gets no frigates, no ships of the line to play with. Can you possibly imagine the harm he'd do, were he to become a junior admiral?"

"Then why not have one of your . . . associates," Lewrie wondered aloud, "stop his business with a knife under the heart?"

"Told you he has a clear head, Peel." Twigg smirked suddenly in glee. "When he thinks, that is."

"Yes, sir," Peel agreed, stony-faced, peering at Lewrie openly, judging, weighing, and balancing.

"He's well guarded, Lewrie," Twigg complained petulantly, as he sipped more wine, made another face. "Made no new friends on his rise with the original revolutionaries. Had damned few from before. Those still alive, that is. Once he'd culled 'em for past slights. Imagined slights, half of 'em. Stays sober, keeps his wits about him, of which I do not have to tell you, he has considerable. Personal guard force, a pack of Breton pets, including this Hainaut fellow we returned to him. As for vices . . ."

"Goes for the windward passage, even with girls," Lewrie stuck in. "So we learned from the Filipina villagers, and Chinese whores."

"The younger and weaker, the sweeter, aye," Twigg snarled with revulsion. "Barring someone doing him in like Marat in his bathwater, he's almost impossible to get at. Our abilities, so to speak, are not that firm in Provence, or along the Riviera. Too much fear, d'ye see, 'mongst adult women, and his tastes run to the small, weak, and helpless. Recruiting a girl-child victim stands little chance, either, that he'd choose her, or that she could summon nerve enough to do the deed. We have a better plan, though."

"Oh, Christ, and it involves me, does it?" Lewrie groaned. "We *played* that card. He'll not fall for it a second time."

"Hot as my hatred for Choundas is, Lewrie, it can't hold a candle to his hatred for you," Twigg cackled, entirely too pleased with himself. "Do you both survive this war, I'd expect he'd be panting to kill you when you're both pensioners. Some things abide. He'll bite."

"And what if I refuse, sir?" Lewrie snapped. "You're Foreign Office, *you* can't order a serving officer, or his ship . . ."

Twigg smirked, reached into his coat, and produced two letters. One from Hotham, one from Nelson, Lewrie noted with horror.

"Not *afraid* of him, are you, sir?" Peel posed, with a barely concealed sneer.

"Name your weapon and place, and I'll show you 'afraid,' sir!"

"Didn't ask were you afraid o' me, sir," Peel egged him on. "I asked were you afraid o' him?"

Lewrie took pause, considering; reading those two sets of orders.

"Aye, I most fuckin' well am fearful of 'im, sir," Lewrie said at last with bald candor. "Anyone who's ever had dealings with Guillaume Choundas has right to fear him. Or should."

"Were you to render me a valuable service, Lewrie," Twigg posed, his pencil-long, thin fingers steepled under his skeletal chin, "which I swear to you involves no physical danger to your ship, your crew, or yourself . . . which helps bring Choundas to book . . . would you do it?"

"You say that now, sir," Lewrie countered, still seething from Peel's goading. And suspecting that it was Twigg's arranging, for Peel to put him off balance with his sneer, his cocked eyebrow. "But things always have a way of going from a walk to a gallop, with you. Once you get the bit in your teeth, there's no stopping you. And there I'd be, clinging to your scheme's tail, half dragged to death. My people right with me, thrown into peril all unwitting."

"Swear it on a Bible, Lewrie," Twigg's eyes twinkled, "no harm will come to this ship you love so much, her hands, nor you. This will not involve artillery, nor steel. A single night's . . . light duties?"

"Means I'm the only one daft enough to listen to you, you mean," Lewrie shot back, topping up his glass. "Or . . . damme!" He showed them a sly grin. "You mean to use me as bait again. Here in Leghorn? We don't have to sail? That sounds like Choundas has learned where *Jester* lies, and has sent some bully-bucks to Leghorn to do me in! Coached to town, did you? You *said* you did. To keep an eye on the assassins he's dispatched, right? Did he come himself? And you want me to trail my colors where you can catch him and kill him?"

"Told you he was imaginative, too, Peel." Twigg sighed in disappointment, like a tutor bored and despairing of a pupil's lack of wit. "Though not *always* clever when he is. No, Lewrie, Choundas has pressing work up north, he can't abandon his duties to suit his personal desires. You run no risk of assassination. Choundas will await your death until he can arrange it by his own hand, a face-to-face *rencontre*. He'll not be satisfied with a report. I don't *believe* that you're in any danger. Your admiral, and Captain Nelson, would never have issued these orders for your coopera- tion with me, else. Besides . . ."

Twigg leaned forward, elbows on the desktop, the cabin shadowed as evilly as a conjured-up companion of Satan. And he was snickering!

"Knowing you as I do, I am certain you'll find this duty to be rather . . . enjoyable, in fact. Now, will you refuse me, sir? Disobey orders from your superiors? I must admit to you, sir, that there is no other person in the entire Royal Navy who may perform this task, since it most vitally *concerns* you, and you alone. It may very well be the last thing I ever ask of you, and we'll call it 'quits' after."

"Enjoyable," he grunted with deep suspicion. "Then quits?"

"As enjoyable as the night in the brothel on Old Clothes Street in Canton, Lewrie," Twigg tempted, like the hoariest pimp in Macao.

"What, the night I got my head bashed in by Choundas's cox'n?" Lewrie griped. "Hellish fun, that was! What's the chore, then? As I seem to have no say in the matter, anyway . . ."

"Why, to allow yourself to be seduced, Lewrie," Twigg replied, beam- ing in triumph of his small victory. "You're hellish-good at that, I know."

"Seduced?" Alan gaped, rocked back on his heels in utter shock. "Have anyone *particular* in mind, then, do you?"

He pictured the ugliest, fubsiest, most-raddled and bewhiskered old mort in all creation who, unfortunately, possessed information just vital to Twigg concerning Choundas's, and French, intentions.

"I most certainly do, sir," Twigg cackled again. "It is my wish that you rattle Senator Marcello di Silvano's mistress, Lewrie. *Signorina* Claudia Mastandrea."

"*What?*" he cried. "Why her? Mean t'*say* . . . ?"

Lord, you'll remember it's orders, for King and Country, he pled. Though suddenly not quite so averse to the duty as he might have been.

"Because we have discovered that she is a French spy, sir."

"*What?*" he reiterated, beyond shocked. "Beg pardon, you . . ."

"Why else do you think she'd *ever* be interested in you, sir?" The old schemer hooted with joy of his revelation.

CHAPTER

2

"TELL HIM, PEEL," Twigg instructed, once Lewrie had calmed.

"You recall the ledger book, sir," Peel began, getting to his feet to make free with a fresh bottle of a much better wine from Alan's cabinet. "The enigmatic heading, 'U-R'? *Not* the initials of a single person . . . rather a corporate entity, Captain Lewrie," Peel said, with a military man's proper deference to a naval officer's title. "As you commented to my employer, he told me . . . a group of three, twenty, even sixty? Quite right, sir."

Peel at least was crisp in his delivery, the perfect soldier, reeling off a situation briefing, compared to Twigg's infernally circuitous maunderings.

"It has two meanings, one for the inner circle, one for the outer." Peel smiled. "It stands for '*Ultimi Romani,*' that is to say . . . 'The Last Romans.' It spans Italy, every kingdom or republic, made of substantial men with what they deem progressive, idealistic Republican and patriotic sentiments. A cabal of romantics quite infatuated with the unification of Italy, first and foremost, like the early Republican era of ancient Rome. Secondly, for the expansion of a unified Italy on the world stage, which will come to resemble somewhat the scope of the Roman Empire. All Italy, of course, all Mediterranean islands, all of North Africa, Egypt, the Levant, Turkey, and the Ottoman possessions in their grasp again, as well as the Holy Land and eastern Adriatic coast. With the Austrians removed as occupiers."

"To achieve this," Twigg interjected, "they've entered into a Devil's bargain with France, to drive the Austrians out, overrun the peninsula

297

and topple every sovereign state, using French occupation as the catalyst for revolution. Become a unified French possession. For a time, only. Until they may negotiate, or take by force, their later autonomy."

"Counting on the Coalition, sir," Peel went on, once Twigg had his nose back in his brandy, "to so weaken France, they can play silly buggers in the Mediterranean. See France so weaken England, Prussia, or Austria that once they have autonomy, by hook or by crook, we'd welcome them as allies at the proper moment, and acquiesce to their greater ambitions, which involve Savoia, the French Riviera, and Provence, maybe even a portion of Spain. They hold that eventually the entire Mediterranean must be Christian, but most importantly, Roman. And that the rest of the great powers wouldn't mind seeing Moslem power kicked back across the Bosporus and the Red Sea. Catholic Christian, o' course." Peel chuckled, with a raised brow.

"So they'd get in bed, so to speak, with revolutionary atheists to gain it?" Lewrie pondered.

"Indeed, sir. Anything to further the cause." Mister Peel smiled. " 'U-R' has an inner meaning, much like Masonry. We're fairly sure that it refers to a particular set of collaborators. They're quite cleverly compartmented, so the exposure of one minor, regional group would never expose the whole. 'U-R' also stands for one man, 'Ultimo Romano,' who may be in charge throughout Italy, or merely the pocket in this region. The Greatest Roman of Them All, sir? *The* Last Roman? From this man's correspondence, we've discovered a tantalizing clue to a larger cabal, to which he seems to be answerable, which goes by the enigmatic notation of 'Pee-Numeral One.' Either a higher council that pulls all the strings, of which he's a member, or a single person. P as in Pope or P as in Papa? Pee-Primo, or the First One? God only knows, Captain Lewrie." Peel shrugged, giving him the honorific title of his post. "By tracing correspondence from Gallacio and Randazzo, we have found the regional leader's identity. *Signore* Marcello di Silvano."

"Why that two-faced, canting . . . hound!" Lewrie fumed. "He's written me, so humble, so supportive . . . !"

"So politically astute?" Twigg laughed. "Who'd be suspected of treason the least, than the patriot who brays the loudest? *Signore* di Silvano wears a half-dozen faces, depending upon whom he's dealing with. I expect he found gulling you with sympathy and friendship to be an amusing exercise, no more. Just keeping his hand in, practicing his pose of hand-wringin', puppy-eyed insincere mendacity."

"So, you want me to bed his mistress, and somehow winkle information from her 'bout his plans?" Lewrie frowned.

"God *no*, Lewrie!" Twigg boomed, almost wheezing with amusement.
"Bless me, but you're far too thick for that! No, sir. *You* are the one to be
winkled. *Signorina* Mastandrea knows what she's about, you let the professional do her work."

"You're certain she's a French spy, then?" Lewrie had to ask.

"No doubt about it, sir," Twigg informed him. "A gift to the senator,
'bout the time Savoia was overrun. Like your Corsican doxy, she's of
mixed parentage, French and Italian. *Not* from Bergamo, as she tells
people, but Breil, near the old French border. Got her marching orders
from my opposite number, to go to Genoa and cozy up to Silvano, who
had the means to pass messages, and was already in contact with the
French. Huge landowner, do you recall, estates all up and down the
Riviera? Estate managers and overseers, goods-carts to and from those
farms pass all the time, even through Austrian-held lands. That's how she
contacts her employers, and how di Silvano services his local Roman
patriots, by land and sea. Intercepted a few of his, found one from her
and read it. Rather laughable encryption, actually . . . wouldn't think a
woman was capable of mastering such, but she did. Were she a man, I'd
have found a tougher code to crack, I expect."

"She doesn't work for Choundas, then?" Lewrie inquired, rather earnestly. Though he couldn't feature a woman so beautiful even being in
the same province as Choundas, much less agreeing to do his dirty work.
Even in his younger days, scrubbed up and looking human!

"Her superiors have sometimes given her tasks that might serve his
interests, and his squadron's," Twigg allowed with a breezy wave of one
hand. "But she is not in *his* direct employ. And what is this concern, sir?
Sweet on her, are you? I forgot, you've already contemplated topping
her. A most fetchin' morsel, ain't she. Sorry that I interrupted your
courtship in Genoa, might have been advantageous for you two to have
an existing relationship. But back then, she had me fooled. I took her as
nothing more than a silly, round-heeled slut, too stupid to stay faithful to
a rich and vengeful master. All sheep-eyed over the pretty young sailor.
There is a risk the senator might not enjoy her chore with you. Taken a
fancy to her, no matter they've a working relationship. She and the
senator are on intimate terms, I know for a fact. So intimate, and exclu-
sive, since he ditched t'other mistress he had, at Paris's bidding, that he
dares to sport with her bareback . . . do you get my meaning? You
might not even need cundums. No, Lewrie. Your job will be to play her

fool, then let slip to her what we *wish* you to let slip, once she's got you in the proper frame of mind."

"And that is . . . ?" Lewrie snorted, still dubious and edgy, no matter how pleasurable his duty might be, how he'd fantasized about Claudia Mastandrea. Twigg had dreamt it up, after all, so . . . !

"Choundas, of course," Twigg sniffed. "Him and the Austrians."

"The Austrians . . ." Lewrie drawled, now totally confused.

"Finest army in Europe, sir," Peel stated, most drolly. "And, the slowest."

"We pay them a hideous sum of money to stay in the Coalition," Twigg sighed wearily, "I do not know whether their emperor has ordered de Vins to delay his campaign another season, so they may touch *another* four million pounds sterling of ours . . . or whether General de Vins is a raging fool. All their damned generals! War is a German's trade, sir. That's when they earn their highest pay, and get the most adulation, so why wrap things up too early, then go back to barracks and be bored to death? Or perhaps General de Vins is much like our poor Hotham, too timorous and dithering to risk failure. Either way, the nub is that we owe the Austrians another installment in gold. No way to ship it downriver along the Rhine, with the Frogs at its mouth, nor through Hamburg overland. It has to come by sea, to Vado Bay, which is de Vins's only link to the sea. A substantial sum of money, Lewrie."

"And so . . . ?" Lewrie asked, getting suspicious again.

"We have allowed *certain* information to be overheard by local informers that such a shipment was forthcoming," Twigg related, going weaselly and twisting in his chair, a sure sign of trouble. "That it was to come from London, to Gibraltar, then to Port Mahon at Minorca, then up to San Fiorenzo Bay, since it carried the coinage to pay Admiral Hotham's fleet. Then it would put into Vado Bay, to be delivered to the Austrians. Should it not arrive, Austria might withdraw troops from the Genoese Riviera. Should France get their hands on it, they'd be dancing in a positive *shower* of 'yellow-boys,' enough to purchase anything they need, and prop up their new currency at home. Restive . . . the Frogs at home, d'ye see. Subsequently, we've revealed the sum to be around £200,000, the name of the ship to carry it . . . and the name of the escort. HMS *Jester*."

"Now wait a bloody minute, you said it was . . . that we'd . . . !"

"Be easy, sir," Peel suggested quickly, "you'll burst a blood vessel, keel over in apoplexy, I swear! What better bait can there be for this fellow Choundas? He was a pirate before, the lure of gold is almost irresistible.

Plus the hope that you are the escort. Two birds with one. Plus what a coup, with such far-reaching repercussions, were he to weaken the Coalition, or lay all northern Italy open to the French Army with a single deed. With his convoys so savaged recently, and his repute in Paris sinking, he must do something to recoup his own estate. There *will* be a ship at sea, a ship much like yours, painted in the same color scheme. The merchantman, though, will be a two-decker 4th Rate, of fifty guns . . . a naval vessel. Even does he fetch *two* corvettes to take her, he'll be confounded. Even does he escape a second time, his fame will be broken. And there are many French officers who'd love to see him come a cropper."

"It will be eminently plausible, Lewrie," Twigg explained with a sly look. "Nelson has lost the services of *Resolution* and *Speedy* for the moment, so he has nothing to spare. Hotham husbands every frigate or sloop of war at San Fiorenzo, and is already short himself. *Jester* is just refitted, though, currently unemployed. And, because of your supposed errors at Bordighera, and Ushant, you're not particularly welcome at either San Fiorenzo or Vado Bay. Yours is the only warship to be spared as escort, or dispatch vessel, for the nonce."

"While the real shipment, I take it . . ."

"None of your concern, sir!" Twigg snapped. "The less you know, the less you might blab, by accident. *Signorina* Mastandrea has already reported to her masters, I know it for a fact. Know their orders to her *verbatim*. She's to come to Leghorn, which she has, confirm reports from local informers anent your ship's state of repair, what orders you might have . . . and when *Jester* may be expected to sail, *and* arrive at Vado Bay."

"Do they know the ports of call, when I could depart to meet the cargo ship at Gibraltar, and when I finish at Vado Bay," Lewrie surmised, "they'd have a rough idea of where we'd be, any given day, assuming seasonal winds and seas. Within fifty miles or so. Two ships patrolling . . ."

Lewrie rose and went to his chart-space, to fetch a large-scale sea chart. He brought it back to the desk and spread it out for Twigg and Peel to look at.

"I'd expect Choundas to be greedy," Lewrie pondered aloud, using a pair of brass dividers to march off legs of a course. "And clever. A little fillip, sirs . . . to not only rob the Austrians, but steal the Navy pay chests. Sailors might be used to being one or two years in arrears in their pay, but soldiers usually aren't. Does he take the ship *before* she reaches San Fiorenzo, both the Army and Navy are cheated. Debts to local chandlers and merchants go unpaid. Troops and ships' crews will be demoralized. Aye, Choundas would like that. And so would his superiors. Might even turn Corsican sentiment against us because of it."

"Very clever," Mister Peel muttered, though speaking more of this sailor's shrewd calculations than of their foe, and sharing a look with his employer, with one brow cocked in reappraisal of all that Twigg had told him of Lewrie's wits. "You would expect him where, sir?"

"West of Corsica, and due south of the Îles d'Hyères," Lewrie replied slowly, stepping off distances. "Were I Choundas, I'd patrol, standing north-and-south along six degrees east, down to the latitude of the Straits of Bonifacio, around forty degrees north, perhaps as high as forty-three degrees," he told them, sketching out a rough box on the chart with a pencil stub. "A ship from Port Mahon in the Balearics on-passage for San Fiorenzo, or Vado Bay, *must* pass through this area."

He was unaware of Peel's newfound regard, nor of Twigg's grudging, hooded smile of pleasure; too lost in speculation. And in *his* own element.

"Two ships, you think, sir? Average-clear days, each could see twelve miles all about from their mast trucks. Ten miles separation . . . so they could read signals betwixt 'em, say . . . they could sweep a moving rectangle thirty to thirty-five miles long, north-to-south, and twenty-four miles wide. Even at a slow six knots, they'd scour the area twice over each day. It's too far west of Corsica to expect interference from Hotham's fleet . . . too far south of France for the escort to expect danger. That's more likely near Corsica's nor'west tip, around Calvi, before they get to San Fiorenzo, just as they enter the fringes of the Ligurian Sea. He may strike sooner, lurk off Minorca, but that's a long way away from his assigned region, sirs," Lewrie said, tossing down divider and rule, looking up at last. "Unless he's been reinforced lately, taking two corvettes, his best most like, will weaken his squadron, and hold up any planned convoys till they're back. He *can't* roam too far afield."

"Nor for very long, does he wish to keep his head," Twigg said with almost a purr of pleasure. "So Choundas may be best expected here in this rough area. Where, I trust, it will be he who is the biter bit. Where he will get the greatest surprise of his life. And his last."

"A good possibility, sir." Lewrie shrugged, hedging his bets.

"Now, all that's wanting is for the *signorina* to get in touch," Twigg beamed hungrily, rubbing his hands together, "so we may arrange your tryst with her. I've taken the liberty of engaging shore lodging, Lewrie.

Somewhere quiet, refined . . . where Mister Peel and I may hide ourselves, stand guard. Observe and listen, so we're sure there's no interference. That the bait is properly taken, hmm?"

"Oh, you mean something like this, sir." Lewrie smirked, opening his
desk drawer and dropping her note atop the chart.

"Why yess, Lewrie," Twigg drawled, most contented that his scheme
was well afoot. "Something very much like that'd do nicely."

CHAPTER

3

IT WAS RAINING that night in Leghorn, just enough to temper the day's balmy warmth, but not enough to cool the evening in the late October afterglow of the Lion Sun season. A sullen, persistent weak rain that made it feel almost as muggy as high summer; just enough rain to gurgle off the roof tiles, trickle down the tiled eaves into the gutters and sigh down the tile or lead downspouts, or plash on the balconies and window-sills. Which made it almost impossible for Twigg or Peel to hear much of what was said in the adjoining rooms, even with drinking glasses pressed to the thin lath-and-plaster dividing wall, ears against the bases. Twigg heaved another huge sigh of grumpy frustration; that a perfectly good gutta-percha stethoscopic tube had been overpowered by the sluicing of the rain and sough of the wind; that he was too old to be stooping against a wall in such a crabbed position; and that he was far too senior now to still be doing a younger legman agent's duties.

"Ah, something, sir," Peel began to say, perking up.

"Sssst!" Twigg hissed, straining to hear. "Damme, just . . ."

Even without their improvised devices, they could now hear what transpired in the apartment adjoining theirs. Not the whispery billing and cooing of muttered pillow talk, which might contain the questions a woman spy had been tasked to ask, nor the beginning of Lewrie's replies in which he'd been strictly coached, to be tossed off casually, feigning alcohol-and-lust-inspired carelessness, either.

"My God, man's a bloody stoat!" Peel whispered, rather in awe of the passionate noises coming through the wall. "Both of 'em. Thrice in the last hour, I make it." He sighed enviously as he went to the table to pour himself some wine, putting his listening device to a more prosaic use. Twigg remained, sitting lumpish, twiddling his long thumbs, with a scowl on his face as the carefully placed bedstead next door, up against the wall so they could hear better, began to cry out—slats, side rails, and ropes creaking. He grimaced as names were whined or mewed, between groans and muffled enthusiasms for impending bliss.

"Doesn't have to make a meal of it," Twigg carped. "Get on!"

"What man wouldn't, given the chance . . ." Peel chuckled to himself, wondering if there would ever come a time in his Duty to Twigg, King, and Country when he was the actor in such a delightful bit of spy-craft—instead of the listener, or the arranger.

"Damn this rain," Twigg muttered, sour. "Damn *him* . . . !"

"Following your last advice, he is, sir," Peel commented, a bit tongue-in-cheek, as he discovered a neglected roast-chicken thigh among the supper plates. "Lay back, grit your teeth . . . and think of England."

"Pahh!" Twigg spat, rueing that cynical parting shot of his.

A soft keening, a frantic yowl of abandon arose, as the headboard began to thump against the wall, in rhythm with audible bull-like pants, and quavery shouts of "God, Claudia darlin', you lovely . . . !" And those ". . . *si, si*, Alan, *Dio mio, si!*"

"Pahh!" Twigg reiterated, swiveling on a hard dining chair.

"Sounds as if *she's* beyond thinking of France, and her revolutionary ardor, too, sir," Peel dared to snicker. Twigg's hugely unamused glower was enough to silence him, to chew on the thigh, as a framed picture on their side of the wall went askew with the last triumphant thuddings, and half screams of mutual rapture. Followed by many groans and weepy, shuddery sighs of content.

"Now get on with it, you two," Twigg snarled, impatient for intelligent speech again.

She really *is* a blonde, Alan thought, most happily spent, and so pleasantly nestled with her sprawled half atop him, his hands stroking such a wee bottom, a cunningly small waist, and the tops of her thighs. Bouncers on his chest, God yes, big as twelve-pounder shot, but Claudia was so exquisite a miniature. Thankee, Twigg; never say another bad thing about ya, he vowed!

"Alan," Claudia huskily whispered, purring and sensuously cat-soft alongside. "I *knew* . . . moment I saw you, we would be lovers, *mi amato*. But I never guessed, so . . . *meraviglioso*, so uhmm!"

"*Cara mia*," he purred back, hoping her clinging fondness, her passion, hadn't been completely sham. Her eyes going so dewy, open . . .

"*Caro mio*," she chuckled gently, after a long soul kiss. "You will have long in Leghorn, to be my *caro mio*, my soul, *si*? And after. We will both be in Genoa, to share this bliss, Alan?" She pressed her face to his shoulder, hugging strong, shifting a thigh across his loins.

"AT BLOODY LAST!" Twigg whispered, glued to the wall again.

Peel remained standing, to finish his wine, so he could put his glass back to King's Service. The rain still trickled, echoing in the spouts or plonking loudly in the collection barrels at ground level. He went to close the balcony doors, though it would be stifling without the faint cooling breeze the rain had brought.

Another damned noise, on a street chosen for light traffic after dark, where carriage wheels on cobblestones wouldn't intrude! Now, at the very worst time, came the clopping, mill-wheel grinding of a coach-and-four in the street below!

"Close those . . . !" Twigg directed, snapping his fingers at Peel, who shut the doors down to a tiny crack, from which he could see, back in the shadows of their darkened room. Hullo, stopping here? he winced.

Warily, he felt in his pockets for a pair of small double-barrel "barkers," in case the coach's occupants were French bully-bucks, despite Twigg's blithe assurances that there was no physical danger.

"Sir!" he alerted in a small voice. "Stopping here, sir!"

"Not now!" Twigg waved off, too intent on listening.

A lodging-house tiler emerged with a lanthorn in the small nimbus of torchlight before the doors, and the postillion boy from the back of the coach alit to open the door and hand down a fashionably dressed young lady. Peel relaxed when he saw her pay off the driver, that she'd come alone. No luggage to speak of, either, just the usual drawstring velvet purse, and a small toiletries satchel shaped like a small chest. A most beautiful young Mediterranean lady, with rich dark hair and eyes, a faint olive hue to her high, excited color. Most fetchin' and handsome, Peel took note appreciatively; quite young, but dressed as grand as any titled London lady—perhaps better. Young heiresses had been ex-Captain Peel's downfall, so he knew best when it came to appraising his woman-flesh; he thought her £10,000 on the hoof! Peel bared his teeth and snickered, thinking a wealthy Tuscan father was in trouble, if his daughter was off to sport the night with a caddish, penniless lover.

"No bother, sir . . . just a single lady," Peel whispered.

"Hmmph!" Twigg grunted, squirming as the coach clattered away, drowning out his vigil. "You try, Peel. You've younger ears."

Peel replaced him at the wall while Twigg stood and stretched to ease the kinks in his back and shoulders, knowing he was definitely too old for this work. He frowned suddenly, turned to share a wary, quizzical look with Peel as footsteps sounded from the stairwell, then from the landing—then in their hallway!

"Damme!" Twigg sighed, drawing one of his own pocket pistols and pulling the right-hand barrel back to half cock. He crossed to the door on cat-feet to press his overstressed ear to the door. He heard voices in the hall, muffled Italian. Light shifted at his feet through the gap above the doorsill. He dared to open the door a crack, to see who it might be, hoping they'd pass on by to other apartments farther along—but no!

He pulled the door open a bit more, stuck his head around it, to see a servant rapping on Lewrie's door! "*Commandante* Lewrie?" he said. And the young lady with him, bouncing on her toes in excitement of her great surprise of her unexpected arrival . . . !

"No!" Twigg gasped, "you silly slut! Why here, why now . . . ?"

He thought of rushing to carry her off, but that would cause an even greater commotion. And it was too late; the door to Lewrie's apartment was opening!

"Sir?" Peel asked with a puzzled look of ignorance. Then Peel flinched away from the wall, almost dropping his glass in surprise, as he had no more need of it. There was sound, and more than enough, to go round!

"*Basta!*" came a loud yelp of outrage. "*Espece de salaud!*"

"Good God!" from Lewrie, over the shriek of "*Dio mio*, Alan . . . !" and the slam of a disturbed headboard. "*Che questo?*"

French, Italian, English; a gabble of curses, mostly feminine voices raised in high dudgeon in three languages. Imprecations, many slurs, some huffy cat-yowlings. Then the sound of something heavy and porcelain shattering against the wall, preceding a manly wheedling.

"It's his Corsican doxy, Peel," Twigg growled. "Why now, why here in Leghorn? Damn her to hell, damn her blood, I say! She's gone and blown the gaff. I'd like to . . ."

Something else, quite possibly heavier and made of more frangible stuff, such as a glass carafe, hit the wall, evoking a redoubled chorus of alarmed yelping from Lewrie, of a certainty, quite possibly Claudia Mastandrea the other. Feet began to drum yonder, bare feet as people were chased, pursued by a constant stream of trilingual invective, or weaker, breathless excuses or pleas in return. Punctuated, of course, by a continual patter and clatter of things being thrown and broken.

Like spear carriers in the opera, from below-stairs there arose a contrapuntal clatter of shod feet on the stairs, the shouts of landlord and servants to hurry up and shut the noise down, discover what was happening, the hired chorus singing under the principal's trio.

Utterly defeated, Twigg went to the table where he and Peel had shared a surreptitious stag supper, to claw a wine bottle to him, and pour his listening device brimful. Lewrie, he thought; just when you counted on him, he'd always let you down; he'd always bungle his way to disaster!

Well, snatch victory from the jaws of defeat, in the end, the old spymaster had to allow, quite grudgingly; but eventual victory had a way with Lewrie of being *preceded* by disaster.

He went to the double doors to the balcony to sip his wine, to lean his weary old cadaver's head against a cool pane, gazing down at the slick cobbles, the dispiritingly meager rainfall winking as drops fell on puddles or slick spots, flickering with the light of distant torches or lanthorns. All seen through the steamed and streaked condensation of the panes. And wondering what to do next?

There really *was* a shipment of gold at sea. The lure, dangled with Lewrie as additional bait to trap Choundas, had also been planned to divert him from the real vessel, the real course. If the Austrians didn't receive it, if Choundas intercepted it, then everything Lewrie had surmised might come true, Twigg thought miserably. Careful as he had been, he was sure word of that ship had reached the Genoese, then the French, soon after. Two rumors; which to believe? Which was the most plausible for Choundas to follow? And they had been so close!

By ear, he could follow someone's progress down the stairs, at last, until their footsteps were drowned out by the continuing battle next door, which showed no signs of abating.

Twigg perked up a bit, stepped back into his proper element—the shadows—as a lady appeared in the small nimbus of light before the lodging-house entry. Claudia Mastandrea, whistling up her coach, still nipping and tucking to complete dressing, concealing her hastily donned state with a shawl, and a large, saucy hat. She looked up at the balcony, and Twigg went rigid with fear that he'd been spotted.

"Hullo," he muttered, though. She wasn't looking at him, she was looking to his right, at the lit windows of the apartment she had just fled. Rather forlornly, he thought in amazement. Even at that distance, in that dim light, her face appeared flushed. She spoke to the ostler, who trotted off to fetch her waiting coach.

Twigg slid sidewise, to peer out the crack between the doors, to have a clear, unmisted view of her, still well back in the shadows.

Claudia Mastandrea, he could see, was dabbing at her eyes, her breathing still deep and hitched. She opened her small string-purse to fetch out a lace handkerchief and . . . and dry her tears?

"Poor little bitch," Twigg murmured, as the entrancing-lovely mort allowed herself a shoulder-heaving sob, and buried her face for a moment in the handkerchief. "Damme, was he *that* pleasin'?"

She seemed to shake herself into composure, stiffen her back and throw up her head, as her coach arrived with a clatter. Almost archly, with what was left of her dignity, she was handed in. But just before the coach rocked and began to depart, there was one last mournful, and almost wistful, gaze aloft, to that beguiling window-glow. Then, away she went, into the night.

And Twigg allowed himself a smile, after all, and a deep breath of satisfaction.

"B'lieve our boy Lewrie came through, after all, Mister Peel," he muttered, going back to the center of the room for a top-up, and a long sip of a rather good red.

"How do you come by that, sir?" Peel sighed. "Thought it was a cock-up?"

"The *signorina* departed in tears, Peel."

"Failed, sir. Make anyone weep." Peel snorted. "And with that Aretino creature about, no more access to 'im, more's the pity."

"In tears, Mister Peel," Twigg pointed out. "Had she failed, I would have expected an aloof stiffness of carriage, a 'so-what?' flouncing. You know women, Peel. You know how much 'cross' they can put into the swish of their skirts. She didn't leave angry, or disappointed, I tell you. Heartbroken, more like. Embarrassed to be caught, but . . . I think she got what she came for. And a great deal more, besides. We will know, soon as we put it to Lewrie," Twigg mused, almost humming with glee. "But I daresay we may 'bank' on it, now, hmm?"

"Her last letter we intercepted gave no hint," Peel complained of the fickleness of women. "Why'd she sail from San Fiorenzo *now*, at the worst possible time! 'Less she's a French agent, too, sir? Half-French, and all? Working for Choundas, not Pouzin? Or someone else?"

"No no, Peel," Twigg pooh-poohed. "Sweet, amusing, but hardly bright enough for this. Just damn' bad luck and timing. Missing her pretty sailor too much, I suspect. Damn her eyes."

"So what do we do about Miss Aretino now, sir?" Peel queried, his brow still creased in concern. "He can't explain this away, without he tells her *too* much. And, can we trust the little mort to keep mum, after, sir?"

"Ah, hmm . . ." Twigg pondered heavily. There came another gust of shrill shouting, the vituperative accusations of a woman wronged—and the gay tinkling of something else going smash. "Does Miss Aretino love him *half* as much as it sounds, Mister Peel, there is the possibility that she'd believe us. And keep mum, for *him*. After all, a few weeks will expose di Silvano and *Signorina* Mastandrea. And net us Choundas. After that, well . . . it's up to them to reconcile. Or not."

"Make her . . . recruitable, sir?" Peel suggested with a leer.

"No, not her, Mister Peel." Twigg grunted. "Consider her former trade, and estate. Entering our trade, Mademoiselle Aretino would be right back where she began . . . *on* her back. She'd never do that, even at Lewrie's bidding. He'd have to be the one to 'run' her, and neither could abide the thought of 'sharing.' He'd warn her off, in any event. To spite me, d'ye see. To protect what she's attained. I gather that Lewrie really *is* fond of her, Mister Peel. In for the penny, in for the pound, is our Lewrie. He's never lukewarm when it comes to his doxies. Damn' fool. Now, on the other hand, there is Claudia Mastandrea . . ."

"Sir?" Peel frowned again in puzzlement.

"A picture to conjure with, Peel," Twigg simpered with amusement. "Nothing feigned, there. More attracted to the lout than ever we could wish. Him for her, so it wouldn't be exactly arm-twisting to get Lewrie to play-up, again. Do they have a *rencontre*, before she's forced to go back to France once she's exposed and di Silvano cuts his losses. The possibilities of a continuing connection, hmm? A chance for us to turn her, doubled-back 'gainst her masters, hmm?"

"Well, possibly, sir." Peel nodded in understanding, amazed all over again by Mister Twigg's ability to consider every possible advantage, every possible use of people's weaknesses; making notes for his career.

The sounds of tumult had died down next door. With his glass to the wall, Twigg could discern weeping noises, some muffled explainings. Then a response from Phoebe Aretino, a hiccupy, louder cursing wail.

"Poor bastard," Peel said softly.

"Yes, Mister Peel, poor bastard." Twigg sighed, though with a wee grin on his face. "It is possible that we have laid their affair, and their mutual happiness, 'pon our sacred altar of Secrecy. Oh, well."

"Well, uhm . . ." Peel shrugged. "Should we go rescue him then, sir? Let her in on our doings? And Lewrie off the hook?"

"Such a verisimilitude Miss Aretino's arrival gave this night's work, Mister Peel," Twigg chuckled. "Now Claudia Mastandrea knows what a total cully he is over women, she may even be considering what use *she* may make of him, in future. Rescue?" Twigg thought aloud, as he found a heel of bread and some sliced *provolone* to savor from their picked-over repast. "Yes, I believe we should, at that."

But sat down at the table and began to root about for something else to nibble on, making a second cold supper, and pouring himself more wine. Sometimes cocking an ear to the ebb and rise of the angry, heartbroken slanging match going on next door.

"Uhm . . ." Peel prompted, after several long minutes had passed. "Will we be rescuing him anytime soon, then, Mister Twigg?"

"Soon, Peel, soon," Twigg said airily. "No rush. After all my dealings with the brute, Peel, I must confess to enjoying the sound of it. Quite relishin', in fact. Music to my old ears, my lad. Music to my ears!"

CHAPTER

4

REDUCED TO T'GALLANTS and jibs, *Jester* stood into Vado Bay at the tail end of November, after a pointless, but necessary, transit; rushed from Leghorn, south-about Sardinia to Port Mahon on Minorca, and then sent off to Gibraltar and back as an errand boy, bearing a heavy packet of dispatches, some pensioned-off soldiers and Marines, and the sea chests or campaign chests of officers who had perished, so they could be sent home to England.

There had been at least one tiny satisfaction; awaiting them at Gibraltar had been a set of orders left with the local Navy officials to allow *Jester* to make good her complement from the pick of hands newly arrived from England in the receiving hulks.

Twigg's way of making some small amends, Lewrie had discovered, though there was little joy of it. Little joy to be found in much of anything, at the rate things were going, he thought. Phoebe . . .

"An' I s'ink you are *not* like ozzer men," had been her parting, wailed, shot, no matter what Twigg and Peel had tried to say to her, no matter his own attempt, and pleadings. "I s'ink I *trust* you, Alain *mon coeur, but . . .* !"

Hoist by mine own bloody petard, he thought to himself, feeling a bit disconsolate, still. Oh, he'd always known their affair was just temporary, an amour eventually doomed by circumstances, but that didn't mean it hurt any less to have it over quite so soon. Or in such a messy way, so shamefacedly . . . or painfully, for the both of them. That long independent cruise had at least provided enough peace and quiet, and an isolated time to mend and ponder.

" 'Bout here, sir?" Knolles prompted.

"Aye, Mister Knolles." Lewrie nodded in agreement. "Round up to the eye of the wind, Quartermaster. Back the fore and main t'gallants . . . and make ready to slip the best bower, sir."

As *Jester* slowly came about, he had time to survey the harbor, and the wide roadstead of Vado Bay's anchorage. There were still some half-dozen prizes moored there, identifiable by being the only vessels stripped of all their canvas, so their crews couldn't make any escape attempts, nor could a French raid from seaward cut them out and sail them away. There were a pair of Austrian supply ships, another brace of British, though little sign that any cargoes were being moved. One small Austrian brig o' war was anchored, with her sails hung slack for airing—seemingly along with her crew, who had what looked to be an idle "Rope Yarn Sunday" going. Only one Royal Navy warship was in the roadstead close inshore, the *Tartar* brig. The rest were probably out at sea, farther west along the Genoese Riviera. Lewrie eyed the hills and pyramids of provisions and munitions for General de Vins's army, a sign his commissary troops and garrison had grown some since . . .

"Signal, sir!" Midshipman Hyde called out. " 'Board *Tartar*! I make it, 'Have Dispatches' . . . 'Urgent' . . . she shows 'Submit' . . . next is 'Close Me' . . . 'Send Boat,' no . . . that's 'I Am Sending a Boat,' sir."

"Does she, by God!" Lewrie growled, irked by the presumption of a junior lieutenant, or a commander farther down the Navy list than him, trying to order him about so.

Pretty much what got me in the mess I'm in, he found wryly amusing, after a moment, though; 'bout half a mile alee? Too far to row . . .

" 'Vast anchoring, Mister Knolles! Back jibs to larboard, brace the fore t'gallant to starboard tack. We'll anchor close to *Tartar*."

"Aye aye, sir."

Jester came around slowly, falling off the wind again, to ghost across the roadstead to within a cable of *Tartar* before turning up to fetch-to. But there would be no need to anchor, since one of *Tartar*'s boats was already down, and stroking hard for her side. Lewrie opened his telescope to eye her. Bowman, eight oarsmen, midshipman in the stern sheets at the tiller, and . . . *damn*!

"Ah," he said, his face stony. "Hmm." He almost moaned as he slammed the tubes closed. And feeling an urge to spit, to cleanse his mouth of a sudden foul taste.

It was ex-Captain Peel in the boat, clinging to a tall hat, with a small clutch of traveling bags at his sides on the thwarts. Peel; no sign of his master, Twigg, but that wasn't cause for much joy. Peel at Vado Bay, as Twigg's urgent emissary, was bad news enough!

"Bosun, man the entry port," Lewrie directed. "We'll not drop anchor, after all, Mister Knolles, till we've sorted this out."

"Uhm . . . trouble, sir, do ye think?" Knolles simply had to ask.

"You might say that, Mister Knolles."

To LEWRIE'S GREAT disappointment, Peel was an agile brute, just as spry as a seaman when it came to departing the boat and scaling the battens to the gangway. Alan had rather hoped he'd slip and break his devious neck—or at least get a good dunking, to wash the spy-stink off.

"Mister Peel, sir," Lewrie grumbled, doffing his hat as Peel doffed his in greeting. Feeling most uncivil, though.

"Commander Lewrie, sir," Peel rejoined, just as stonily. "I am required to give you this, at once . . . to be read at once, sir."

Peel produced a square of vellum, folded over from the corners and sealed with a large blob of candle wax. Lewrie took it and turned away, took a few paces to larboard for privacy, wondering what new vat of shit he'd tumbled into. He peeled it open.

"Well, damme . . ." He frowned in puzzlement.

It was from Captain Nelson, in his own hand, not his clerk's. Lewrie and *Jester* were to consider themselves under his orders again. But the next paragraph instructed him to place himself and his ship at Mister Peel's service until further notice, and to render to him, and his superior Mister Twigg, any and every service and assistance they requested.

"Shit," he whispered, hoping he'd seen the back of them, that Twigg had told the truth for once that his duties ashore at Leghorn had been "quits." He'd lied, o' course. Again. And what else was new?

"Very *well*, Mister Peel, sir," Lewrie drawled, stalking back to the man. "What assistance do you require from us?"

"That I am only allowed to tell you in the strictest privacy, sir," the stolid ex-cavalry officer replied rather guardedly, muttering only as loudly as necessary; as if sharing even a cryptic conversation with Lewrie was too much to bruit about in public. "Might I be allowed to urge you to do whatever it is you do, to return to sea, though, sir?"

"Get underway?" Lewrie hinted, with a faint grin.

"If that's how sailors phrase it, sir, yes."

"To where, sir?" Lewrie inquired.

"Uhm . . ." Peel darkened, clamming up.

"*Point*, if you can't say it," Alan suggested resignedly. "East, is it? Very well, sir. That wasn't so difficult, now was it. Mister Knolles? Secure the anchor party, and make sail. We'll stand out to sea. Get way on her and ready to come about to larboard tack. Once we make an offing, come back to starboard tack, course due east."

"Aye aye, sir! Bosun? Hands to the braces! Topmen! Trice up and lay aloft! Make sail!" Knolles bellowed.

It took half an hour to work *Jester* back to sea, to scoot along inshore, rounding up and gathering enough speed to tack, to stand away from the coast until it was about six miles astern, then come about to the east. Once assured that *Jester* was secure, Lewrie could head below at last, his simmering anger, and his dubious curiosity, both at a fine boil, by then.

"So where is it you wish to go, Mister Peel?" Lewrie asked, as he opened the wine cabinet, after shooing his steward and servant out.

"Genoa, sir," Peel announced finally.

"But didn't you just come from there?"

"I did, sir. To await your arrival and deliver those orders to you," Peel admitted, accepting a glass. "My employer said to extend to you his compliments, Commander Lewrie. And his apologies. For the uhm . . . upshot of Leghorn. And for not being able to fulfill his word to you that he would pester you no longer. But it's quite urgent that you assist us just this *one* last time, sir."

"So?" Lewrie snapped.

"It's a total, bloody cock-up, Commander Lewrie," Peel confessed, his shoulders sagging in defeat. "The trap we so carefully laid . . . went amiss. Choundas never even went near 'em! They didn't see anything on their voyage. Put in at Vado, then had to scamper back to San Fiorenzo to rejoin Hotham."

"So I am still your *bait*?" Lewrie fumed.

"No, sir, we're a bit beyond that, I fear." Peel groaned as he took a seat, looking as if he needed one. "The real ship . . . the vessel that was really carrying the gold for the Austrians . . . well, sir, it's been taken! That Choundas bugger outsmarted us, after all!"

"Well, damme!" Lewrie exclaimed in surprise. Though he really didn't think it much of a surprise, that Choundas had once more shown himself to be fiendishly clever. "Where, and how, sir? And how much'd he get away with?" he demanded, suddenly all impatience.

"As to where, Captain Lewrie," Peel sighed, "soon after she left San

Fiorenzo Bay. 'Least the solid coin for the Navy, and our garrison on Corsica was safely landed. Perhaps within a hundred miles of Vado Bay? As to when, five days ago, we think. At any rate, *four* days ago, a French privateer put into Genoa . . . sailed right into Genoa itself, I tell you, sir! Put all the gold and silver ashore. As for how much? Nigh on £100,000! Which is now being used, sir, to pay the recruiting bounty, and to purchase boots and small-clothes at least, to raise volunteers to serve in the *French* Army! They're drilling and mustering on the main plazas all over the city, Lewrie . . . swaggering and swilling as bold as brass! Singing their version of 'La Marseillais,' damn' 'em!"

"But they can't do that, Genoa's neutral, that'd . . ."

"The bloody Genoese colluded with the French to *take* it, sir!" Peel snarled back, still simmering with anger and chagrin, days after. "Senator di Silvano and his cronies, we're certain. The Senate allowed the privateer the right to anchor and unload, and they're claiming she has a right to stay as long as she likes, 'stead of enforcing any time limit on a belligerent . . . since she isn't a French national warship formally commissioned, they *say*, sir! But, do we do anything to take *her*, they'll scream bloody murder. Your Nelson sailed in, to see what the hell was going on, but he was too late, and there's little he can do about it but complain. They're shamefaced enough to not demand that *he* treats the port as a neutral, but does he do anything to seize the privateer, it'd be just the sort of incident the traitorous faction wants. We don't have the force to make Genoa cooperate with us, either. Bloody devious, two-faced . . . !" Peel sneered, and took a sip of wine—which gave Alan time to sardonically muse that for Peel to deem anyone devious and two-faced was a rare irony, after all *he'd* been up to!

"So what does Twigg think I can do about it, Mister Peel?" he pressed.

"Things are coming to a head, sir," Peel insisted anxiously. "General de Vins has finally stirred himself and his army into motion. Like the gold was his, personal . . . took from his own quarters! Before I left, with the hope you'd be returning soon, he'd thrown his outpost line right to the gates of Genoa. To show them who's in charge, we may suppose, and marched his forces west of Vado, at last, into contact with the French outposts. He's going to fight, finally, before winter."

"You still aren't telling me . . ." Lewrie huffed.

"It's Choundas, sir," Peel announced suddenly, stone-sober, and bitter. "It was he, took the gold, himself. He's aboard the privateer, at Genoa. He shows no sign of coming ashore, so there's no way for us to get to him. Nelson can't get at him, since Genoa won't tolerate any belligerent action in their bloody 'neutral' harbor. We can expect to be held to the convention that Nelson can't sail for twenty-four hours after he does. Though the Genoese can turn a blind eye to Choundas going out, anytime he pleases, once Nelson sails. Which he was going to do, Mister Twigg told me, sir. The only problem is, I was also told not to expect too much from Captain Nelson's ship. That she was so slow and badly in need of a refit. Practically held together with rope, a foul bottom . . . you'd know better what they were talking about, sir. I will never understand naval matters."

"But the rest of our ships, the frigates, Mister Peel," Lewrie inquired. "Surely . . ."

"All far to the west, sir, to keep an eye on French ports, where rumor has it that they may be preparing a landing from the sea." Peel shrugged again. "Take a day or two for a tender to gallop off to find them, and a day or two for them to return. And Choundas might be away by then, d'ye see. *Meleager* left for Leghorn for her own refit. Put in there a week after you left. *Speedy* and this *Tartar* are too weak to deal with the privateer, your Nelson thought. *Speedy* is the one rushed off to whistle up the frigates, anyway, so . . ."

"His ship against mine again, then." Lewrie frowned, hesitant to cross swords with Choundas, especially after the last drubbing. "My sloop of war 'gainst his twenty-two-gunned corvette . . ."

"No, sir!" Peel exclaimed, with a small sign of glee. "Not his flagship . . . *La Vengeance*, we think she's named. Maybe she was used for taking the merchantman with the gold, but he came to Genoa 'board a privateer, what they call a *xebec*. Fast as the wind, I heard . . ."

"Aye, they are." Lewrie nodded, feeling a little surge of hope. "Three-masted, lateen-rigged, much like a pirate's galley. Long, lean, and very fast. Fairly low freeboard and bulwarks, though . . . tell me, Mister Peel. Have you seen her?"

"Well, yessir," Peel allowed cautiously. "Though I know nought of boats and such, I was told what Choundas now looks like. Mister Twigg had me boat past his ship, to confirm he was there. And he is, Captain Lewrie. Seemed to know who I was, too, damn his eyes . . . eye, rather." Peel snorted with faint amusement. "Christ what an ugly bugger. Carve damn' well, you do, sir, I must say! How he knew to go after the right ship, we *still* can't understand, when the bait was so temptin' . . . ignore what the *signorina* gathered for him . . . ?"

"*Too* tempting, perhaps," Lewrie sniffed. "Once bitten, and all that. A mite too convenient, and overly clever a ruse."

"We're supposing Choundas was forced to depend on Mister Twigg's opposite number, a civilian spymaster," Peel admitted softly. "And they do not get along, we've heard. Suspect each other . . ."

"No matter, now," Lewrie snapped, opening his desk to fetch out a chart-pencil and a blank quarto sheet of paper. "Since you've seen her close-aboard, could you sketch her? Recall how many guns she carried . . . and an idea as to their caliber?"

"S'pose so, sir." Peel shrugged again, bending over the desk to begin drawing. " 'Bout as long as your ship, I think. Not as tall . . . I think I saw only five or six openings along the one side for guns. One was open . . . fairly good-sized stuff at either end, though. Big as some siege artillery I once saw at Woolwich. Hellish good weekend, that . . ."

"Short barrels, like mortars?"

"No, I don't think so, Captain Lewrie." Peel frowned, cocking his head as he bent over his sketch. "Looked average-long barrels, to me."

Lewrie went to the wine cabinet to refill his glass, riding the easy motion of his warship as she tore through the sea, sails set "all to the royals" in her haste. For once, there was enough wind aloft in the fickle Ligurian Sea to make speed, when speed was vital. He could be off Genoa Mole by sundown.

A *xebec*, he pondered; about *Jester*'s length. Shoal-draught, she could stand much closer inshore of *Jester*, should they discover her, to escape. Draw about three feet less, perhaps? Long and lean, built low to the sea, and very wet along her gunwales and gangways. Sail-tending was done amidships, fore-and-aft, on a central walkway, and some *xebecs* were oar-driven, still . . . Spanish, Venetian, Genoese, Barbary Pirates . . . they still depended on them as armed, oared galleys. With guns mounted on their forecastles and stern platforms, primarily. Nothing more than twelve-pounders, he thought, anything else'd be too much end weight.

Why had Choundas come himself? he fretted. Let's say he already knew that de Vins would take action, that the French Army was ready for a battle, too, and that stealing the gold would precipitate it. Wasn't his prime responsibility with his squadron? Wouldn't that be where any diligent senior officer would be, if things were indeed coming to a head?

"Rub our noses in it," he muttered. What had Peel said? It was as if Choundas had known who he was already. Might even have known that Twigg was in the area! And no *wonder* he'd failed to take the best bait! But why do the dirty work, himself? Alan still puzzled. When that would isolate him from his squadron, get him penned in at Genoa for days, even

weeks? And not bring his own ship? Rely on a privateersman, not under
naval discipline, unreliable, untrustworthy, sure to pocket . . . !

"Here you go, Captain Lewrie," Peel interrupted, rising to go for the
wine cabinet himself. "Dusty work, sketchin' from memory, do ye mind?
I can't get it out o' my head, though, that those guns along the side, well
. . . looked no bigger than galloper guns. Four, perhaps six-pounders.
'Bout like horse artillery."

"Not carronades? Not squat and stubby pestles?" Lewrie pressed as he
regarded Peel's handiwork. "Like those on my quarterdeck?"

"Nossir," Peel rejoined, certain. "Definitely long barrels."

"Too few French copies of carronades to go around, yet," Lewrie said,
feeling even more hope. "Nothing they'd sell or share with the war-for-
profit mob." Peel had produced a fairly good drawing, complete with
arrowed notes regarding the *xebec*'s paint scheme. Dark green hull, with
red gunwales and upper works. "She'll be fast, but *Jester*'s quick-work is
clean and new-coppered. With a good slant, should she sail, we stand a
good chance of bringing her to battle. If I stand off Genoa to the
sou'west, about five or six miles inshore. He has to sail soon, to the west,
if he wishes to rejoin his squadron. He *can't* be absent when the big
battle's about to come off. Can't count on his army taking the city right
off, either. One warship could bottle him up for a month!"

"Unless he does something else clever, sir," Peel griped moodily. "I'm
coming to fear just how clever he really is. Abandon the privateer and go
overland in civilian dress, perhaps? Senator di Silvano's farm carts and
estate agents could smuggle him out. Then should this ship . . ."

"Aye, should we close her and take her, he'd be ashore, laughing his
bloody head off," Lewrie sourly agreed. "I assume Mister Twigg has
already made arrangements against that?"

"He has, sir," Peel assured him—sort of. "Though we're thin on the
ground when it comes to people we can trust, besides the pair of us,
Mister Drake, and a few of his hired agents. The Austrians . . ."

"I'm sure their army has spies in plenty," Lewrie gloomed. "In business with Italians all this time, some bad habits must have rubbed off by
now, surely!"

"Unless the rumor of a large French invasion convoy was another
sham, Captain Lewrie," Peel pointed out. "It was a good-enough rumor
to draw most of your Nelson's ships off to the west, to counter it. If the
French are just as ready for a decisive battle as the Austrians, it may be
possible that Choundas doesn't expect to have to go very far, to rejoin. Or

wait a week till Genoa is theirs. He knows *something*, that much is certain, this Choundas. Something we don't, yet."

"Large crew, this privateer of his?" Lewrie asked.

"About a hundred or so, that I saw, sir," Peel told him.

"Had to have promised half the booty to them, else they'd never have taken the job on." Lewrie sighed. "Why should they risk all that, to sail out at once? *They* could wait for Genoa to fall. Doesn't mean Choundas would. Fearsome as he is, he couldn't count on a crew of mercenaries to protect him. And she's not a proper warship, disciplined . . . did you see any uniformed men aboard? Any soldiers, their versions of Marines? Any naval officers, besides him?"

"Nossir," Peel replied. "Though what might have been hidden . . ."

"Not much depth of hold in which to hide anything, aboard shallow-draught vessels such as *xebecs*," Lewrie interrupted impatiently. "No . . . I expect what you saw was all they had. Hired for the one job, perhaps . . . but only to *transport* the gold, not take it, d'ye see, Peel?" Lewrie enthused. "Choundas couldn't use his flagship to fetch it to Genoa. I *hate* the man . . . but I understand him, a little, I think. He's a sailor! *La Vengeance*, d'ye say? Wager he named her, himself. Chose her paint scheme, so she'd look just like his old'un, the one he lost in the Far East, in eighty-five. Lost her, and two others, too! The greatest shame any captain can stomach. No, he'd never risk *her*. Never take the chance of losing another command, especially to me . . . or your Mister Twigg. This privateer's expendable, now she's done his chore for him. She's civilian, not Navy. Does she sail, and we take her, I'll sport you any odds you like, he'll *not* be aboard. She'll swan off sou'east, *paid* to lure us on a false scent. While he takes passage west, close inshore. On one of Senator di Silvano's fishing boats or coasters, more like."

"Well, I'm damned, sir!" Peel breathed out, the victim of twice the surprise; that Choundas could be that clever. Or that Lewrie, for all the deprecating things his employer had said about him, was showing signs of being just as discerning and quick-witted. "O' course, it makes *eminent* sense. Once he gets to Genoa, he knows he's a quick way out . . . *that's* what he had up his sleeve that we couldn't hope to know!"

"He's a sailor," Lewrie reiterated. "Wasn't born to Frog nobility, Mister Peel. Brought up in the coastal fisheries. Not many good horsemen spring from that lot. He won't go overland, 'less forced to."

"And you knackered his leg, sir, long ago. Make a ride that far all but impossible for him. Though a cart, or coach . . ."

"A *sailor*, Mister Peel!" Lewrie laughed. "He'd feel lost on the land, no matter how he goes. But he knows the sea. With a small crew of experienced Genoese, supplied by *Signore* di Silvano . . . seamen just as dedicated to the conspiracy as their master is . . . he's still in his proper element."

"A fish *in* the water, so to speak, Captain Lewrie." Peel japed.

"Exactly."

"Though . . ." Peel sobered. "That would mean we're only one ship. And we'd have to stop and search every bloody rowboat 'tween Genoa and Vado. *And* intercept the privateer if she comes out."

"That, too, exactly, Mister Peel," Lewrie snapped, losing every hope he'd conjured up. "Needle in a bloody hayrick. Damn!"

CHAPTER

5

AGAMEMNON WAS ALREADY at sea, lurking a few miles south of the harbor approaches to Genoa. Like a reunion with a parent after years apart, Lewrie was shocked at how she'd aged in the months that *Jester* had been away. Paint faded and streaked, her gunwales gone filthy and her sails turned weary brown, and much patched. Worst of all, thigh-thick anchor cables had been bound about her hull to keep her together.

A quick, shouted conference with Nelson, across the fifty yards that separated them after *Jester* came under her lee, both captains too impatient to waste time transferring from ship to ship, so they could lay their plans in the idle comfort of the flagship's great-cabins.

Nelson had to admit that *Agamemnon* was too weeded to catch the privateer, should she come out. He would take her to Vado Bay at once, send *Tartar* out to watch the coast closer inshore east of Vado, rearm little *Bombolo*, which had been swinging idle since *Meleager* had abandoned her so she could go off to Leghorn for her refit, put a crew in her, and reinforce *Tartar*. The privateer would be Lewrie's "pigeon," when or if she left port.

To aid his own search, Nelson gave Lewrie the use of his barge, a thirty-two-foot ten-oared boat, which could be rigged with two masts and carry a two-pounder boat gun and a pair of swivels. With an admonition not to scratch her paint, *Agamemnon* departed, leaving *Jester* to stand guard at Genoa by herself, until *Tartar* and *Bombolo* could join her. A day and a night, perhaps, before she was reinforced. *Speedy* would have encountered at least one or two of the frigates by then, and summoned them back from their wild-goose chase to the west. With all the luck in the world, they'd then sew a net so snug about Genoa and its approaches that Choundas would never get out.

The first use Lewrie made of the barge was to man her, and send Midshipman Hyde inshore with her, to carry a message to Twigg or Drake to keep an eye on the privateer, hire a swift local boat, and send out an alert if Choundas transferred to another vessel, and its description and course.

Then, five miles sou'west of the Mole, he could do nothing more.

Except fret, of course.

As *Jester* continued her pacing, standing off and on that coast as the evening gathered, Lewrie paced his quarterdeck on the windward side. Back and forth, from the hammock nettings overlooking the waist to the corner of the taffrail by the night lanthorn. Fretting a safe and swift return of the barge, Mister Hyde and its crew; though he doubted the Genoese government would be silly enough to delay her or seize her. They were in enough bad odor, already; had practically thrown in with the French! Fretting the delay of fresh information from Twigg, which Hyde would surely have for him. That Choundas would confound them one more time, and stay snug and safe aboard the privateer, after all. Or take the overland route, disguised as a misshapen Gypsy, or something.

But mostly, fretting that Choundas would realize that *Agamemnon* had departed, and make his move before any reinforcement arrived. Had Choundas planned to sneak out aboard a nondescript fishing boat, rush back to his beloved corvette, and his neglected duties, flush with new triumph, he'd have to do it soon. Surely, he'd feel the noose drawing tighter, the bastard had the survival instincts of a bread-room rat . . . and was just about as hard to kill for certain.

Depart just after twilight, Lewrie pondered, hands in the small of his back, glaring down at the toes of his fashionable boots, pacing almost hunchbacked with impatient gloom. Show no lights, maybe a wee lanthorn . . . one fishing boat 'mongst a fleet of 'em?

Speed, though . . . has to get back, soon. Dash along the coast to be west of Vado Bay before tomorrow's dawn? French lines begin where? Can't count on anything tubby as *Bombolo*—she's typical of boats hereabouts—to get him through the area where he'd be most vulnerable. A larger vessel, then. Longer waterline, schooner-rigged. A *tartane* or pencil-thin . . . he *might* try with the privateer. She's armed, *and* fast enough. Does that damned senator have himself a yacht? He looked like the sort to afford one . . . ruddy-faced. Hunting, I thought. Owns ships and such, so he *must* do some sailing, maybe it comes from . . . *damn!*

He stopped to scrub his face with dry hands and peer shoreward. *Jester* was on the easternmost leg of her patrol line, barely two miles off the harbor entrance. There were few signs of activity. Some small fishing boats about *Bombolo*'s size working their way back into harbor. Few sail visible at all, save for them, and some even smaller with one lugsail or lateen, little bigger than *Jester*'s jolly boat or gig. All heading in as sunset approached, or idling bare-poled close inshore for a final cast of the nets. And a two-master heading out! He crossed to the binnacle cabinet by the wheel to snatch his telescope and inspect it.

The elegant barge, at last! Within half an hour, she'd be alongside with news. Then he could arm her before full dark, put more hands into her, and double his patrol.

"Helm up a point, Quartermaster!" he snapped. "That'll be our Mister Hyde returning. We'll stand down to her."

"Aye aye, zir," Brauer crisply agreed, feeding spokes a-weather.

"A NOTE FROM Mister Drake, sir," Hyde offered, once he was back on deck. "His compliments to you, Captain, and said for me to inform you that he already had the privateer under close scrutiny. Of yet, there's been no sign that anyone has left her. Though he also bade me tell you that they'd hoisted an 'Easy' pendant this morning, and allowed traders' bumboats to come alongside. Rather a lot of 'em, sir," Hyde contributed. "Saw 'em myself. So many it's hard to keep track, that Mister Drake also said to say, sir."

"Do you carry any message for me, sir?" Mister Peel asked from the side.

"Aye, sir, I do." Hyde nodded, reaching into another pocket for a wax-sealed note. "Mister Drake gave it me, from some *banker* fellow?"

Kept in the dark so far, Hyde could only raise his brows and wonder why a commercial letter was just as important as one from the Consul representing HM Government at Genoa. Having this stranger Peel aboard, with the right of the quarterdeck, and put aboard so urgently, had Hyde and the rest totally mystified.

"Any vessels follow you to sea, sir?" Lewrie asked quickly. "A vessel of *any* kind that looked in the way of readying for departure?"

"None that I took note of, sir." Hyde frowned.

"Very well, Mister Hyde." Lewrie sighed, deflated. "Mister Buchanon, sir? We'll arm the barge before dark. I wish you to take charge of her. Mister Crewe? A two-pounder with round-shot and canister in the barge, with two swivels and ammunition. Four extra hands besides boat crew, Mister Cony. The sharp-eyed, and some decent gunners. I'll want a pistol, musket, and cutlass for every man, as well. Mister Peel, with me for a moment, if you please, sir. Let us compare . . . notes."

They stepped aft to the taffrails for privacy. Peel had already perused his, and crumpled it up to toss overboard, astern.

"My employer has contacted the Austrian headquarters. They're to keep a close watch on all roads, looking for a scarred man with a limp. They're to particularly inspect any wagon or cart going to one of our Senator di Silvano's estates. Mister Silberberg has also placed a watch upon the senator's mansion, should Choundas be spirited there. But we don't have the willing agents to follow every coach coming or going to his house. The rest of the conspirators' houses aren't covered. Even with things coming to a head, Mister Silberberg doubts di Silvano will tip his hand that directly, I'm sorry to say, Captain Lewrie. I doubt we'd be able to watch close enough should this be happening in London."

"Mister Drake says there've been so many bumboats alongside the privateer, coming and going, that it's impossible to say if Choundas was in one of them, disguised, either." Lewrie groaned. "She's her sails harbor-gasketed, and her crew ranti-poling with the local whores, as drunk as lords. She's not coming out tonight, at any rate. Or in the morning, either, the way he says they're celebrating their new fortune."

He crumpled up his own note and tossed it over.

"Their heads'll be too thick." Lewrie chuckled without amusement. "The senator does have a yacht. But then, so do almost all of the other conspirators. It's a local sport, yachting."

"Those we know about, sir," Peel cautioned in a covert mutter. "And them we still can't link to the plot, direct. A fishing boat, or a yacht. By dawn, there could be hundreds of 'em out here."

"Does Choundas come out tonight, Mister Peel," Lewrie schemed, trying to put himself in the wily Frenchman's head, "it'll most like be around nine or so, after full dark. Combined with us being close off the approaches, I should think. We'll be turning away, to stand west on our leg. He could idle just off the mole . . . no lights showing, and *follow* us, damn his eyes! Close inshore, with a local pilot who can *smell* a shoal or rock. Not much moon to speak of . . . him black against a dark coastline. Trail us as far as Voltri. That'd take a couple of hours, then we'd have to turn back east, and he could scoot along the twenty or twenty-five miles to Vado Bay and be just a few miles west of there by false dawn tomorrow morning. A fishing boat, 'bout the same size as yon barge, would be too slow for him. He *must* know that Vado Bay'd be well-patrolled. There's a decent wind tonight, and night winds are fairly steady in strength and direction. From the nor'east, for once. A perfect wind to ghost out on, and broad-reach west on. He'll want a longer, faster boat for that. I would. If he doesn't make it to Vado, he can't expect to lay up for the day along this coast, not with Austrian troops about. Where are the French, last report? How far east?"

"East of the inland road that comes down to Finale, sir." Peel shrugged. "How far East, I . . . of late, I have no way of knowing." He gave Lewrie a quick grimace before turning bland again. Hating to say "I don't know" as bad as any secret agent. "Along the coast road, we must assume they've advanced closer to Vado."

"Other side of the headland?" Lewrie grumbled in surprise when Peel told him that. "That'd be only ten miles west of our anchorage!"

"It's possible, sir. Sorry I can't enlighten you further."

"Forty miles, at most then," Lewrie puzzled. "Genoa to Finale or thereabouts. Seven hours to safety, at six or seven knots. *Damme* if I'll play his game!"

But not knowing how he was going to accomplish that, yet. That barge could never catch up a larger, faster vessel, once she got to sea, with a bone in her teeth. He'd have to place *Jester* more to the west, if he hoped to get a decent slant at interception. With his ship tied too close to the harbor entrance, though, Choundas might gain a precious lead that he could never make up, once Choundas slipped past them close inshore. Yet, to remain far enough west to counter that, *Jester* couldn't guard the entrance, could not spot any vessel leaving in time to overhaul her and inspect her.

Or could he?

"Mister Buchanon, 'vast your packing, sir," Lewrie called out. "I apologize, but I'll need you aboard, after all. Mister Hyde, you're still in charge of the barge."

"Aye, sir!" Hyde grinned, proud to have a temporary "command."

"Pass the word for Mister Crewe to come to . . ."

" 'Ere, sir!" Crewe replied from the gangway above the tethered barge, which was still being loaded and armed.

"Mister Crewe, you're familiar with fire-arrows? *Darde-au-feu?*"

"Well, aye, Cap'um . . ." the gunner replied, creasing his brow. "Don't 'ave no spring-iron t'make th' arms t'catch in sails, though."

"Forget the spring-arms, Mister Crewe," Lewrie countered, with a leer on his face. "Just make me up a half dozen that can be shot up high in the air, that we can see for, oh . . . six miles, at night? Shot at extreme elevation from a swivel gun. Like a signal-fuzee that Mister Hyde can light off like a fireworks."

"Oh, like a Roman candle, sir!" Crewe beamed. "I can do that, sir. Half dozen, no work a'tall, Cap'um."

"Pass the word for Mister Giles. My compliments, and he is to supply the barge with two days' dry rations and water, biscuit, cheese, and small-beer. And enough wine for two days' 'Clear Decks and Up Spirits.' You'll not be splicing the main brace, Mister Hyde, till I tell you. You're to loaf about just off the entrance, showing no lights of any sort. Stay furtive as mice, till any vessel leaves larger than a rowboat. You're to fire off one of Mister Crewe's fuzees from a swivel, soon as one does. Almost straight up, but in the general direction of her course. Anything heading west is what we're interested in."

"Aye aye, sir," Hyde agreed, though not sure what it was he was agreeing to.

"The captain of that corvette we fought, Mister Hyde, that's the bastard we want. He captured a commissary ship full of British gold . . . and he now thinks he'll slip away and go back home to crow about it," Lewrie told his senior midshipman first, before he explained things to the rest of his crew before dark. "I want him, Mister Hyde. And with your help, I mean to have him, this time."

•

CHAPTER

6

A HOT SUPPER, for which he had little appetite, almost uncivil a host to Mister Peel and Lieutenant Knolles who dined with him, talking "shop" for once. And so eager for news that most of what he heard wasn't an awkward conversation, but the loud ticking of his chronometer in the chart-space on the starboard side of the great-cabins.

Then back on deck, wondering if Choundas had made a total fool of him, of them all, no matter how cleverly they'd schemed. Alan had always come a cropper, whenever he'd thought himself especially sly—didn't matter at what, he'd always tripped over his own wits—hoping against hope that just this once, events would prove an exception. A gelatinous crawling of time, an *age* between the half-hour watch bells. Nine o'clock, then three bells at nine-thirty, four bells at ten . . .

"*Signal!*" a lookout screamed, as a tiny phosphorescent spark leaped into the inky night sky, trailing an amber train of embers. At a fifty-degree angle, Lewrie estimated. Pointing toward *Jester*, four miles offshore and ten miles down the coast, near Voltri. Pointing to the West! "*Got* 'at bastid, sir! We'uns got 'im!" A cheer rose from the decks, the duty watch, and the gunners standing idle in the waist. Ferociously satisfied, their blood up for the hunt, a kill. Sure that *Jester* would avenge herself, prove herself a lucky ship once more.

By God, we'd better, Lewrie thought! But not a very good night for it. Perversely, the winds had risen a trifle, the sea was surging and creaming now and then in tiny whitecaps—cat's paws and horses. What there was of the moon was occluded by scudding clouds coming down from inland, some storm rushing downslope off the Alps. Their view of the coast was only a black smear against a cold-ashes evening, merely a matter of degree.

"Fetch-to, Mister Knolles," Lewrie commanded. "We go galloping off east, he's sure to slip past us."

"Aye, sir! Duty watch, hands to the braces and sheets!"

A quarter-hour later, riding cocked up into the wind, bows almost due north, the ship making no headway. Still nothing to be seen.

"Signal!"

Another fuzee skyrocketing into the night, pointing west, a bit closer to them, as Hyde sailed in pursuit of whatever had aroused him. No hope of catching his Chase, of course, whatever she turned out to be. Safe enough for Hyde and his men, Lewrie thought, relieved; Choundas did not have night enough to turn and make her pay for alerting the blockade he'd have to thread. Assuming that so-far unseen vessel was his; if it was, he'd gotten a late start, and lost a precious hour already.

"We'll begin to stand inshore, Mister Knolles," Lewrie said with impatience, after another quarter-hour had passed. "Slowly, at first."

"Aye, sir."

Another half hour, Hyde's barge making no more than five knots at best, even with that stiff broad-reaching wind on her quarters. An hour, so five miles closer to us he's come, Lewrie plotted, almost frantic, but concealed by darkness on the quarterdeck, as *Jester* prowled without even a single glim burning. A *tartane*, lateen-rigged, he thought; she'd go around seven knots off such a goodly wind . . . two miles closer to us than Hyde? Yet not a whiff of her, not hide nor hair?

Another fuzee, this time fired slantwise, as if Mister Hyde was firing a very long, up-the-stern shot, as a miniature comet arced up and down like the trail of a burning carcase shot from a mortar. Within two miles of *Jester*'s bows, so the Chase surely must be in smelling distance!

"Haul our wind, Mister Knolles! Time to stand in directly. Due north, Quartermaster!"

"Sail *Ho*!" from a larboard forecastle lookout. "*One* point awrf th' lar-b'd bow! 'Gainst th' town's lights! D'ye *hear*, there?"

Lewrie dashed to the larboard side, leaned out over the bulwarks to peer into the gloom as *Jester* swung. The town of Voltri was three miles north, almost dead ahead, by then. They might have been holding a *festa* to celebrate the recent harvests, or some saint's day, for the waterfront and main streets were lit with torches, lanthorns, and a big bonfire, producing a pencil-thin smear of light. And suddenly, there was a ship; a quick, eye-blink glimpse of a ship atop the amber, scintillating fire-glade of the town's lights, stark and black in a second of silhouette—high-pinked stern, sharp bow, and three crescent moon sails, low to the deck; two large lateens, and a long lateen jib!

"Haul our wind, Mister Knolles, come about to west by north!" he howled. "A *tartane*, no error! And she's already west of us!"

Hellish-fast, too, Lewrie shivered, as the night wind went cold; fearing he'd left it too late. Seven knots mine arse, she had to be going eight or *nine*, or I'm a Turk in a turban! By the time we get turned in pursuit and settled down, she could have a mile lead on us.

Six bells of the Evening Watch chimed up forrud; eleven o'clock on a dark, filthy night. *Jester* was quick with the wind on her quarters, he knew, but this *tartane* would be fast as a witch. He rolled his eyes, to peer without straining or staring, for a glimpse of her, but blackness had swallowed her up, once more.

He looked astern as *Jester* came around on her new course, the sea swashing down her flanks, the babble of water 'neath her forefoot, under her transom an urgent mumbling. Hyde was to return on-station till daybreak then come west to safety in Vado Bay. Pray God there were no more signals from him! Had Choundas sent a first vessel out as a false lure, to test the waters and draw any watcher away, there was little he could do about it. For better or worse, he was now committed.

"WE ESCAPE HER," the captain of the *tartane* crowed to his crew, to his lone passenger the "Brutto Faccia" Francese huddled deep in his warm boat-cloak. "Barge, *signore*? Pretty barge of a *capitano*, I say. I see her before. Ah-gah-mem-non," he pronounced carefully in a poor French, mingled with quick native Italian. "She was only Britannici I see off Genoa. And she is slow. *Big* and slow, *signore*!"

"You are quite certain?" his passenger demanded, unused to being an idle commodity to be carted about, fretful that he had not been given charge of the saucy yachtlike coaster by Pouzin's cabal of plotters, but was now at the mercy of this filthy, unshaven brute with his dark, liquid eyes, olive complexion, and harsh Arabic face. Mongrels, he thought them all, unwanted Persian, Turkish, Egyptian polluters of the ancient Etruscan, Celtic blood of the first Latins.

"Only Brittanici we see, days and days, *signore*," the tartane's commander insisted. "Barge, come in today then go back out. Watchers, in fishing boats see ship of this Nel-eh-son-ey go west, meet another, but do not return. We are safe now, *signore*!" he boasted, thumping his chest. "I sail *circle* around big, slow ship-of-line! *Ecco*, we go out to sea. Coast come down to us, at Vado there are Brittanici patrol. We reduce sail, too. No one can catch us."

"No, we should press on," Guillaume Choundas curtly replied. He almost felt a mythic prickling in his thumbs, an unease that would not be stilled until he was ashore, or back aboard his ship. "I order . . ."

"No one order me," the other barked. "I am *capitano*, you are the passenger. We reduce sail. It is blowing almost too good. We go out from the coast. We get to Finale before sunrise, we go so quick, and cannot land you on that coast in the dark. Lay still, off Finale, and wait till the dawn, we meet Brittanici patrols, you see? If more wind comes, we are safe out at sea, not on rocky coast. You want to live, *signore*? We do what I say. Angle out, stand back in, go fast all the time. But not too fast, *si*? Shut up and drink some wine, *signore*. I am best *capitano* in all of Genoa, the *senatore*, he knows this. Why he hires me to carry his letters to you Francese. I command his *yacht* if he did not give me so many orders. I do not *like* orders."

"Whether you like them or not," Choundas protested, "your employer told you to get me to a French-held port. If we're making such good time, then it could be Loano, even Alassio. It doesn't have to be Finale. Stay inshore, keep up your speed, and land me at the port where dawn finds us."

"Too far for us," the captain objected, turning surly. "There is too much risk coming back to Genoa. I do not ever see ships of you Francese to protect me, *signore*. You are *capitano importante*, in such a *little* navy. There are ten of us . . . one of you. You do not tell *us* what to do, *Capitano grande*."

With that, he turned away to shout orders to his crew, to reduce sail, and went to the tiller-bar aft, to direct the helmsman to wear out to sea. The *tartane* slowed, began to slough and rock. Lateen rigs were horrid when it came to sailing so fine downwind. A square sail, off the wind, would belly full, strain equally from corner to corner, and reduce the excess wallowing motion, which robbed a ship of speed.

Shop clerks, Choundas was forced to fume in silence! Eager for their own beds tomorrow evening, no stomach for a long voyage. Working for the gold, the excitement . . . but with no sense of discipline, purpose, or loyalty. Mongrels, he added to the list of their sins. Just as bad as those swaggering, cockscomb mercenary privateers; all bluster and brag. Once Genoa was theirs, Choundas vowed, and the guillotines came, to winnow out the "aristos," the usurers, those opposed to the new regime, he would be sure that this captain's name was found in the book of the damned.

Mongrels, he thought, squinting his eyes in fury; so dumb they cling to barbaric Arabian lateens, when even the most famous man of Genoa, Christopher Columbus, knew to change over to square rig! An ignorant, mongrel race!

"I'D NOT BE pressin' closer ashore, sir," Buchanon warned him. "Too dark t'see what we're about. Nor whether we're still chasin' yon *tartane*."

"There's depth enough, Mister Buchanon?" Lewrie countered. "A nor'east wind to drive us offshore, for once? Not a lee shore . . ."

"But th' coast trend's southerly, sir," Buchanon insisted. "I suggest we come t' west by south, Captain. E'en does our Chase stand inshore o' us durin' th' night, the coast'll shoulder her out."

"It's the coast he *wants*, to land on, Mister Buchanon," Lewrie spat, as two bells of the Middle Watch chimed at one a.m.

"Which he'd be a purblind fool t'do, with such a sea runnin'," Buchanon countered. "He can't close it till dawn, same'z us, sir."

"Very well, Mister Buchanon. West by south it is. Mister Knolles, we'll haul our wind a mite more, to west by south. Hands aloft, take in sail. First reefs in the main course, mizzen and maintop'sls. I don't wish to shoot past her in the dark. Nor be blown too far loo'rd of the coast by sunrise . . . by this nor'east wind."

Should there be a wind shift, which usually happened along such a coast, should it moderate or clock northerly, he'd be headed, robbed of power when he needed it most, and badly placed for pursuit.

Assumin' there's somethin' t'see at dawn, he sighed, frustrated. *Jester* had logged a steady eight knots since espying their Chase around Voltri. Three hours later, and they were almost level with Vado Bay, at that speed. And still had no further sighting of that spectral *tartane*. He had to admit that Buchanon was right to be cautious. Rocks aplenty inshore, the sea not so boisterous they'd be warned of risk by white foam breaking on them, the moonlight too weak to give them first sight to steer clear. Stout as the wind had blown, he'd expected some rain with it, such a pall of storm cloud overhead that what poor view the lookouts had would be blotted out entirely; but that hadn't come. The solid black of the shore could still be guessed at, if one didn't peer too long or hard at it; whitecaps could be espied all about, by the faint moon. But no sign of that damned *tartane!*

Jester slowed as her sail was reduced, even with the wind fine on her starboard quarter. Purring now, as three bells chimed, solidly surefooted and ploughing. But to where?

CHAPTER

7

"Sir?" Knolles prompted, a little closer to Lewrie's ear, and giving him a "gentlemanly" nudge. "Sir?"

"I'm awake, sir," Lewrie grumbled, rising from a treacly sleep from his wood-and-canvas deck chair. He fought the constricting folds of his boat cloak, sensing immediately that the weather had changed.

"Wind's died out, sir," Knolles reported, fighting a yawn himself. "The last five minutes, it went scant, then . . . nothing."

Jester was rocking and heaving, her timbers and yards groaning in protest, and her sails slatting like flapping laundry amidst all the squeaking of parrel blocks and pulleys. Lewrie marveled that he could have slept so soundly through all that. "What's the time?" he asked.

"Two bells of the morning just went, sir," Knolles informed him. "I make it about a quarter-hour to false dawn, sir. Sorry, sir, but as we kept both watches on deck all night, I held off on pumping and swabbing, and let the hands caulk for a bit. Do you wish me to . . ."

"No, no, you did quite right, Mister Knolles." Lewrie shivered, wrapping himself in the boat cloak again. "Galley fires going? Soup's the thing. Soup and gruel. Cold . . . but clear."

"Remarkably clear, sir." Knolles grinned. Or fought a yawn, it was hard to tell. "The sea's moderating, too."

"Just what I feared." Lewrie groaned. "Good as stranded, much too far to seaward. Northerly, or a Levanter easterly to come, after sunrise proper. Beat for hours to get back inshore, against the land breeze. I s'pose there's no sign of our Chase?"

333

"Uhm . . . not yet, sir," Knolles had to admit. "But we can see a bit better now."

The moon had set, but their world was a nebulous charcoal gray, disturbed only by an occasional whitecap. The coast was definable . . . just barely. About ten miles off, that solid blackness? he thought. Off which a morning's land breeze would flow, dammit to hell. Maybe a nor'wester, to begin with, before the ocean heated and countered, from whatever capricious direction the Ligurian Sea had in mind today?

"If the galley fires are going, I'd admire some coffee," Lewrie said. "And an idea how far west we were blown during the night."

"I'll send a messenger down to roust your steward, sir," Lieutenant Knolles offered. But Aspinall clomped up the larboard ladder from the gun deck, having already made a trip to the galley. For a warm-up, if nothing else, Lewrie thought, uncharitable that early in the morning. He cradled a battered old lidded pot, and bore some tin mugs on a string.

"Coffee, sir? Coffee, Mister Knolles, sir?" He beamed. "Got enough fer all, sir. Thought th' gennlemen'd relish a spot o' hot."

Toulon had gone with him on his errand, for a bite of something from the cooks, who ever would spoil him. Now he came prancing up the ladders to the quarterdeck, tail stiffly erect and *"maiwee?"*-ing for a good-morning rub. He leaped atop the hammock nettings to greet Lewrie with loud demands for attention. After a warming sip or two, Alan went to him to give at least a one-handed tussling and stroking.

He stiffened suddenly, stopped his frantic purring, and turned to look to the north. His ears laid back, his back hairs and tail got bottled up, and he craned his neck, whiskers well forward.

A faint whicker of wind came from there, the worst direction of all, to Lewrie's lights, just as Knolles extracted his pocket watch to state that it was now time for false dawn.

"Sail *Ho!*" a forecastle lookout yelped. "*Four* points off th' *star*-b'd bows!"

"Due north?" Lewrie gulped. "Due north of us?" He looked at the cat, wondering whether he'd sensed the wind's arrival, or caught a scent of that ship . . . Toulon was now busy washing himself, intent on a paw, and the side of his face that Lewrie had tussled.

"What *sort* o' sail?" Knolles bellowed back.

"*Tartane*, sir!" came the quick reply. "Close-hauled t'th' nor-east! 'Tis *her*, d'ye hear, there!"

"Get us underway on starboard tack, Mister Knolles. Sheet home and brace in. Full-and-by to weather," Lewrie demanded. Coffee mug in one hand, telescope slung open in the other, and laid on the mizzen shrouds to starboard, he espied her. Aye, a two-masted *tartane*, about three miles off, showing them her stern as she ghosted against a faint land breeze, pointing higher than *Jester* ever could but riding so slow her decks were level, even with her bows as close to the wind's eye as she could lie, with her lateen yards braced in almost fore-and-aft.

Slowly, just as painfully slowly as the *tartane* crawled, *Jester* began to gather headway, to pinch up point at a time to the wind, her bows at last aimed west-nor'west, as close as *she* could lie. Two knots were reported, then three, when the log was cast astern.

"Good mornin', sir," Buchanon reported to the quarterdeck.

"I'm happy someone can find something good about it," Alan said as he finished his coffee. "Do you give me a rough idea of position, I would be much obliged, Mister Buchanon."

"Aye, sir," Buchanon replied, crisply cheerful as Aspinall gave him a mug as well. "But I make 'at cape off th' larb'd bows t'be th' one guardin' Finale. 'At isle t'th' north'rd, 'at'd be sou'-sou'west o' Vado Bay, sir. 'Bout ten mile offshore, we are. Didn't get blown half so far'z I'd thought, Cap'um. 'At our Chase, at last? Th' poor bugger's on th' wrong tack, don't ya think, sir?"

"She's three miles ahead, sir, that's what I think," Lewrie shot back. "Up to windward, safe as houses."

On a hugely diverging course, too. The *tartane* was beating to the nor'east, but had bags of room in which to tack, safely two miles out of gun range. She could turn nor'west for the coast *between* the island and the western headland, and there were inlets aplenty for a beaching, in shallow water where *Jester* could never dare go.

"Four knots! Four knots t'this log!"

The best Lewrie could hope was to stay on this starboard tack, gain speed as the wind rose, as it seemed to be wanting to, to deny her a shot at tacking further west. It wasn't over yet . . . there might come a patrol from Vado Bay. But so far, though, they had the morning sea to themselves.

"Five knots, sir!" Spendlove shouted.

"We'll tack, sir?" Knolles asked. "There's wind enough."

"No, not yet, sir," Lewrie decided, feeling an urge to chew on a thumbnail. "We'd lose ground on her, she'd tack once we were on a new course, and force us to do it all over again. We'd fall even more behind. Hands aloft, and shake out the night reefs. Let's fill every sail bellyful."

"Aye aye, sir!"

❀   ❀   ❀

Six knots, then seven at times; nothing to write home about with pleasure, but *Jester* was increasing her speed, two miles nearer to that coast,
pointed just east of Finale's headland. Now and then the winds grew a
tiny bit stronger, backing a little east of north, and Spenser and Brauer
luffed her up into it to wring every inch of advantage from the puffs.

"Deck, there!" a foremast lookout called down. Once the dawn had
come, men could be posted aloft, once more. "Chase is tackin'!"

"Had to, sir," Buchanon opined. "She stood any more east'rd . . .
she'd end up in Vado Bay. She was a'ready level with th' island."

"We're at west-nor'west, she's making nor'west, two points higher to
windward, though, Mister Buchanon."

"But closin' th' range, sir. Closin' th' range."

Lewrie eyed her again with his telescope. The *tartane* was hard on the
wind, on starboard tack now. Her decks were still fairly level, though,
which puzzled him. *Jester* was beginning to heel, as if being two miles
farther out at sea they'd caught a stiffer wind than what it might be like
closer inshore, under the shadow of the rugged coastal heights.

"Run out the starboard battery, run-in larboard!" Lewrie barked.

"Seven-and-a-half knots, sir!" Spendlove shrilled.

Jester was really moving now, no matter how average the winds. With
her longer waterline and greater weight, once she got a way on she
tenaciously held it, in even the lightest winds, as the *tartane* could not.
For once, she was the shorter vessel, the one more prone to fall off, to
slough and slow. As she did, even as he watched! To sail as fast as she
needed to, she'd have to fall away from close-hauled, let the wind cross
her decks a little more abeam, on a close reach. Slow to gather way, and
quick to lose it, beating to windward could result in her crawling at a
snail's pace, cocked up but going nowhere.

Was it his imagination, did she appear to be falling off? To the same
compass heading as *Jester*, west-nor'west? And trending aft.

Jester was outfooting her to the coastal shallows, which were now only
five miles off!

"Abeam," Lewrie said with satisfaction a half hour later, now within two
miles of that rocky shoreline. The Chase was almost abeam, and closer to
Jester, as she'd pinched up and luffed to weather, every opportunity; at
least a half mile nearer, though still tantalizingly a half mile outside the

most optimistic shooting range. "She'll not get to Finale, at this rate. If that's where she was headed."

Had the *tartane* been on starboard tack when the wind came back, had she tacked immediately, she'd have been gone long since, but it'd still be a close-run thing. The closer *Jester* got under the lee of a tall range of coastal hills, the more fickle and weak the wind was for her, too. His telescope revealed no shelving beaches ahead, no inlets in which to flee. Behind the island, yes, there was a deep inlet, but they'd have to tack soon, if they wished to get back to it.

"Deck, there! Chase is tacking!"

"Reading my bloody mind," Lewrie grumbled. Now, she's able to steer nor'east by east, run along the coast to pick her spot . . . "Mister Knolles, we will—at last—tack ship!"

"Aye aye, sir!"

Around *Jester* came, thrashing and flogging, carrying her way into the turn smoothly, pivoting, it seemed, almost in her own length, it was so quickly done by a well-drilled ship's company. Slowing as sails were laid aback, of course, as fore-and-aft sails flagged and fluttered lift from themselves. But surging back to seven, almost eight knots within a scant couple of minutes. Now the Chase lay just one point off their larboard bows, and within a mile-and-a-quarter.

"Run out larboard battery, run-in starboard to the centerline," Lewrie shouted, once *Jester* was stable. That made a tiny difference, though the *tartane* still pointed about ten degrees higher to windward, even sailing "a point free" of close-hauled for more speed.

"Lookit th' sea, Cap'um!" Buchanon shouted suddenly, pointing ahead. "Lookit th' sea!"

"Meet her, Spenser, meet her!" Lewrie warned, as the wind laid a brush on his left cheek. There was a rising zephyr, one which backed a point or more, with which they could luff up to claw at least a cable of advantage to windward.

There were ripples on the slow-heaving wave tops around *Jester*'s bows, out ahead and inshore of her. There were *not*, out where the Chase lay! There, the sea was oily-smooth, glittering with many small inshore chops, but the tops of the wavelets were undisturbed. Beyond, tempting but unreachable yet, the winds rippled the waters, but the *tartane* had staggered into a flat, limpid circular pool of calm.

"I see it, Mister Buchanon!" Lewrie almost laughed with glee. The *tartane* would take a long minute to coast through the calm patch of water, slowing all the time, her shorter waterline shedding speed while

Jester stood on through it. She could tack, but tacking might slow her even more. And did the winds return to that calm patch, they might be perverse and "head" her more westerly than she wished.

"I make her no more'n a mile off now, Cap'um," Buchanon said, after taking her measure with a sextant. "Almost gun range. An' th' shore, maybe a mile and a half off."

The *tartane* rode it out, coasting through the calm, with *Jester* marching up her stern relentlessly. Then caught the edge of the wind beyond, her sails luffing as it took her bows-on.

"Headed, by God!" Knolles cried out with delight.

She fell away, crossing to dead on *Jester*'s bows, poised over a rhythmically rising bowsprit and jib boom, having lost at least a half-mile lead, and forced down more easterly. Unless she tacked, she'd be thrown below and east of the island, toward the western headland that marked Vado Bay. She'd shave the island, on her present course.

"Mister Crewe?" Lewrie shouted. "Fetch Mister Rahl from the magazine, and try your eye with one of the foc's'le carronades. Upwind of her, so she won't tack inshore on us!"

"Aye, sir!"

"Wind's veerin' ahead, sir!" Spenser told him from the wheel. " 'Ave t' ease her a point."

"Very well, Mister Spenser." Lewrie chuckled. "That'll keep us honest. And from running ashore on the island, bows-on."

" 'At it will, sir!" Spenser snickered, easing his spokes.

Rahl marched almost stiff-backed like a Grenadier guard to the forecastle, still in his list slippers and powder yeoman's apron, keenly aware of the crew's eyes on him. He fiddled and fussed, weighing a charge, turning a ball to check how perfectly round it was. Tinkered with the elevation screw, the compressors.

"Bloody hell!" Knolles groaned as he stood back at last, with the firing lanyard taut, awaiting the perfect moment.

Sailing "a point free," Rahl had a good portion of gun arcs to work with, instead of firing right over, or through, the forestays or jibs. Up *Jester* rose a trifle, then sagged bow-downward; then up once more, poised and . . .

Boom! As Rahl jerked the lanyard. He stood ramrod straight to spot the fall-of-shot, one hand shading his brow. A pillar of ricochet spray leapt into the sky, tall and so prettily symmetrical it resembled the finest white goose feather. Within a short pistol shot of the *tartane*'s windward side! His fellow gun captains gave Rahl a lusty cheer as their Chase veered off the wind as if recoiling from that strike, to duck down to dead-ahead of *Jester*'s bows, where no more round-shot could be hurled at her. But that forced her to leeward, just a little farther from shore and safety.

"Well shot, Mister Rahl!" Lewrie shouted. "Man the starboard . . . the lee carronade! Spenser, back on the wind, close-hauled, quickly."

As Rahl and the forecastle gunners readied the other eighteen-pounder, *Jester* clawed back up to windward a full point, right on the razor-edge of luffing, to put the *tartane* almost two points alee of her. To claw *Jester* inshore of the Chase!

Boom! Another shot soared out, raising a second feather of spray; again, close-aboard the *tartane*, which ducked back up to windward, this time to escape, weaving an Ess-shaped wake before *Jester*'s bows. Boom! went the larboard carronade once the *tartane* had ducked upwind enough.

"*Ja!*" Rahl shouted in triumph. "*Eine schön Gott-damn hit!*"

I'M SURROUNDED BY fools! Choundas raged; incompetents! Filthy-arsed mongrel defectives! Goddamned . . . *farmers*, who haven't a clue to the sea! Forced to remain silent, forced to depend on a leering cretin, who should have *known* a night wind off the land would fade, and stranded them too far from shore. Failed to tack once they saw that "Bloody" ship and didn't seem to know that the heights would muffle what breeze there was. Chances for an escape looked rather bleak at the moment, but they had one shot left—to tack at once and run inshore, get into shallows where the "Bloodies" couldn't go. Brave their guns, and flee.

The impact of the shot took him by surprise, muffled in his boat cloak on the weather deck below the high-pinked quarterdeck. Cold made his ravaged leg throb with agony, but he was about to fight it back, as he'd done for years, mount the quarterdeck and take charge. The aching delayed him a fateful second as he rose to stand, to mount the ladder.

The *tartane* shuddered, jerked and rolled as if she'd run aground. Men were screaming, even men on the weather deck around him who weren't even in the line of fire! There was a frightful smash of shattered timber, the parroty *Rrwawrk*! as the taffrail and upper stern transom, and a portion of the larboard rails were ripped away in pieces, and whickerings as foot-long wood splinters of the transom and quarterdeck planks whirled in the air. Choundas forced himself up the first step, to peer over at nose height as the lateen above his head was quilled with splinters—and spattered with gore.

Serves you right, he sneered! That boastful Araby-looking nasty of a captain had been slain, along with the helmsman on the tiller, and the other two on the quarterdeck had been blown off their feet.

"Silence!" he boomed, almost crying out at each step as he went to the quarterdeck. "Listen to me! I am captain now, and I will save you. Do what I say and you will live. Lose your heads, and you all are dead men! As dead as your fool of a captain is!"

That stopped them in their tracks, as he took hold of the tiller sweep and began to force it leeward again, to hold them close-hauled on the wind.

"Trim us in to beat, then hoist the rowboat over the side. The lee side, where the 'Bloody' ship cannot see it," Choundas roared. He used his free hand to sweep back his boat cloak to reveal the pistols in his waist belt, the hilt of his sword. "Once around the island, we are out of its lee. There will be wind. There we will tack, and run into shore. Then we will get in the boat and row in, with this ship as our shield. They will not see us doing this, until it is too late. Do you understand me? *Bien. Très bien.* Now, do it!"

Out of desperation, with no other option they could agree to in their fear of capture and death, they obeyed. Choundas forced himself to smile, which made him look malevolent, but competent enough to save them. Though some made the sign against the "evil eye" as they crossed themselves for luck. Feral, brutally ugly . . . but he looked like a real officer who knew what he was doing; they obeyed him.

Too bad I didn't have Hainaut with me, Choundas thought, leaning his hip against the long tiller bar; with four pistols, I'd have killed that idiot, and done this hours ago!

CHAPTER
8

"HELM A'WEATHER, MISTER Spenser," Lewrie was forced to say. "Ease us two points off the wind." The shore of the island was coming up fast, and he'd have to bear away to avoid its shoals. The *tartane* was only a half mile ahead of him now, but she was able to shave closer inshore . . . still hard on the wind, and brush *Jester* off, recapturing the windward advantage. He'd have to cede her the inshore route.

"Mister Rahl!" he shouted through cupped hands. "Grapeshot and scrap, to damage her rigging! Cripple her, sir!"

Rahl tried, firing at extreme elevation, but it was too far for grapeshot, and *Jester* had no star-shot, bar-shot, or chain-shot for the carronades that could whirl across the half-mile gap. Rahl could hit her, evident by the multiple froths of small hailstorms in the waters around her, but it was too light to do crippling damage. And she wasn't ducking high and low anymore, either, but was being unflinchingly steered as close to the wind's edge as she could be. And beyond the island, there was a narrow channel that led to a deep inlet, winding back west, the tall headland at the western edge of Vado Bay. There was a village at either place, a beach below the headland where fishing boats landed, where the pounding of surf had created a gravelly shingle. More rocky would be the narrow channel, with few places to land safely.

"*Herr Kapitan!*" Rahl announced in a parade-ground bark. "I go back to der solit-shot, ja, zir?"

"Aye, Mister Rahl!" Lewrie shouted back.

"We've almost got him," Mister Peel said. "If he's aboard, after all, that is, Captain Lewrie."

"Thankee, Mister Peel, for reminding me what fools we might yet be," Lewrie groaned, most happily unaware of Peel's existence for the last few hours.

"I borrowed Lieutenant Knolles's telescope, sir," Peel told him. "The last few minutes, there's been a fellow steering her who's wearing some sort of uniform. It could be that's part of a deliberate sham but I rather hope not."

"No more'n me, I assure you, Mister Peel." Lewrie yawned, badly in need of more coffee, though the galley fires had been extinguished, once they'd opened fire. "Oh, well shot, sir! Serve her another!"

Rahl's round-shot from the larboard carronade had slammed into the sea so close-aboard the *tartane* that she reeled leeward, her masts shaking and her deck heeled almost a full forty-five degrees for a moment!

But she came back upright, slowed by the drag of the knockdown but sailing doggedly on. Not turning for the narrow, rocky channel!

"Right, she's for the beach on the headland!" Lewrie exulted as the island came abeam, and he could see the wrinkly cat's paws stirring the waters beyond it, a fluke spiraling off the headland. "The town, Mister Peel. Know it? Who holds it now?"

"Genoese troops, I *think*, sir. Don't think the Frogs have come over the heights this near Vado yet." Peel perked up. "Inland might be a different story, but . . ."

"Deck, there! Chase is tacking!"

"Damn him, damn him!" Lewrie groaned. *Jester* had to sail more than half a mile farther before she had enough clearance from the coast to come about! The *tartane* was just a little east of the tip of the headland, and could come back to nor'west by north and run in.

"Wind's *backin'*, sir!" Spenser exclaimed, feeding spokes alee to keep *Jester* on the wind's edge, as he'd been ordered.

"He's tacked right into a shift!" Knolles screeched. "Headed, *again*, by God, sir!"

"Stand on, and ready the larboard battery," Lewrie ordered.

The *tartane* had run into an invisible wall, almost coming to a full stop as she met the wind change head-on, forced to bear away more and more westerly to find the proper angle, fall away at a huge angle even beyond *that* to get some speed up before she could come back to a beat. The wind was now out of the nor'west, and *Jester* could turn up nor'east to run in much closer to the headland and the beach. And the struggling *tartane*.

Chases were like that sometimes, Lewrie realized; plod astern of a ship for hours, never fetching her a yard closer, but all along, gaining slowly. And suddenly, one's ship seemed to leap forward, and there she was, close enough for point-blank broadsides, as if someone had conjured the Chase to reappear within spitting distance. Within the blink of an eye, there she was, not a quarter-mile off, just back to speed but set too far west of the now-visible beach to ground upon it, and forced to tack again to the nor'east, slowing her even more!

"They've a boat alongside, sir!" Knolles shouted as he lowered his glass. "Starboard side!"

"It's him!" Peel cried. "Looks like Choundas, at any rate."

Lewrie raised his own glass. Yes, so close now, he could fetch that ant-figure on her quarterdeck to almost fill the ocular, head-to-toe, he could recognize his foe of old, in the red breeches and waistcoat, the gold-laced blue coat and boat cloak of a French Navy officer!

"Mister Crewe, run out the larboard battery, and open fire!"

It was rushed, too rushed, with the range closing so quickly it made accurate aim impossible, going from a quarter-mile to two hundred yards in a trice. Round-shot went whizzing far overhead, splashed too far short, and too steep to ricochet. Only a few ball struck the *tartane*. And missing the rowboat completely! Men were tumbling down into it, Choundas among them, just as it was cast off to wallow astern, the *tartane* bumping and grinding alongside as it fell away, with no one at the helm. Falling down toward *Jester*, and just big enough to present a danger of collision! And mask her fire!

"Shift fire to the rowboat, Mister Crewe!" Lewrie howled, hot for murder. "Cony, hands forrud to fend that damn' thing off! Mister Spenser, your eye, sir, to match course with her. Where's Andrews?"

"Heah, sah," his cox'n answered, leaving his lee side carronade.

"Go below and fetch me my Ferguson rifle, the one with the screw breech," Lewrie snapped. "There's a shot pouch, cartouche box, and a powder flask stowed in my smaller sea chest in the bed space. Before that bastard rows out of range, hurry!"

Crewe got off another ragged broadside, rushed again, but a lot more accurate. Feathers of spray flayed the sea around the rowing boat, short, wide, a little over, so close-aboard they skipped once, caromed over the oarsmen to Second Graze near the headland's shoals. But nary a bit of harm could they do!

"Luck of the Devil, that'un," Peel spat. "Uncanny, ain't it."

"Gotta fall off, sir!" Spenser announced, as the *tartane* came careening in toward their bows. *Jester* was doing about six knots and the *tartane* no more than four, her close-trimmed lateen yards strained and her sails flat-bellied the way her crew had left them, scudding to a beam-reach by then, heeled over by the unnatural press of wind.

"Cease fire, Mister Crewe!" Lewrie groaned in defeat. The guns were masked as *Jester* had to turn away from the coast, out of range of even his rifled Ferguson he'd kept since his escape from Yorktown. It came up from his cabins with Andrews, just a half minute too late!

Gun crews leapt from the waist to scramble up on the gangway as the *tartane* fell alongside. There was a shiver and scrape, a thud, as the hulls met. But Spenser and Brauer had judged it to a nicety, laid *Jester* parallel to the collision, and falling off the wind had slowed her to almost a match.

"He's going to get away," Lewrie griped. "Again!"

"Sir, you recall the orders you received," Peel snapped, stony and crisply military again, and fearfully impatient to complete Mister Twigg's bidding to him. "To render me every and all assistance to take or kill Captain Choundas."

"Christ, yes, Mister Peel, but . . ."

"Can't count on the Genoese holding him, sir," Peel rapped out. "Can't count on him runnin' into an Austrian cavalry patrol, and being took, sir. The village may have horses. He could ride west, till he's in the French lines. You must land me at once, sir. Me, and any men of your crew who're horsemen, to pursue him. This minute, sir!"

"Sailors who can ride, my God . . ." Lewrie sighed, looking about the deck. Knolles, being a country gentleman, had his hand up. So did his clerk, Mountjoy. Cony could, but he couldn't spare the bosun.

"This minute, sir!" Peel demanded. "There's not a jot o' time to waste!"

"Mister Knolles, you are in command, sir," Lewrie snapped, taking the Ferguson and its accoutrements from Andrews. "Mister Mountjoy, I hope you ride better than you scribble?"

"Country hunts and steeplechasing, sir." Mountjoy swore.

"Andrews, fetch my pistols. Both pair, for me and Mister Mountjoy," Lewrie decided. "My hanger, and the Frog smallsword. Bring 'em to the larboard gangway, midships. Cony, grapnels! Keep the *tartane* alongside for a minute! You have money to rent or buy mounts, Mister Peel?"

"Some, sir."

"Got me purse on me, sir," Buchanon offered. " 'Bout twenty or so pound, an' change."

"God bless you, Mister Buchanon." Lewrie smiled. "Mister Knolles, you will stand out to sea to clear the headland, then enter Vado Bay to report to Captain Nelson. Hyde should be along, sooner or later, you should recover him and his crew, and wait our return. Well, let's go, then. 'Board the *tartane*. She's trimmed for a beat, and that'll take us ashore."

"Spare hands, sir?" Knolles asked.

"Not for what I have to do, no, Mister Knolles." Lewrie smiled grimly, trotting to the gangway entry port to scramble down the battens to the main chains. "God speed, sir. And don't muck up my ship."

"God speed to you, too, sir," Knolles replied, suddenly feeling a lot older than his years.

CHAPTER
9

THE *TARTANE* DRIBBLED down *Jester*'s side as she got a way on her, with Lewrie alone on the quarterdeck, shoving the helm hard over to the starboard corner, alee, to force her back onto the wind. Mountjoy and Peel sorted out weaponry below the ladders, amidships; a souvenir from Lewrie's Florida adventure in '83, a long-barreled .54 Cal. fusil musket, and a French cavalry musketoon, six brace of assorted dragoon, pocket or naval pistols, and their various reloads.

Finally, clear of *Jester*'s side, falling astern, and turning up to use the wind, instead of being wafted aimless by it. He eased the tiller sweep as Peel came to the quarterdeck, complete with a battered-looking saber and scabbard at his hip. They both gazed shoreward, as Choundas's rowing boat cocked and surged over the beginnings of feeble breakers within fifty yards of the beach, another quarter-mile inshore.

"Hell of a lead on us." Peel grimaced, baring his horsey teeth. "Village around the point, 'bout another quarter-mile, I recall. We'll sail around and put in there, I take it?"

"Thought we'd do things direct, Mister Peel," Lewrie said, with a humorless laugh. "He's lame. He can't scamper too far. Or quick."

Lewrie swung the *tartane*'s bows a touch off the wind, her decks canting over a mite more, but making more speed, as if he was aiming to shave the point by the thinnest of hairs, east of where Choundas would ground.

"Ah, land us 'twixt him and town, so he can't get a horse," Mister Peel supposed aloud.

"Something like that," Lewrie agreed.

"But, uhm . . ." Peel demured, "we don't have a rowboat. They . . ."

"We *have* a boat, properly speaking, sir." Lewrie beamed, humming to himself. "Why I didn't want any extra hands along. Bit iffy, this. But you said 'this instant,' so, 'this instant' it'll be. Looks steep-to, around there, not so much sand in the shallows so we'd not reach the shore. Yon rocky notch? Maybe six feet of water within musket shot of the shingle. Remind Mountjoy to keep his powder dry, sir. When we hit, and when we go over the bow."

"Good God, you . . . !" Peel went quite pale. "I can't swim that . . ."

"Mister Peel, I can't swim at all!" Lewrie hooted, grinning at him maliciously, happy to be getting some of his own back. "Just lie back, grit your teeth . . . and think of England, hey?"

"You're daft, you're . . . !" Peel gasped.

Lewrie put the tiller hard-over for the shore. He looked about for the rowboat; it was already ashore, abandoned, bows grinding upon the strand. A flash of white shirt on a rocky path above the beach was the tail end of the escapees, scrambling around the point to the village where they could blend in with their fellow Genoese, perhaps prop their feet up in an *osteria*, sip some wine, and pretend to be simple fishermen. Choundas, though . . . ! He hadn't a hope, except to find a way to hide or flee. And if there were troops in the village, as Peel seemed to recall, they might persuade them to remember their "neutrality" and hunt for the French officer who violated it.

"Dear Lord, sir!" Mountjoy screeched as he learned what Lewrie had in mind, as the *tartane* arrowed in toward the beach.

"Hang on!" Alan warned. They were back up to at least five knots. Rocks were visible underwater to windward as she went in at a sixty-degree angle. There was a shudder as she scraped over something, a slither of sand, then a thunderous roaring and groaning as her bow and forefoot planking tore away, as her keel shattered forrud, and stout ribs of her hull timbers almost exploded into kindling! Her bow pitched high, then came crashing down again, she canted to starboard amid the shrieking of her masts and yards, stays, taut halliards and sheets twanging and snapping loud as gunshots, as everything came down in ruin!

Her motion came to a stop in an eye-blink, throwing everyone off their feet. Lewrie fetched up at the forward edge of the quarterdeck, rolling over to get back upright, and regretting his precipitate action just a tad; after all, she'd been a pretty little thing, worth a pretty penny at the Prize

Court. For all the good that would have done him if his previous experiences with those thieves was anything to go by.

The *tartane* was firmly aground, canted hard-over to starboard and wrecked beyond repair, her forward third splayed open and her back broken, with her long outthrust rectangular Dago-fashion bowsprit platform hanging over the top of the surf line and some shallow rock pools. When the wind did come from seaward later in the day, she'd grind and pound to death, until she resembled a dead whale, all spine and ribs.

"Well, let's go ashore!" Lewrie urged, trotting forward to find some loose bights of line to ease their scramble down the starboard end of the sprit platform to shin-deep water.

THERE WERE NO troops in the village. Peel's and Mountjoy's fluent Italian gathered that much from the locals; they'd ridden off a day before. No, no smugglers had come ashore, *signores*, they were assured; only honest fishermen and herders, here. Though more than a few tarry sorts eyed the heavily armed trio nervously from the lone tavern's windows or doorway. A uniformed man, *si si, signores*, and very ugly, he'd come but he had gone quickly; hired a horse and ridden off, too. Their village didn't attract many visitors, and they rarely stayed for long in any event. Horses? *Si, signores*, there is a man who has horses to buy, they are *"molto costoso"* . . . very expensive, they were told, with many villagers rubbing their fingers together in a universally understood sign.

"Bloody rejects," Peel said, as he pawed a chocolate gelding's chest for defects. "Austrian, Genoese, maybe French . . . sound-enough, once, I s'pose. Girth galls and saddle sores, almost healed? Cavalry remounts. Stolen, I shouldn't wonder. Maybe this bastard's fattening 'em up to sell back, later."

"No matter," Lewrie snapped, impatient for a gotch-eyed, gangly ostler lad to put saddle and pad on the likely dun mare he'd picked. "He admits he sold a horse to Choundas? He recognizes our description?"

"Yessir, best of his lot," Peel replied, doing his own saddling. "Our boy, 'Brutto Faccia' was here, right enough. Paid in gold, didn't quibble. Didn't wait for change, either. Now, price he asked for ours you'd think we'd just bought blooded Arabians, 'stead o' these. In the Household Cavalry, we'd deem these Welsh coal-pit ponies."

"I had a pony once." Mountjoy crooned to his choice to calm her as he sat her back, already mounted. "Bit me, rather often, he did."

"Paid for information, too, this brute tells me," Peel went on, kneeing his horse to tighten the girth. "Don't hold yer breath, damnye. So we had to, as well. There's the coast road . . . east to Vado, or west to Finale, pick it up 'bout a mile inland. Another road at the junction . . . goes inland, northwest." Peel swung up into his saddle and leaned down to adjust his off-side stirrup.

"Which did he take, does this fellow know?" Lewrie pressed, as he swung a leg over, his Ferguson rifle muzzle-down across his back.

"Asked about Austrians," Peel said, sitting upright. "I doubt this man really ever knew, but he told him there *had* been Austrians on the Finale road, to the west. That much gold gettin' slung about, he told him anything he wished to hear, more than like. But I can't remember reports of Austrian patrols this far away from Vado. I wager he took the northwest road, inland. For certain, the French Army is that way. Let's go. Catch him up before he finds them."

They set off at a brisk trot, posting in their saddles, finding Latin saddles' high pommels and backs awkward. The horses were awkward, too, too long unexercised and fractious; taken too soon from their period of recuperation to be strong. The road junction was uphill all the way, less than a mile, but their mounts were already breathing hard.

A quick halt for Peel to study clues in the wheel ruts and hoofprints that went in every direction, those partly obliterated by boot marks of the soldiers who'd left the village.

"Sir!" Mountjoy yelped, having ambled down the Finale road for about two musket shots' distance. He came cantering back, waving something aloft. "Tricolor cockade, sir. Just lying in the middle of the road. Off a Frenchman's hat, do you think, Mister Peel?"

"Yessir, I do." Peel squinted down the road. "You stayed in the middle, or on the verge, sir?"

"Middle, sir." Mountjoy groaned. "Did I err?"

"We'll see. You wait here for a bit."

Peel walked his gelding down the left side of the road, peering at the ground. He stopped where he saw fresh shoe prints that Mister Mountjoy had made when he dismounted, then crossed over to the right-hand side, kneed his mount through the brushy undergrowth, and disappeared! Minutes later, though, he emerged; on the northwest road!

"Clever, this Choundas!" Peel laughed, waving them to join him. "For a sailor, I'd not expect it. Tossed his cockade to lure any pursuit down the Finale road, then doubled back through these woods to hide his prints. With that uniform he wears, under a cloak, he could almost pass as an Austrian artillery officer. Or Genoese, Piedmontese . . . as little as most have seen of 'em. Yet, here's his prints, leading right up this inland road. There's still a chance! Must we kill our horses, so be it, but we can still catch him! Follow me!"

CAPITAINE DE VAISSEAU Guillaume Choundas was not a horseman. He had never owned one. His father couldn't afford one when he was growing up; even if their principal diet came from their catches at sea, grain for a horse's nourishment was better put in the bellies of the Choundas family, than such an extravagance.

Yet a man who'd aspire to the level of the aristocracy or those untitled rich, as his father had schemed for him to do, the brightest of his sons, *must* ride. There'd been a retired Norman cavalry officer who'd drilled him, hours and hours in a paddock or the countryside of St. Malo, for a small fee, but young Guillame had never taken to it as he had the skill of the sword, pistol, or mathematics. What need had a naval officer-to-be with a good "seat," except to impress the ladies? Equipoise was nothing to him but a regrettable means to an end, an onerous task to perform until he'd been deemed reasonably competent, and quickly abandoned as he focused on the knowledge necessary for a naval career. His time at the Jesuit school as an impoverished charity student, pretending to espouse their vows of poverty, chastity . . . Bretons made the world's best seamen, perhaps stout infantry. Let the rest of the Franks, Normans, and effeminate Gauls who had come to dominate the ancient, original pure Breton race have their love of horses! Let the other lads prate and pose on their expensive living toys! He would be a Breton, with his feet firmly planted on the ground, or an oak deck.

So he sat his horse lumpishly, his crippled left leg too weak to tolerate a trot. He could post with his overdeveloped thighs, but a few minutes' work with his calf created a burning, engorged numbness before it went slack and nerveless. A canter or lope was much better, but even a poor horseman such as he could see that this horse was not up to a fast pace for long. After the road junction, he'd rested his gelding, gone down the Finale road and torn off his Republican cockade to leave a false scent, as he'd read that Rousseau's Noble Savages did. He'd then loped for three-quarters of a mile inland, until his horse began to toss its head, and slowed to a steady, long-legged, distance-eating walk. Once on the north-west road, the going was more level and easier, the inclines gentler among the rock-bound pastures filled with goats and sheep, the gleaned-over fields of stubble, the orchards and patches of forest. Easier on the horse . . . and him.

"Maniac," Choundas whispered in uneasy awe, recalling again the *tartane* driving ashore, with that madman Lewrie at her helm. Choundas had recognized *Jester* after their first tack, from three miles off, and had known at once who it was pursued him. But he'd bested Lewrie one more time, in spite of his best efforts. He'd gotten ashore, and then gotten away! But why, he asked himself, would such an idle rakehell turn manic, insane? Was it possible that Lewrie's hatred was just as hot as his own for him? Even though it had been Guillaume who'd suffered at *his* hands? No, someone must be ordering him, driving him to chase me. Even at two hundred yards, he had smelled defeat, and fear, the last time their ships had dueled off Alassio. But for that damned frigate, he'd have had him, at last. Lewrie would not come after him so lustily, unless pressed to it. For at heart, he was surely afraid of him, by now! A cowardly English gentleman-"aristo" weak-wrist!

British agents? How pleasurable it had been, to send Pouzin's spies off on a false errand, knowing from the first which ship carried the gold. His next report would damn Pouzin for being led astray by a "Bloody" plot, for failing, as he had concerning Alassio, and the loss of the convoy and warships. Choundas suspected British agents, and a vague description of a Jew from London, a banker—he sounded like a cadaverous butcher who'd confounded him in the Far East—Twigg! It was more than possible. And with Pouzin gone, himself installed as a replacement, he could recall that whore Claudia Mastandrea to France—to answer questions! Lewrie had had her, so he must. Then lure Lewrie to his death, with her the bait, this time. His bait!

But that death would be a long time coming, Choundas vowed to himself. Oh, yes! First he must scream for mercy, for forgiveness, that he'd maimed me, and made me so ugly! Months, it could last, no torment, no agony too great. Then leave him just as ugly, crippled, and abhorrent! A slug, trailing useless legs behind him, so ugly his pretty English wife and adoring children would shriek to see him, and that handsome, cocksure, swaggering brute slashed and carved into so hideous a creature, he'd be as repulsive as a leper! His whore from Corsica—Mastandrea, too?—have them in front of him, make Lewrie wail and gnash his teeth in impotence? *Was* death too good for him?

Choundas was so intent on his revenge, so rapt in savage dreams, that he missed the fact that the road began to curve north as it wound through a stretch of wooded hills, and did not wind back, but kept on trending more to the east, following the path of least resistance.

"ONLY ONE HORSE has been along here, this morning," Peel stated with certainty as they took a rest at the northern edge of a copse of wizened trees so interlaced and convoluted they looked woven together. Before them stretched about a half mile of small woodlots and orchards, some small grain fields, to the beginnings of a series of winding hills covered in tall pines. "Were I out on vedette, I'd say some guns were along here yesterday . . . perhaps a troop of cavalry."

"Yes, but whose?" Lewrie asked, beginning to question what he was doing away from his ship, this far inland, playing at soldiers with the French Army in the offing. As far as he was concerned, if Choundas wanted to keep on riding, he'd be more than happy to let him. As long as he never heard from the bastard again.

"Well now, that's the question, isn't it, sir?" Peel chuckled.

"Another good'un would be 'where does this road go,' sir?" Mister Mountjoy muttered, sounding as if he was experiencing his own reservations about their little outing.

"Perhaps your captain might know, Mister Mountjoy," Peel hinted. "After all, he's been staring at more maps of this coast than we."

"Charts," Lewrie corrected, shifting his saddle to ease an ache. It had been two years since he'd been astride, and his inner thighs and buttocks were reminding him of it, rather insistently. "Sea charts, do you see, Peel. Prominent stuff to steer and navigate by. But what's behind 'em, out of range-to-random shot, don't signify. I haven't the faintest clue where we *are*, much less where this road goes. Frankly, I was hoping you did!"

"Well, all roads lead somewhere." Peel frowned. "If it's good enough for Choundas to follow, it's good enough for us."

He heeled his mount and clucked, and they lumbered into motion once more, working their way back to an easy lope for those far woods.

CHAPTER
10

GUILLAUME CHOUNDAS EMERGED from the woods at last, after a serpentine journey in the shadow of the pines. The day was warming up, and he threw his boat cloak back over his shoulders. Before him was a wide valley with low hills to either side, covered with broader grain fields and shrouded on three sides with bush-covered boulders, with more woods to the north and east. The road led straight on. Wary of being out in the open, he checked the priming of one of his three pistols, then rode into the sunlight. About 300 yards off there was a wayside shrine, at a crossroads. He rode to it, warily looking about, but he was quite alone. The shrine was footed with a stone watering trough, but it was dry, filled with crumbly leaves and a green-brown rime. His horse nuzzled it, snuffling disappointedly. A tapering stone column at a list as it sank into the ground, a small altar covered with brittlely dry flowers, surrounded by fluted columns and topped with a steepled roof. It had a cross, but that was a recent addition, he thought, for the moss-filled inscription was Roman, like some legionary burial sites he'd seen in his childhood Brittany. The figures, though, on the original stele, much effaced by time, were far older. They were Celtic! he gasped with pleasure. He took that as a good sign. Till the raven came.

The raven glided in from his right, flared its wings and alit atop the steepled roof that was streaked with bird droppings. One of Lugh's birds, he shivered; old Bretons still knew who'd built the dolmens, and worshiped at them. Lugh was the greatest old god, and his raven was a harbinger—an ominous one! It preened its feathers, shook and settled, then cawed once at him, silhouetted against the morning sun.

The sun! Choundas sat bolt-upright, twisting his head to scan the empty valley. It was a bit past midmorning, yet the sun was in his eyes! He was facing southeast! All the time in the woods where the sun didn't reach, had he missed a trail, gotten turned around? His stomach chilled as he saw a patch of blue through a notch in the woods—the sea. Vado Bay! The cart track by the shrine led down to Porto Vado; or back to the west. But it might take him back where he needed to go. He strung out a rein to guide his thirsty horse, as the raven cawed once more, spread its wings, and lifted away, not six feet over his head, winging off to the west. Choundas then heard what had disturbed it—the thud of hooves, the jingle of chains and scabbards, and the clomp of feet. In the woods there was movement, shakoed infantry, and a troop of cavalry on the tracelike Vado road, lance pennants fluttering and points glittering above their heads. Austrians!

The raven's flight was the only clue he needed to turn away, and begin to ride off again, a good sign, he thought; that here in the land of the Roman conquerors of his ancient people, he was not alone, that a Celtic influence still resided. He dug in his heels, to urge the horse to get him out of sight before those lancers spotted him. A shout . . . ?

"VIEW HALLOO!" PEEL cried as they left those maze-y woods, loped out into the broad valley. "There's our fox, gentlemen! Tally ho!"

Heedless of their horses, they kneed them into a gallop, aiming to cut off the fleeing rider with the cloak flying behind his back, Mister Peel in front, with Lewrie and Mountjoy behind, neck and neck.

Almost at once came the shrill call of a trumpet to the right-rear as the troop of Austrian lancers entered the valley and wheeled to form two ranks across as they trotted forward, quickly changing to the canter.

"Peel!" Lewrie warned. "We've got company!"

"Bugger 'em!" Peel threw over his shoulder, drawing his saber and laying it point-down, extended beyond his horse's neck. "On!"

"They think we're French . . ." Lewrie panted, "runnin' away . . . and you'll *think* buggery!" He turned his head to see the front rank lower its lances and break into the charge at the urging of a trumpet. "They're after *us*, you damn' fool! Speak . . . bloody German . . . anybody?"

"I do, sir!" Mountjoy called, his clothes filthy with clods of earth and grass thrown up by Peel's horse's hooves. "Some, anyway. I . . . picked up a few phrases . . . from Rahl and Brauer!"

And before Lewrie could tell him not to, Mountjoy reined in and turned away to trot back toward those glittering lance points, into the teeth of the charge, with his hands up, screeching *"Meine herren, meine herren, bitte! Hilf mir! Eine Fransozich spion wir verfolgen! Bitte!"*

"Bloody damn' . . . !" Lewrie yelped, knowing it was suicidal, but unwilling to abandon the hen-head! He reined back himself, slowing his horse so quickly it crow-hopped after its skid, quite willing to throw him off! He swung back to join Mountjoy, at an inoffensive canter, his hands empty and outstretched. The only thing he knew that might identify himself was to break into a loud song—"Rule, Brittania"! The lancers came on, like an imminent collision between two ships, lances still lowered as Mountjoy continued yelling. He had a childlike urge to cover his eyes, and only watch the outcome through his fingers!

At the very last second, though, the front rank parted, raising its lances and sawing back to a lope, to circle him and Mountjoy. Alan let out a *huge* whoosh of relief, and plastered a grin on his phyz.

"Guten morgen, mein herr," Mountjoy was babbling to a pimply faced young officer. *"Herr leutnant? Mein kapitan,* Lewrie . . . *König* George, *Britisch Königlich Kriegsmarine? Wir verfolgen ein spion."*

"Parlez-vous Français?" the blotch-faced young lieutenant said.

"Well, *oui . . . certain, s'il vous plais, mein herr."*

"Good." the officer laughed. "German is *so* inelegant. What do you say you do, m'sieur?"

"Thank bloody Christ," Lewrie muttered under his breath, once Mountjoy got to slanging. Grateful that it wasn't just the Russians' aristocracy who hated their own tongue, and mostly spoke in French.

"They'll help us pursue, sir!" Mountjoy announced. *"Leutnant* Baron von Losma will follow us with his troop. I've told him that he shouldn't mistake Mister Peel for Choundas, when we catch him up."

"Bloody good. Let's be at it, then." Lewrie beamed.

"Trupp!" von Losma piped, his teenaged voice breaking with the effort, though damned elegant in his movements. *"Vorwarts!"*

OFF THEY WENT again, the lancers in a column of twos, thundering up through those bouldered, bushy hillocks, through a patch of forest, and out into another, smaller valley, where they caught up with Peel, perhaps only a half mile from where they'd split off from him. He was circling his horse at a breather-trot, waiting for them. Beyond, they could see Choundas, just as he put his struggling horse to a slope.

"What'd you stop for?" Lewrie demanded, reining in.

"Them, damn 'em," Peel spat.

"Oh." Lewrie cringed.

A little beyond Choundas, at the top of that grassy slope sat a troop of French dragoons—heavy cavalry. It wasn't 150 yards off, but it might as well have been the distance to the moon! A column of blue-coated infantry could be seen to the north, at the head of the small valley, marching for the low, bouldery ridge they'd left.

"Goddamn the man's shitten luck!" Peel cried. "After all we've done, got so close on his heels . . . now *this*! It's as if he's in league with the Devil, damn his blood."

"Still a chance," Lewrie muttered through a dry mouth. He alit from his horse, trotted to the tumbled ruin of a rock fence just beside the road, and unslung his Ferguson rifle. He'd killed Lanun Rovers at 200 yards with it—winged 'em, anyway.

One complete turn of the trigger-guard lever, to lower the screw breech and open the barrel's hind end.

"Lewrie, it's over," Peel pointed out. "We sit here, this dumb and happy, they have the slope of us. Sooner or later, they'll charge. And lancers ain't meant to tangle with heavy cavalry, head-on."

"It's not over yet, Peel," Lewrie snapped. "Sooner he's dead, the sooner you and Twigg leave me the hell alone."

He bit off the folded end of a premade cartouche, the powder bitter on his tongue. Bullet end up the spout. Crank the breech shut and pull the flint striker's dog's jaws back, checking to see that the flint was firmly seated and didn't slip against the leather under the clamping screw's face. At half cock, he flipped open the frizzen, to bare the pan, and primed it with a measure from the powder flask that held the very finest, talclike igniting powder.

"Er, sir?" Mountjoy bickered. "The Herr Baron von Losma says we should hightail it. Soon, sir. He's *found* the Frogs, so . . ."

"A minute." Lewrie sighed. "A minute."

He pulled the Ferguson back to full cock and put it to his eye, resting the barrel on the rocks, settling himself. It looked to be at *least* 200 yards, maybe more? And there was Choundas, stopping beside a French dragoon officer, pointing back to the valley. Smiling like everything, he suspected. Bragging about his escape, too!

There was the wind to consider; it was blowing from behind the cavalrymen on that far slope, and a little to Lewrie's right. A shot uphill, almost into the wind? He held high, aiming a foot above his nemesis's hat, a touch to the right, maybe a foot beyond Choundas's shoulder.

"Might as well shoot at the moon, sir, the *herr leutnant* says," Mountjoy interrupted. "With a musket, at this range . . . ?"

"Shut *up*, Mister Mountjoy!" Lewrie barked. "*Not* a musket."

There was a raven's caw off to his left, so near his ear that he almost jerked the trigger. Tramp of marching feet, thud of a drum. Another column of infantry emerging far to left of the slope where the cavalry sat and stared. At least a battalion, coming to use the road they were on.

The raven swooshed past, zooming upward, gliding and tilting to gain altitude before beating its wings, again. Flying toward Choundas. Once it was past, the wind faded, the grass tips before Lewrie stilled their slight wavering, and he inched the barrel a bit more left. Took a quarter-inch more elevation.

"MY CONGRATULATIONS ON your breathtaking escape, *Capitaine*," the dragoon officer enthused, offering Choundas a silver brandy flask. "Though it is not every day we see our Navy among us. Do you wish me to sweep those Austrian scum who chased you away? Just sitting there, counting heads, the damned fools. Lancers . . . they're insane!"

"Their infantry is not far behind them," Choundas cautioned as he slurped down a restoring measure of brandy.

"We wait for the rest of the squadron, then," the dragoon said in disappointment. "For the infantry to flank them away."

"We march on Vado Bay, at last?" Choundas beamed.

"Indeed, *Capitaine*. Soon, your ships will anchor there."

Choundas turned to look at the Austrian troop, and at the men in civilian dress who'd accompanied them, hoping that one of them was his *bête noire*, Lewrie. Was that him, kneeling down? So close, at last, so far from his ship, and all aid. With a word, he could urge this cavalryman to gallop down and take him for him. He could have Lewrie in chains in his cellars at Nice by the next evening, to begin the exquisite revenge he'd planned so long. Just a word, and . . .

There was a puff of smoke from the fence, from the kneeling man.

"It *is* him!" Choundas crowed. "The desperate fool!"

"Far past even the best musket shot," the dragoon officer cried in derision, and his troopers guffawed at the hopeless gesture.

"*Capitaine* Jonville, perhaps . . ." Choundas began to say.

A raven came soaring up the slope, flaring and riding the thermal off the hillside, climbing, climbing, then beat its wings, beginning to circle—

to Guillaume Choundas's right hand. He raised his right arm in supplication, remembering what the old people had told him . . .

". . . couldn't hit a house, at that . . ."

A second or two in flight, arcing up, then down, as it lost its momentum, plummeting like a howitzer shell and regaining velocity . . .

The .65-caliber ball slammed into Guillaume Choundas with the impact of a heavy, hard-swung cudgel, smashing into the flesh and bone of his upraised right arm, just below his armpit! His horse screamed, almost as loud as he did, as he was flung sideways in the saddle, and dragged to the right and down by the force of it! His horse whirled as if to bite its own haunches, rearing and backpedaling for balance and slinging Choundas's total weight onto that weak left leg caught in the stirrup, shuddery and nerveless from his desperate gallop, caught by the iron brace that stiffened the thick left boot. He flailed to stay in the saddle, but his right foot was free, and he was falling, to land on that right shoulder and arm, and the back of his head, get dragged for a few paces in a maddened circle before a trooper sprang down to grab the reins, and another rushed to free his foot.

"*Merde alors!*" The dragoon officer breathed in stupefied awe. "Miraculous!"

"Eatttt thatt, you *bassttardd!*" Lewrie screamed as he rose to his feet, his face mottled, and split by a feral, heathen grin. Alan trotted back to the horse Mountjoy held, took the reins, and slung the Ferguson over his back before mounting. "That's all for *him!*"

"*Gott in Himmel!*" Lt. Baron von Losma peeped, turning pale.

"Good *shot*, hey?" Lewrie crowed, riding in an impatient circle.

There was a sudden sputter of musketry up the valley, among the trees. A platoon firing, at first. Then what sounded like a whole regiment lit off. The flat bangs of a three-gun battery of light artillery joined them . . . followed by another regimental volley.

"*Heraus!*" Lt. von Losma shouted, waving his arm in the air in a signal. "*Mach schnell, heraus! Wir zurückziehen . . . zur ruck, jetzt!*"

The French infantry column on the road, still 300 yards away, lumbered out from column to line, four deep, and began to load for a volley of their own, their skirmishers out in front already firing.

"Time to scamper, sir," Mountjoy translated as the lancers with them wheeled away, almost in a headless panic. As the French dragoons came flowing from the trees, down off that far slope's crest.

"Lewrie," Peel breathed, half in awe, but his face hellish-dark with concern. "Just what the bloody hell have you *started*?"

They sawed at the reins and kicked their horses to a gallop, back the way they'd come, whooping to scare them to greater effort, eating a shower of flung clods from the rapidly retreating lancers. The French helped, whooping and keening with blood lust. As they began to climb that bouldery bare ridge, Lewrie looked behind, to see the dragoons in full charge, sword points hungry, and not fifty yards astern!

They almost flew over that low ridge, down into the broad valley to the crossroads and past the filthy, slow-toppling shrine, whooping with relief to see at least a brigade of Austrian infantry drawn up at the edge of the far woods, another quarter-mile away. The drumming of dragoon hooves didn't seem to falter, though, thundering loud as gunfire. And, to speak of it, there was rather a *lot* of gunfire. Waves and volleys of it, full broadsides of musketry.

They blazed past the infantry brigade's left flank as trumpets sounded and drums beat to stand the soldiers to attention and begin to load. Lewrie dared look back once more, grateful beyond all expression to see the French dragoons slowing and circling across the face of that stout brigade's lines, just out of musket shot.

"Think we're safe, now," Peel informed them, checking his horse. The troop of lancers, though, was still rushing pell-mell down the road to Porto Vado. The last they saw of them were the winks of lance points and colorful pennants, the flash of shod hooves as they thundered away.

The brigade began to volley by ranks, and a sudden fog-bank rose before them. More blaring of bugles could be heard.

"That stopped 'em, cold!" Mountjoy gasped happily. "Thank God, I say, for the Austrians. Slow or not, they were there when we needed."

He was not quite so thankful a moment later when infantrymen in gaudy Austrian uniforms came streaming back from the firing, out of the smoke of their own muskets in a ragged mob, as fast as their legs could carry them. Some mounted officers appeared, a few flailing with their swords to turn their troops, or stop them. Other officers galloped on past, just as intent on escape. They could hear cheering far beyond . . . over the wails of alarm closer to them . . . the drums and tootling of a military band, and harsh voices baying out "La Marseillais"!

"What the bloody hell?" Mountjoy yelped, as the straggling mob of fleeing infantry became a positive flood as the brigade broke.

"Christ, they panicked at their own bloody volleys," Peel spat; figuratively, and literally. "A brigade, routed by a *troop* o' cavalry?"

"Maybe we should try to ride back to that village where we began," Lewrie suggested, fingering the brace of long-barreled pistols stuffed in his waistband. He looked down that way, but there seemed to be the plumes and pillars of gun smoke above those woods, too.

"Doubt it," Peel groaned. "The Frogs'd have taken the junction above the village before we got there. They need the coast roads most of all. This way, I think." Peel waved, down the sketchy path to Vado Bay the lancers had used. "And quickly," he added, seeing the sparkle of bayonets atop the far bare ridge, the blue coats and white trousers of a French brigade deployed in line across the road they'd just ridden.

"How far do you think it is, sir?" Mountjoy asked nervously.

" 'Bout three dead Italian horses," Peel replied, leading them into motion, kicking his already-weary mount to a trot.

But isn't anybody goin' to congratulate me? Lewrie thought. Or will we live long enough for that?

CHAPTER

11

FROM WHAT THEY could see of it, the finest army in Europe had turned itself into a panic-stricken horde. After all General de Vins's dithering, it had also gone from what they'd deprecated as the slowest in Europe, to one of the very fastest. Now, going the wrong way, its speed of retreat was breathtaking!

The few poor roads were strangled by trains of wagons, bullock teams dragging heavy guns. Lighter civilian carriages and coaches were strewn along the sides of the roads, broken down after they'd tried to bypass the tangled messes. Large artillery pieces stood abandoned by the side, left in artillery parks lined up wheel to wheel as if for an inspection, but their gunners and their dray horses were gone, commandeered by the first takers who could get to them.

There were mounted color bearers clattering along to save their regimental symbols—but without their regiments. Officers dressed in a dizzying assortment of brightly martial uniforms; infantry, artillery, cavalry, Commissariat, medical units . . . dragoon, lancers, grenadiers or fusiliers, light infantry or line, all mixed together, all clopping off toward the sea, or the east, without their troops. There were soldiers in dribs and drabs, here a platoon, there a company, together, shambling away to the rear without officers, and it was rare to see a full battalion that had kept some sense of order.

Or their weapons. The road and ditches, the fences and fields, were littered with abandoned muskets, pistols, hangers and knapsacks, cartridge boxes and powder flasks, cross-belts, hats, neck-stocks, and belts. Anything and everything that might slow them down they'd left behind.

There were camp followers who accompanied every army to a war;

wives, children, laundry-women and officers' servants, fiancées, amours, and whores, mothers and fathers come to see their sons win glory on the fields of honor—all running, riding, or clinging to wagons, or an offside stirrup, to escape the French. From raggedy barefoot peasant girls who slept with the privates to lordly, aristocratic courtesans in court dress, they lined the road, crying and begging for a ride, a seat behind a cavalryman, for water, for a clue as to where to go, or a word of encouragement, or an explanation of what it was they witnessed.

Hard-hearted, they rode; Peel, Lewrie, and Mountjoy, with pistols in one hand, swords in the other, and reins in their teeth to prevent a swarm of desperate soldiers or civilians from swamping them and taking their horses. Children held up to *them* had to be denied, no matter how pitiously a young, still-pretty mother might plead. Their mounts were barely able to carry them at the moment, judder-legged and blowing, so slick and foamy with ripe ammoniac sweat that Lewrie's thighs and boots were damp with it; reeking, too, with the rotting meat stink of saddle sores and girth-galls that had never completely healed, and were now rubbed raw and open, leaving blood and pus stains on the saddle pads to trickle to the corners and drip in the dirt of the road.

Every rill, every creek or well, was thronged with people eager for a drink, with artillerists or cavalrymen fighting their way through to water their horses before they died on them. Villages had to be avoided, too crammed with the weak or defeatist almost elbow-to-elbow; or sprinkled with potential murderers who'd have killed their children for a horse.

"Piedmontese," Peel pointed out, once they'd found a shady spot far off the road, downhill by the side of a small brook. "They were up north, thirty miles or more. And here they are, running to the sea. I think I spotted some Austrian uniforms of regiments garrisoned at Vado, too. Going the other way. That don't bode well, I tell you."

"It looked to be four or five miles to the coast," Lewrie said, forcing himself to be brutal and jerk his horse's lips from the water, before it foundered itself. "Last view we had, that last clear hill."

"We'll be on foot long before then, if it's that far," Mister Peel said with a fatalistic shrug. "*If* the Austrians haven't abandoned it, yet. God, the French ain't pursuin' them . . . they're *herdin'* 'em!"

"We've left the ones streaming down from west-to-east," Lewrie pointed out as they had to lash with their reins to get their mounts to leave the brook and begin a shaky walk again. "Think we'll run into a new wave, coming up from Vado?"

"Fight our way, cross-current, then." Peel sighed. "Might even be easier, who knows, Lewrie?" He drew up, as his horse began to limp, unable to put weight on its left foreleg. "That's that, for this'un," he said, dismounting at last. He stripped off the saddle and pad, the bridle and harness, to discourage anyone else forcing the poor beast any farther, and began to march beside them, leaving it spraddle-legged and head-down in utter exhaustion.

A mile later, it was Lewrie's that sank under him, too weak to stand, much less walk anymore. They stripped it, but it could not rise. Just lay in the road, its sides heaving, and whickering in pain. Lewrie drew a pistol and shot it behind the ear. He was an Englishman, adored horses, of course—and had never been forced to be so callous to one, ever. Hoped he never would again, either.

A mile more, and it was Mountjoy's that began to favor a forefoot. They were all three now on "shank's ponies," and perhaps a long three miles from the sea, still. It was almost all downhill, and they could see it, winking and glittering so invitingly, now and again, from a vantage point. The traffic was coming up to them, fleeing Porto Vado. They could see a mass migration heading north and east. Perversely, it was easier to work their way across the flow of traffic, cross fields ignored by the retreating army and its train of followers, who desperately clung near the roads.

"Porto Vado's out," Lewrie said, pointing south one hour later. They were within a mile of the sea, with the last strings of stragglers left behind them. Yet the port town swarmed with military activity, a constant coming and going in French uniforms. "Strike the coast over to the east, perhaps. Might find a boat on the beach, a scrap o' sail? We might have to go as far as Genoa. Fancy a shore supper in Genoa, Mister Mountjoy?"

"Fancy a horse, sir," Mountjoy muttered back, waving them to get low. "There's a French cavalry patrol yonder."

Half a dozen riders came up a dirt path from a distant village on the sea, swaying in their saddles and laughing loud enough to be heard from 200 yards off, waving foraged straw-covered wine bottles.

"Still have that cockade that Choundas dropped, Mountjoy?" Alan inquired.

"Yessir, but . . ."

"You wanted a horse," Lewrie grunted, taking it and wedging it beneath the gold loop of his hat. "So do I. Come on. Act superior."

He stood up and began to walk toward them, rifle slung on his shoulder, loaded and primed to fire, his pistols in his waistband. A march pace, nothing hesitant or suspicious about him.

"*Mes amis!*" he shouted loudly to get the cavalrymen's attention. "*Alors, mes amis!*" From the corner of his mouth, he asked a question; "Mountjoy, how do you say, 'come here, you drunken fools'?"

The cavalrymen straightened up in their saddles, adjusting the undone collars of their shirts and stocks, corking their bottles and trying to hide them in their forage bags.

"Come here! I have need of you!" Lewrie shouted sternly, this time by himself, in what he hoped passed for decent French. "I am *Capitaine* Choundas . . . Navy! Come here!" Softer; "Pistols, lads."

They rode up to them, a sergeant and five privates, cutty-eyed and abashed at being caught drunk, cringing at the harsh tone from the officer with the cockade on his hat. They didn't recognize the uniform, but he had an epaulet, and his coat was blue, the same as theirs.

Quite close, within fifteen feet.

"*Mes amis . . .*" Lewrie began to smile, holding out his arms to admonish them. "Now!"

Peel shot first, and the sergeant went backward off his horse, a bullet in his chest. Lewrie drew a pistol, pulled it to full cock, and fired at the next-nearest man, who was just reaching for his musketoon. He went down to be dragged, whimpering, and bounding behind his terrified horse. Mountjoy dropped another who'd drawn a saber, dashed in and snatched the reins as the man toppled into the dirt. Peel shot his second, a private who was trying to control his rearing mount. A shot in return that went wide, Lewrie missing with his second pistol, but Mountjoy, now mounted, popping off at another who swayed in the saddle, left arm useless. The last wheeled to gallop away, but Peel had the .54-caliber musketoon to his shoulder and snapped off a shot that took the fellow in the kidneys, spilling him onto the stubbly grain field he'd tried to cross.

They managed to snare the reins of two more mounts, swung up in the saddles, and lashed away from their hastily improvised ambush before the rest of the cavalry unit the patrol had come from were alerted.

"East!" Peel shouted, lashing with the reins. "Far as we can! Whoo!" he exulted for all of them; to have killed without a scratch. And to be astride strong, fresh horses . . . still alive and free.

TEN MORE QUICK miles, going cross-country above the coast roads, any pursuit left behind, it looked like, and beyond the reach of French soldiers, still encountering streams of Austrians headed away as fast as they could hobble on foot, mostly going inland and nor'east, running from nothing. Running away from the sea. Going almost as far as Savona, and hoping it was still in Genoese hands, daring to dip down to the coastal road, finally where the traffic was blessedly both sparse and civilian again.

They drew up on a low, shingly bluff, at last, just 100 yards from the surf. There were ships out there, not a mile off, which had fled Vado Bay themselves. Lewrie recognized Austrian colors, and Genoese under Red Ensigns, in sign of their captures.

"No boats," Mountjoy groaned, as spent as his stolen horse, by then. "No way off."

"Yes, there is," Lewrie said, stripping off his coat and hat. "There, sir! There!" he insisted, wigwagging his coat over his head. "Come on, you blind son of a bitch! See me! Be a *little* curious!"

Around the next point came a rowboat under two lugsails and jib, not a half mile off the beach. Lewrie began to shout, and urged them all to wave their coats, to fire off their weapons and scream.

The boat turned in, began to slant shoreward, close-reaching on a sea wind that had at last come up from the sou'east. The boat stood in cautiously, until almost level with them, as they dashed down to the surf line, still yelling and waving. The sails were lowered, and oars appeared to stroke her in. Within a cable, Lewrie could make out the dark red hull, the neat gilt trim of *Agamemnon*'s borrowed barge. And the incredulous face of Midshipman Hyde in her stern sheets, surrendering the helm to a more experienced able seaman who'd beach her proper, without risk.

They waded out to meet her, the last few yards, splashing up to their thighs as some oarsmen stroked her sideways, to turn her bows to the sea, while others jumped over to push her around quickly to take the surf from forrud, not abeam, and to help them scramble over the side to the safety of a solid oak thwart.

" 'Bout given you up, sir!" Hyde yelped. "Been up and down this coast for hours, looking for you, Captain! Mister Knolles told me to wait till dusk, if you didn't . . ."

"Thankee, Mister Hyde." Lewrie sighed, glad for a sip of brackish ship's water, and a hard biscuit to rap, then gnaw dry. "And for Mister Knolles's perseverance. Thank him in person, soon's I meet him, and be damned glad of the doing."

"You get the bastard that stole the gold, sir?" Hyde asked, as the oarsmen strained to the helmsman's shouts of "Give way, together!" and "Put yer backs in it!" to keep the barge moving forward, up, over the dangerous breaking surf to calmer water beyond the breakers.

"Aye, we got him, Mister Hyde." Lewrie sighed with relief, and weary satisfaction. "We got the bastard. It's over. Now, take us to *Jester*, Mister Hyde. Take us home."

Epilogue

THERE HAD BEEN so few casualties, for which the good doctor on duty had thanked a merciful God, that he and his compatriots had spent mostly an idle day, celebrating an almost bloodless victory over those much-vaunted Austrians. The coast was theirs, now, the entire Genoese Riviera, as far as Voltri, the surgeon had heard boasted, within easy ride of Genoa itself. The Austrians and Piedmontese had fled like so many terrified children, far inland; maybe thirty miles, he'd heard a cavalry chef du brigade crow. Once spring came, once the weather was suitable, the Republican Armee d'Italie would march, to complete their conquest of all of the northwest. Paris was sending a new general to put life into things, some newly risen pet of the Directory, with the improbable name of Napoleone Bonaparte. He was reputed to be impatient and aggressive; rare in an artillery officer, the surgeon thought. Till then, though, through the long Ligurian winter, there'd be peace and quiet, some skirmishing but nothing of consequence, nothing that tasked his skills to the utmost. He could drink his wine, smoke his pipe, and sleep peacefully, to ready himself for the horrors to come.

The surgeon made his last rounds among the pitiful, whimpering wounded who lay in the large tents that the Austrians had been so good as to abandon so hastily. French casualties under canvas, of course . . . and the few Piedmontese or Austrians under the stars or the trees. It was almost cozy in the cavernous pavillion tents, glowing like so many amber jewels, lit from within by a single lanthorn.

"This one, sir?" his assistant said with a sad *moue*. "The poor fellow's left us, I'm afraid."

366

"Both legs." The surgeon shrugged philosophically. "Too much stress, too quickly, for his humors to restore their balance. *C'est dommage*. And that one?"

"Feverish, but better, sir," the assistant said, gesturing for orderlys to remove the dead infantry officer.

The surgeon took the lanthorn to peel back the blanket and look at his handiwork. A neat bit of sewing, he grunted with pleasure, as he puffed on his pipe.

"You are with us, sir?" the surgeon whispered as the man opened his eyes and groaned in pain. "I do not recall treating anyone from our Navy before, sir. You came up to headquarters to see the battle, *hein*? And saw too much of it, *quel dommage*."

"I . . . will I live?" the officer croaked, gritting his teeth to withstand his pain, now that he was awake to feel it roar and gibber.

"A fairly clean wound, sir," the surgeon assured him, chuckling a little. "Your coat and shirt easily extracted from it. Nothing left behind to cause sepsis. So few casualties, the water still very hot in the instrument pails . . . I have noted that there is less later infection when the water is bloodless, and the water is scalding hot. Why it is, I have no idea, but I think it may be worth a letter to Paris, *hein*?"

"Ahh . . . !" The naval officer grunted, screwing up his horribly disfigured face in torment for a second, then almost seemed to find it amusing. "Ahh . . ." he sighed as that wave of agony subsided. "I have cheated him again. I *beat* him, after all!"

"It does not pay to boast of beating the Angel of Death yet, I suggest, sir." The surgeon laughed. "A week or more, before we count you free of fever, and able to be moved to the rear, to complete your recovery in nicer surroundings, *hein*? For your stump to drain, to show a laudable, healing pus."

"Stump?"

"*Certainment, Capitaine*, uhm . . ." The surgeon frowned, not sure if that was even the proper title of rank, and not knowing his patient's name. "Your arm was so completely smashed, the bone in shatters . . ."

Guillaume Choundas tried to raise up, to raise his arm, against the surgeon's entreaties and pressing hands. It was gone! There was a thick wrapped bandage over absorbing batt, the whole once white but now pink or dull red, crusted with oozed blood. So short, almost *all* . . . !

"Nnnoooo!" Choundas screamed. "Nnnoooo!!! Lewrie! Lewrie! You . . . *Lllewwrieeee!!!* Lugh . . . Lugh's bird! The raven. That bass-tardd!"

✿ ✿ ✿

"C'EST DOMMAGE." THE surgeon sighed minutes later, after giving the distraught fellow a cup of laudanum-laced wine. He took a seat on an upturned crate by the fire, under the flyleaf of his wagon, with the tailgate boards for a rough table. "Bernard, pass the wine, *hein*? So good, this. Real Provence, not that Italian muck."

"What was that all about, Jean-Claude *mon ami*?"

"Some poor fellow lost his arm." The surgeon sighed, bourgeois happy in his bear-skin slippers, at last, instead of those ridiculous boots the army insisted he wear. The tailboard and the fire wasn't as comfortable as his old café back home, once the shops, and his offices, were closed for the night, but it could be rather pleasant, this life of an army surgeon, so far from home. "You know how they can be, once they know it. A fellow scarred as he, you'd expect he's used to pain and loss, but he raved like a madman. Not many unman themselves so."

"Loss of his looks, anyway," Bernard snickered. *"Une hideux."*

"Kept ranting about Lugh, Lir, Lewrie, and ravens," the surgeon muttered over his wine. "Whatever those are. Ever heard the like?"

Surgeon Bernard had not, so he merely shrugged. "Nonsense words, alliterative ravings. Was there a head wound? Hmm. Might keep an eye on the poor fellow, Jean-Claude. Recommend he's kept longer, once he's well enough to transfer. Then he's someone else's worry. Cards?"

NIGHTFALL ON THE sea, aboard a sloop of war that surged surefooted and secure, serene for once, her young captain pacing the decks bone-weary but unable to contemplate sleep as she made her way among a gaggle of escapees from the anchorage at Vado Bay. A bath, a shave, a clean uniform, and a more than ample supper had gone a long way toward physical recovery, though he could not be sure what the next days might bring him, or his ship.

"Excuse me, sir," Mountjoy said, interrupting his solitary musings with an apologetic prefatory cough. "Could I speak with you?"

"Aye, Mister Mountjoy?" Lewrie replied pleasantly.

"I, uhm . . . I rather loathe to cause you or your affairs any disruption, or distress, but . . . well, Captain Lewrie," Mountjoy said with a sheepish gulp, "I'd like to resign my position as your clerk, sir."

"I'll not put you in danger again, Mister Mountjoy, if that's . . ."

"No, sir! Quite the opposite, in fact!" Mountjoy gushed. "Going ashore with you and Mister Peel was the most exciting thing I've ever done, sir! For the first time in my life, I felt active and alive, useful and . . . *doing* something other than scribbling. As if I'd discovered my true calling, do you see, sir. To shed another man's blood . . . strive to shed Choundas's, too, well . . . Mister Peel has suggested that his employer, and their, uhm . . . 'department,' would find my skills very useful. Forgive me, but I intend to hold him to it, and take service with that Mister Silberberg. As an assistant in training, as it were."

"They'll bloody get you knackered," Lewrie countered. "Knife in the back some night. It'll be dry, Mountjoy. What we did today isn't the usual. More skulduggery, like whist or chess, creeping . . ."

"God, I hope *so*, sir!" Mountjoy laughed. "Like *that*, I did, as a climax to the intellectual, though I'm not a born soldier. I enjoy both sorts of action, what Mr. Silberberg described? Never make a sea officer, sir, you know that. Have to start very young for that. Not enough money for an Army commission, but . . . this I'd be good at, sir. And be able to make just as grand a contribution. Padgett, Mister Giles's jack-in-the-bread-room, could move up to be your clerk, sir, and he's diligent. More so than I, we both know. Would it be all right, Captain? Do I owe the Admiralty a term of service, or . . ."

"No, you don't, Mister Mountjoy." Lewrie sighed. "You serve me, at my pleasure. And, eventually, yours. You're *quite* determined . . ."

"I am, sir. Completely," Mountjoy said, with fervent certainty.

"Very well then, Mister Mountjoy," Lewrie said, offering a hand to the young man. "I'll accept your letter of resignation. And may God protect you in your new career. You may go ashore with Peel at Genoa."

"God *always* sends the Right, sir." Mountjoy beamed. "Thankee."

WISH I WAS that certain, Lewrie thought; of anything. With France holding almost all of the Genoese Riviera now, *Jester* could be sent God knew where. There was still the matter of false colors to settle, with Hotham to decide whether it was glory, or infamy and a court.

He was just bone-weary enough, though, to suspend disbelief, to feel a small, heretical sense of hope that things would work out, in his, and *Jester*'s favor. After what Buchanon had said over supper.

"The sea!" he'd shouted in the heat of pursuit; look at the *sea*! He thought he'd meant that broad, perverse windless river of calm that had doomed Choundas's *tartane*. But Buchanon's real meaning had been a lot more, he'd whispered only one hour ago, over port and biscuit.

"A seal, Cap'um, I *saw* it!" he'd hissed. "Close-aboard. What 'at Mister Peel told, o' th' raven ashore, too? Dear Lord, sir! Made me go ice all over when I heard. 'Twas th' Old'uns, sir. Lugh, and *Lir!*"

"But really, sir . . . mean you really, or just *thought* . . . ?"

"All the way from home t'here, sir," Buchanon had whispered so reverently, shivering with wonder. "Lir's eye 'pon ya—'pon *her*, sir! An' you, an' me, an' all o' us, in his hand, still. Swear t'Jesus, sir, I think where'er we sail, Lir means t'follow. Mayhap he meant t'use ya, Cap'um . . . t'settle this fellah Choundas's business. Must've rowed Lir sore, over somethin', for him t'grant ya good cess ashore. But once he uses ya, he don't forget his favorites."

ME, LUCKY ASHORE, Lewrie wryly mused; now *there's* a new'un!

Still, he went to the bulwark to gaze out at the swelling, dark sea, and raise one hand, almost in supplication, as eight bells began to chime up forrud, so blissfully routine, so fragile, thin but brassy-mellow.

"*If* you're out there, thankee," he whispered. "You've your eye on us, spare a glance for Mountjoy, too. He'll need it. What comes . . . good or ill . . . so be it. But, thankee . . . for *Jester's* Fortune."

And the night wind breathed in the shrouds, as if in a soft and sympathetic, assuring response.

Afterword

IT WASN'T THE usual thing for individuals to be awarded medals in the eighteenth century; those were reserved for successful campaigns or battles, given only to the few. Quite unlike today's "medals for migraines." So Lewrie wasn't recognized for his small part at The Glorious First of June. Admiral Howe's Flag Captain, Sir Roger Curtis, created a storm of controversy by recommending only those few of his personal favorites who had closed the foe, and the rest of the ship captains went without, which put them into a snit fit. There is a large group portrait of Howe and others at the National Maritime Museum, Greenwich, England, showing Howe (suffering too-tight shoes in asperity), the wounded Captain Sir Edward Snape Douglas with his hand to his head, distracted as if he was hearing some phantasmic voices, and at the extreme left, Sir Roger, who looms like a Nixon White House aide. The Lt. Edward Codrington went on to fame with Nelson at Trafalgar, and once he made flag rank, commanded the victory at Navarino, the last sea battle fought completely under sail in 1827.

Yes, Hotham was just about as huge a drooling idiot as I wrote of him. He was one of those people who could literally snatch defeat from the jaws of victory. Not that he tried very hard, mind. He was replaced in the Mediterranean by Admiral Sir John Jervis, "Old Jarvy," the following year. Jervis was a bit on the grumpy side, a disciplinarian whose harshness saved the Mediterranean fleet from the rot of the Great Mutiny in '97, even if he had to hang a few conspirators to keep his fleet functioning. Do you imagine, gentle reader, that Lewrie and Jervis will get along like a house afire? Hmm . . .

As for those shocked that Captain Horatio Nelson could be portrayed as angry, crude in his speech, even blasphemous, or that the man I wrote about isn't the marble demigod atop that pillar in Trafalgar Square (I mean, I've heard of putting people, women especially, on pedestals, but that'un rather takes the cake, doesn't it?) let's remember that it's a long way from his father's rectory at Burnham Thorpe to a harsh life in the Royal Navy, and Nelson spent the greater part of his childhood and all his adult life around . . . sailors.

Drawing principally upon Oliver Warner's *Portrait Of Lord Nelson*, I found that yes, Signorina Adelaide Correglia of Leghorn existed, that she was as goose-brained as I described, and that Nelson was just as silly over her as I wrote. More to the point, what Capt. Thomas Fremantle wrote, in his laconically terse entries in his diary, which mentions dining aboard *Agamemnon* several times the mort was present. Fremantle was so terse he wrote of his marriage to Mistress Betsy Wynne later in one rather spare sentence! He refers to the "happy couple" as "Nelson and his doxy." Though there is a letter to Sir Gilbert Elliot from Nelson that cites "one old lady" who tells Nelson everything *they* wish to know. So it is possible that Adelaide Correglia was someone in Twigg's line of work, with whom, like Lewrie, Nelson could combine the business of intelligence, and pleasure.

To further cite Oliver Warner's work on Nelson, Warner used the earlier work of James Harrison, who wrote a biography with the Lady Emma Hamilton ("That Woman!") as his source, who claimed that:

"Nelson . . . only had two faults; venery and swearing. Harrison said of him that 'it is not to be dissembled, though by no means ever an unprincipled seducer of the wives and daughters of his friends, he was always well known to maintain rather more partiality for the fair sex than is quite consistent with the highest degree of Christian purity.' "

Hmm . . . sounds rather like Lewrie, in that respect.

Further, " 'Such improper indulgences, with some slight addition to that other vicious habit of British seamen, the occasional use of a few thoughtlessly profane expletives in speech, form the only dark specks ever yet discovered in the bright blaze of his moral character.' "

And, I'd imagine that Lewrie was the sort who could get so "up his nose," as to rouse a saint, much less a Nelson, to intemperance.

The Lt. Thomas Hardy of *Meleager* was indeed the man whom Commodore Nelson would risk battle with Spanish frigates to rescue, *that* Hardy of Trafalgar fame. At the time, he was a junior officer aboard *Meleager*, later following Captain Cockburn into the *Minerve* frigate.

Cockburn, hmm . . . There may be some who could say that I have not been exactly charitable to him. He *was* one of Nelson's favorite officers, held up as a paragon. Nelson even forgave him for shouldering *Agamemnon* aside, and putting his commodore aground under fire, later at Oneglia, in his zeal to close the foe. He was the diligent sort who'd not have cared very much for Lewrie's sort, though—never married till he was forty-seven, and that to a cousin, and died without issue—and I think, for the reasons stated in the book, that Lewrie wouldn't have cared for him very much, either. More to the point, I don't, since he was that bugger who invaded the Chesapeake and burned Washington, D.C., and the White House to the ground during the War of 1812!

THERE WAS NO raid on Bordighera that I know of. I made it all up. That's what writers tend to do when things get slow. Same as "Surf's Up!" when the plot broke down in all those old "beach movies" with Annette Funicello; "Beat To Quarters!", do twenty or so rather easier pages and let the good guys slaughter a s . . . load of Frogs.

YES, THE AUSTRIANS did win the Vado Sweepstakes. General de Vins acted like Confederate Gen. Braxton Bragg and came down with vapors, a migraine, or something, turning things over to his second-in-command the morning of his battle. They ran like the Yankees at both Battles of Manassas. Nelson lost a lieutenant, a midshipman, and sixteen men at Vado, and his purser was forced to stagger eighteen miles with the fleeing Austrians. There were some units *thirty miles* from any French outposts, who took off like greased lightning without ever having *seen* an enemy, without a shot being fired—by them, or at them.

Was *that* Lewrie's fault? Could a single rifle shot (deuced *good* 'un, you have to admit!) have been the cause of such a rout? Stranger things have happened. Ask the Yankees again, at that bridge at First Manassas, as we unreconstructed Confederates call it. Yeeeeh-hahhh!

Besides, I think we all know by now that whenever Lewrie turns up, things just sorta kinda happen, and not always for the best. Nor, intentionally. After all, he *means* well, but . . . !

So what will happen next? Will Lewrie reconcile with Phoebe? Will Twigg throw him and Claudia Mastandrea together? Will Guillaume Choundas be a raving one-armed lunatic in some French Bedlam, or will he return to plague Lewrie once more? Will Alan settle him, once and for all? Or will he face that court-martial?

Tune in tomorrow . . . same station, to discover what comes amiss with Lewrie's, and *Jester*'s, Fortune. In the meantime, I will be at Wrightsville Beach, North Carolina, pondering these matters and trying to find some radical feminist bullies in thong bikinis who wish to kick sand at me.